When Life Gives You Lululemons

A Novel

LAUREN WEISBERGER

Simon & Schuster Paperbacks

NEW YORK LONDON TORONTO SYDNEY NEW DELHI

Simon & Schuster Paperbacks
An Imprint of Simon & Schuster, Inc.
1230 Avenue of the Americas
New York, NY 10020

This Simon & Schuster Canadian export edition June 2018

SIMON & SCHUSTER PAPERBACKS and colophon are registered trademarks of Simon & Schuster, Inc.

For information about special discounts for bulk purchases, please contact Simon & Schuster Special Sales at 1-866-506-1949 or business@simonandschuster.com.

The Simon & Schuster Speakers Bureau can bring authors to your live event. For more information or to book an event, contact the Simon & Schuster Speakers Bureau at 1-866-248-3049 or visit our website at www.simonspeakers.com.

Interior design by Ruth Lee-Mui

Manufactured in the United States of America

10   9   8   7   6   5

ISBN 978-1-9821-0135-0
ISBN 978-1-4767-7846-4 (ebook)

To my entire family, with love

Part One

Part One

1

Again with the Nazi Getup?

Emily

Emily racked her brain. There had to be something to complain about. This was New Year's Eve in Los Angeles, one of the most annoying nights of the year in arguably the most annoying city known to humanity. So why couldn't she think of a thing?

She sipped her skinny margarita from her chaise and watched her husband's beautiful body cut through the water like a moving art installation. When Miles emerged, he propped himself on the back of the lit infinity pool, where the turquoise water appeared to spill over the side and straight down the mountain. Behind him, the lights from the valley twinkled for miles, making the city look alluring, even sexy. Night was the only time Los Angeles really shone. Gone were the smog and the junkies and the soul-crushing traffic, all replaced by an idyllic vista of night sky and silently twinkling lights—as if

God Himself had descended into the Hollywood Hills and selected the most perfect Snapchat filter for His least favorite city on earth.

Miles smiled at her and she waved, but when he motioned for her to join him, she shook her head. It was unseasonably warm, and all around her, people were partying in that intensely determined way that happened only on New Year's Eve after midnight: *This will be the most fun we've ever had; we will do and say outrageous things; we are loving our lives and everyone around us.* The massive hot tub was packed with a dozen revelers, all with drinks in hand, and another group sat around the perimeter, content to dangle their feet while they waited for a few inches of space to free up. On the deck above the pool a DJ blasted remixed hip-hop, and dancers everywhere—on the patio, in the pool, on the pool deck, streaming in and out of the house—all moved happily to his playlist. On the chair to Emily's left, a young girl wearing only bikini bottoms straddled a guy and massaged his shoulders while her bare breasts dangled freely. She worked her way down his back and began a rather aggressive handling of his glutes. She was twenty-three, twenty-five at most, and while her body was far from perfect—slightly rounded belly and overly curvy thighs—her arms didn't jiggle and her neck didn't sag. No crepey anything. Just youth. None of the small indignities of Emily's own body at thirty-six: light stretch marks on her hips; cleavage with just the smallest hint of sag; some errant dark hairs along her bikini line that just seemed to sprout now willy-nilly, indifferent to Emily's indefatigable waxing schedule. It wasn't a horror show, exactly—she still looked thin and tan, maybe even downright hot in her elegant Eres two-piece—but it was getting harder with every passing year.

An unfamiliar 917 number flashed on her phone.

"Emily? This is Helene. I'm not sure if you remember, but we met a couple years ago at the Met Ball."

Emily looked skyward in concentration. Though the name was familiar, she was having a hard time placing it. Silence filled the air.

"I'm Rizzo's manager."

Rizzo. *Interesting.* He was the new Bieber: the hottest pop star whose fame had skyrocketed when, two years earlier at age sixteen, he'd become the youngest male to win a Grammy for Album of the Year. Helene had moved to Hollywood to join an agency—either ICM or Endeavor, Emily couldn't remember—but she'd somehow missed the news that Helene now represented Rizzo.

"Of course. How are you?" Emily asked. She glanced at her watch. This was no ordinary call.

"I'm sorry I'm calling so late," Helene said. "It's already four a.m. here in New York, but you're probably in L.A. I feel terrible interrupting . . ."

"No, it's fine. I'm at Gigi Hadid's childhood mansion and not nearly as drunk as I should be. What's up?"

A shriek came from the pool. Two girls had jumped in together, holding hands, and were splashing Miles and a couple of his friends. Emily rolled her eyes.

"Well, I, uh . . ." Helene cleared her throat. "We're off the record, right?"

"Of course." This sounded promising.

"I'm not sure I understand the whole story myself, but Riz appeared on Seacrest's Times Square show earlier tonight—everything was fine, it went off without a hitch. Afterward, I went to meet up with some old college friends, and Rizzo was headed to some party at 1 OAK. Sober, at least when he left me. Happy about his performance."

"Okay . . ."

"And just this second I got texted a picture from a colleague who works in ICM's New York office and happens to be at 1 OAK right now . . ."

"And?"

"And it's not good."

"What? Is he passed out? Covered in his own puke? Kissing a guy? Doing lines? Groping an underage girl?"

Helene sighed and began to speak, but she was drowned out by shrieking laughter. In the shallow end, a girl with hot pink hair and a thong bikini had found her way atop Miles's shoulders for an improvised chicken fight.

"Sorry, can you repeat that? It's a little chaotic here," Emily said as she watched the tiny piece of suit fabric wedge even tighter between the girl's naked ass cheeks, themselves spread straight across the back of Emily's husband's neck.

"He appears to be wearing a Nazi costume."

"A *what*?"

"Like with a swastika armband and a coordinating headband. Storm trooper boots. The whole nine."

"Oh, Jesus Christ," Emily muttered without thinking.

"That bad?"

"Well, it's not great. Prince Harry pulled that stunt forever ago—but we have to work with what we have. I'm not going to lie, I would've preferred drugs or boys."

In the pool, the pink-haired girl on Miles's shoulders reached behind her back, yanked the tie of her bikini top, and began swinging the top around her head like a lasso.

"First things first: who knows?" Emily asked.

"Nothing has shown up online yet, but of course, it's only a matter of time."

"Just so we're clear: you're calling to hire me, yes?" Emily asked.

"Yes. Definitely."

"Okay, then right now I want you to text your colleague and have him get Rizzo into the men's room and out of that getup. I don't care if he's wearing a gold lamé banana hammock, it's better than the Nazi thing."

"I already did that. He gave Riz his button-down and shoes, confiscated the armband, and let him keep the trousers, which apparently are bright red. It's not perfect, but it's the best we can do, especially since I can't reach Rizzo directly. But someone will post something any second, I'm sure."

"Agreed, so listen up. Here's the plan. You're going to jump in a cab and head over to 1 OAK and forcibly remove him. Bring a girl or two, it'll look better, and then get him back to his apartment and don't let him leave. Sit in front of the damn door if you have to. Do you have his passwords? Actually, forget it—just take his phone. Drop it in the toilet. We need to buy ourselves time without some idiotic drunken tweet from him."

"Okay. Will do."

"The first flight out of here is six a.m. I'm going home to pack, and then I'll head to the airport. The story will definitely break while I'm in the air, if not before. Do not—I repeat, do not—make a statement. Do not let him talk to anyone, not even the delivery guy who brings up the food. Information lockdown, you understand? No matter how bad the photos are, or how horrified the reaction—and trust me, it's going to be bad—I want no response until I get there, okay?"

"Thank you, Emily. I'm going to owe you for this one."

"Go *now*!" Emily said, managing not to utter what she was actually thinking—namely, that the charge for her time and the holiday and the travel was going to take Helene's breath away.

She took the last sip of her margarita, set the drink on the glass table next to her, and stood up, trying to ignore the couple beside her who may or may not have been having actual intercourse.

"Miles? Honey?" Emily called as politely as she could manage.

No response.

"Miles, love? Can you please move her thighs away from your ears for thirty seconds? I have to leave."

She was pleased to see her husband unceremoniously lower the girl into the water and swim over to the side. "You're not mad, are you? She's just some dumb kid."

Emily knelt. "Of course I'm not mad. If you're going to cheat, you better pick someone a hell of a lot hotter than *that*." She nodded toward the girl, who looked not at all pleased with her wet hair. "I got a call from New York. It's an emergency with Rizzo. I'm running home to get a bag and hopefully get to LAX for the six a.m. I'll call you when I land, okay?"

This was hardly the first time Emily had been called away in the middle of something—her surgeon girlfriend claimed Emily had worse call hours than she did—but Miles looked positively stupefied.

"It's New Year's Eve. Isn't there anyone in New York who can handle this?" His unhappiness was obvious, and Emily felt a pang, but she tried to keep it light.

"Sorry, love. Can't say no to this one. Stay, have fun. Not too much fun . . ." She added the last part to make him feel better—she wasn't one iota concerned about Miles doing anything stupid. She bent down and pecked his wet lips. "Call you later," she said, and wove through the throngs to the circular driveway, where one of the cute valets motioned for a Town Car to pull around. He held the door for her, and she flashed him a smile and a ten-dollar bill.

"Two stops, please," she said to the driver. "First one is on Santa Monica Boulevard, where you'll wait for me. Then to the airport. And fast."

New York, her first and truest love, awaited.

2

Living the Dream

Miriam

It was only the beginning of mile two, and she felt like she might die of suffocation. Her breaths came in jagged gulps, but no matter how deeply she took in air, Miriam was unable to slow her heart rate. She checked her Fitbit for the thousandth time in the past sixteen minutes—how could it have been only sixteen minutes?!—and briefly worried that the reading of 165 might kill her. Which would officially make her the only woman in all of Greenwich, or perhaps all the earth, who had dropped dead after running—really, if she were being honest, walking—a single lousy mile in sixteen minutes.

But she had shown up! Wasn't that what all the feel-good bloggers and motivational authors were always screeching about? *No judgments, just show up! Show up and you've already won the battle! Don't expect perfection—showing up is enough!* "Fuckers," she mumbled, streaming massive puffs of steam in the freezing January air. Motivating for a jog at seven o'clock in the morning on January 1—was more than just showing up. It was a downright *triumph*.

"Morning!" a woman called as she raced by Miriam on the left, nearly jolting what was left of her heart into immediate cardiac arrest.

"Hi!" Miriam shouted to the back of the woman, who ran like a black-clad gazelle: Lululemon leggings with elaborate mesh cutouts that looked both cool and extremely cold; fitted black puffer that ended at her nonexistent hips; black Nikes on her feet; and some sort of technical-looking hat with the cutest puffball on top. Her legs went on forever, and her butt looked so firm that it wouldn't possibly hold so much as a bobby pin underneath, never mind a full-size hairbrush, which Miriam had once tucked successfully and devastatingly under her left ass cheek.

Miriam slowed to a walk, but before she could regain anything resembling composure, two women in equally fabulous workout outfits ran toward Miriam on the opposite side of the street. A golden retriever pulled happily on the leash of the hot pink puffer coat while a panting chocolate Lab yanked along the woman in the army green. The entire entourage looked like a mobile Christmas card and was moving at a brisk pace.

"Happy New Year," the golden owner said as they sprinted past Miriam.

"You too," she muttered, relieved it was no one she knew. Not that she'd met many moms in the five months since they'd moved to town just in time for the twins to start kindergarten and Benjamin to start second grade at their new public school. Beyond saying hello to a few moms at school drop-off twice a day, she hadn't had much opportunity to meet a lot of other women. Paul claimed it was the same in wealthy suburbs everywhere—that people stayed holed up in their big houses with everything they needed either upstairs or downstairs: their gyms, their screening rooms, their wine cellars and tasting tables. Nannies played with children, rendering playdates unnecessary. Housekeepers did the grocery shopping. Staff, staff, and more staff to do everything from mow the lawn to chlorinate the pool to change the lightbulbs.

The heady smell of burning wood greeted Miriam the moment she stepped into the mudroom, and a quick peek in the family room confirmed that her husband had read her mind about wanting to sit next to a fire. It was one of the things she loved most about suburban living so far: morning fires. Otherwise bleak mornings were instantly cozy; her children's cheeks were even more delicious.

"Mommy's home!" Matthew, five years old and obsessed with weaponry, shouted from the arm of the couch, where he balanced in pajamas, brandishing a realistic-looking sword.

"Mommy! Matthew won't give me a turn with the sword and we're supposed to share!" his twin sister, Maisie, screeched from under the kitchen table, which was her favorite place to sulk.

"Mom, can I have your password to buy *Hellion*?" Benjamin asked without looking up from Miriam's hijacked iPad.

"No," she said. "Who said yes to screen time right now? No iPad. It's family time."

"Your fingerprint, then? Please? Jameson says it's the coolest game he's ever played! Why does he get it and I don't?"

"Because his mommy is nicer than me," she said, managing to kiss her son on top of his head before he squirmed away.

Paul stood at the stove in flannel pajama pants and a fleece sweatshirt, intently flipping pancakes on the griddle. "I'm so impressed," he said. "I have no idea how you motivated this morning." Miriam couldn't help but think how handsome he was despite all the premature gray hair. He was only three years older than she, but he could have been mistaken for being a decade her senior.

Miriam grabbed her midsection, ending up with two handfuls of flesh. "This is how."

Paul placed the last pancake on a plated pile nearly a dozen high and turned off the stove. He walked over and embraced her. "You're perfect just the way you are," he said automatically. "Here, have one."

"No way. I didn't suffer through twenty minutes of sheer hell to kill it all with a pancake."

"Are they ready, Daddy? Are they? Are they?"

"Can we have whipped cream on them?"

"And ice cream?"

"I don't want the ones with the blueberries!"

In a flash, all three children had gathered at the kitchen table, nearly hyperventilating with excitement. Miriam tried to ignore the epic mess and focus on her children's joy and her husband's kindness, but it was tough with flour covering every inch of countertop, batter splattered on the backsplash, and errant chocolate chips and blueberries spread across the floor.

"Anyone want some fruit salad or yogurt?" she asked, pulling both from the fridge.

"Not me!" they all shouted in unison through mouthfuls of pancake.

Yeah, me neither, Miriam thought to herself as she scooped some out. She spooned a bite into her mouth and nearly spat it into the sink. The yogurt had clearly gone bad, and not even the sweet strawberries could mask the rancid taste. She scraped the entire bowl's contents into the garbage disposal and considered hard-boiling some eggs. She even nibbled one of those cardboard-like fiber crackers, but two bites in, she just couldn't.

"Live a little," she murmured to herself, grabbing a chocolate chip pancake from the top of the pile and shoving it into her mouth.

"Aren't they good, Mommy? Do you want to try it with whipped cream?" Benjamin asked, waving the canister like a trophy.

"Yes, please," she said, holding out her remaining piece for him to squirt. Screw it. She was setting a good example for her daughter that food wasn't the enemy, right? Everything in moderation. No eating disorders in this house. She had just popped a pod into the coffee machine when she heard Paul mutter, "Holy shit."

"Daddy! Language!" Maisie said, sounding exactly like Miriam.

"Daddy said a bad word! Daddy said 'shit'!"

"Sorry, sorry," he murmured, his face buried in the newspaper Miriam had set on the table. "Miriam, come look at this."

"I'll be right there. Do you want a cup too?"

"Now. Come here now."

"What is it, Daddy? What's in the newspaper?"

"Here, have another pancake," Paul said to Maisie as he handed the paper over to Miriam.

Below the fold but still on the very first page blared the headline: MADD: MOTHERS ALL-FOR DRUNK DRIVING! SENATOR'S WIFE SLAPPED WITH DUI . . . WITH KIDS IN THE CAR!

"Holy shit."

"Mommy! You said 'shit'!"

"Daddy, now Mommy said a bad word!"

"Shit, shit, shit!" sang Matthew.

"Who wants to watch a movie?" Paul asked. "Benjamin, why don't you go down to the basement and put on *Boss Baby* for everyone." Again, there was a mad scramble as they bolted toward the stairs, and then, seconds later, blessed silence.

"This can't be right," Miriam said, studying the mug shot of her old high school friend. They had overlapped senior year of high school in Paris at the American School. Karolina was there modeling and learning English on the side, and Miriam was forced to follow her parents there on a posting. "Karolina would never do that."

"Well, it's right here in print. Failed roadside sobriety test. Empty bottles of booze in the backseat. Refused to take a Breathalyzer. And five kids in the car, including her own."

"There is no way that's possible," Miriam said, scanning the story. "Not the Karolina I know."

"How long has it been since you've spoken to her? Maybe she changed. I don't imagine things are so easy being in the spotlight, like they both are now."

"She was the face of L'Oréal for ten years! The mega-model to end all supermodels. I hardly think she has issues with the spotlight."

"Well, being the wife of a United States senator is something else entirely. Especially one who plans to run for president. It's a different kind of scrutiny."

"I guess so. I don't know. I'm going to call her. This just can't be right."

"You guys haven't spoken in months." Paul sipped his coffee.

"That doesn't matter!" Miriam realized she was nearly shouting and lowered her voice. "We've known each other since we were teenagers."

Paul held up both hands in surrender. "Send her my love, okay? I'll go check on the monsters."

Karolina's number rang five times before sending her to voicemail. "Hi! You've reached Karolina. I'm not available to take your call, but leave me a message and I'll get back to you just as soon as I can. Bye, now."

"Lina? It's me, Miriam. I saw that hideous headline and I want to talk to you. I don't believe it for a single second, and neither does one other person who's ever met you. Call me as soon as you get this, okay? Love you, honey. Bye."

Miriam clicked "end" and stared at her screen, willing Karolina's name to appear. But then she heard a scream coming from downstairs—a real pain scream, not an I-hate-my-siblings scream or an It's-my-turn scream, and Miriam took a deep breath and stood up to go investigate.

It had barely even begun, and already this year was shaping up to be a loser. She grabbed a now-cold pancake off the plate on her way to the basement: 2018 could take its resolutions and *shove* them.

3

Like a Common
Criminal

Karolina

"Hey, Siri! Play 'Yeah' by Usher!" Harry called from the back of the Suburban. A chorus of cheers went up from the boys when Siri chirped, "Okay, playing 'Yeah' by Usher," and the bass blasted through the speakers.

Karolina smiled. Never in a million years would she have thought having a car full of twelve-year-old boys could be fun. They were loud and rowdy and even sometimes smelled bad, yes. But Harry's friends were also sweet and quick to laugh and made an attempt at manners, at least when she was around. They were good kids from nice families, and once again she felt grateful for the move that had taken them from New York—the city of social land mines—to Bethesda, where everyone seemed a little more easygoing.

Sweet boy, Karolina thought for the thousandth time as she sneaked a look at Harry from the rearview mirror. Every day he was starting to look more and more like a teenager: broadening shoulders, dark fuzz above his lip, a smattering of pimples on his cheeks. But just as often he seemed like a little boy, as likely to spend an hour playing with Legos as texting with his friends. Harry was outgoing and confident, like his father, but he had a softer, more sensitive side too. Right around the time they moved to Bethesda, Harry started asking Graham more about his late mother: where she and Graham had met, what she liked to read, how she'd felt when she was pregnant with him. And always Graham put him off, promising to tell Harry about his mother later. Later, when he was finished with a report he needed to read. Later, that weekend, when they had more free time. Later, during their ski vacation, because his mother had loved to ski. Later, later, later. Karolina wasn't sure if it was laziness or avoidance or genuine pain causing Graham to put off his son, but she knew Harry needed answers. It took her nearly three days while Graham was at work and Harry at school to assemble all the scattered pictures and letters and clippings she could find, but when she presented Harry with the memory box of his mom, his relief and joy made every minute worthwhile. She reassured Harry that his mom would always be his mom, and that it was okay to talk about her and remember her, and Karolina's big, strong tween had collapsed into her arms like a kindergartener returning from his first day away from home.

"Guess what?" Nicholas, a lanky lacrosse player with shaggy blond hair, called from the third row. "My dad got us tickets to the 'Skins/Eagles game next weekend. First playoff game. Who's in?"

The boys hooted.

"Hey, Mom, do you think Dad will take me?" Harry asked.

"My dad said tickets weren't that expensive," Nicholas said.

Karolina forced herself to smile, though the boys couldn't see her in the driver's seat. "I'm sure he'd love that," she lied, and sneaked a peek at Harry to see if he could hear it in her voice. Despite the fact that Harry was passionate about professional football in general and the Redskins specifically—and Graham, as a sitting U.S. senator, could name his seats anywhere in the stadium—father and son had never attended a game together. Every year Graham swore to Karolina and Harry that they'd sit in the owner's box, fly to an important away game, or invite a bunch of Harry's friends and get seats on the fifty-yard line, and every year another season went by without the Hartwell boys in attendance. Harry had been to a game exactly once, two years earlier, when Karolina took pity on him and bought tickets off StubHub. He'd been thrilled and cheered like crazy in his head-to-toe gear, but she knew he would have preferred to go with Graham: Karolina had unknowingly gotten tickets on the visitor side, and she couldn't totally follow who had the ball, and in spite of her best intentions, she kept cheering at the wrong times.

"Mom! Hey, Mom!" Harry interrupted her thoughts. "There are cop cars behind us with their lights on."

"Hmmm?" Karolina murmured, more to herself. She glanced in the rearview and saw two police cruisers with their lights ablaze, so close to the Suburban that they were nearly pushing up against the bumper. "My goodness, it must be important. Okay, okay, give me a second," she said aloud. "I'm moving over."

She was grateful Harry was safely beside her, because she always got nervous when she saw an emergency vehicle in her neighborhood. Their house might be on fire, but so long as Harry was safely in her sight, she could deal with anything. She put on her blinker and eased the unwieldy truck onto the side of the road as gracefully as she could, sending a silent apology to the Crains, who lived five doors down and owned the beautiful lawn her tires were probably digging up. Only the cruisers didn't quickly pass her on the left, as she'd expected; they too pulled to the side and came to a stop directly behind her truck.

"Ohhh, Mrs. Hartwell, you're busted!" Stefan, another of Harry's friends, yelled as all the boys laughed. Karolina did too.

"Yes, you know me," Karolina said. "Going twenty in a residential neighborhood. Crazy!" She watched in the rearview as the officers stood next to her license plate and appeared to type it into an iPad-like device. *Good*, she thought. They would see the United States government plates that were on all three of their cars, and this whole silly thing would be over.

But the two officers who approached her window weren't laughing. "Ma'am? Is this your vehicle?" asked the female officer, while the male cop stood behind her and watched.

"Yes, of course," Karolina said, wondering why they'd ask her such a ridiculous question. She was driving it, wasn't she? "Officer, I really don't think I was speeding. We literally just pulled out of the driveway. See? We live right back there. I'm just taking my son's friends—"

The female cop looked hard at Karolina and said, "I'll need your license and registration, please."

Karolina checked the woman's face. She wasn't kidding. Karolina carefully removed her driver's license from her wallet and was relieved to find the car's registration tucked neatly in the glove compartment. "I, um, as you may recognize the name from my license there . . . I am actually married to Senator Hartwell," Karolina said, giving her best smile. She wasn't usually one to name-drop, but then again, she wasn't usually being pulled over by angry-looking cops.

The male officer furrowed his eyebrows. "Ma'am, have you been drinking?"

Karolina was vaguely aware of the boys going quiet with this question, and her mind flashed back to an hour earlier, when she'd deliberately opened a bottle of Graham's outrageously expensive cabernet that he'd been buying by the case lately. Harry and his friends had been polishing off pizzas, and of course she'd known she'd be driving them home shortly, so she'd had half a glass. If that. She hadn't even wanted it, really, but it had been satisfying to open the bottle and know that it would likely go bad before Graham got home from New York. He'd asked Karolina to join him for a New Year's dinner at a friend's apartment in Manhattan, but Karolina didn't want to leave Harry behind on New Year's Eve. She'd been upset that he'd gone without her, although she wasn't completely surprised.

Summoning her most dazzling smile and her most direct eye contact, she said, "Officers, I have children in the car. I assure you that I have not been drinking. I didn't think I was speeding either, but I suppose it's possible. If so, I'm very sorry about that."

At the mention of children, the male officer took his flashlight and began walking the perimeter of the car. He didn't seem to care that the light was shining directly in the boys' eyes. Karolina could see them all squint.

"Mom, what's happening?" Harry asked, sounding nervous.

"Nothing, honey. I'm sure it's just a misunderstanding. Just let them do what they need to do."

With this, the male officer called to the female officer and gestured to something with his flashlight. They exchanged looks. Karolina felt her heart do a little flip-flop, though there wasn't a reason in the world she should be nervous.

"Mrs. Hartwell, please get out of the car. Slowly," the female officer said.

"Excuse me?" Karolina asked. "Why on earth would I get out of my car? I'm not even wearing a coat—"

"Now!" the male cop barked, and it became immediately clear that this wasn't a routine traffic stop.

Karolina jumped out of the driver's seat so quickly that she didn't bother to use the running board, and as a result she twisted her ankle and had to grab the door to keep from falling.

The officers exchanged another look.

"Mrs. Hartwell, we have observed both reckless driving and empty bottles of alcohol in the backseat of your vehicle. Keeping your arms down by your sides, please walk in the middle of the street for a distance of approximately twenty feet. Our officers are stationed down the road, so there will be no oncoming traffic."

"Wait—you found what? In my car? You must be mistaken," Karolina said, trying not to shiver. "My husband is going to be livid when he finds out about this!"

The female officer gestured toward the very road Karolina lived on, now slick with rain, and motioned for her to walk. Immediately and without thinking, Karolina wrapped her arms around her chest to keep warm in her too-flimsy silk blouse and began to stride confidently toward her house. If there was one thing Karolina could do better than nearly anyone else on earth, it was work a catwalk. But what she hadn't expected was seeing her neighbors' doors and curtains open, their familiar faces squinted toward her, recognition dawning on their features as they realized who was performing a field sobriety test like a common criminal on their beautiful, quiet street.

Is that Mrs. Lowell? Karolina wondered, seeing an elderly woman peek out behind a crisp linen curtain. *I didn't realize she was visiting now. I can't believe she's seeing me like this.* Karolina could feel her cheeks start to color despite the cold, and somehow she must have missed the small pothole in the road, because the next thing she knew, she'd stumbled and nearly fallen.

"Did you see that?" Karolina said to the officers, who were watching her closely. "We've been telling the town forever that this road is badly in need of repair."

They gave each other that look again. Without a word exchanged, the male cop approached Karolina and said, "Ma'am, you're under arrest for suspicion of driving while under the influence. You have the right to remain—"

"Wait—what?" Karolina shrieked, before noticing that Harry had stuck his head out of the Suburban's window and was intently watching the entire scene. "Under *arrest?*"

"—silent. Anything you say can and will be used against you in a court of law. You have the right to . . ."

The words were familiar, of course. So many police procedurals she'd watched with Graham, and nights of *Law & Order* marathons in her single days, but who knew they actually said those things in real life? Was this actually happening? It seemed so surreal: one moment she was just another mom driving home her son's friends, and the next she was being escorted into the backseat of a police cruiser.

"Wait, excuse me! *Sir!* Listen please, I can't just leave the children in the car!" Karolina called as the car door slammed closed. She was alone in the backseat, entirely cut off from the world with a thick layer of presumably bulletproof glass.

The officer's voice came through some sort of speaker. "Officer Williams will look after your son and his friends and ensure that everyone gets home safely. I'll be taking you to the station now."

The engine started, and with it, the sirens went on. She couldn't hear Harry, but she could see that he was screaming "Mom" and trying very hard not to cry. Hand against the window, she mouthed to him, "Don't worry, everything's fine," but Karolina knew he couldn't see. With lights and sirens blaring in the quiet night, the cruiser pulled away from Karolina's son.

"How dare you!" she screamed at the officer, before noticing a camera with a blinking light mounted in the corner right above her window, but the officer didn't so much as glance up. Never in her life had she felt so completely helpless. So totally alone.

They hadn't allowed Karolina a phone call until nearly two hours after she'd been arrested. Was that even legal? she wondered, trying to keep calm. At least the woman officer had come by the holding room to tell Karolina that Harry and his friends were all home. The parents of the boys had each come to the station to retrieve their sons, and when Graham didn't answer his phone, Harry had suggested they call his grandmother Elaine, who had swept in to take Harry back to her house. Karolina was relieved that Harry was safe, but she was filled with dread at the idea of retrieving him from her mother-in-law.

"My husband isn't answering," Karolina said to the officer overseeing her phone call.

He was slumped over a desk filling out paperwork. He shrugged without looking up. "Try someone else."

"It's almost midnight on New Year's Eve," Karolina said. "Who am I supposed to call to come pick me up in the middle of the night from the local police station?"

With this, the officer looked up. "Pick you up? No, sorry, Mrs. Hartwell. You'll be staying here tonight."

"You can't be serious!" Karolina said, nearly certain he was joking.

"Strict orders from above. All DUIs have to sober up for at least five hours before they can be released. And we only do releases between the hours of seven a.m. and midnight, so I'm afraid you're out of luck."

"Do I look drunk to you?" Karolina asked him.

The officer glanced up. He looked barely old enough to buy beer, and the blush that spread across his neck didn't help. "Sorry, ma'am. Those are the rules."

She dialed the only other number she had memorized. Trip, who was their family lawyer and Graham's best friend, answered on the first ring.

"Lina? Where did you say you're calling from?" he asked groggily. Leave it to Trip to be asleep before midnight.

"You heard me, Trip. The local drunk tank at the Bethesda County Jail. Sorry to wake you, but I figured you'd understand. I tried Graham, but he's nowhere to be found. Surprise, surprise."

Trip and Graham had been roommates at Harvard Law and best men at each other's weddings and were godparents to each other's children. She'd always thought of Trip as almost an extension of Graham, an extra set of eyes and ears, an acceptable substitute, a brother figure. Usually they shared a warm, mutual affection. But tonight she didn't even try to mask her displeasure that she was talking to Trip and not Graham.

"Can you please get me out of this hellhole?" she whispered into the phone. "They said they won't let me out of here until morning, but that can't be possible."

"Sit tight. I'll call a few people and get this sorted out," Trip said with reassuring confidence.

"Hurry, please."

But either he didn't hurry or there was nothing he could do, because Karolina didn't speak to Trip again until he showed up to bail her out at seven the following morning. Without Graham.

Trip read her face immediately. "Graham wanted to come, of course. I was the one who advised against it."

Karolina took a seat in one of the plastic chairs next to Trip. Her entire body ached from lying on a bench in the holding room—not a cell, exactly, more like an outdated boarding gate at an old airport.

"I'm not an idiot, Trip. I understand pretty clearly that the optics of a sitting senator walking into a county jail to bail out his wife aren't great. But you can't blame me for wishing he'd done it anyway," Karolina said, trying to hold back tears. "Can you tell me what the hell is going on?"

Trip's cell phone bleated, and he silenced it without looking at the screen. "I'm going to be honest with you, Lina. This is a first-rate shit show."

"You think I don't know that? *I'm* the one who slept in jail last night. *In jail*. And where is my *husband*?"

Trip's brow furrowed. He cleared his throat. "Lina, it's not—"

Karolina held up her hand. "Don't. First I want to know who has Harry. Who's getting him to school?"

Another throat clear. Karolina almost felt bad for directing her anger with Graham at Trip. Almost. He looked so miserable. "Harry stayed the night at Elaine's house."

"He's still there?"

"You know Harry called her when they arrested you last night. Naturally, some of the journalists picked up the story from the police scanner, and a few cameras were waiting outside your house when Eleanor went to drop Harry off. She just kept driving and took him back to her place. The media has staked out your house, and we didn't want to put him through that. At least now no one knows where he is."

Karolina nodded. As much as she disliked her mother-in-law and the idea of her son having to hide out at Elaine's house, she had to agree it sounded like the best option. "Fine. Now, how are we clearing up the rest of this nightmare? This is entrapment! False arrest! We should be talking lawsuit!"

Trip coughed, looked at Karolina, and coughed again.

"Trip? What's going on?"

"It's just that . . . Well, it's complicated."

"Complicated? That's a funny word. I would say confusing, perhaps. I'm certainly *confused* that I was arrested for drunk driving when I was not driving drunk. And even if I were driving drunk—which I absolutely was not—my husband happens to be a United States senator with more connections than a teenager on Instagram, and I know *full well* that if he wanted this to disappear, it would have already," Karolina hissed.

A garbled announcement came over the loudspeaker, and a female police officer hurried past them and out the front door.

"Why don't you take me through it, Lina? Tell me exactly what happened."

It was only now, many hours into her ordeal, that Karolina felt like she may not be able to control her tears. She'd been stoic through the arrest and braver than even she would have predicted when she realized that no one was coming for her. But in the face of Trip's familiar kindness, his obvious concern—even though it should have been her husband sitting there—it was all she could do not to weep.

"Sorry," she said, swallowing a sob. "I'm just . . . overwhelmed."

Trip cleared his throat. "Did you and Harry go out at all last night?"

"Out? Of course not. I mean, only if you count running to the grocery store at about five to stock up on chips and salsa for the boys. He invited four friends over to hang out. I ordered them pizza, and they played Xbox and God knows what else twelve-year-old boys do. Face-Time girls? Each other? I don't know. I'm not proud of it, but out of spite, I opened one of Graham's thousand-dollar bottles of cabernet and poured myself half a glass. I knew that was all I was having, but it felt very satisfying to stick the barely drunk bottle into the fridge—he would have a heart attack when he saw it, and truthfully, I was looking forward to it. But that's all I had. Half a glass."

"Okay, and then what?"

"And then nothing! The boys wolfed down an entire Carvel ice cream cake in, like, thirty seconds, and they all piled into the Suburban around nine-thirty. Before I got to Billy Post's house less than a mile away, two cop cars appeared out of nowhere. Full lights and sirens, like a real emergency. I pulled over to let them pass, but then they came up to my window."

Trip nodded as though Karolina were confirming a script he already knew. "What did they say?"

"They asked if I'd been drinking. When I said of course not, they said I was driving very erratically. Which is ridiculous, because I was actually driving very slowly in our residential neighborhood."

"They said they saw empty bottles of champagne rolling around in the back of the Suburban." Trip said this quietly, looking down at his hands.

"Oh, did they? Well, that's *impossible*. Because I don't even like champagne. Neither does Graham. It gives us both headaches—" She paused. Unless the kids had gotten into it? Karolina scrunched her nose in consideration. Was it possible? Twelve was hardly too young to try sneaking alcohol for the first time. Was she being delusional in thinking Harry would never try a drink? No, she knew her kid. She knew he'd be exactly like every other teenager and experiment with all kinds of things, but she was also positive that he wasn't there yet. And even if she was completely off-base and the boys had gotten into Graham's prized wine cellar, there was no way five twelve-year-old boys could even open a bottle of champagne undetected, much less polish off two bottles. She remembered back to the night before. Both Harry and his friends had all seemed completely normal: rowdy, yes, but certainly *sober*. "No. That wasn't it. I have no idea how the bottles got there."

Trip placed his palm over the top of her hand, and it felt warm, comforting. "I'm so sorry, Lina. This can't be easy."

All it took was that small expression of sympathy for the tears to start freely flowing again. Karolina was certain she had dragonlike streams of mascara running down her cheeks, but considering she'd just spent the night in jail, she figured it wasn't the worst of her appearance problems.

"But here's the part that makes absolutely no sense. They brought me back here. Then without giving me a Breathalyzer or anything, they throw me in that room for the night. On what grounds? Empty bottles in my car? How is that even allowed?"

Trip's phone rang again, and the force with which he pressed "decline" startled her. He cleared his throat. "The police said you refused both the Breathalyzer and a follow-up offer of a blood test. Maryland is an implied-consent state, which means that by even having a driver's license, you consent to be tested. Refusal to participate in all chemical testing immediately results in a DUI."

"You can't be serious."

"I do mostly corporate work, Lina, you know that. Barely any litigation and certainly no criminal. But I did consult with a colleague before coming here, and he took me through the laws."

"No, I mean you can't be serious that they're saying I refused a Breathalyzer. It was the exact opposite, actually—I asked for one. *Begged* for one. I knew it would put this entire misunderstanding to rest if I could just . . ."

"Lina? You know Graham and I will have the very best people on this. So long as we all stay calm, I know we will work through—"

The rest of his words garbled together as the repercussions of what had happened began to play slowly, full color, in her mind. She could practically see the headlines—SUPERMODEL-TURNED-SENATOR'S WIFE DRINKS WHILE DRIVING KIDDIES—and predict the intense media scrutiny and the humiliation of people believing she would do something like this. And Harry. Mostly Harry. Twelve-year-olds should be embarrassed by their stepmothers because of the jeans they wore, not because they were arrested for driving a car full of kids around drunk.

Then another feeling, one that surprised her with its brute strength: a yearning for her husband that was so visceral, it nearly took her breath away. How had they gotten here? To a place where she'd spent the night in jail and her husband—her lifelong partner—had left her there and then sent his friend to retrieve her in the morning. No, this couldn't be right. Something was going on, something out of their control. Yes, there had been some distance lately. She'd felt more disconnected from Graham than usual. There was less intimacy. She even suspected he might be cheating on her again. But this was *Graham*. The man who had made meticulous arrangements to ensure her entire extended family's financial security. The person who told her at least ten times a day how gorgeous she was. She could remember their wedding like it was yesterday. The vibrant green vineyards had provided a gorgeous backdrop to the unexpected rain, which might have ruined the day for another couple, but not for them. They'd barely noticed, they were so wrapped up in dancing and laughing and each other. She'd sat at their shared table and looked up at her strong, handsome husband as he thanked everyone for celebrating with them. When he'd turned to her and extended his hand, she could see the tears in his eyes, and the toast he gave was so clearly heartfelt and true. And now this.

Trip was still talking. Something about legal precedent. The fatigue was beginning to hit her, and the sadness and the humiliation and the loneliness all at once.

"I'm exhausted," she said, again wiping her eyes. "Can you take me to get Harry?"

"Of course. Let's get you out of here."

They drove in silence to her mother-in-law's house in Arlington. Trip pulled away the moment Karolina reached the front porch.

"Karolina," Elaine said when she opened the door, as though she'd just tasted something bitter.

"Elaine. Thank you for picking up Harry," Karolina forced herself to say as she placed her coat on the hallway bench and followed her mother-in-law, without invitation, to the kitchen.

"Someone had to. And contact the parents of those other boys."

"Yes, well, thank you again. Where's Harry?"

"He's still sleeping," her mother-in-law said. "It was a traumatic night for him."

Karolina pointedly ignored the woman, and when no offer was forthcoming, she rose to fix herself a cup of coffee. "Would you like one?" she asked Elaine, who merely waved her off.

"You've got a real . . . situation on your hands, Karolina. It's none of my business, but if you're having trouble, you should have sought help. But a DUI? The wife of a senator? Of the future president of the United States? It's one thing not to think about yourself, but how could you not have considered Graham's career?"

"You mean Harry's safety? I must have heard you wrong."

Elaine waved her off again while making a clucking sound. "You know I don't like to get involved in things between you and Graham, but this time the circumstances—"

"Mother, *please.*"

Graham's voice caused Karolina to jump just enough to spill coffee down the front of her sweater. "Graham?" she asked, although he was standing right there in front of her, looking handsome. Karolina waited for him to run and embrace her, and she extended her arms to receive him. He didn't move. He stood in that doorway, glancing between his wife and his mother, looking like there was nowhere else on earth he'd less rather be. Everything about him was immaculate, from his custom shirt and pressed chinos to the thick dark hair he had cut every third Friday. Cashmere socks. Professionally clean-shaven. Hermès overnight bag. And the subtlest crinkle of crow's-feet around his green eyes, just enough to lend him gravitas. He was six feet and two inches of expensively groomed masculine perfection.

"I didn't know you were here," Karolina heard herself squeak out, self-consciously pulling her arms back in. "Trip said you were on an Acela."

"I was actually just leaving," he said, walking past her into the kitchen. His voice was as cold and impersonal as the stainless fridge doors.

"Where are you going?" Karolina asked, shocked by his distance. He was mad at *her*? Of course he didn't think she'd driven the children while drinking—he of all people knew she was practically a teetotaler these days. Shouldn't *she* be the aggrieved party right about now, what with him leaving her in jail *overnight* for a crime she didn't commit?

"Here, darling, let me get you a cup of coffee," Elaine said to Graham, leaping out of her chair with newfound vigor.

"Elaine, would you mind giving us a minute?" Karolina asked.

The woman, appearing greatly offended, looked at Graham, who nodded his approval. "Thank you, Mother."

Elaine made a big show of gathering up her coffee and banana; the moment she walked out, Karolina practically ran to Graham. "Hey, what's going on with you?" she asked. And then, trying very hard to keep her voice light, "Not sure if you heard or not, but I spent New Year's Eve in the slammer."

He turned sharply to her and shrugged her hands off his arm. "Is this some kind of a joke to you? Is that what this is—funny?"

Karolina could feel her mouth open in shock. "Funny?" she sputtered. "Of course not. It was horrible, every minute of it. And where have you been? You send Trip? You know I—"

"All I know is what I heard from the Bethesda Police Department, Karolina. According to Chief Cunningham, you were detained during a routine sobriety checkpoint after failing a roadside test."

His use of her full name, Karolina, instead of Lina, hit home.

"Graham, I know what they *said*, but I also know that—"

He slammed his palm against the countertop. "How could you do that? How could you possibly be that stupid?" His face and neck were a mottled red. "And with my son in the car, no less!"

"*Your* son?" Karolina asked. "You meant to say *our* son. He may be my stepson, but you know I've never called him or thought of him as anything less than my own."

Graham tossed his full mug in the sink and held a finger inches from her face. His eyes were slits. "You need to wake Harry up right now and get him home safely. Can you manage that? Obviously, by Uber, since you're not driving anywhere. Those leeches"—he motioned toward the manicured Bethesda street out front—"will find you. I hope it goes without saying that you are not to speak to a single one of them. Not a word. Don't even make eye contact. Do you understand me?"

Karolina moved closer to him, hoping to see him soften. "Why are you acting like this? You know I didn't drive drunk. You know how private I am. You know I would never, ever do anything to put Harry—or anyone else's children—at risk." Karolina sounded desperate, pleading, but she couldn't help it. It was one thing for her husband not to pick her up from jail, but it was another for him to be so livid over a crime she obviously didn't commit.

He had a brand-new hardness in his eyes. "I'll be home tonight. Remember—talk to no one." And with that, he left the kitchen.

4

Some of My Best
Friends Are Jewish

Emily

When the elevator doors opened directly into an apartment with floor-to-ceiling views of the Freedom Tower and both the East and Hudson rivers, Emily tried to arrange her expression into one of nonchalance. She'd been in some impressive homes in her time. The Kardashian spread in Hollywood wasn't too slouchy. George and Amal's Lake Como spread didn't suck. And no one could say that Miranda Priestly's Fifth Avenue townhouse wasn't spectacular. But there was something about this $12 million fifty-eighth-floor-penthouse glass magnificence that took her breath away. Since there weren't many skyscrapers in Tribeca, it felt like they were floating alone in the clouds. There was so much natural light she had to squint, and the starkly modern furnishings and complete openness of the enormous space gave it an otherworldly feel.

"Thank you so much for coming," Helene said, pushing her hair back. For as long as Emily could remember, Helene had worn her hair in the most spectacular Afro—wild, massive, and fabulous—but today it was tamed into a trillion tight, shiny ringlets that framed her entire face.

"Of course," Emily said, setting her overstuffed Goyard tote down on the entryway bench. She'd received six panicked texts from her assistant, Kyle, on the way from the airport. Apparently Helene was having a meltdown. "Is he here?"

Helene nodded, ringlets shaking. "His trainer is with him. They should be done in a couple minutes. Can I get you anything? Some coffee? A stiff drink? I could sure use one."

"How about both together? I won't say no to that."

Emily followed her into the blindingly white lacquered kitchen where a uniformed Hispanic woman stood in front of a Starbucks-level espresso machine. "Clara, could we each get a flat white with a shot of Baileys, please?" If Clara thought it even a tiny bit strange that these two professional women were requesting a spiked coffee at three in the afternoon, she gave no indication. The woman expertly prepared their drinks and led them to a white leather couch that looked directly out at the spectacular view.

"So, I guess we should start with the obvious," Emily said, taking a sip. "Why did he pick a Nazi outfit to wear to a costume party?"

Helene looked at her hands as if searching for strength. "It wasn't a costume party."

"Come again?"

"What can I say, Emily? He's a kid. A dumb kid with too much money and too much time and too many people exactly like you and me to cover his ass. It's not a new story."

"No. But it makes everything that much harder." Emily glanced at her watch. Not that she had anywhere else to be, but she had flown cross-country with zero notice to help this boy, and it was high time to meet him.

Helene noticed. "Here, come with me. I'll introduce you."

The women walked down a long white hallway lined with street art–inspired paintings and down a winding staircase. Another hallway, this one covered with graffiti, led to a set of glass French doors. Inside she could see Rizzo in a set of boxing gloves, furiously punching a red bag that hung from the ceiling. A beautiful girl wearing only hot pants and a fuchsia sports bra hopped around yelling at him.

Helene rapped on the door. Both Rizzo and the girl glanced up but didn't stop punching or jumping.

"Riz? Can you take a break for a minute? There's someone I'd like to introduce you to."

Emily should have been staring at his sweaty, shirtless, six-packed chest, but her eyes were immediately drawn to the trainer, whose sports bra featured a cutout all along its band, resulting in two inches of below-the-nipple bare breasts bulging out, threatening to emerge from their flimsy cover at any moment. It was so interesting, Emily thought, to wear a sports bra—which by definition was supposed to contain and support one's breasts—and then cut away most of the fabric that would actually do either one of those things. She suddenly felt ancient.

"Hey, great work, Riz," the girl said, swatting him on the ass with a towel. Her breasts heaved. Emily noticed she wasn't alone in staring at them—Rizzo and Helene were captivated too.

"Thanks, baby. See you tomorrow." Rizzo yanked the towel out of her hand and draped it around his neck. All three of them watched as the girl grabbed her duffel and her boxing gloves and walked toward the door.

"Damn," Rizzo breathed as he stared after her.

"Hey, Rizzo? I'm Emily Charlton. Helene brought me in to help manage the . . . situation from last night. It's really nice to meet you."

His eyes met hers, and for a split second Emily was torn between feeling like the only woman in the world and feeling like a complete pedophile for finding an eighteen-year-old so damn sexy. No one had eyes like that; could that shade of green even be real?

"Hey, thanks for coming. Very cool of you, but I do think Helene is overreacting a little."

Rizzo twisted open a bottle of SmartWater and drank the entire thirty-four ounces without taking a breath. Helene gave Emily a look that said, *Why don't you take this one.*

"I'm sure you didn't mean anything . . . nefarious by it, Rizzo, but especially after what happened in Charlottesville last year, the public tends to make a pretty big deal out of anti-Semitism, which is typically how wearing a Nazi costume is interpreted. So we should definitely get out in front of this."

He waved his hand and started on another bottle. "All just for laughs. People get it. My fans get it."

Emily took a deep breath and tried to keep her voice even. "Okay, maybe. But some fans might not. The Jewish ones in particular. Or any-one who was not in favor of the Holocaust, which is probably a lot of people. Certainly your sponsors—Uniqlo, Lexus, SmartWater—won't be thrilled. And I don't imagine Sony will be either. So I've come up with a plan to extricate you from all this ugliness. One hundred percent clean, a do-over. As long as you listen and play your part well, this will all go away, I promise."

Rizzo didn't appear particularly impressed, but he looked at her and waited.

"I'll call all my contacts at the usuals: the *Post*, *HuffPo*, TMZ, *Variety*, etcetera, and explain how you thought the swastika was an ancient Buddhist symbol of peace. We'll play the idiot card. Just a role, but im-portant to play up: you're young and inexperienced and horrified that you offended anyone. You read about the symbol in a Buddhist text you were studying for a meditation class and really connected with its peace-ful message."

"Young and inexperienced?"

"You're not, of course," Emily said. "That's just the part you're going to play." When he didn't say anything, she continued, "You will make yourself available for all respectable interviews, where you'll be contrite and apologetic. You'll make a massive donation to the ADL. You'll pay a very public visit to the Holocaust Museum in D.C., where you'll meet with Jewish clergy and issue a formal statement stressing that this was all a mistake and a misunderstanding and not at all representative of who you are. You'll repeat it a thousand times, or however many it takes, with genuine sincerity, until the story shifts gears and you suddenly become a champion of peace and a defender of persecuted peoples everywhere. Trust me, we can get there so long as we all follow the script."

"That's smart," Helene said, nodding. "Emily's plan sounds like exactly what we need."

Rizzo snorted. "Really? I think it sounds asinine. I'm supposed to go out there and pretend like I'm some sort of idiot?"

Emily could feel Helene trying just as hard as she was not to exchange any glances.

"I mean, this is all such bullshit. Total overkill."

"Do you have another suggestion?" Emily asked, her voice as neutral as she could manage. He really was as huge a fucking idiot as she'd imagined he would be.

"Yeah, dude, I'll post an explanation—that I was just having fun on New Year's and never wanted to piss anyone off. I mean, I don't have anything against Jews. My agent is Jewish. My accountant is Jewish. Hell, *all* of my lawyers are Jewish. My fans know I'm not a hater."

"Rizzo, I can't express strongly enough that the best response is definitely *not* 'some of my best friends are Jewish,'" Emily said. "I really don't think you can get away with Snapchatting a 'my bad' and expect it all to go away. Because it won't."

"If I post it to Linger, that's exactly what will happen."

Emily had no idea what Linger was, but she wasn't about to admit it. "Rizzo, this is what I do. Affleck after the nanny. Bieber after the wanker pictures. Kevin Spacey after the fourteen-year-old. DUIs. Drunken rants at cops. Political rants at Oscars. Shoplifting. More sex tapes than I could ever count. I can *help* you."

"Cool," he said. "I'll think about it and get back to you." And before Emily could mask her shock, he strolled out of the gym and closed the door behind him.

Emily looked to Helene, who shrugged. "He's just like that," she said. "He knows you're right."

"Really? I didn't get that impression. And this isn't something that can wait. I've already seen the pictures on Radar Online. Has he?"

"I know, I totally agree with you. Let me talk to him after he cools down, and I'll call you. You'll be local?"

Emily nodded, although she hadn't given one moment's thought as to where she was headed next. She'd come directly from JFK with her suitcase, figuring she'd be working out of Rizzo's apartment for the rest of the day and night, at which point she'd check in to a hotel. But now? With no confirmed job?

Helene walked her to the foyer, and the maid appeared with Emily's rolling suitcase. "Thank you for coming on such short notice. I'll call you within the hour, okay?"

But Emily's phone rang before the elevator reached the lobby. "That was fast."

"I'm really sorry, Emily, but I wanted to tell you right away. He wants to . . . go in a different direction."

"A different direction? What, is he planning to join the KKK? Because even I would have a hard time smoothing that one over."

Helene didn't laugh. "I told him you were the absolute best, but he wants to go with Olivia Belle. Apparently she called him this morning and he liked what she had to say. I can't tell you how sorry I am. We'll of course cover your flight and time, just invoice me."

"Are you serious?" Emily asked, not able to help herself.

"I think he's making a mistake, and I told him as much. But if he listened to me, we wouldn't be in this situation."

"No, I get it," Emily said, even though she didn't. She mumbled something about talking later and hung up as soon as she could. Thankfully, the lobby furniture was both welcoming and empty, because she sank into an armchair without even looking.

Olivia Belle? If that was even her real name. Was he fucking kidding? *She was a child.* Granted, one with an Instagram following of more than two million people, compared to Emily's twenty thousand. But still. Instagram didn't fix crises. Followers didn't manage megacelebrities. Tweeting was not a sufficient solution to a catastrophe.

Still, this was the third big job she'd lost to that bitch. Olivia Belle was twenty-six and gorgeous and popping up at every worthwhile party and event on both coasts. She was loud. And all over every social-media platform. And moving in on Emily's clients as if she owned the industry.

Emily started dialing Kyle before she remembered it was New Year's Day. She could call Miles, she supposed, but he was probably working out or hanging with friends. Instead she pushed "Miriam" on her favorites list and laughed, as she always did, when a picture of her friend grinning in the dorkiest way popped up on her screen.

"Hi!" Miriam said. Kids were yelling in the background. "Isn't it early for you to be awake? What, like noon?"

"I'm in New York, actually. I hate that you left the city. Why didn't you think about me for one second when you made this asinine decision to be a suburban housewife?"

"Aw, sweetie. I miss you too!"

"I'm serious. I'm here, what? Like, twice a month? And you just left."

Miriam laughed. "I'm thirty minutes away, Em. There are trains that come here, like, every five seconds. How long are you staying? I'll come meet you tomorrow as soon as the kids are back in school."

"I don't know. I just got fired by Rizzo Benz. Or not ever even hired, I'm not sure which. Olivia Belle is ruining my life."

"She's a child. She doesn't have anything on you. And Rizzo Benz is an idiot for thinking she does."

"Three jobs now. And that's not even counting the other two I lost to her last year. Whatever," Emily said, glaring back at the doorman, who shot her a look for cursing or talking too loudly or using the lobby like her personal office or all of the above.

"How many times has Miranda called you now?"

"I cannot go back to *Runway!*" Emily blurted.

"Director of special events sure sounds huge to me."

"I know, but I'd feel ridiculous going back. New York, sure. But to give up my autonomy? I decide where and when and how I work, for whom, and how much. It feels like the wrong move to give that up and go back where I started."

"I hear you. But it's Miranda Priestly. Think of the wardrobe budget. The parties . . . It's the job a million girls would die for . . ."

"You did not just say that."

"Sorry, I couldn't help myself."

Emily heard a loud crash in the background, followed by crying. "Which monster is that? I'll let you go."

"Matthew! How many times do I have to tell you that you may not touch the fireplace poker? It's not a toy!" And then to Emily in a whisper, "Sorry. He can be such an asshole."

Emily smiled. Anyone who could call her adorable five-year-old an asshole was someone she wanted to be friends with.

"Em? If you really have nothing to do, why don't you come here? We have a guest suite with your name on it. Totally sequestered, up on the third floor, with no children anywhere nearby. Stay a night. Or as long as you like. I'll text you the train information."

"The train?" Emily spat, as though Miriam had just suggested she walk from Tribeca to Greenwich.

"Everyone takes it, love. It's not just for unstylish people."

Emily harrumphed. "Fine. I'll come. I can't bear to get on a plane right away. And of course I'd like to see those rug rats of yours. But only one night," she said, and clicked her phone off before she could change her mind. Then she swiped it open once more and punched her location into the Uber app. Emily Charlton might be a washed-up, middle-aged Luddite, but she most definitely did *not* take the train.

5

Just Give Up. I Have

Miriam

As the door quietly closed behind her, Miriam surveyed the tangle of toys in the garage that, in New York, her children hadn't even known existed—bikes, sleds, skis, Rollerblades, scooters, even an old-fashioned wooden wagon—and smiled. They were so lucky to live in a place like this, and even six months in, she didn't take it for granted.

The mudroom, as usual, looked like a hurricane had hit, with overflowing cubbies of puffers and mittens, raincoats and hats and snow boots and scarves and umbrellas, and the kitchen after breakfast always looked like a starving rabid raccoon had nosed its way into every single cabinet and drawer.

"Hey," Miriam heard from the couch before she could see the source of the voice.

"Em?" she asked, although she knew full well that was the only person who would be watching *talk shows* in the family room on a Tuesday morning. Emily had been with them for three days now, poring over gossip sites and newspaper articles about Rizzo Benz and Olivia Belle; she showed no signs of leaving. "Thanks for cleaning up—you shouldn't have."

"What?" Emily turned and glanced at the kitchen. Miriam could see she was in a ratty T-shirt that read BUT FIRST, COFFEE, and a borrowed pair of Miriam's flannel pajama pants that looked like they were three sizes too big. An open laptop sat on the couch beside her. "Oh, I wasn't getting near that disaster. Please. Don't you have someone to handle that?"

Miriam rolled her eyes and stuck a pod in the machine. "Do you want a coffee?"

"Are you coming from actually working out?" Emily asked. "Or are Lululemons considered getting dressed around here?"

"Both, actually. I went to a nine o'clock SoulCycle class."

"Wow, I'm impressed. The Miriam Kagan I know is not the Soul kind of girl."

"Yeah, well, I try to go a couple days a week. Not like the other moms. The instructor asked today who was 'doubling,' and half the class raised their hands. Three of them were *tripling*."

"Three hours of your day and a hundred and twenty bucks—aggressive. Even for Greenwich," Emily said. "At least in Santa Monica, they don't admit to it."

Miriam dumped in a splash of half-and-half and grabbed a croissant from the plastic bucket of assorted Trader Joe's breakfast pastries.

"You can't outrun a bad diet, you know," Emily called.

Miriam gave Emily the finger and shoved the croissant in her mouth.

"A minute on the lips, a lifetime on the hips."

"These hips can handle one croissant, trust me." Miriam grabbed a love handle with one hand while balancing her coffee cup with the other. The croissant hung out of her mouth as she carefully lowered herself into the chair opposite Emily, trying to ignore the sensation of her stomach fat rolling over the waistband of her yoga pants. The high-waisted waistband. With extra compression. "What are you working on?"

"Trying to get my career back. I'm being Snapchatted to irrelevance. When did we get so old?"

"We're thirty-six. It's hardly ancient."

"Look around. You have three kids. And a professionally decorated house." Emily surveyed the family room. "It's lovely, but whoever did this clearly hates color. It's like fifty shades of gray without the S and M."

Miriam nodded. "Exactly how I like it. So, what's going on? I hardly think it's fair to say that your career is in the toilet just because Rizzo Benz went with Olivia Belle. Or are we still not allowed to talk about it?"

"It's not just Rizzo." Emily sighed. "Maybe I'm losing my touch."

"Your touch? You went from being the top stylist in Hollywood to managing top celebrities in crisis. But if you don't like it, do something else. You clearly *can*." Miriam polished off the last of her croissant. "What does Miles think?"

Emily shrugged. "He thinks like you. I'm overreacting. I'm great. But he's not even around these days. He's about to go to Hong Kong for three months."

"Go with him," Miriam said.

"I'm not going to Hong Kong."

"It's a great city."

"Maybe I'm depressed. Look what I'm wearing," Emily said.

"Looks fine to me. Move in here and you can live in your pajamas all day. Just give up. I have."

"Yeah, you have," Emily said. "I never thought I'd see Ms. Editor of the *Harvard Law Review* doing school drop-off followed by SoulCycle class."

"That's harsh. But fair, I guess. You should hear my mother. She's literally embarrassed by me."

"Your mother won a Pulitzer when she was twenty-eight and ignored you until you were in college."

"Last week Matthew told us, 'When I grow up, I want to be an inventor just like Daddy.' And then Maisie, without missing a beat, says, 'Well, when I grow up, I want to go to the gym like Mommy.'"

Emily laughed. "Ouch."

"Yeah, I know. Like, 'Sweetie, Mommy has a JD/MBA from Harvard. She made partner at the most prestigious firm in the city at thirty-four. Up until a lousy six months ago, Mommy worked eighty hours a week helping multinational companies and was the breadwinner for this family.'"

"Did you say that?"

Miriam snorted. "She's five. And the goal is *not* to become my mother, right? I said something inane about whether she grows up to become a mommy or a musician or an architect or a firefighter, all that matters is that she's happy."

"And you believe that?" Emily asked, eyebrows raised.

"Yes! I do now. I've been operating at a hundred percent since I was *her* age. I blinked, and my kids went from newborns to school-aged real human beings with their own thoughts and feelings, and I missed most of it because I was always at work. Now that Paul's sold his start-up everything's upside down, like we hit the lottery. How do I explain that having the chance to take a breather midlife and evaluate everything is rarer than a double rainbow?"

"Tell me you didn't say all that." Emily brushed hair out of her eye.

"I didn't say all that. I asked if she wanted a bag of cheddar bunnies, and she broke down hysterically crying because she only likes the cookie ones. But seriously, Em, how lucky am I right now? I have choices. Not a lot of people can say that. You can too."

"It's been, what? Six months out of the city? Another six and you'll want to step directly in front of one of those Range Rovers out there."

"Maybe. But for now it's okay. Besides, I'm doing some freelance stuff on the side. Local projects, to keep my edge."

"Like?"

Miriam could see that Emily's attention was already starting to drift back to the TV. On the screen, Hoda and Kathie Lee were drinking rosé.

"Like nanny tax law. Prenups. Estate planning. That kind of thing."

"Sounds scintillating."

"Don't be a bitch."

"That's exactly what you said to me during the summer we met when you thought I was making fun of that nitwit. What was her name? Rosalie?"

Miriam laughed, remembering how everyone else at camp was scared of Emily, who wore lipstick despite the no makeup rule, slept in boxer shorts she claimed belonged to her older boyfriend, and said "fuck" with abandon. Miriam had never met someone who would flat-out refuse to play lacrosse for "personal reasons," or insist on wearing stilettos to the weekly dances on the basketball court with the boys' camp, or convince the CITs to sneak her cigarettes. The first week they met, Miriam thought Emily was mocking a bunkmate's weight, and Miriam told her in front of everyone to stop being a bitch. By visiting day, they were introducing each other to their parents as best friends, and by summer's end, they clung to each other when it came time to say goodbye.

"How do you remember that? I was convinced you were calling her fat," Miriam said.

"She may have been a little bit of a chunker, but I was walking like an elephant because I was imitating that buffoon who worked in the office—what was his name? Something rapey."

"Chester."

"Yes, Chester! Have you ever looked him up? We should Google him. I bet he has more pedophilia arrests than we can count. I'm just sure of it."

"He was the grossest man ever," Miriam said. "He leered at all the girls whenever they went in to pick up mail or drop off postcards."

Miriam's phone rang. "It's her. Finally!" she said, and snatched her phone from the table. "There you are!" Miriam said before Karolina could say a word. "How are you? Where are you? I've been leaving messages for you stalker-style for three days!"

"You saw the papers," Karolina said, her slight Eastern European accent sounding more pronounced.

"Of course I saw the papers! The whole universe saw the papers! But I didn't believe them for a second. Where are you? I must have left a thousand messages."

"I'm in Greenwich."

"What?"

"To 'collect myself.' "

"Oh my God. I'm coming over." Miriam glanced at the wall clock. "I need to shower, but I can be there within the hour."

At this, Emily looked up. "Who is it?" she mouthed.

"You don't have to rush over. I'm sure I'll be here for a while," Karolina said, her voice breaking. "I just miss Harry."

"Oh, honey, I'm on my way. Same address?"

Karolina sobbed. "Yes, the hideous house with the gold-enameled mailbox."

Miriam pictured the McMansion . . . splashed across the cover of the *Post* that morning with the headline WHERE WILL HIGH-FLYING MRS. HARTWELL LAND THIS TIME?

"Okay, I'll see you soon. Can I bring anything?"

"Maybe some pills? What do people take these days? You wouldn't know it from the news, but I'm out of the loop. Valium? No, that's old-school. Percocet? I feel like now is an excellent time to develop a prescription-pill problem. I'm a drunk, apparently. No one will be surprised."

"Sit tight, I'll be right there."

"What? A mommy friend calling to commiserate about her maid stealing the silverware?" Emily asked, typing furiously on her laptop.

"Karolina Hartwell calling to say that she's here in Greenwich."

Miriam was halfway to the stairs when Emily called, "I'm coming with you!"

"No, it's not a good time. She sounds really upset. I don't think she would want a stranger showing up at her house."

"I'm not a stranger! I met her a hundred times when I was at *Runway*. She must have been on the cover, what, five times while I worked there? She was in and out of the office every three seconds. I can *help* her!"

"I don't know . . ."

"Trust me, it'll be good to have me around. You go shower. I'll change and pack a few necessities. Between the two of us, we can cheer her up."

Miriam nodded. As usual, she felt powerless to stand in the way when Emily made her mind up. "Meet me in the car in twenty. And please, no booze until we hear what's really going on with her."

Miriam was halfway up the stairs but could hear Emily in the refrigerator. "Moët is hardly booze!" Emily called after her. Miriam smiled to herself and thought how much she loved that crazy bitch.

6

Just a Cottage
in the Country

Karolina

As it neared eleven, Karolina peered out the window near the door that faced the grand circular driveway, working her hair into twisty knots. When they'd bought the Greenwich house a couple years into their marriage, Graham had insisted they add the automated wrought-iron gate to the driveway for security purposes. She remembered feeling like it was a prison but hadn't wanted to start another fight. "It's the smart move," Graham had said. "It's what people do." He'd sounded both supremely confident and totally vague.

Karolina had had a hard time understanding Graham's obsession with the house in the country. They were living in a lovely apartment in a full-service building on Sixty-Third and Park, close to the midtown law office where he was working backbreaking hours as a new associate. Who needed Greenwich? They did, Graham swore. Acres of manicured lawn and great restaurants and fabulous shopping and only a stone's throw from Manhattan. They could have a garden and a pool and enough space to host all their friends over snowy winter weekends or long vacations in the summer. She remained steadfastly unconvinced until he had played his trump card: Harry would have a place to roam and explore without fear of getting hit by a taxi or kidnapped in plain daylight. Was she really going to say no to that? The boy was two when they got married and still wouldn't walk barefoot on grass. Harry was motherless—Graham's first wife had died tragically of a rare type of stomach cancer when he was an infant—so how could Karolina possibly be the one to deny him this opportunity? Wasn't it time that Harry had a swing set?

Those were some of the sweetest times of their marriage. She was still swept off her feet by Graham's charm and social connections, his private clubs and the ease with which he navigated his world. He was a twenty-first-century JFK Junior, dashing and handsome and wealthy. She knew he could have chosen anyone, but he'd chosen Karolina. As successful a model as she'd been through the years, deep down she was still just a poor girl from Wrocław. Beautiful, yes. But also sheltered by a protective mother and surrounded by friends and family who had lacked education. How could she not fall for a man who swept her into private clubs where Rockefellers and Carnegies dined? It was a glimpse into an entirely different world than modeling afforded her. It was storied.

In those early years they threw lavish parties and extravagant dinners and booze-heavy cocktail hours. They laughed all the time and liked watching the same shows. It was hard to pinpoint exactly when things began to shift, but Karolina thought it had a lot to do with searching for the perfect Greenwich house.

It didn't take long for Graham's wish list to balloon in both size and grandeur: the quest for a modest four-bedroom home on a cul-de-sac quickly became an intense hunt for a minimum of seven bedrooms, two acres, a pool, and a tennis court. And although at the time Graham drank exclusively beer or whiskey, it was suddenly imperative that they have a humidity-controlled wine cellar with a tasting room. Newest. Biggest. Fanciest. Karolina should have listened to those warning bells. But she didn't.

On the fourth visit, a spectacular October weekend at peak foliage, Graham fell in love with a house that was designed by a famous architect. It was ultra-modern, with jutting angles and miles of glass: 35 Honeysuckle Lane sounded like it fit the bill, but it looked like it belonged in a movie featuring a sociopath. It was perhaps the least child-friendly home she'd ever seen, but she couldn't argue with Harry's obvious glee as he sprinted across the beautiful backyard and giggled uncontrollably as the oversize fish in the koi pond leapt up as he tossed them bits of his bagel. They'd closed fifteen days later, a record, according to the blue-haired realtor. Karolina had the good sense to require that the house be in both their names. The money was entirely hers, earned from nearly a decade of modeling while Graham was still living off the interest from the trust fund he couldn't touch until he was forty. He tried to argue it would be better for "tax purposes" to list only his name on the deed, but she had insisted. If only she had known how many weeks and months the house would sit empty and unloved save for a quick trip out to pay the caretakers and groundskeeper and make sure it was still standing. The last time they'd stayed there as a family was before Graham had won the Senate race four years earlier and they'd all relocated to Bethesda, and that was only for the night.

Karolina checked the picture window facing the lawn once again. She'd been in Greenwich a few days, not enough time to get lonely, but there she was, desperately waiting for Miriam. Usually an elderly couple lived in the house as a kind of caretaker-and-housekeeper team, but Karolina had asked if they'd like to take some vacation time, and they'd been all too happy to go visit their daughter. She didn't feel like making polite conversation. Or, honestly, showering. And the solitude had been healing. It was a relief to look out on one's front lawn and see only empty stretches of space after the paparazzi crush in Bethesda.

A text came in from Harry.

what do i wear to a school dance????

She smiled and typed back. *Your navy Brooks Brothers suit with your white dress shirt.*

Tie????

Yes. Winter Party! Your first dance!

He replied with a *"Y."*

Is Daddy going? He knows that parents are invited, right?

This time the three dots popped up, disappeared, returned. Then: *No, he's dropping me off. Your sure about the tie???*

Karolina felt her throat tighten. Wasn't it obvious? This boy needed her. To advise on outfits, yes, but also to accompany him on his first time being a guest at Sidwell's Winter Party. Who was going to help him choose shoes or cheer for him beside the dance floor when he competed in Coke & Pepsi, or chat with all his friends and their parents? She knew Harry was growing up, that soon he would start to negotiate these things on his own, but good God—the boy was only twelve! And twelve-year-olds needed their mothers.

Finally the doorbell rang, sounding like a Buddhist monk hitting a giant gong. Karolina yanked the front door open and found Miriam smiling, looking very suburban in jeans and Uggs and a massive puffer coat, holding her arms outstretched. It was strange to see Miriam in something besides a suit. The women embraced, and as Karolina inhaled the vanilla-scented moisturizer Miriam had been wearing for twenty years, she thought how wonderful it was to be with someone who didn't hate her. Miriam motioned toward the Highlander, where Karolina saw a woman in the passenger seat smoking a cigarette and screaming into her cell phone. Karolina raised her eyebrows.

"Sorry. It's Emily Charlton. She's staying with me now for . . . I don't know how long. She's an old camp friend. Anyway, she overheard me on the phone with you and insisted she come too. She says she knows you from *Runway*? I feel terrible bringing her by unannounced, which is why I told her to wait in the car while I—"

Karolina held her hand to her forehead, shielding her eyes, and squinted. "Emily?" she said. "Hey! Come on in. And bring those cigarettes!" She turned to Miriam. "I totally remember her from *Runway*. Miranda Priestly's senior assistant. She was such a bitch!"

"Oh, I know it. Emily has told me all the stories . . ."

"No, I meant Emily! She was a first-rate ball-buster and funny as hell. I could use funny right now."

Both women watched as Emily jammed her finger into the phone screen to end the call and opened the door in a cloud of smoke. "Am I cleared to enter? Did I pass?" she called as she walked toward the house.

Karolina and Emily exchanged double cheek kisses. "It's so good to see you! How long has it been? Years," Karolina said as she escorted them to a sitting room. She pointed a remote toward the fireplace and flames leapt to life. "Here, sit. I made some tea, I'll bring it in."

When she returned holding an enamel tray with a glass teapot and three glass mugs, both women assessed the room. "Welcoming, isn't it?" Karolina asked, acutely aware of how it looked to outsiders: the couches low and stiff and uninviting; the surfaces devoid of books or knickknacks; the walls bare except for a few fine-art black and whites.

"I fucking love it," Emily breathed, looking around. "It's like no one lives here."

"No one does live here," Karolina said. "Although I guess I might soon."

Miriam's face crumpled. "I'm so sorry about everything that's happening."

"Yeah, quite the drama," Emily said. "That headline this morning: 'Most Hated Celeb: Rizzo Benz or Karolina Hartwell?' My God. I haven't seen the press this excited since Harvey Weinstein."

Karolina opened her mouth to talk, but she felt the now-familiar knot in her throat. "It's been . . . hard. And confusing. I just didn't expect it to be so vicious in Washington. Reporters . . . are . . ."

"Staking out the house, I imagine?" Emily asked.

"Oh my God. They're everywhere. I've never seen anything like this. Not when they thought I was having an affair with George Clooney pre-Amal. Not even when Graham was elected to the senate. They were three deep at our home in Bethesda." She motioned to the front door. "Thank God for that hideous fence Graham had installed here."

"How is Harry?" Miriam asked, sipping her tea.

Karolina shook her head. "I don't know. Graham insisted we take an Uber from my mother-in-law's house, and literally, a mob of people descended on us as soon as we pulled in. And you know what the first question was? 'Are you drunk right now, Mrs. Hartwell?'"

"They're animals," Emily said knowingly.

"Thank God we could pull directly into the garage, because I don't know what would have happened if we had to walk through it. They literally mobbed the car. Harry was crying."

"Where was Graham?"

Karolina took a deep breath. "He couldn't risk being seen with me."

She told Miriam and Emily how she had tried Beth, her best mommy friend. The phone had rung and rung until finally going to voicemail, which wasn't particularly strange: no one answered the phone these days. Karolina had felt self-conscious even calling. But when her first text had gone unanswered, and then two more, she'd started to feel a little queasy. *That* wasn't like Beth, who joked that her phone was practically welded to her palm. Nearly two hours later, Karolina finally received a reply text: *Cole may no longer play with Harry. Please don't contact either of us again.*

Karolina had gasped as though she'd been punched. For nearly a full minute, she'd struggled to catch her breath, wondering if she was having a heart attack. When her breathing had finally slowed to something resembling a normal rate, she'd fired off a group text to the mothers of the boys from the night before: *Hi all. I'll call each of you individually, but I just wanted to let you know that I was NOT drunk and last night was a huge misunderstanding. Your children were never in danger. Love, K.*

The responses came back fast and furious:

We trusted you with our son!

How can you even look at yourself after what you did?

And the worst one of all, although it was the only message that didn't include any angry exclamations:

Please, please, please: get some help. I've been there too. You can't do this without the professionals and you're deluding yourself if you think you can.

These four simply worded text messages had broken Karolina in a way that being pushed into the back of a squad car, feeling the rage of her husband, and spending an entire night in a county jail had not. Her phone slipped from her hands, and she succumbed to the sobs. These were her *friends*. Not the catty frenemies she'd made in her twenties. Not the New York society women who were alternately intimidated by her appearance and put off by her lack of pedigree. The group of women she'd met after they had moved to Bethesda had been easy from the start. Some of them worked, some of them didn't; there was a big variety of education levels and backgrounds and income; most of all, they were all trying to raise their kids as well as they could manage and have some laughs along the way. No one cared that she used to be a famous model. No one cared that her husband was a senator. And certainly no one cared that she wasn't Harry's biological mother. They got together for birthdays and took the kids trick-or-treating and carpooled to softball practice. Their husbands shared beers during weekend barbecues. Their kids all mostly got along and treated one another's houses as their own. It was easy. It was natural. And it was over. She felt ill.

Miriam's hand on her arm brought Karolina back to the charmless living room where she sat with two women who didn't despise her. "How long are you staying?"

Tears sprang to her eyes. "Graham says it's better with me here in Greenwich, so that Harry doesn't have all the stress of the media attention, but I don't know."

"When was the last time you spoke to Graham?" Emily asked.

"Last night. I'm so confused. Do you know I actually asked Harry about that night?"

"What about it?" Miriam asked.

Karolina dabbed her eye with a tissue. "I couldn't help myself. I asked if he remembered what I had to drink. He said he saw me having one glass of wine—I called it 'mommy juice,' which he found totally humiliating in front of his friends. He even remembered I poured it for myself right after I gave the boys their Sprite, and he was worried that Graham would be upset because I'd opened a new bottle. What he could not answer was why there were two empty champagne bottles floating around the back of the Suburban when the police pulled me over."

"You don't think it's possible he and his friends got into it?" Miriam asked. "I'm sure he's a good kid, but he *is* twelve, and he wouldn't be the first."

"Those boys weren't drinking champagne. None of us were. And I begged for a Breathalyzer once the boys were out of the car, but the police are saying I refused. It's a nightmare."

With this, Emily slapped her hands in her lap. "I can't stay quiet another second. Why are we all freaking out right now? DUIs are totally recoverable! If you just get in front of this, you can make it go away."

"Go away?" Karolina asked. "Have you turned on a television or opened a newspaper in the last three days?"

"Yes, I get it. The former face of L'Oréal and current wife of New York senator Graham Hartwell gets busted for driving drunk. Big fucking deal! You didn't kill anyone. That would be *way* harder. The kid factor complicates things a little, I admit, but let's keep the focus on what's important: no one got hurt; no one died; no one even crashed. This is all a lot of hysteria for nothing."

Karolina saw Miriam give Emily a look telling her to shut up. She remembered enough about Emily to know that was unlikely. And besides, when Emily phrased it like that, it didn't sound quite so horrific.

"Go on," Karolina said.

Emily shrugged. "I'll tell you what I would tell a client. No one cares if you were drunk or not. You need to apologize for having a problem and putting children at risk. You'll definitely need to do thirty days inpatient somewhere—the optics for that are just unbeatable, especially when we tip the press off ahead of time—but there's one in Montana that's downright fabulous. Like an Aman."

"Thirty days inpatient? Like *rehab*? But I don't have a drinking problem!"

"That's totally irrelevant," Emily said, glancing at her buzzing phone. "There's a protocol people follow, and this is it: everyone loves to forgive a repentant sinner. Look at Mel Gibson. Reese Witherspoon. John Mayer. Graham's affair complicates things a tad, but it's nothing that can't be dealt with. They'll forgive you too."

"His . . . affair?" Karolina whispered.

"I'm just assuming. Am I wrong?"

Karolina sat quietly for a minute and then said, "If he is, it's with Regan Whitney." Karolina could see Miriam's face register shock before she tried for a more neutral expression. Was she surprised that Graham might be cheating on Karolina or just surprised that it might be with the young, beautiful, and polished daughter of former president Whitney? Karolina's suspicions were based solely on a handful of texts she'd seen that were more suggestive than actually incriminating. That and the fact that he'd lost all interest in sex over the past six months.

"She's not nearly as pretty as you," Emily said authoritatively. "Not even close."

"She's nearly a decade younger than me," Karolina said. "Does she really even need to be pretty?"

"No," Miriam and Emily agreed simultaneously.

"Being connected is more appealing to Graham than being pretty," Karolina said flatly. "Anyway, right now Trip advised us to keep quiet. Supposedly he's working the phones on my behalf, and he thinks we have a shot at getting the charges dropped."

The sound of a buzzer broke the silence.

"That's the gate," Karolina said. Her mind flashed back to the hordes of camera crews and reporters camped outside their Bethesda home. "You don't think the police have let them through, do you?"

Thankfully, the neighbors on either side of the Hartwells' house had complained about the disruption from the paparazzi, and the Greenwich Police Department had very thoughtfully closed the road to all traffic except those who could prove their residence and their invited guests. It was the only thing saving her sanity.

Miriam jumped up from the couch. "Where can you see the gate camera? The kitchen?"

Karolina merely nodded. It was starting to feel like she would never escape this nightmare.

"It's just two Girl Scouts!" Miriam called. "Can I buzz them in?"

"No cookies at a time like this!" Emily called back. "The last thing she needs is an endless stream of empty calories!"

Karolina took a sip of water. "I guess not even the cops can say no to Girl Scouts."

Miriam walked back in and shot Emily a disgusted look. "I buzzed them in. You can't refuse a cookie solicitation, it brings seven years of bad luck."

"Oh, well, we sure wouldn't want that," Emily said. "I mean, not with how gorgeously everything seems to be going right now."

This time Karolina burst out laughing. She was crazy and emotional, and her life was spiraling completely out of control, but damn, it felt nice just to laugh. "Bring on the Samoas. This girl is ready to *eat*!"

Vodka and Tampax:
A Match Made in Greenwich

Emily

"Emily! Half-caf skinny latte for Emily!" The Starbucks barista had a ring through the cartilage of her left ear and a line of small silver cuffs all the way up her right one. Emily wanted to hug her for merely existing in Greenwich without either a blond bob or a pair of Sorel Joan of Arctic boots.

"Thanks," Emily said, grabbing the cup and beelining back to her corner seat before one of the women trolling for tables snagged her spot.

She sipped her coffee and tore herself away from a photo of Olivia and Rizzo lunching at a brasserie in the East Village, instead scrolling through a list of designers to approach last-minute for Kim Kelly. Kim Kelly, the actress made famous by risqué roles (read: willingness to take her clothes off anytime), was having a dress crisis. Kim was Emily's first client after *Runway* and remained, to this day, her craziest. The

SAG Awards were less than two weeks away, and according to Kim, the Proenza Schouler Emily had commissioned for her was a "total fucking nightmare." Nearly ten years of dressing the woman had taught her to expect this behavior at least fifty percent of the time—but she was annoyed by the total about-face. Kim had loved the dress at her first fitting a few weeks earlier, twirling in front of the three-way mirror, giggling to herself. The shoes were Chanel, the jewelry Harry Winston, and the only thing left to source was the perfect beaded clutch—hardly a difficult task. Emily's phone buzzed with yet another hysterical text from Kim.

Will you look at this? Total fucking nightmare, Kim had written.

Emily squinted at the iPhone picture of Kim looking exactly the same in the dress as she had two weeks earlier: gorgeous. *Nightmare? WTF? You look like a Disney princess, only hotter.*

I look like a wildebeest. You know it, I know it, and soon everyone who watches E will know it!

Stop! This is Proenza we are talking about. They don't do wildebeests.

Well then they fucked up this time b/c I am huge. I can't wear this. I won't.

Okay, I hear you, Emily typed, although apparently she said this out loud, because one of the women sitting next to her turned and said, "Excuse me?"

Emily looked up. "What? Oh, sorry, not you. I'm not hearing you."

The woman turned back to her friend, only now Emily couldn't help listening. She sneaked sideways glances as both women pulled out their phones and opened their calendar apps.

"So, yeah, it would be great to get them together. I can't believe it took until first grade to get them in the same class! Elodie can do Wednesdays. Does that work?"

"No, Wednesdays aren't great. India has fencing. How are Mondays?"

"Mmm, Mondays are tough. I have to drop my older two at swim, get back to the school to pick Elodie up from violin, and then take all three of them to this healthy-cooking class they're taking together. What about next week?"

The woman shook her head. "We're in Deer Valley next week. I know, I know, I shouldn't be pulling them all out of school right after Christmas break, but Silas is insistent. I was, like, 'But, honey, we're going to Vail over Presidents' Week. Can't we go somewhere *warm*?'"

Her friend nodded. "I hear you. Patrick is the exact same way. I had to fight tooth and nail for Turks in February. The only place he wanted to go was Tahoe. I was like, 'Enough Tahoe! You are not eighteen anymore. It can't just be all about your boarding! The kids *need* to swim outside at some point this winter.'"

The ping of an incoming email was the only thing that dragged Emily back to reality. She clicked open the email from Kim Kelly and began to read.

Camilla,

I tried again, exactly like you said, and I CANNOT work with her anymore. I love Emily, you know that. She's done great things for me over the last decade, but she's lost her edge. I don't know how anyone with eyes could think I look good in this total fucking nightmare of a dress. And now she says I have to find something RTW because there's not enough time?????? RTW to the SAG Awards, are you fucking kidding me? I've been hearing great things about Olivia Belle. Can you get in touch with her and see what her availability is for the next 24 hours? And please write to Emily and let her down easy. I like her, I really do, but it's time for me to move on. Fire her nicely, please. Xx KK

Without even realizing it, Emily was blinking at the screen and then rubbing her eyes. Camilla was Kim Kelly's manager, and it couldn't be more obvious what had just happened. It took only a split second to decide whether she should wait for Camilla's email or write directly to Kim.

Kim,

While it's obvious you didn't have the nerve to fire me yourself, I don't
happen to suffer from the same condition. So I will gladly tell you straight
to your face that the problem isn't the dress or the designer or me. It's
you. Namely, your raging eating disorder that allows you to think that at
104 pounds and a size two, you look like a wildebeest. I hope you get help
before it's too late. I'm sure Olivia Belle will be the *perfect* fit for you.

Sincerely,
Emily Charlton

She punched "send" without rereading it. *Good riddance*, she
thought. But then the deflation. The dread. Another client lost to Olivia
Belle. Another humiliating and high-profile firing. Another step closer
to having to shutter her business altogether. She fired off a quick, slightly
panicked email to Miles, giving him the update, but she had no idea what
time it was in Hong Kong.

Next to her, the women had given up on trying to schedule a play-
date. They had somehow segued into an uninhibited conversation about
vodka-soaked tampons.

"I mean, I've, like, read that the college girls all love it. But I can't
bring myself to actually do it," the mom of Elodie said. She had on
workout wear, head to toe: running shoes, yoga pants, a performance
fleece, and a reflective headband, topped off with a down vest.

Her friend wore a variation of the exact same outfit, only she had
swapped out the headband for a knit hat with a massive fur ball on top.
This woman—India's mommy—leaned in and said, "Oh, it's amazing.
OBs definitely work best because of the no applicator. All of the buzz,
none of the calories!"

"Wow," the headband mom said reverently. "That sounds amazing.
Have you ever tried tequila? I'm not a huge vodka fan."

"But that's the best part!" crowed the fur ball. "It doesn't matter what you use—you can't even taste it! And I haven't noticed that any one type is easier on my vag than any other, so . . . as long as it's not flavored, I think you can use whatever you have lying around."

"I'm trying it. This weekend. Wait—does that mean you would pass a Breathalyzer? Like, if no alcohol goes into your actual mouth, you should be fine, right?"

Emily was about to respond—they were raging idiots to think that alcohol absorbed through their vaginas instead of their stomachs didn't have the same effect on their blood alcohol level—but she stopped herself. After ten days in Greenwich, Emily had seen the same faces over and over again. Telling people off in her favorite Starbucks was probably not the best way to go.

She glanced around. It was as though someone released a man-repelling chemical weapon at seven a.m. each weekday and didn't turn off the spigot for a full twelve hours. The only men able to survive it were the ones older than eighty or too rich to even pretend to work anymore, but they didn't spend their time in Starbucks. It was women as far as the eye could see. Women in their thirties, pushing strollers and chasing toddlers; in their forties, eking out every second before school let out at three; in their fifties, meeting for a cappuccino and a chat; in their sixties, accompanying their daughters and grandchildren. Nannies. Babysitters. The odd twentysomething who taught a local yoga or spin class. But not one damn man. Emily noticed how different it looked from L.A., where everyone was freelance and flexible and sort of working and sort of not. She missed L.A., but it was not missing her back. Olivia Belle had probably signed half the city by now.

Her phone rang and flashed MILES.

"Em? Hey, sweetie."

"Hi. I'm so glad it's you and not the bitch who just fired me."

"You got fired? Who fired you?"

Emily laughed. "Kim Kelly. In an email that wasn't even intended for me."

"Kim Kelly's a cunt."

"I appreciate the sentiment, honey, I really do. But can you not use that word?"

"What, 'cunt'? Since when does that bother you? You've been in Greenwich too long."

"Probably."

"Have you always hated 'cunt'? How could I possibly not have known that about you? I mean, my God, we—"

"Stop saying 'CUNT'!" Emily all but shouted into her phone, causing Elodie's and India's mommies to turn and stare. "What are you looking at?" she asked them.

"Me?" Miles asked.

"No, not you." Emily raised her voice and said into the phone, "I prefer 'cooch.' As in, next time you want to get drunk, you should consider sticking vodka-soaked tampons up your cooch. That's what all the *cool* moms are doing."

This time the women, dumbfounded, exchanged a look.

"What? Vodka-soaked tampons? What are you *talking* about?" Miles said.

"Nothing, never mind." Emily took a gulp of her now-cold latte. "So where are you now?"

"Just got back from dinner to the hotel, which is insane. I can't wait for you to see it."

"Yeah, me neither. The pictures look incredible."

"I'll be back in L.A. a week from this Friday. You'll be home by then, right?"

"Of course. Unemployed, washed up, and humiliated. But home."

"Oh, come on, Em. Who even cares that Kim Kelly fired you? She's a shit actress anyway."

"She's won three Oscars and two Globes. She was one of my best clients."

"She's a hack. And getting older and fatter by the second. You, my love, are the queen of the crazies. I know it, and so does everyone else."

Clearly he was trying to make her feel better, but it only made Emily desperate to hang up. "Miles? I've got to run. Miriam's expecting me home soon."

"Okay. I miss you, honey. Remember, Kim Kelly is a bad car accident, and you're lucky you escaped that one. I'll see you in a couple more weeks, and I'll take you out to cheer you up. Just remember— you're a rock star."

"A rock star. Right. Check." She couldn't remember feeling this down on herself, possibly ever, but then again, she'd never been fired by three big clients right in a row. She managed an "I love you" before hanging up.

Then, as Emily went to close her laptop, another email came in. Camilla's subject line said: *Please read immediately*.

The official firing email. Well, that had taken all of three minutes. "Fuck you," she said as she jabbed the "delete" button without even opening it. Two women who had taken the table of the other moms— and who were also clad in head-to-toe Lululemon—turned to stare at her, mouths agape.

"Mind your own fucking business," Emily snapped. "And just so you know, getting drunk through your cooch instead of your mouth will result in an identical DUI, which will inevitably force you to sell your house and change your name and move straight across the country, since no mommy around here will ever speak to you again. Even though they all do it too. Just a friendly FYI."

Emily grabbed her computer bag and slung it over her shoulder. "Have a great day!" she sang as she left, flashing just the quickest middle finger as she walked past their table. Making new friends was overrated. Especially in the suburbs.

8

Happy to Sip
and Not to See

Miriam

Miriam tiptoed back into her still-dark bedroom and slipped under the covers. It felt so supremely indulgent to crawl back in bed. Like when she and Paul had first met and would sleep until eleven on the weekends, venture out in their sweats to pick up coffee and bagels, and then head straight back to bed with their favorite sections of the *New York Times*. Now Wednesdays at eight-fifteen were the new weekend: Paul worked from his home office that day and made it a point not to start until ten, since most other days he was up and out early. She snuggled up with him, pressed her body against his, and inhaled. Something about his neck in the morning always smelled delicious.

He smiled without opening his eyes and murmured, "What did you do with our children?"

"All three off to school. It's just you and me. And Emily, but she doesn't count. What do you think about that?" She reached her hand under the covers and into the waistband of his boxers, but he turned away.

"I've got to get up. An earlier-than-usual call today." He gave her a dry peck on the lips, headed into the bathroom, and closed the door behind him. A moment later, she heard the shower turn on.

Miriam kicked off the covers and sighed. She'd had the idea to strip off her stretched-out leggings and yogurt-splattered T-shirt before waking him and had even slipped into what qualified as lingerie after three kids and seven years of marriage: a sleeveless cotton nightshirt and no underwear. What more could the man want?

She followed him into the bathroom and appraised him as he stepped out onto the bath mat after his usual quick rinse. There was no denying it, he was still handsome: broad-shouldered and small-waisted, annoyingly so. His close-cropped hair was starting to turn salt and pepper, but that just made him look more distinguished. And he still had the body of a runner—lean, ropy, and tight—despite the fact that Miriam ran more than he did these days, which really wasn't saying much.

"What are you up to today?" Paul asked as he tied his towel around his waist and swiped on some deodorant.

Paul had never shown anything but complete support for her decisions. Whether she was working eighty hours a week at Skadden or enjoying her new, more leisurely life, he was completely behind her. He didn't mean it now in a snarky way, he was just expressing interest in her day. Still, she felt a little stupid telling him that she was planning to attend a sip 'n' see at eleven.

"That sounds nice," he said through a mouthful of toothpaste.

"I mean, who does that? A formal baby viewing at eleven a.m. on a Wednesday? Does no one have anywhere else to be?"

He spat and rinsed. "Go and enjoy yourself. You deserve it." Another unsexy peck, this one on the cheek. "I've got to jump on this call. I'll see you at the school at three. And have fun at the party!"

"Thanks," she muttered, but he was already gone.

A scan through her own closet revealed a lot of leftover work clothes and plenty of workout clothes, but not much else. She pulled out a pair of black pants, boot-cut and professional, with a white silk blouse, kitten-heeled patent-leather shoes, and her late grandmother's gold-leaf necklace. Miriam glanced in the mirror and nodded with approval. Totally inoffensive. Blending in. Perfect for anything from a conference room to a Hadassah luncheon. But when she walked into the kitchen, Emily turned around from her perch in front of the cabinet-mounted TV, coffee mug in hand, and said, "Really? You look like a cater-waiter."

"Thanks. You always know just what to say." Miriam stuck a mug in the coffee machine and hit "start." "Where are *you* going?" she asked Emily, taking in her leather leggings, chunky cardigan tied off at the waist, and four-inch booties.

"With you," Emily said.

"Like hell you are." Miriam splashed some leftover milk from one of the kids' cereal bowls into her coffee and took a sip. "Seriously, where?"

"I can't sit here anymore. Please."

"I'm hardly tying you to the bed each day. You're free to go anytime. I've even offered you a ride to the airport."

"I know, I know. Miles isn't home to visit for another couple weeks, and you know I hate being alone. Plus, I can't face everyone after this whole thing with Kim Kelly. Don't make me leave. I even kind of sort of like it here. In a weird, fucked-up way."

"I'm not making you leave! But there is no way you're coming with me to a sip 'n' see. You weren't invited. You don't even *like* babies."

"I'm sure there'll be plenty of wine, so I'll be fine. Please? I won't embarrass you." Emily motioned again to Miriam's outfit with a look of pure disgust. "Although I hardly think I'll be the problem."

Miriam couldn't help but laugh. "You are such a bitch. Fine. I'll say you're my pathetic, childless, out-of-town friend who's going through a really hard time right now. But promise me you'll keep your mouth closed. It'd be nice to meet some new people without you scaring them all off."

Emily headed to the mudroom. "Come on, we don't want to be late."

The drive to the sip 'n' see took them through Greenwich's downtown, which upon first glance resembled a charming version of a pedestrian-friendly, all-American Any Town—until you noticed the storefronts: Tiffany, rag & bone, Baccarat, Alice and Olivia, Joie, Vince, Theory. One of the only mom-and-pop stores sold and serviced fur coats. Range Rovers and Audi SUVs occupied at least fifty percent of the metered spots.

But soon they were past it and weaving through the more rural part of town, on the outskirts closer to Bedford, to a pretty street that snaked through the woods. Miriam turned onto a road with a very small and subtle PRIVATE sign and followed it up and over a steep hill, then down into a more densely wooded area until the woods cleared to reveal a gorgeous, sprawling estate. A handsome valet who looked more like he belonged on a surfboard than in a uniform materialized at the driver's side and took Miriam's keys.

"Now we're talking!" Emily said, staring. "Who did you say this was for?"

"One of the moms in Maisie's class. Just had her fourth baby. I don't really know her, but my co–room mom, Ashley, is organizing it, and she invited me."

"I'm no expert, but I thought you didn't get a shower after baby number one."

"It's not a *shower*. It's a *viewing*. Plus, this is Greenwich, where we embrace all excuses to drink during the day."

A heavyset woman in black pants and a pressed white shirt opened the front door as they approached. Emily took one look at the maid's uniform, turned to Miriam, and raised her eyebrows.

They were escorted through a sprawling kitchen and into the most spectacular greenhouse, a massive room with a glass ceiling and all-glass walls that overlooked acres of snow-covered backyard. Exotic cacti and tropical plants in hand-painted planters; succulents of all shapes and sizes; orchids and birds-of-paradise in bright bursts of color. Among all this natural beauty, sixty or so of the most meticulously put-together women Miriam had ever seen lounged on upholstered chaises, perched on sofa backs, stood in groups of three and four, and sipped mimosas and Bloody Marys, each looking like her own version of perfection with a glossy blowout and an outfit just like Emily's. More attractive waiters floated around refilling drinks and offering fruit skewers and Greek-yogurt mini-parfaits and other assorted carb-free goodies. The decorations were shades of pink, but nothing else was baby-themed: not a diaper or a baby bottle in sight.

"I feel like we just stepped into an episode of *Housewives*," Emily hissed. "Only without all the screaming. And with much better taste."

Before Miriam could respond, her co–room mom, Ashley, bounded over, an absolute vision of perkiness: perky blond bob, perky boobs, perky smile. Veneered teeth. Pretty in a girl-next-door way and just stylish enough not to be intimidating in a short dress with ankle booties and a cropped leather jacket. Her diamonds were gorgeous without being ostentatious, her tan was just right, and her perfume was detectable but not overwhelming. She seemed so *happy*.

"Miriam! I'm so glad you could make it!" Then, turning to Emily but without a hint of disapproval, she said, "Hi there, I'm Ashley. I don't think we've met."

Miriam started to explain why she'd brought an uninvited friend, but Emily turned on her own beaming smile. "Ashley! Miriam has told me so much about you. She said you're showing her the ropes with . . . everything. I'm Emily Charlton. I'm visiting from L.A., and Miriam took pity on me sitting at home alone and invited me along. I hope you don't mind?"

Ashley appeared thunderstruck. "Wait. You're Emily Charlton? Not *the* Emily Charlton?"

Miriam tried not to laugh as she watched Emily's face transform from fake happiness to genuine joy. "Do we know each other?" she asked with faux humility.

"No, no! I mean, of course you don't know *me*," Ashley said, looking flustered for the first time Miriam had ever seen. "But I'm very into fashion—not that you can tell by this old thing—and, well, I have totally followed your career from your *Runway* days. I think it's just incredible what you've done for Kim Kelly. She was a hot mess before she met you!"

Miriam noticed Emily's jaw tighten at Kim's name. This could very easily take a turn for the worse. Quickly, before Emily could say anything appalling, Miriam grabbed her by the arm. "Ashley, we'll be right back. I want to introduce her to the guest of honor." She yanked Emily to the other side of the room and shot her a warning look. "Best behavior," she said in a low voice.

"Yes, *Mom*," Emily said. "But you can't keep me from my adoring fans forever."

The sound of a utensil clinking against crystal interrupted them. "Ladies! It's that time!" Ashley called out, beaming.

Everyone held aloft a drink and clinked. Miriam heard a woman behind her say quietly to another, "She spun for a girl with number three, and when that didn't work, she had in vitro with this one. Why are we all acting like this is some sort of big surprise?"

"Let's have Christina open her gifts," Ashley announced. "Chris, which would you like to start with?"

Everyone turned to the gift table, which was surprisingly sparse. Miriam counted exactly three gifts, one of which she knew to be her own.

Christina ripped the card off the first box, which was wrapped in the most beautiful floral paper and tied with a bunch of live peonies. She read the card and, after announcing it was from her mother-in-law, opened the package to reveal a sterling silver rattle, baby spoon, and sippy cup.

"And they're engraved with Rose's name," a thin woman in a Chanel skirt suit announced from her seat.

Christina blew her a kiss and then opened the second gift. "Oh, Marta, you shouldn't have!" she squealed, holding up a generic hooded-towel-and-washcloth set trimmed in itchy-looking pink lace. She motioned for the uniformed maid who had greeted the guests at the front door to enter the room, and the woman shyly approached. "I love it. Thank you so much!" The housekeeper bent down for an awkward hug and then scurried away. Christina handed it off to Ashley. It was not monogrammed. It was not woven from Egyptian cotton. It did not originate in a French boutique. Even Miriam knew the chances that the towel or washcloth would ever so much as graze an inch of that baby's skin were nil.

"Here you go," Ashley chirped, handing over the last wrapped box: Miriam's.

Christina quickly unwrapped it and revealed the contents to the crowd. Two pink onesies with zippers—Miriam had loved the zippers instead of snaps with her own babies—a coordinating newborn hat, and a pair of furry pink booties. "Oh, how precious. I love it! Miriam, thank you—that was so sweet."

Christina seemed to appreciate and admire the outfit, and Miriam felt a wave of relief that she had chosen well. But where were everyone else's gifts? Why was it only Miriam, the mother-in-law, and the maid?

A hush fell over the room. Christina looked eager, anticipatory.

"Okay, ladies! The moment you've all been waiting for. It's time for the group present!" Ashley called as though she were the head cheerleader at a football game.

Only then did Miriam notice a gigantic pink sheet thrown over something large in the corner. A baby swing, she figured. Probably one of those new high-tech ones that you could control with your phone through an app and have it link to Spotify. Who knew these days? It could come with a camera or an aromatherapy diffuser, for all she knew.

"So, this is from the rest of us," Ashley sang. "Because we know it's only two weeks until you can work out again, and with four kiddos it might not be so easy to get to the studio, so . . . Ta-dah!" And with a great flourish, Ashley yanked off the blanket to reveal a brand-new Peloton spin bike. Perched on a side table next to it, collected in a gigantic wire-mesh basket, were an extra set of clippable pedals, wireless headphones, sleek white spin shoes, a YETI water bottle, and a pile of Lululemon workout clothes so massive that it looked as though someone had purchased the store's entire size-four stock.

"Oh my God, it's *exactly* what I was hoping for!" Christina squealed with obvious delight. "Thank you! Each and every one of you! You are all just so amazing!"

The entire room clapped and cheered and lined up to receive their grateful hug.

"Where's the *baby*?" Emily hissed. A little too loudly, Miriam thought. "Even in L.A.—which I previously thought was the most fucked-up place ever—women bring actual babies to a viewing party!"

Miriam was scanning the room when she felt her phone vibrate. Worried that it was one of the kids' schools, she pulled it out. A meeting reminder. She'd set it when she first started working at Skadden so she never forgot the weekly lunch meeting, where the partners would take turns presenting their case updates to everyone else. Twelve-thirty on the dot, every Wednesday. She had hated that meeting, absolutely dreaded it, but for some reason, she had never deleted the automatic reminder. Now she looked around the beautiful room at all the beautiful plants and the stylish women, nibbling gourmet treats and sipping morning cocktails, and she felt a pang of yearning for that drab conference room with its droning partners and dry turkey club sandwiches. Only for a split second. But still.

Emily raised her champagne glass. "Don't get me wrong, I'm *fine* sipping and not seeing, but good God."

They were interrupted by Ashley, who was cradling an armful of the most sumptuous-looking cashmere blankets in a very tender way.

"Oh! Is that baby Rose?" Miriam cried, moving closer for a peek just as Emily stepped away.

Ashley looked confused. "What? Oh, this?" She tossed the pile on the couch, and both women gasped. Ashley stared at Miriam and Emily as if they were crazy. "Those are gifts."

"Got it," Miriam said.

"Listen, do you two have a minute? It would be so great if you could help me hand out the favors. We had white S'well water bottles personalized with 'Rose,' and we had them wrapped with a bottle of Whispering Angel for each guest. Get it? Rose and Rosé? They're *so* cute."

"Got to keep our sip going," Emily said, raising her eyebrows in Miriam's direction.

Miriam shot Emily a warning look and turned to Ashley. "Of course. We would love to help."

9

My Romantic Relationship

Karolina

Karolina was sick of playing the good girl. What the hell had Trip done other than remind her that she had no rights? She was still in limbo and without any substantive information. How long was she expected to hide away in Greenwich, playing nicely, as instructed, in hopes of seeing Harry?

She could not get out of bed. Her comforter was made from eiderdown, but it seemed to weigh a thousand pounds. As did her legs, which felt barely strong enough to take her the ten feet to the bathroom. She hadn't showered in two full days and nights; there was stubble in unacceptable places and a furry feeling to her tongue. She knew this was depression. She'd had a bout with it during her endless struggle to conceive, but this felt ten times worse.

Since even holding the remote was too exhausting, Karolina couldn't turn off CNN, where it was obviously a slow news day because they were looping coverage on the new health care bill Graham was spear-heading. So-called experts on both sides of the bill kept appearing and disappearing from Anderson Cooper's table, arguing whether the bill would single-handedly save or disastrously ruin the United States for all eternity. She had watched it four times over now. No one said any-thing new or interesting. She would so much rather be watching *Ellen* or Bravo or nothing at all, but the remote was lost somewhere in the im-possibly heavy comforter, and it would take too much energy to find it. Exhausted, Karolina stared at the hideous modern light fixture Graham had chosen when they bought the house. The sleek automated blinds made the room feel about as warm as a hospital ward. One day, if she could ever find the motivation, she would rip them out and everything else too.

Karolina didn't even realize she had fallen asleep until she awoke to the sound of Graham's voice.

"Graham?" she nearly shouted, bolting upright faster than she'd thought possible.

He didn't answer. Karolina looked around the room, but all was just as she had left it. And then she saw him: alone at Anderson Cooper's table, the rest of the talking heads cleared out so the man himself could have the full stage.

"I hear what you're saying, Anderson, I do," Graham said, nodding gravely. "And that's a concern for me as well—and all Americans. But now is the time for us to put our hesitation and fear aside and do what we all know is right."

Karolina collapsed back against her pillows and exhaled. When had he gotten that suit? She bought all of his clothes, and she was certain she'd never seen that one before. Even more irritatingly, it looked great on him.

The show went to commercial break, and Karolina made a serious attempt to find the remote—no one should have to endure the sight and sound of her estranged husband on television while trying to wallow in self-pity. It had been nearly three weeks since she'd seen him, but it felt like three years.

"If you're just joining us, I'm here with Senator Graham Hartwell, the junior democratic senator from the state of New York and the sponsor of the Hartwell–Connolly Bill. Senator, thanks for joining me."

"Always a pleasure, Anderson." Graham offered an easy smile. He was completely comfortable on live national TV. Hell, he was completely comfortable everywhere.

"So, before the break we were discussing the impact the Hartwell–Connolly Bill will have on a specific population. How will your bill offer protection when Republicans want mental health and addiction provisions removed from standard coverage?"

Graham appeared to consider. "Well, you know, Anderson, I think Americans are more concerned about mental health and addiction than those of us in Washington would like to think. Take my own personal situation, for example. As you may have heard, my wife got in some serious trouble earlier this month."

The camera zoomed in on Anderson's face, which registered shock and then unbridled joy, in that order. Had the senator just *willingly* brought up his famous wife's very notorious DUI? Had he actually uttered the words "as you may have heard" to address the single most covered topic in the United States so far in the month of January? Was there a political pundit or journalist or comedian or talk show host or news anchor or gossip columnist who *hadn't* commented on Karolina's run-in with the law? Jimmy Fallon had dedicated an entire opening monologue to it.

Anderson collected himself—it wasn't easy to surprise the Silver Fox, and if the circumstances had been different, Karolina would have admired Graham for it. "Yes, of course," he said, his voice reflecting the gravitas of the situation. "I'm sure it hasn't been easy."

"Most certainly not. My wife is very ill. It's taken me a long time to understand that alcoholism is an illness, but I do now. That said, she has had every opportunity to get help—certainly many more chances than the average American ever has, I recognize that—but still she continues on with this risky behavior. I've tried to help her for many years. If it were just me . . ." Graham allowed his voice to trail off, and the average viewer couldn't be blamed for thinking he was actually choked up.

It had felt difficult to move before, as if she were swimming in a resistance pool, but now Karolina's entire body felt paralyzed, and her brain had ceased processing certain words. *Illness? Alcoholism? Risky behavior?*

"I'm . . . sorry?" Anderson said, newly flustered. Had there ever in his entire career been a guest—a United States senator, no less—who had so willingly broached the subject of his deliciously salacious personal life?

"But it's not only about me. I have to consider my son. I would be remiss as a father if I allowed my romantic relationship to further put my child at risk."

A howl escaped from Karolina's lips. Had she just made that noise? Had Graham just called their ten-year marriage his romantic relationship? And referred to Harry as *his* son and not theirs?

Anderson cleared his throat. He looked edgy, like a hunting lion about to strike. "Are you saying that your marriage—"

Graham clenched his hands together and stared solemnly at his lap. "You make all sorts of exceptions for the people you love. But I no longer see a path forward for us."

"I see," Anderson said, although he clearly did not.

"Does anyone remember you were talking about the fucking Hartwell–Connolly Bill?" Karolina screamed.

It was as though Anderson heard her through the TV. He said, "I have to take a quick break, Senator. I hope you'll stay with me to discuss this—and everything else—in further detail?"

Graham nodded. "Of course, Anderson. I'd be happy to."

Her phone rang immediately. It was her former agent, Rebecca, the woman who had mentored her through all her top years of modeling. Karolina knew Rebecca always kept CNN running in the background of her office, had done so for years, and clearly she was watching the Graham interview. As Karolina was debating whether or not to answer, it went to voicemail. A call from her aunt quickly followed. After sending that one and the next two directly to voicemail, Karolina switched off her phone. She yanked the covers to climb back in bed and almost sat directly on an apple-size spot of bright red blood. One glance down at her stained-through underwear confirmed it. How had she not even realized?

Sighing heavily, Karolina stripped in the bathroom, threw her soiled clothes into a sink full of cold water, and climbed into the shower. Although it required superhuman amounts of strength, she grudgingly scrubbed and shaved all the parts that needed attention and wrapped herself in a massive Frette bath sheet. It wasn't until she went to pull on a pair of fresh underwear and clean flannel PJ pants that she discovered she was fresh out of tampons.

"Christ," she muttered, stuffing a wad of toilet paper in her underwear the way she used to do in middle school when she found herself without supplies.

It wasn't even five in the afternoon, but she was entirely alone: the caretaker couple had already called twice to ask if she needed them to return, but Karolina had insisted that she was fine by herself. A local woman came a couple mornings a week to clean, but she didn't come on Fridays. With no choice but to actually leave her house, Karolina padded to the kitchen. Unable to resist, she swiped open her email on her iPad and scrolled through the new messages. She didn't make it past the first one, a note from her aunt that contained only two items: an attached photo with a long chain of question marks preceding it. The quality was grainy, since her aunt had taken a picture of the picture using her phone and then emailed it—surely on the lowest resolution—to Karolina, but it didn't take long to make out the players. Seated at Capitol Prime in D.C., known as the power lunch place for politicos, were Trip, Graham, and Joseph, Graham's chief of staff. The interesting addition was the striking woman seated to Graham's left. *Regan. The Ice Queen.* The camera caught her only in profile, but she was gazing at Graham while tossing her head back slightly and laughing. Graham was cutting his food and grinning a smile much wider than his grilled salmon probably warranted. All four wore business suits. To the normal onlooker, it appeared to be exactly what it was: a business lunch among colleagues. Your average Joe would not look at that photo and immediately think, *Those two are fucking*, but Karolina would bet her life they were. And so, obviously, would her aunt.

Close it, close it, close it, she coached herself, possibly aloud. Her hands moved to flip the screen cover back on, but she couldn't stop herself. Up came Google and in went the woman's name: Regan Whitney. Karolina paused for a moment, knowing that she couldn't undo what she was about to discover—simultaneously proud for never having given in to the temptation before and ashamed for being too weak to resist it now—and then hit "return."

Karolina skipped over the Wikipedia entry, the Facebook link, and a handful of the most current news articles and clicked directly on "images," where she was rewarded with thousands of photos. Regan Whitney at four different inaugural balls, wearing four different gowns, posing with four different guests. Teaching English at a mud hut schoolhouse in rural Nigeria. At a gala benefiting the Make-A-Wish Foundation. Holding hands with a small, sad Syrian child who had been granted a visa to the United States. Looking positively luminescent in all white at a Hamptons clambake.

Karolina clicked back to the nitty-gritty bio details that she'd never allowed herself to read. Some were familiar, because as the daughter of a former president of the United States, Regan had been in the public eye since childhood. Like the fact that Regan's mother had died in childbirth and she, the youngest of five children but the only girl, was her father's favorite. But some she hadn't paid much attention to years earlier, during President Whitney's administration. Karolina either didn't know or didn't remember that Regan had gone to Sidwell Friends and played two varsity sports and graduated with a 4.0 GPA. There were pictures of her being picked up at the White House on prom night by her date. Princeton. The Peace Corps. Then finally a master's at Harvard. The closest thing to a scandal Karolina could uncover was an embarrassing photo of Regan clutching a bong and exhaling a long stream of smoke in what was obviously a fraternity room with half a dozen other well-scrubbed, white, and preppily clad college kids.

Karolina snorted. Regan Whitney was the closest thing to real live political royalty in this generation. Twenty-nine years old, brilliant, accomplished, gorgeous, polished, and a humanitarian to boot. As pretty as the young woman was in her blue-eyed, blond, all-American way, Karolina knew Regan couldn't compete with her in the looks department—not even with the advantage of being nearly a decade younger. At thirty-seven, Karolina still turned heads each and every time she stepped outside. While Regan's body was trim and fit, Karolina's was slamming: curvy and tanned and sexy and tight—quite literally the stuff of fantasies for boys and men worldwide. Regan's bouncy bob framed her pretty face and showed off her translucent skin; Karolina's wild brown waves tumbled down her back and grazed the very top of her buttocks and seemed to suggest that she had always just climbed directly out of someone's bed. Pretty versus hot. Brilliant versus sexy. Ivy League humanitarian versus high-school-dropout lingerie model. All-American privilege and upbringing versus peasant roots and a slight but persistent Polish accent.

Karolina may have stayed there all day, clicking madly, but she had female matters to address. She slipped on her favorite boots, a massive Canada Goose down jacket, and a pair of outdated glasses from the kitchen drawer. In the car, she commanded Siri to take her to the nearest drugstore, which directed her to Whole Foods instead. Unwilling to continue driving, Karolina parked and braced herself against the frigid January wind as she made her way to the front door in the darkness. As though the cold wasn't bad enough, it had to get dark in the middle of the day. Had that happened in Bethesda too? Why did it seem so much worse here? And was that creepy guy standing just inside the entrance

FaceTiming someone, or was he holding his phone up like that because he was taking her picture? She shivered, unwilling to know the answer, and had begun a frantic search for the toiletries aisle when she heard a familiar voice.

"Oh my God. Karolina!" Miriam materialized, pushing a cart, her cheeks adorably red from the cold but her expression one of concern.

"Hey, fancy meeting you here."

"Karolina! You look *homeless*. What's going on with you?"

"I have my period."

Miriam frowned. "Is that code for something? Or—wait. Are you relieved? Or upset? Are you *still* trying?"

Karolina laughed and it sounded bitter even to her own ears. "Yeah, only for seven years now, and you can see how well that went."

"I'm sorry. I didn't mean—"

"No, please, it's fine. I'm here to buy Tampax."

Miriam looked relieved. "How are you doing otherwise? I've called and texted you the last two weeks, but . . . Anyway, I didn't want to stop by unannounced." She made a show of looking Karolina up and down. "But I probably should have."

Karolina waved her hand but the tears had already begun. "I'm fine," she said, wiping her eyes.

"Oh, honey. Come here," Miriam said, and although Karolina was embarrassed to be sobbing at the local Whole Foods, it felt so wonderful to be hugged. "It's going to be okay. I'm here now."

A petite woman in a workout outfit pushed a cart with a toddler past them. As the little girl shoved Cheerios in her mouth, the woman couldn't disguise the fact that she was staring at Karolina. Not sneaking little glimpses but staring openly, head swiveled, mouth agape.

"Yes?" Karolina asked her. She was certain that directly confronting the woman would shame her into looking away, but it had no effect whatsoever. The toddler screeched and pulled at her mother's sweat-wicking shirt, but still the woman stared at Karolina.

"You're Karolina Hartwell," the woman murmured, trancelike.

"Can we help you with something?" Miriam asked more politely than Karolina would have liked.

"It's just—you were my favorite model ever. I'll never forget, I saw you at the Victoria's Secret fashion show . . . what? That was like a hundred years ago. When you were Angel of the Year."

Karolina forced a smile. "Not exactly a hundred. But close to fifteen. You were there?"

The woman nodded, completely ignoring her child as the little girl dumped the bag of Cheerios on the floor. "You were spectacular. My God! The face of L'Oréal, right here in Greenwich! I thought it was amazing when you became the ambassador for Save the Children. It brought a lot of attention to a cause that not enough people care about."

"Thank you," Karolina said, wiping under her eyes with a fingertip despite the fact that she wasn't wearing any makeup. "I appreciate that."

"But what happened to you?" The woman's face contorted into angry accusation. "From Save the Children to *drunk driving with children*? Innocent *children*?" At that moment she seemed to remember her own and placed a protective arm around her daughter. "You should be ashamed!" This last part was yelled loud enough that other shoppers turned.

Karolina's face flushed and her heart beat faster. She was about to defend herself when she felt a stream of blood seep through her flannel pajama pants. She froze.

Miriam grabbed her arm and pulled. "You have no idea what you're talking about!" she called to the woman from halfway down the aisle.

"It's all over the news! I know exactly what I'm talking about!" the woman yelled back, and her child started to cry.

Karolina allowed herself to be led to the front of the store, where Miriam extracted a car key from her purse and pressed it into Karolina's hand. "It's the blue Highlander in the first row to the left when you walk out. There should be a towel for the dog in the back. Maybe sit on that? I'll get what you need and be right back."

Karolina nodded. Miriam, always capable, always reliable.

"Go. Before this turns into a whole thing," Miriam said, hurrying off.

Karolina found the car and the slightly muddy dog towel exactly where Miriam had said. She had barely hoisted herself into the front seat before her friend returned.

"Here, I got you two kinds. I don't know what you like," Miriam said, handing Karolina a plastic bag and climbing into the driver's seat.

"Wait. Where's your stuff?" Karolina asked.

"I'll come back later. First I want to take you home."

"No, I'm fine. I can drive myself—you don't have to drop me off. Maybe I can borrow the towel, though?"

"I'm not dropping you off. I'm taking you to *my* house. And I don't want to hear another word about it."

"But my car! And I'm in PJs—blood-soaked PJs. I need to go home."

"I'll bring you back to the car later. Right now you need some TLC, and you're not going to get it alone in your glass mansion," Miriam said, already turning in to traffic.

Karolina was too exhausted to argue. Although she wasn't sure how Miriam's house, with the dog and the three kids, qualified as TLC, she was happy not to have to make any decisions.

When they walked into the house, they nearly tripped over piles of wet snow pants and jackets, muddy boots, and heaps of gloves and hats and scarves spread across the floor and bench. It barely ever snowed enough in Bethesda for Harry to play in the snow—and he was certainly too grown up lately to do anything so childish—but the sight of kids' snow gear nearly took Karolina's breath away.

Miriam, being Miriam, noticed immediately. "You must miss him so much."

"I can't believe it's been almost a month. This is the longest I've ever gone without seeing him."

"But you're talking to him, right?"

"Every night. And we FaceTime. But it's not the same."

"No, of course not."

Maisie spotted her mother. "Mommy! Did you see what we built out-side? It's a real snowman. His name is Bobsy. Isn't that funny?" The little girl's cheeks were red with cold and her nose and lips were covered in mucus, but Karolina still had an overwhelming urge to kiss her.

"Bobsy looks terrific, honey. Tell Ben and Matthew they have ten more minutes until dinner, okay?"

When Karolina saw Paul sitting in the kitchen, clicking away on the computer, she nearly had a heart attack. Again, Miriam read her mind. "Don't worry," she whispered. "If he thinks it's just me, he won't even look up. Just take the back stairs to the guest room. There are towels in the bathroom, and I'll bring you some clean sweats. I'll be up in a few minutes."

As predicted, Paul called out a hello to his wife but didn't glance up from the screen. When Karolina came back downstairs, hair wet from its second washing in two hours, wearing a super-comfy sweatsuit that was at least three sizes too big, the entire family was assembled around two large pizzas at the kitchen table.

"Karolina!" Paul said warmly, walking over to embrace her. He'd clearly been prepped, because he didn't utter a word about her appear-ance. "It's so good to see you."

"Thanks for letting me crash your Friday-night dinner. I think it's my fault you're having pizza tonight and not whatever Miriam was plan-ning to buy at the grocery store."

"Pizza, pizza, pizza!" Ben sang out through a mouthful of half-chewed food. "I love pizza!"

"Yeah, you can see how devastated we all are." Paul smiled and pulled out a chair for her. He turned to Miriam. "Is Emily back for dinner?"

"No. She's staying in the city. She'll be back in the morning to pack. Her flight is tomorrow at three out of JFK."

"Where's she going?" Karolina asked.

"Home, can you believe it? One night turned into three and a half weeks. I thought she'd never leave." Miriam laughed. She didn't seem to notice Matthew pouring a small stream of milk onto his side of steamed broccoli.

"Oh, come on. You've loved having her," Paul said. "I hear you two cackling like witches late into the night."

"Of course I have! It's been great. This is the longest time we've spent together since we were fifteen. What's not to like?"

Karolina forced herself to smile. She asked each of the children questions about school and friends, and even managed to get down a slice of lukewarm pizza despite feeling like she might vomit.

"I'll just Uber back to my car," she announced, not caring that it was either rude or a complete non sequitur. "A driver can be here in three minutes."

"Nonsense," Paul said, waving her off. "Miriam said you were sleeping over."

Miriam nodded. "I already changed the sheets in the guest room. You're staying."

Karolina wanted to argue, but she couldn't get the words out. It was freezing and dark out, and Miriam's house was homey and warm, and the idea of not being alone another night sounded rather nice. She nodded and allowed Miriam to walk her upstairs.

"I'll be back after I get the kids to bed, okay? Then we can watch something bad on Bravo? I'll light us a fire."

"Thank you," Karolina murmured. She closed the door and immediately climbed under the covers. She briefly thought about turning on the TV but didn't want to risk stumbling across another news show. Instead, she picked up her phone. There on the screen saver, in honor of her wedding anniversary, was a wedding portrait: Karolina in a filmy custom Vera Wang; Graham so handsome in bespoke Tom Ford. He'd been thirty-two then, and he looked like an absolute baby. And standing beside him, Harry, just two, clutching his raccoon lovey and holding tightly to his father's hand. Karolina had been twenty-six when she met Graham at a dinner party in the Hamptons, and they'd gotten engaged six months later. She remembered feeling ill prepared to become an overnight mother to this sweet, motherless boy, but Harry had made it so easy. Loving him was the most natural thing in the world, and she remembered thinking that one day they would give him a whole flock of brothers and sisters.

They'd honeymooned together, the three of them, in an oceanfront suite that opened directly onto the turquoise waters of the Caribbean. She loved how devoted a father Graham was. Parrot Cay was astronomically expensive and exclusive but not super-posh. It was the kind of place you could be barefoot from breakfast to dinner, wearing nothing more than a bikini and a muslin caftan, the pace as slow and languid as the heat. Harry spent hours splashing in the warm shallows, shrieking with laughter as he raced in and out of the waves, while Graham and Karolina looked on from chaise lounges, hand in hand. In the evenings they would feed Harry spaghetti or chicken fingers early, then all rinse together in the outdoor shower behind their suite. When Harry was in his striped pajamas, hair wet and smelling deliciously of coconuts, Graham would read to him while Karolina dressed. A couple of nights a kind older lady from guest reception came to stay with Harry, but since Karolina hated to leave him, they would carry him to the oceanfront restaurant and pull two chairs together to create a sort of criblike bed where Harry would curl himself around his blankie and immediately fall asleep. After a meal of fresh fish, they would walk back to the suite, Harry asleep and cradled in Graham's arms. Giggling from too much wine, Karolina and Graham would make love like it was the most natural thing in the world, which back then it was. They'd fall asleep on top of the cover as the breeze from the ceiling fan cooled them.

Now, lying in Miriam's guest bed, Karolina wondered if she'd imagined the whole thing. But no! Things hadn't always been like this. The wedding and the honeymoon had been real, as had many of the years they'd shared afterward. Naturally, there had been disagreements, even a few all-out screaming fights, but those early years had been filled with mostly happy memories: Harry's first day of kindergarten; Graham's promotion to partner; all the birthdays and dinners and cocktail parties

Karolina thoughtfully planned and executed, every detail perfect, every guest feeling wanted and welcomed. Graham had bought her beautiful, expensive jewelry for her birthdays, and yes, his secretary had probably chosen it all, but the tennis bracelets and diamond-drop earrings had come with store-bought Hallmark cards on which he'd scrawled heartfelt words about how much he loved her. He'd looked at her with both lust and adoration when she'd glided around those dreadfully boring lawyer parties, and he'd told her she lit up the room. When was the last time he had looked at her like that? Maybe this entire thing had been a misunderstanding. Maybe she was too suspicious of Regan Whitney. She didn't have any *proof* that they were having an affair, and God knew her instincts weren't always a hundred percent accurate. Could the Graham she had shared a life with for the better part of a decade—the same man who'd sworn that he would always take care of her—actually announce their divorce on national television? Or, as she was starting to suspect, could there be another explanation? Something she just hadn't considered yet?

Karolina bolted upright in bed. This was about a lack of communication, not a shortage of love—not a deliberate sabotage. She hit Graham's name in her Favorites and listened as it rang and rang. Voicemail. She left something rambling, perhaps a tad incoherent, but loving. The gist was "Let's work out this mess together; this has all been a misunderstanding; I love you and miss the way we used to be."

"Call me back?" she said, but it sounded more like a plea. "I've realized so many things and want to talk to you." Then she texted him the same thing. Twice.

She watched her phone for a while, but there was no return call or text. She must have fallen asleep at some point, because when she woke up five hours later, it was nearly two in the morning and someone had turned off the lights and pulled up her covers. The memory came back: she had reached out to Graham to reconcile, to work through this horrible misunderstanding. She would apologize for thinking the worst of him; he would beg her forgiveness for leaving her overnight in jail. They would vow to get to the bottom of this whole situation together. As a team. She saw her phone sitting peacefully on the night table, charging with its ringer thoughtfully turned off. Miriam. Always considerate Miriam. No wonder she hadn't heard him call back! But when she scrolled through the Recents list, there were no missed calls. It wasn't until she clicked on her texts that she saw his message:

Karolina, you're obviously ill, but I'm sorry to say that I can't help you. Once you put Harry's life at risk, you sealed your fate. Going forward, please only contact me through Trip.

The sky had already begun to lighten by the time she fell back into deep, dreamless sleep. And when she woke again at nine, pillow soaked with tears and eyes bloodshot from crying, she felt like she'd been run over by a bus. But there was something else there, something that felt equal parts terrifying and healthy. Something that felt a lot like rage.

10

The Suburbs
Make You Fat

Emily

The train lumbered out of Grand Central, the conductor calling future stops like an auctioneer on speed, and Emily practiced a deep-breathing technique to zero effect. How the hell can you shut down I-95 at evening rush hour? For a terrorist attack or something real—fine. But a gas spill? Jamming up the entire highway from Manhattan to Fairfield? Forcing innocent people to *take the train?* It was beyond comprehension.

Emily had just loudly exhaled when a man in a rumpled but clearly expensive suit asked if the seat next to her was available. She needed peace and space to sift through the stack of headshots she'd just been handed by the city's preeminent talent manager. Singers making their Broadway debut, first-time actors who'd impressed seasoned directors, musicians who stood out from the crowd. The list of up-and-comers was long and varied, but Emily was hopeful her next new star was in that pile. Emily needed the Next Hot Thing, and she needed him or her now, so she didn't try to hide her annoyance as she heaved her overflowing Goyard tote from the seat next to her onto her lap, turning to stare out the window. The Greenwich train was full but not packed. Could he really not find anywhere else to sit?

"I probably could have," the man said with a posh British accent. He was cute, there was no denying it. "But the only seats I can see from here are next to obese people or babies. So you're the lucky winner."

"What?" Emily asked. Had she said that out loud?

"If you don't want people to sit next to you on Metro-North trains, you should probably consider gaining a few stone. It would be an enormous help." And with that, he pulled a pair of earbuds from his briefcase and stuck them in his ears.

She sat there, dumbfounded, for nearly a minute before turning to him. "You picked here because I'm thin?" she asked stupidly.

He pulled one bud out of his ear and leaned in close enough that she could smell him. It was a clean, preppy smell, despite the rumpled look. And then he smiled and she noticed how his eyes crinkled. They were a bluish green, not so bright that they were the first thing you'd notice about him, but a lovely color that probably changed according to the undertones in the shirts he wore. Emily was so intent on studying his eyes, examining his teeth, breathing in his smell, that she almost didn't catch his teasing.

"I hope you don't mind, but I'm not really a train talker."

"What?" she asked. *Stop it!* she berated herself. *Can't you say anything except "what"?*

"You seem like you want to chat. Nothing personal, I'm just not really the type." He said this with the smallest hint of a smile.

"*You're* not the type? You have no idea who you're talking to. I do not talk to people on trains. I don't even *ride* trains."

He raised his eyebrows. "I don't know you well enough to say that you sound mental, but if I did know you better, that's probably what I would say."

"Best compliment I've had in weeks. Even if it's coming from a guy who still manages to look homeless in a Brioni suit."

With this, he laughed. "Hedge fund asshole, at your service. My name's Alistair, because really, what else would it be?"

In spite of herself, Emily laughed too. "I'm Emily. Former fashion phenom headed unwillingly for total obscurity thanks to my refusal to live entirely on social media."

"Hmm."

"Hmm what?"

"I guessed wrongly about you."

"What did you guess? That my name was Kelsey or Kinley or Lulu?"

He smiled again. "No, I was certain you were a Greenwich stay-at-home mum with a full-time nanny, married to some bloke like me."

Emily knew this was where she should have at least mentioned Miles, but why ruin the fun? An innocent flirtation on a train she'd never again take with a guy she'd never again see. Why not enjoy it? "Wait—you think I live in Greenwich? That may be the most offensive thing you've said yet."

His laugh was deep and sexy. "It's not that bad."

"Clearly you haven't spent any real amount of time there."

"That's where you're wrong. I live there. Have for five years now."

"I'm sorry."

"I wasn't offended."

"No, I mean I'm sorry you live there. That must be rough."

Again the laugh, and Emily couldn't help but smile back. She felt like she'd do anything to make him laugh again.

"What's rough is living there as a divorced dad. Let's just say it wouldn't be my first choice for having a wide pool of single women to meet."

So he was *divorced*. Interesting how he put it out there like that. He was probably only in his mid- or late thirties—how on earth had he already had time to marry someone, have children, get divorced, and start to date?

The train stopped at 125th Street, and a few more people straggled on. One, a sweaty overweight man, eyed Emily before lumbering toward the back of the car.

"You can thank me for that," Alistair said.

"So why'd you get divorced?" Emily asked, not so much because she thought it was any of her business but so she could try to wrest a bit of control back. He was out-charming her, and she wasn't used to it.

"Isn't this where you ask me my children's names? Or how old they are? Something more benign?"

"I don't really like kids."

"All right, then. If you must know, my wife and I met in a nightclub in Istanbul and eloped three months after that. She liked to party, but I thought mostly the usual stuff: booze, weed, a little ecstasy every now and then. How could I have known she was going to fall in love with Adderall and then oxy and then smack? That I'd find her shooting up in our shower? That was fun. That she'd be in and out of rehab for a decade, all while I'm wondering when she's going to overdose? And then the kids came along, and she couldn't stay clean even for them? That the final straw was when I came home early from work one day to find her in our bed with our dealer while our daughters watched TV in the family room? Probably more than you wanted to know."

"Oh my God. Really?" Emily asked, suddenly feeling super-guilty for dredging this all up.

"No, not really! We met senior year at Brown and dated on and off for years."

It was Emily's turn to laugh. "You are an asshole."

"Yeah, she thinks so too. I mean, we were happy for a while, but apparently I pressured her a lot: to get married before she was ready, to move back to London with me when she didn't want to leave her family, to give up her job and stay home with the girls. Nice, right?"

"I've heard of worse crimes. And I'm sure it wasn't just you."

"No, it wasn't. She had a big-time anxiety disorder that medication barely put a dent in. A lot of irrational fears and limitations—wouldn't fly, refused to drive on highways, that kind of thing. Whatever, that's all in the past. Now we are very happily divorced. We have one of those highly functional co-parenting relationships where we think of each other as mostly good and decent and we put the children first and serve only organic food and everyone is happy."

"I call bullshit," Emily said.

"It's all rather dull, if you must know. The girls are well adjusted, we both go to all their sporting games and co-host their birthday parties, and we'll often spend weekends together. I had an early client meeting in the city today, but I'm headed to her house now so we can all go skiing together this weekend."

"How progressive."

"Yes. Lots of therapy. Supposedly this is how our generation separates, did you know that? We are all so knackered from our parents' vicious divorce battles that we refuse to subject our own children to it. We don't even put down our ex-partners, can you imagine? Just support and kindness and 'family love.'"

"My parents got divorced when I was ten, and they definitely hated each other."

"Naturally," Alistair said. "My mother found my father shagging the housekeeper one day and he was gone the next. It was proper. Expected. But anyway—"

At that exact moment the train screeched to a halt at the Greenwich station and the doors opened. They scrambled onto the platform, barely making it before the train pulled away. They stood looking at each other as the crowd dispersed around them.

"Well, Emily, it was a pleasure to meet you," Alistair said, extending a hand. It felt warm, dry, strong.

"You as well. Have fun skiing. I'm not going to lie, that sounds like a terrible time."

He laughed. "What? A freezing weekend away with your ex and two kids doesn't sound like a dream? I hope you have something far lovelier planned, Emily." And with that, he turned and walked to the stairs.

She stared after him. Had he really just left? After a conversation like *that*? Without so much as asking for her number or if he could see her again?

Miriam was not impressed when Emily climbed into the passenger seat and complained about this fact. "You're *married*!" Miriam said while she navigated the hideous, crumb-laden SUV out of the station parking lot.

"He didn't know that!"

"Well, aside from the fact that you should have told him, you do happen to be wearing a wedding band with, like, blinding diamonds in it. I doubt he missed it."

"Men don't notice things like that."

"What did you want? Would you have slept with him if he called? Or is this an ego thing?"

Emily sighed. She loved her friend like a sister, but Miriam could be so exasperating. How was Emily friends with someone so perfect? Sure, appearance-wise she had the extra fifteen pounds and the frizzy hair and the vile suburban-mommy addiction to athleisurewear—but Miriam was just so *good*. So even-keeled and rational. So smart and sensible. So considerate of those around her. And the doting husband and the three kids and the perfect house in the perfect suburb? With no visible signs of marital fracture or life dissatisfaction or even run-of-the-mill depression? If Emily didn't love her so much, it would be really fucking annoying.

"Never mind. Can we get a Starbucks?"

"I have coffee at home."

"Your pods don't compete with the real thing."

"But they're Starbucks brand. They *are* the real thing."

Emily sighed loudly.

"Fine. But just the drive-through. Karolina is upstairs. She stayed over last night."

"Stayed over? Why?"

"I found her wandering around Whole Foods last night, looking like she'd just stepped out of a crack den. I couldn't let her go home."

"Is she okay?"

"She's fine. But I'm guessing her general demeanor had something to do with Graham announcing on *Anderson Cooper* that their marriage is over."

"Oh shit, of course. I saw the clip."

"Yeah, it was bad. He basically called her a drunk in front of the entire universe and said she was beyond help and that he had to think of his son. Not *their* son. *His.*"

"He's a real first-class pig. And he must be super-serious about this other woman, because that was an aggressive move. I wonder who's advising *him.*"

Miriam shrugged.

"Well, if Karolina were my client, I'd tell her to go on the offensive. She can't just sit back and let him decimate her reputation. Who's her agent? Where's her lawyer?"

"I'm not positive, but I think she and her agent parted ways right before all of this went down and she hadn't hired someone new yet. Her lawyer is a family friend. Graham's best friend, actually, so I've offered to help her with anything in that area. She really doesn't have anyone; it's kind of surprising."

Emily rolled her eyes. "Well, then, she really needs to get someone. Like, stat. If anyone can convince her, Miriam, it's you."

Miriam pulled up to the Starbucks drive-through, and Emily leaned over her friend and shouted out the window, "Grande skinny vanilla latte, please. Extra hot and no foam." She turned to Miriam. "What are you having?"

"I'll just get it at home."

"You are so like my mother. Live a little, have a coffee!"

Miriam sighed. "Fine. Just a drip, please. Small."

"Sexy!" While they waited, Emily tapped her fingers. "What's Karolina going to do next?" And then, watching Miriam take the cup: "There you go, rock star. Enjoy it."

Emily had downed her entire coffee by the time they got to Miriam's and wished she'd ordered a venti. Her phone bleated with a text message, and although they hadn't exchanged numbers or even last names, she found herself hoping it was from Alistair. When she read Miles's text (*Hi baby. Safe flight back to L.A. today. Missing you so much and can't wait to see you. xoxo*), she felt a pang of guilt. But it had just been fun, innocent flirting. The kind that Miles engaged in pretty much every minute of every day, often right in front of her. They were both secure enough in their relationship that they could have fun with other people. Not a big deal.

"I'm excited to see Miles," Emily announced as they walked into Miriam's mudroom.

Miriam turned to look at her. "I'm glad to hear that," she said slowly.

"No, really. I am. It's been nearly a month."

"Well, we're going to miss you around here. It's been great having you—we've loved it and so have the kids."

As if on cue, Maisie came bounding down from upstairs. "Mommy! Daddy said Aunt Emily is leaving today!" she shrieked, a look of panic on her small, rounded face.

"I am, lovey. It's time for me to go back to Los Angeles." Emily held her arms open and Maisie ran into them. While she wasn't particularly enamored with Ben or Matthew—even when they were clean, they seemed kind of gross, with constantly runny noses and dirt under their fingernails, not to mention their exhaustive nonstop motion—Maisie had really grown on her. The little girl was drawn to Emily, always showing up in her room and asking if she could try on her heels or help put on her makeup. One evening Emily had applied some blush and lip gloss and a bit of eye shadow on Maisie, and she thought the child might faint from excitement. Naturally Miriam had sent her daughter back upstairs to wash her face, and Emily had muttered something not particularly nice about being the mom where fun goes to die, but from that moment on, Maisie had remained steadfastly devoted.

"Why do you have to go back?" Maisie whined.

Emily opened her mouth to answer and was surprised that nothing immediately came to her. She was looking forward to seeing Miles, but he was only going to be home for a few days before heading back to Hong Kong. And her job? Well, that was a shit show. With Kim Kelly and Rizzo Benz now gone with Olivia Belle, all she was left with were a few reality-TV stars she could manage in her sleep. So long as she scored them designer labels to wear for free and made a few half-assed phone calls on their behalf to the tabloids, they were happy. Emily needed to step up her game if she wanted to stay relevant.

"It's time" was all she could come up with. She'd been avoiding her voicemail and had told Kyle to tell everyone that Emily was on a silent meditation retreat. With a famous monk. In a faraway country.

"Are you sure?" Kyle had asked, her doubt coming across loud and clear.

Emily had paused just long enough to make the girl squirm. "Am I *sure*? Are you asking if I know what I'm doing? Celebrities eat that crap up, especially if it makes me seem hard to get. You'll get the word out right away, do you understand?"

Kyle quickly agreed, but Emily had to make a mental note to log in and check the girl's work email. She couldn't have her beautiful and socially connected assistant blabbing to everyone that Emily was in *Connecticut*, for Christ's sake. There was only so much damage her reputation could weather.

Paul jogged into the room wearing spandex tights with a pair of athletic shorts over them, a super-fitted long-sleeve performance tee, and new sneakers.

"You've adjusted nicely to suburban life, Paul," Emily said, giving him a once-over. "How sporty."

Paul laughed. "Hey, I'm headed to the gym. I'll be back around two.

Do you need anything?" he asked Miriam while grabbing an apple from the bowl on the kitchen island.

"Say goodbye to Emily," Miriam said. "She's leaving for her flight."

Paul kissed Emily on the cheek. "Safe flight, sweetie. Say hi to Miles for me, okay?"

"Will do. Thanks for putting up with me for so long. Three weeks is above and beyond. Very appreciated."

They exchanged a warm hug and Paul went into the garage.

"He looks great," Emily said, looking after him. "Being an Internet millionaire totally agrees with him."

Miriam rolled her eyes. "He can't stop working out. You should see this gym he joined. It looks like a luxury Asian hotel. It costs more per month than our first apartment. Who would have ever thought my husband would . . ." Her voice trailed off and she looked alarmed.

"What?" Emily asked.

"You don't think . . ."

"What? That he's having an affair? No, of course not. Not Paul," Emily said, and hoped she sounded convincing.

"Mommy, what's an affair?" Maisie asked.

"Nothing, sweetie. Can you go upstairs and ask Karolina if she wants some breakfast? Make sure she's okay?"

The little girl grinned with delight at the assignment and ran off.

Emily watched Miriam as she sliced an apple. "That wasn't a serious question, was it, Miriam?"

Her friend shrugged. "No, not really. I mean, of course I don't think he's having an affair, but the wife never really does, right?"

"What's your evidence?"

"Evidence? I don't have any evidence. Just that he had a huge windfall of money and has recently started taking an interest in his appearance, which he certainly never cared about before."

"And sex?"

"What about it?"

Emily sighed loudly. "Are you having it?"

"Of course," Miriam said. Then she held the knife frozen in midair and furrowed her brow. "Actually, it's been a while . . ."

"Define 'a while.'"

More furrowing. "I'm thinking," Miriam said.

"Not great." Emily opened the fridge and pulled out a container of Greek yogurt. "But not the end of the world. Everyone gets in ruts. Going a week or two without doesn't necessarily mean . . ."

"A week or two?" Miriam hissed. "A week or two? Are you serious? Is that what life is like without kids? Because if you define a week or two without sex as a problem, I should have been divorced six years ago."

"You only got married seven years ago."

"Exactly," Miriam said.

"Christ. It's that bad? I mean, I've heard from other moms that things slow down, but I had no idea . . ."

"So he might *really* be having an affair. That's what you're saying."

A voice surprised them both from the stairs. "I didn't think you two would be talking about it behind my back," Karolina said, holding on to the banister, looking pale and disheveled in Miriam's oversize sweats.

Emily gave her a little wave. "We're not talking about you and your potentially cheating husband. We're talking about Miriam's!"

With this, Miriam hissed at her, "Lower your voice! The kids hear everything."

"Paul?" Karolina asked with obvious incredulity. She accepted the cup of coffee Miriam handed her.

"Of course he's not," Emily said.

"I mean, I don't *think* he is, but who ever really knows?" Miriam asked.

"I always knew," Karolina said quietly.

Emily glanced at Miriam, who glanced back at her. No one said anything.

"It's the only time he would stop wanting to have sex," Karolina said. "It's a total cliché, but it was true."

"So, this isn't the first time?" Miriam asked. She looked like she was trying hard to keep the judgment from her voice, but Emily didn't think she was being particularly successful.

"No. There have been two others that I've known about. He confessed to both of them. I—I kind of assumed it was going to be the same thing this time."

More silence.

"Maybe it will be," Karolina continued. "Both other times he begged for my forgiveness. Told me that he couldn't live without me, that Harry couldn't, that he was an idiot for jeopardizing our marriage. The second time we went to counseling—it was his idea. I'm not making excuses for him, but I almost think he can't help himself. My mother always said my father was the exact same way, that he would have these meaningless flings and then throw himself at her feet. She said all men are like that . . ."

"Well, they're not," Emily said, not meaning to sound quite so harsh.

"Emily!" Miriam reprimanded.

"What? I shouldn't be honest? I should let her believe that all men are cheating scumbags? A lot are. But not all. Take Miles. He parties, he flirts, he goes to strip clubs and would never turn down a chance to see some hot girl's nipple piercing. But he is as loyal and committed as the day is long. He has a lot of flaws—trust me, I could name them one by one, and we'd be here for hours—but he's not a cheater. Not all of them are."

It got so quiet in the kitchen that Emily could hear the fridge humming. Had she gone too far? She wasn't the greatest at judging that, she knew. Karolina looked stricken. Miriam picked the remnant of a blueberry muffin off one of the kids' plates and popped it in her mouth, and Emily glared at her.

"Leave me alone," Miriam said through a full mouth.

"I'm going to remind you of that muffin when you complain about your weight later."

"The suburbs made me fat. Remember how thin I was when we

lived in the city?" Miriam said. "I walked everywhere. And worked all day. And what do I do here? I eat."

Karolina took a sip of her coffee. She seemed to be off in another world. "I think I put too much pressure on us to have a baby," Karolina said, completely ignoring Miriam. "We used to have mind-blowing sex before it became all about getting pregnant. But it can't be just that, can it? I think Graham will come to his senses. He can't really want a *divorce*, can he?"

Emily stretched her arms over her head. "I'm going to lay out the facts for you, Karolina. It's what I try to do with clients when they find themselves in messy, ugly situations that are difficult to grasp when they're right in the middle of it."

"Em, I'm not sure that's going to be super-helpful right now," Miriam said, grabbing another chunk of blueberry muffin.

"No, let her talk," Karolina said.

Emily cleared her throat. "Graham has cheated two other times that you know about. Both times he confessed and begged for your forgiveness, am I right?"

Karolina nodded.

"This time, although we don't have hard proof that he's having another affair, you suspect it?"

Another nod.

"But this time is obviously different: he's not just some horny guy who screwed up and regretted it. This time it's something more."

"What do you mean by 'more'?" Karolina's voice was close to a whisper.

"Either he thinks he's in love or he needs something from her. I'd lean toward the latter. Regan Whitney, picture-perfect poster child of a former president, is a serious catch. She's too controlled to have meaningless flings, especially with married men."

"I'm not sure why we have to do this right now," Miriam said, looking supremely uncomfortable.

"How can we not?" Emily asked impatiently. "Anyone who has ever picked up a newspaper knows how ambitious Graham is. He's WASP royalty. Harvard, Oxford, partner at Cravath, and now senator from New York. He gave that brilliant speech about family values at the Democratic National Convention, and suddenly everyone started talking about him as a front-runner for 2020."

"That caught him by surprise," Karolina said. "He couldn't believe the attention he got for that."

Emily looked hard at her. Contrary to stereotypes, Karolina was not dumb.

"So now Graham, possible Democratic front-runner for *president*, is entangled with another woman—one who is even more politically connected than he is. What's Mr. Family Values going to do? Just up and leave his wife? Trade in one model for a younger version?"

At this, Karolina visibly flinched.

Emily ignored it. "Of course not! He has to find a no-fault way out. So he sets *you* up to look like the happy-marriage-home-wrecker."

Karolina's eyes widened. "What?"

"Graham. Set you up. So he could divorce you and still look like the good guy. It's obvious."

"It is?" Miriam asked. "I can think of a hundred—"

"Miriam, get your head out of the fucking sand!" Emily said. No one ever benefited from denial. "Karolina, you say you had one lousy glass of wine and then got pulled over thirty seconds after leaving your house. I don't know, but I'm presuming you live in a beautiful residential Maryland neighborhood with huge family houses—not where the police are customarily setting up so-called sobriety checkpoints. Despite the fact that neither you nor your son knows where they came from, there were empty bottles floating around your SUV. Then you're given some bullshit field sobriety test, which apparently you failed, and you're carted off to the police station, where no one gave you a proper Breathalyzer or blood test, which would actually *prove* you weren't drunk."

Karolina stared at her, expressionless.

"At the station—despite the fact that you are a senator's wife with absolutely no previous record who is also decidedly *sober*—you are locked up like a common criminal and kept there all night long. Does any of that make any sense to you?"

Again Karolina didn't move a muscle.

"Yeah, me neither. It only works like that if someone wants it to. Someone powerful enough to plant a few bottles of booze and then call in his buddies at the Bethesda PD to 'check things out.' Someone like Graham. The only thing I don't know is *why*, but I'm absolutely certain he's the one responsible."

"Emily, stop!" Miriam said, but didn't refute her.

"She's right," Karolina whispered.

Both women turned to her.

"You're right," Karolina said to Emily. "It explains everything. The bottles, the no Breathalyzer, the way the police treated me. My so-called lawyer, Trip, doing zero to contest this. Graham basically kicking me out of my own house. And then that, that . . . garbage about *his* son's safety. It's all a big setup. How did I not see it?"

The room was silent.

"Oh my God. I feel sick. He did this," Karolina said, placing a hand ominously on her throat.

"He wants a divorce," Emily sang. "What's he going to do, just ask for one like a normal human being? Of course not. Americans don't vote for divorced men! Not after Donald Trump. They vote family values! They vote decency! They do *not* want their future president casting aside his beautiful wife just because he found a new and improved version."

The pain hit Karolina's face.

"Sorry if I was too . . . blunt," Emily said.

She was met with more silence.

"Okay, then." Emily stood up. "I've got to start packing if I have any hope of getting to the airport on time . . ."

She was on her way up the stairs, literally counting the seconds until she could climb into an Uber and pitch some more work, when she heard Karolina call her name. "Emily?"

The fierce look on Karolina's face took her breath away. There were no tears in sight, only cold, hard determination. *Good girl*, Emily thought. *You're never going to survive this if you sit around crying all day. Time to get mad.*

"Yes?"

"Will you help me?" Though Karolina's question was plaintive, her tone was anything but.

"Help you?" Emily asked, although she knew immediately—hoped—what Karolina was asking.

"Help get my son back. And also? Help me nail that asshole to the wall and show the whole world that he's a fraud and a monster," Karolina said.

"Karolina, darling." Emily smiled widely and gave a half-bow. "It would be my pleasure."

11

Mom's Night Out

Miriam

"Mommy? Mommy?" Miriam tried to gauge the desperation in Maisie's voice, half-heartedly praying her daughter would miraculously forget what she wanted and go to sleep, which of course was ridiculous. "MOMMY!"

Miriam took a deep breath and reminded herself to be patient. The child was only five. Bedtime delay tactics were a fact of life. "Yes, sweetie?" she asked, opening Maisie's door ever so slightly and peeking her head in.

"I need you."

"I'm right here, love. What can I do?"

"Come here."

"Sweetie, we read three books and sang two songs. You have water. We found your mermaid PJs in the hamper and changed into them. I took the scary Gruffalo off your shelf and checked under your bed for foxes. It's time to sleep now."

"I want a cuddle," Maisie cooed in her sweetest voice. The child was no dummy—she'd learned long ago that it was the one thing to which Miriam would never say no.

How many years more would her girl beg her to snuggle? She climbed under Maisie's covers and pulled her daughter's warm little body into her own. So she wouldn't have time to put on makeup for the Moms' Night Out? Big deal. She inhaled her daughter's still-damp hair and smiled. She gave her daughter one final kiss and murmured "I love you" and then was able to tiptoe out of the room and close the door without further protestation. Maybe she'd have time to do her makeup after all.

Her phone bleated with a text from Ashley saying she was in the driveway.

"Dammit." Miriam caught a glimpse of herself in the full-length mirror: not great. She'd managed to dig out a clean enough turtleneck sweater in a nice shade of light blue, but the leggings were pilled, and her effort at a chic messy bun had resulted in a ratty-looking topknot. She still hadn't figured out what she was supposed to wear around town.

Whatever, she thought. This wasn't some gala. It was a Thursday night in the suburbs, and all the invited guests were women. Ashley had been vague about the theme of the get-together, but she'd insisted it would be lively and there would be plenty of wine and lots of nice women. Who was Miriam to say no when she barely knew anyone in town? It would be fun.

"Hey, sorry to keep you waiting. Maisie was clingy tonight," Miriam said, hearing her own breathlessness as she pulled the passenger door shut. "Thanks for picking me up."

"Of course, honey! Look at you—so cute!" Ashley cooed. She was also wearing a turtleneck sweater, but hers was camel-colored and looked like it was spun from the eyelashes of baby lambs. She had paired it with tight white jeans, the most delicate diamond pavé jewelry, and a pair of gorgeous black leather boots. Her blond hair looked professionally blown out. She even smelled delicious. Everything about her just glowed.

"How do you get your hair like that?" Miriam asked, touching her own bun. She'd recently gone to a guy in the city who was renowned for cutting kinky, curly hair—he styled without wetting it and called it "The Diva Cut"—but it had looked fantastic for only thirty-six hours before all signs of diva-ness had exploded back into a frizzy disaster.

"Oh, this? Please. I haven't washed it in a week. I go through so much dry shampoo, I can't even tell you. Lucy told me the other night that it smells."

Miriam laughed. "Well, if it makes you feel any better, I found a drawing of me in Matthew's folder from school. When I asked him to tell me about it, he took great pride in pointing out the three deep lines running horizontally along my forehead and the shading under my eyes. 'Like when you're really tired, Mommy,' I think was what he said."

Ashley laughed. "Classic."

"So, who's going tonight? I brought a bottle of Malbec, but I wasn't sure what else . . ."

"No, no, that's perfect! Just a fun group. We'll do some drinking and a little shopping. You'll love everyone."

A little shopping. There it was. Miriam smiled to herself as Ashley weaved through the dark, winding roads. She should have known—she'd heard all about these events in the suburbs: all-female "parties" where the hosts provided wine and nibbles and then, in a feigned-relaxed but actually hyper-aggressive way, tried to sell you whatever product she was now a "stylist" or "consultant" for. Ashley once told Miriam she had bought everything from stackable bangles to workout wear to wrinkle cream at events that were initially presented as book club meetings or Girls' Nights Out.

When they arrived at their hostess's home, all the women were gathered in the family room, sipping and chatting in front of a gorgeous fire. Miriam recognized a few from the baby shower and a few more from the kids' school, but mostly they were strangers: beautiful, confident, coiffed strangers.

"Hey, everyone! Some of you might know her, but for those who don't, this is Miriam Kagan. She has the cutest twins in kindergarten, Maisie and Matthew, and also Benjamin in second grade. They just moved here from the city."

Miriam could feel the heat rise from her neck to her cheeks. She desperately wanted to disappear. After over a decade knowing exactly where she fit in city life, she was finding this harder than she would have thought. But all the women smiled kindly at her and gave little waves and then went right back to their conversations. Almost immediately, Ashley vanished, and Miriam found herself standing awkwardly alone in the kitchen. She helped herself to a glass from an open bottle of merlot. Then, unsure what to do next, she popped a small chunk of Parmesan into her mouth and looked around.

The home was spectacular, of course. Vaulted ceilings, a double-high fireplace, enough fur throw blankets and accent pillows to open a boutique. The rug under the live-edge coffee table was made from animal hides, all shades of gray and white and carefully stitched together to create a kind of modern floor quilt that stood out starkly against the trendy gray-washed wood floors. Diptyque candles burned everywhere. Low, sexy music played from invisible speakers. Women with long hair and long legs floated between the rooms, kissing each other's cheeks and inquiring after each other's children, workout regimens, and vacation plans.

"You're Miriam, right?" An elegant woman with a jet-black bob and porcelain skin offered her a smile. "I'm Claire. I'm so glad you could make it tonight."

"Claire? Oh, this is your home, right? It's beautiful, I was admiring your taste. I love everything."

Claire's smile widened. "Thank you, darling. So, Ashley said you have three little ones, all in elementary school?"

Miriam nodded.

"And you stay home with them?"

Miriam opened her mouth and then closed it again. "Yes, I do. I haven't always, but it's been really great having these last few months to—"

"It is, isn't it?" Claire interrupted. "Hey, maybe you want to join me on the board of Opus? It's not an enormous financial requirement—although all the money does so much good—and we put on great events. Plus, the funds raised make such a stunning difference in the lives of children who live so nearby yet suffer so much."

"Hmm, that sounds so interesting," Miriam murmured. It did—who didn't want to help children?—but she wasn't clear on what Claire was suggesting.

"Hello, girls," Ashley trilled as she approached and refilled her glass. "I'm glad you two have met. Claire, it's been so great having Miriam as co–room mom with me. I just knew you two would love each other."

"You were right, of course!" Miriam said, perhaps a bit too loudly.

A brief moment of awkwardness followed before Ashley leaned in and stage-whispered to Claire, "You look amazing. I can't even believe you're only a month out."

Miriam pretended not to hear, but Claire looked at her and said, "I got the full mommy job a few weeks ago: boobs, belly, and vagina. It was torturous but definitely worth it." She gently ran a hand over her concave stomach. "I've had so much sodium today *and* I should be getting my period momentarily, and look: flat as a board."

Ashley gazed at Claire's midriff. "I *so* regret not doing my stomach when I did the boobs. And not to do the vag! I wasn't thinking. What, just because I had three C-sections didn't guarantee my entire pelvic floor wouldn't get demo'd. Tampons fall out when I do jumping jacks."

"I hear you." Claire nodded. "Sex was like throwing a hot dog down a hallway. I didn't care so much, but my God, Eddie could not stop bitching about it. I mean, like, two perfect children aren't enough, now he wants me tight as a teenager?"

"Of course he does. They all do. And he got what he wanted!"

Claire feigned embarrassment. "He sure did."

Miriam laughed along with everyone, but inside she felt a stab of panic. Was that why Paul had seemed so uninterested lately? She'd had a vaginal delivery with Ben and then a C-section with the twins. She didn't outright wet herself when she laughed or sneezed or jumped—wasn't that enough? Or was she missing something crucial?

Claire glanced at her watch and gasped. "Oh my, nearly eight-thirty." Then, in a louder voice to the crowd: "Ladies? Join me in the living room?"

The doorbell rang before they could all take a seat. Someone gave a little squeal. Miriam wondered who could be so exciting. Maybe someone famous? She'd heard a rumor that Blake Lively had moved to town, but nobody seemed to know for sure. She'd overheard someone mention that Karolina, the senator's wife, was hiding out in Greenwich, but thankfully the subject had changed almost immediately.

When a woman appeared at the door, Miriam recognized her as one of the moms from Ben's second-grade class. She had a little girl, if she remembered, with fiery red hair and what Miriam's mother would definitely call a "fresh mouth." Sage. That was the woman's name. Sage wore a flowy maxi dress topped with a cashmere cardigan and a tangle of delicate gold chains. Her red hair was loosely braided into a crown that framed her face, and her skin was nearly translucent, flawless, and devoid of makeup. She looked like she belonged at Coachella, where she could take a long, sensual drag off someone's joint, shake off her sweater, and languidly dance the night away with desert bonfires and younger men with pierced tongues. Sage offered a smile to the room of lovely women and, in a surprisingly baritone voice, announced, "Let's get this party started!"

"Oooh, I can't wait to see what she brought this time," Ashley said, pulling Miriam's arm toward a prime spot on the couch. "I hope you brought your credit card."

The rolling suitcase Sage tugged behind her seemed rather large for jewelry, but what did Miriam know? She sipped her wine while Sage settled herself.

"First of all, a huge thanks to Claire for hosting tonight's . . . festivities. Honey, I promise not to get lube on your linen."

Laughs all around.

"Isn't she a pediatrician?" Miriam whispered to Ashley, who didn't take her eyes off Sage's suitcase.

"Was. Not practicing anymore. The call schedule was hell, apparently."

Miriam nodded. Sage looked around the room. "Ladies, first I'll tell you what I'm not going to do. I am not going to play some asinine icebreaker game. I am not going to push you to buy chocolate body paint. Or anything, for that matter. And I am most definitely not going to pull out some disgusting plastic dildo and tell you why it will change your life."

A few women laughed, but to her relief many looked as uncomfortable as Miriam felt.

"Think of me as your intimacy concierge for high-end luxury products only." Sage paused dramatically. "How many of you expect your husband to stay interested?" she asked, looking around.

Some called out, "I couldn't care less," but most of the women tentatively raised their hands.

"And how many of you put every effort into making that happen?"

Silence. No hands.

"Can anyone remember the last time she wore a proper negligee to bed?"

"If by 'negligee' you mean an old T-shirt from college and a pair of my husband's boxers, then I would have to say last night," a woman called out.

Everyone laughed. Miriam quickly took another big sip of wine, worried that she'd laughed a little too hard.

"And dare I ask when was the last time anyone in this room gave a blow job?"

"To my *husband*?" Ashley screeched.

That elicited laughs from the entire group.

Sage shook her head as though the women had greatly disappointed her. "I guess I don't even have to ask about anal. But I will say, you're really missing out on a hot spot of female pleasure."

The lone pregnant woman in the group said, "My husband just can't get enough, especially with this." She rubbed her enormous belly and grinned. "Who doesn't love some good pregnancy hemorrhoids? Or the fact that I talk about how constipated I am over dinner?"

Suddenly things didn't seem so dire between her and Paul.

Sage held up her hands in mock defeat. "You, Leesa, are the only one with an excuse. But the rest of you—if you're not going to put in the time and effort to keep your husbands satisfied, they're going to look for it somewhere else."

"Promise?" asked a petite woman in jeans and a leather jacket.

The women laughed and a few even clapped, but Sage ignored them and began pulling tubes and jars and bottles from her bag. They were beautifully packaged, like the kind of products at Barneys makeup counters. "Here we have our bath-and-body product line. Bath salts, aromatherapy diffusers, scented massage oils, and hydrating moisturizers. Everything is paraben-free and made exclusively in the U.S. using formulas developed by world-class cosmetic dermatologists. Nothing here will give you a yeast infection or cause your skin to break out, but they're specially formulated to appeal to men."

Miriam examined a delicate glass bottle when it was passed to her. The small block print on the front read SENSUAL MASSAGE OIL, and when she twisted off the top to smell it, she wanted to douse herself in it. Yes. She would happily buy some massage oil and offer Paul a shoulder rub. How long had it been since she'd done that? She accepted a refilled wineglass from Ashley and sank back into the couch.

Sage kept pulling out brightly colored objects in every imaginable shape and size. Like the bath products, these were all packaged beautifully in sleek, minimalist boxes with little indication as to their contents. "Please, feel free to open and touch all of them."

Miriam examined a box that could have been mistaken for something you'd buy at the Apple store. It featured a picture of what looked like a lavender-colored egg and boasted the ability to vibrate in response to pressure. There were ten preset vibration patterns, or you could program it to remember up to six of your own personal patterns. When she opened it, she could see it charged on a sleek white base and came with a white silk carrying case. It felt as smooth as a river stone, just softer and a bit flexible.

"That one there— Sorry, I don't know your name," Sage called out.

Miriam was too engrossed in examining the purple egg to realize that Sage was pointing at her.

"Miriam. Miriam Kagan," Ashley called out.

Miriam snapped her head up and saw the entire room looking back at her as she cupped the vibrator. The heat that started in her chest and moved straight to her face felt nearly overwhelming.

"The one Miriam Kagan has is a bestseller. Miriam, will you hold that up, please?"

Miriam lifted it six inches in the air.

"That little gem is a triumph of design," Sage declared as though talking about a new Gehry building. "It's more responsive than your Porsche, and trust me, it will make *you* much happier. It's perfect for partner play, given the fact that it's not some crude imitation of your husband's private parts. The medical-grade silicone is nonporous, making it easy to clean, and it's completely waterproof for fun in the shower or a nice hot bath. Miriam, what do you think?"

"Think?" Miriam squeaked. Why was she acting like such a prude? It was a vibrator, for Christ's sake, not a set of leather whips, and yet all she wanted to do was crawl under the couch.

"It's very . . . nice?"

Everyone laughed. Sage smiled beatifically.

"It's yours," Sage said. "A gift from me. Make sure you put it to good use!"

The room broke into applause. Miriam managed an embarrassed

thank-you before she dropped the vibrator, complete with its charger and packaging, into her purse like a dirty secret.

Everyone's attention shifted to a vibrator shaped exactly like a tube of lipstick, complete with a YSL logo on the side, and Miriam slipped out of the room and into the kitchen, where she grabbed the biggest hunk of Parmesan off the cheese tray and jammed it into her mouth. She'd gone for her second massive piece when Ashley appeared in front of her.

"How fun is this?" she said, laughing, refilling her wineglass for the third time. Miriam didn't want to act like anyone's mother, but Ashley *was* her ride home. "It's so good. We all need to keep it fresh in the bedroom."

"My bedroom is stale," Miriam blurted out, then was promptly mortified.

"Oh, honey, I'm sure that's not true. Things always slow down with young kids. But then they pick up again." Ashley helped herself to the smallest baby carrot on the tray and dipped a millimeter of it into the hummus. "How often do you and Paul do it?"

"Not often."

"What, like, once a week? Once every week and a half?"

Good God, Miriam thought. Ashley sounded as bad as Emily, only this woman had three children of her own.

"Something like that," Miriam lied. "How often do you guys?"

Ashley laughed. "Not as often as Eric would like to, that's for sure. He climbs all over me, and I probably give in three, maybe four times a week." Miriam must have looked shell-shocked because Ashley rushed to add, "If I say yes in the middle of the night, I'm allowed to just lie there."

Miriam forced a laugh. "Totally," she said, although she didn't think that Paul had ever woken her in the middle of the night for sex.

"I'm glad Paul and Eric are hanging out tonight," Ashley said. "It's so crazy hard to make couple friends where you both like both people, you know?"

"Not tonight," Miriam said, although now she wasn't sure. "Paul is home babysitting. Scratch that—he's parenting. I hate when people say the dad is 'babysitting' his own children."

Ashley pulled out her phone and showed Miriam a text from Paul that read, *Guys are coming over to play some poker. Invited Paul, like you said. He's in.*

Miriam grabbed her phone. *Where r u?*

Three dots appeared and then . . . *Poker night at Eric's house. The Miller girl from across the street came over to sit w/ kids. Everyone asleep. You having fun?*

Yes, she wrote, and tried not to be annoyed that Paul had arranged a babysitter and gone to a friend's house without so much as a text.

Another minuscule carrot dipped into another millimeter of hummus. Ashley shook her head as she chewed. "They say they're playing poker, but it's total bullshit. They are ogling our new au pair."

"You have a new au pair?"

"Boobs up to here and an ass to die for. We all went to one of those disgusting indoor water parks last weekend, and I thought Eric would have a full-on heart attack when he saw her. She was wearing one of those Brazilian-cut bikini bottoms that's not quite a thong but almost? And what was I in? A rash guard. And water socks. Can you picture it?"

"No," Miriam said, wondering what this au pair must look like if she made Ashley—size two, perfect figure, gorgeous blond hair, and Botoxed within an inch of her life—feel less than.

"She's our third one, and the last two were perfection: awkward, chubby, one even had bad acne. It didn't stop her from having sex in Tyler's room with a guy she brought home from the city, which is why we had to fire her. Ugh, I'm still trying to get that visual out of my head."

"She did not!" Miriam said, not bothering to hide her delight.

"Yes, but when you need to rematch in the middle of the year, who's going to be left? Only the hot ones. No moms want them. The ugly girls go like hotcakes, and by August, only supermodels are left. Claire had one last year that was a legit clone of Scarlett Johansson, only prettier."

"My God."

"What are you going to do? Take care of your own children? God forbid." Ashley laughed, and it was obvious that she understood exactly how she sounded but didn't care.

Claire appeared in the kitchen. "I certainly didn't leave my job on Wall Street to be a stay-at-home mom without a full-time nanny!" she said, and winked. "Where's the fun in that?"

"Hear, hear!" Ashley raised her wineglass and, without waiting for anyone else to toast, dumped it down her throat. Miriam made a mental note to call an Uber.

"Miriam? Sage is looking for you."

At the mere sound of Sage's name, Miriam blushed, picturing the lavender egg resting in her bag. "Me? I'm, uh, I don't really . . ."

"It's probably your turn in the private room," Ashley said, refilling. "After the demonstration, Sage takes each woman into a separate room so you can make your purchases in private. And you're up."

"Oh, I'm fine. Thanks, but I already got that one thing and—"

"Come *on*!" Ashley said, grabbing Miriam's arm, sloshing some of her wine onto the counter. "Stop being such a prude. Trust me, Paul is going to thank you for this. Think of the jewelry. Men are often overcome with a desire to buy their wives diamonds when sex is reintroduced to the marriage!"

"It's not that we're *not* having sex," Miriam muttered, but she stopped herself. Why had she said anything to Ashley about something as personal as her and Paul's sex life?

"Go on. Buy whatever looks good—he'll like *anything*, I promise."

Before Miriam could protest again, Sage swooped out of nowhere, yanked Miriam into a room, and closed the door behind her. "Welcome to my boudoir," Sage said, waving her arms expansively.

The juxtaposition between the masculine mahogany of Claire's husband's office and the objects that occupied every centimeter was comical. On the wall behind the desk was an old-school oil portrait of some titan of industry who appeared to be gazing out on a desk filled with sex toys of every imaginable shape and color. The velvet tufted couch was strewn with naughty black lingerie, and the windowsill served as a staging area for various types of lube.

"Thank you for tonight," Miriam said, trying to keep her gaze directly on Sage. "It was so . . . informative. And thanks also for the lavender . . . thing. But I think that's all I'm interested in for right now."

"No pressure!" Sage sang, pulling Miriam around the room in a small circle. "Just look around. I know it can sometimes feel a little embarrassing, but trust me, I can't even tell you how many marriages I've saved with a few well-chosen items."

Miriam's laugh sounded hollow and uncomfortable. "Oh, Paul and I are totally fine. Just young kids, you know? Nothing more serious than that."

"Of course not," Sage agreed. "But those—lean years, shall we call them?—can quickly become the norm if you aren't vigilant. One minute you're blaming it on nursing and the next minute your youngest is four and you can't remember the last time you've had sex."

Five, Miriam thought.

"Then the next thing you know, your husband's sexting the nanny or the tennis coach or his nurse or his secretary, and bam! End of life as you know it. Clichés exist for a reason."

Miriam's thoughts flashed to Paul, who was likely sitting around another multimillion-dollar home at that very moment, staring at the gorgeous, unsuspecting au pair who'd made the mistake of stopping by the kitchen for a banana or a can of Coke. Miriam glanced around at the lingerie, which looked microscopic. "I can't wear any of that," she said, waving her hand toward a mesh catsuit that may or may not fit a ten-year-old.

Sage nodded in agreement while Miriam tried not to be offended. "No, that's not what I'm thinking. Here, look at this. It's my all-time bestseller and just a great, nonthreatening way for the bashful to jump right in."

"What is it?" Miriam asked, accepting the beautiful navy box that read *love is art* in small script.

"It's a gigantic white canvas—think the size of a shower curtain—and it comes with completely safe and organic body paint. You lay it out on the bedroom or bathroom floor, apply the paint to each other, and then make love right on top of the canvas. When you're finished, you get to shower together and soap each other up to get off all the paint. I bet you used to shower all the time together. Can you even remember the last time?"

"No," Miriam murmured, staring at the box.

"The best part is that you'll have made a masterpiece that you send back to the company, and they frame it in a color of your choosing and you mount it over the bed. Every time you go to sleep, you'll both remember that night. It's literally the best date night ever."

"That actually does sound cool," Miriam said, trying to envision her and Paul covering each other in black paint and rolling around on the canvas together. It seemed fun. It didn't require her to jam herself into anything binding or itchy, nor insert anything into her body—or his. She wouldn't have to pretend to be a cowgirl or a schoolgirl or an any other kind of girl—just herself having some old-fashioned sexy fun with her husband. Yes, Sage was right. This was a good start.

"You can't even imagine how many of these I've sold tonight. You're going to walk into half the master bedrooms in Greenwich and see these hanging on the wall."

"I'll take it!" Miriam said, yanking out her Amex.

"You'll love it," Sage promised, tucking the box into a discreet brown paper bag. "And so will your husband. Here, sign with your finger and you're good to go."

Miriam accepted the iPad from Sage and nearly passed out when she saw the total: $475.

"Um, I didn't realize . . . I thought . . . It's quite a bit of money . . ."

"Oh, that's just because it includes the framing, sweetie! Trust me. It's going to change your life for the better. And you can't put a price on that."

There was a knock on the door. "Just a moment!" Sage called out. "We're nearly finished here."

So much for "I won't pressure you to buy anything," Miriam thought as she scrawled her name with her fingertip. Watching over Miriam's shoulder, Sage pressed "submit" and flashed her an enormous smile. "Enjoy it, okay? And come back again soon. He's going to be hooked!"

Miriam half-staggered back out to the living room, where Ashley was sitting with three or four other women. They were all laughing so hard that tears streamed down their faces.

"What'd you get?" Ashley called to Miriam.

"Oh, nothing, really," Miriam said, trying to hide the telltale brown paper bag behind her leg.

"I bet you got the canvas!" called a woman Miriam recognized as co-president of the school's PTA. The women all nodded.

"Hey, not to pry," said the one who had twins the same age as Miriam's. "But Ashley said you're friends with Karolina Hartwell. Is it true she drank an entire bottle of tequila and then got in the car with all those kids?"

"No, that's actually not true at all," Miriam said. She noticed the room had quieted, but she wasn't sure what she should say next. It was hardly the right time or place to announce that the senator had set her up. So she quickly helped herself to another sip of wine and held her breath until the group changed topics.

It took a minute for Miriam to realize that she was a little tipsy, yes, but in a good, warm way, and besides, how long had it been since she'd gotten buzzed with friends? Ashley was high-energy, but she was kind and so willing to introduce Miriam around and make her feel welcome. And most important, she had taken a first positive step to improving whatever temporary weird thing was going on between her and Paul. She took a few deep breaths, pulled her phone out of her bag, and sent her husband what counted in mommy world as a racy text: *At sex-toy party and all stocked up. Hope poker night is fun. See you later. xoxo*

Smiling, she gathered up her things and went in search of another glass of wine.

Miriam flashed on Karolina. She was glad Karolina had hired Emily, since it was obvious that all of Greenwich believed Karolina was a drunk. There was work to do there. But other than that, even Miriam had to admit: as far as nights went, this one wasn't a total bust, and Greenwich wasn't shaping up to be such a bad town after all.

12

No Good
Deep

Karolina

"I'm so sorry. So, so sorry. I really wish it could be different." Natalie folded her hands and looked at the table.

The coffee shop in Georgetown where they were seated buzzed with the lunchtime rush: young professionals in suits, college students in hoodies, and mommies clad in spandex. Karolina was both surprised and grateful that she hadn't yet run into anyone she knew.

"I understand," Karolina said quietly, although she didn't.

"You know that if it were up to me, there would be no question. But the board was unanimous. And let me stress that it's temporary. Only until this whole . . . situation can be cleared up."

"Uh-huh."

Natalie reached across the bistro table and placed her hand on Karolina's elbow. "Lina, say something. Please. Is there anything I can do?"

"You can give me my position back. You know firsthand that I would never do what I'm accused of, and that I care about helping this school more than anyone else does."

"I wish I could, honey. But the school is one hundred percent reliant on the generosity of its donors, the largest of whom make up the board, and they voted to suspend you temporarily—until this can all be cleared up. Any type of legal trouble or negative media attention detracts from our mission. You must understand that."

"I do. I just hate it."

"I hate it too."

A moment of awkward silence followed before Natalie pressed her palms to the table. "I'm sorry to cut this short, but I have parent meetings all afternoon."

"Of course," Karolina hurried to say, although she was caught off guard by how abruptly Natalie was ending their meeting.

"Stay in touch? And let me know if there's anything I can do."

Karolina stood up to hug her goodbye and could feel the eyes of the surrounding customers on her. She was accustomed to it—if you were six feet tall and a former cover girl, you got used to people staring—but now she had to wonder if they recognized her because of the news. Today's *Post* was particularly nasty: a photo of Karolina from the Greenwich Whole Foods with HOT MESS! in all caps and size-100 font. Emily had talked her down when Karolina called, half-hysterical; said she was working on a plan.

"Will do," Karolina said, but Natalie was halfway to the door. Karolina sat back down and blew into her tea. A man in his forties wearing an ugly gray suit diverted his eyes when she looked at him.

Her phone rang. "Trip?"

His voice was familiar but distant. "Lina? Hi. Okay, I spoke to Graham, and it's all worked out. You're welcome to attend Harry's swim meet today." He said this as if he had secured primary custody for Karolina. "I think, under the circumstances, that's a fairly generous—"

"Cut the shit, Trip. You know exactly what's happening here and so do I."

"Lina, it's not quite that—"

"I'll be at the meet at four."

"One more thing . . ." Trip sounded apprehensive. "Graham insists that the visit be supervised."

"*Supervised?* It's at the middle school pool! With his entire team and all the other parents and coaches. Come on, Trip. That's ridiculous."

"Those are the terms for a visit with his son."

"*His* son? Whose side are you on here?"

"I'm trying to remain impartial and represent both of you fairly." Trip paused, and his voice softened. "I really am sorry, Lina, but we both know that he has sole custody of Harry."

Karolina inhaled sharply, as though she'd been punched. "How many times did I ask Graham to adopt Harry? A hundred? Three hundred? There was always an excuse why it wasn't a good time, but now I see exactly why: so when he inevitably traded me in for his next girl, he wouldn't have to waste time with messy custody battles. *What a stand-up guy your best friend is.* And you're right there with him."

"Lina, we've all talked about this through the years, and I know that—"

"Stop calling me Lina! That's for friends. Which you no longer are. And while your definition of a parent might be who has legal custody, my definition is the person who wakes up in the middle of the night to check the closets for monsters and who watches endless hours of *Transformers* when the child is home sick and who holds his hand when he gets his first cavity filled. Not to mention packs the school lunches and knows all his friends and drives him to all his practices and hugs him when he cries because the boys are picking on him at school. Graham sure as hell isn't doing any of that."

"Lina, I really—"

"Karolina!"

"Karolina," he said slowly. "I took the liberty of calling Elaine to meet you today at Harry's school."

"I don't know how you live with yourself."

"It's who he felt . . . comfortable with."

"I have nothing else to say to you. Tell Graham I'll be there today and I look forward to seeing his cold fish of a mother. Goodbye." She pressed her thumb into the "end" button with force and then immediately dialed Trip back.

He answered on the first ring.

"One last thing. You no longer represent me. You're fired."

Karolina didn't realize she was crying until the man who'd been staring at her walked over and handed her a clean napkin. She thanked him and dropped a twenty on the table before he could invite himself to sit. "I have to run," she said quickly, grabbing her coat and bag. She held it together until she got to her car, parked right in front of Georgetown Family Medicine, where Jerry Goldwyn, their family doctor and a close friend of Graham's from childhood, had his concierge practice. It was one of the perks of moving to Washington, Karolina thought—personalized medicine from a dear family friend. He had spent dozens of hours counseling Karolina and Graham on their fertility struggle, even when they lived in New York. In his early fifties, Jerry wasn't quite their parents' generation or their own, so he existed in a space between friend and family.

Karolina wiped her mascara as well as she could and walked up the stairs into Dr. Goldwyn's townhouse office. His receptionist, Gloria, greeted her warmly.

"Karolina! Sweetheart, do you have an appointment?"

"Hi, Gloria. No, I was just walking by and wanted to see if Jerry was in."

The older woman mimed wiping her forehead. "Phew! I thought the senility was advancing. I know he would love to see you, but he stepped out to lunch. Do you want me to give him a message?"

The waiting room *was* empty, but Karolina couldn't help but wonder if that was an excuse and Jerry had somehow given Gloria instructions to turn her—this embarrassing drunk—away should she show up look-ing for anything. Just as she'd almost convinced herself of this, the door to the street opened behind her and Jerry walked in.

"Karolina? Sweetheart? Is that you?" Jerry's voice was as warm and welcoming as always.

"In the flesh. Sorry, I was parked outside and wanted to come say hello. Is now a bad time?"

"A bad time? For you? Come, let's go to my office. Do you want any coffee or anything?"

"No, I'm fine."

"Gloria, don't put any calls through unless they're genuine 911 emergencies, okay? Thanks, love."

Karolina followed him into his cluttered office, which had books from floor to ceiling and massive piles of patient charts on the desk. "Forgive the mess. I must be the last practicing physician in the Western world who hasn't gone digital. I just can't wrap my mind around it . . ." He pulled a lab coat off a guest chair and tossed it in a corner. "Please, here, sit. Let me get a look at you."

"Not much to see, I'm afraid."

"Nonsense. You're always radiant. Glowing."

"Pregnant women glow. Not women who have been thrown out by their husbands."

"Right." He looked physically pained. "I'm so sorry to see what's been going on in the press. How can I help?"

Karolina hadn't come in here in search of anything other than a friendly face, but she had a sudden realization: Jerry certainly knew—and could likely testify—that she did not now, or ever, have a drinking problem.

"Well, clearly you know that despite what my husband would have you believe, I am not an alcoholic. Almost the opposite! With all the hormones and IVF cycles and specialists, I've barely had a drink the past five years."

"Of course. I know that."

"Then maybe you would, like, testify to that effect? Not in court or anything, but maybe you'd go on the record saying as much? To a newspaper or a TV anchor or something?"

She could tell from his reaction that he was going to say no. "Lina, sweetheart, I would bet my entire practice on the simple fact that you don't have an alcohol abuse problem. I know that. What I don't know or understand—and what's really none of my business—is what's going on between you and Graham. I know that you're separated because I read it in the papers, not because I heard it from him. I hope you can understand, but as both your and Graham's doctor and, more importantly, friend, I really can't get in the middle of this. I love and adore both of you." Jerry gave her a sad smile. "I know this can't be easy for you. But you're an amazing woman, and I know you'll get through it. Not just get through it—transcend it. Of that much I'm sure."

"Thanks, Jerry. I appreciate hearing that, especially from you. And I do understand," Karolina said, although she wasn't sure she did.

The phone on Jerry's desk rang. He pushed a button on the front face and said, "Yes, Gloria?"

"Sorry to bother you, Dr. Goldwyn, but it's Mrs. O'Dell calling. Little Aiden fell out of his high chair and split open his lip. She's wondering if she should go to the ER, and if so, what plastic surgeon you recommend?"

Jerry's brow furrowed. "Wait, let me see who's on call right now. Have her hold just a second . . ."

Karolina stood up. "It was great to see you. Sorry to barge in like this."

He looked up. "You're never barging in. I'm so sorry, I have to help this woman—"

"No, of course. Send my love to Irene." She gathered her bag and coat and walked back to reception. "Wonderful to see you, Gloria."

Gloria gestured to Karolina with a stack of papers.

"For me?" Karolina asked as Gloria transferred the call.

"For you. A couple of old bills. We'd put them through insurance, but they were returned. I thought it was just a problem with the coding, so I recoded and resubmitted—twice, actually—but they still didn't go through. You may want to make sure nothing went to collections."

"Thanks," Karolina said, and tossed the small rubber-banded pile of envelopes into her purse. "I'll deal with it."

Maybe Graham would pick up her call if it related to finances? He certainly hadn't deigned to do so for any other reason. Emily had made her promise to stop trying to contact him. But he was her *husband*. How was this happening to her? When had her husband changed into this person she barely even recognized?

As Karolina eased out of her parking spot, Aunt Agata's number flashed on her dashboard screen.

"Hi, Auntie," she said, instantly switching to Polish. "How are you feeling?"

"Fine, dear. Just fine. I'm not calling to talk about me. I want to see how *you're* doing."

"Me? I'm okay. I'm down in D.C. now, heading back to Bethesda to go to Harry's swim meet. It feels like I haven't seen him in forever."

"I heard on the news that you and Graham are getting divorced." This was not a question.

"Yes, apparently that's how we're all finding things out these days," Karolina said as she merged onto the highway.

"He's a *dupek*!"

"I won't argue with you there."

"Always has been, always will be."

"Now, that's not exactly fair, Auntie. Graham was different when we met. Decent."

Her aunt hooted. "That may be what your mother and you thought, but I could always see the writing on the wall. Yes, missy, this was clear as day! Not that I'm saying 'I told you so,' because I love you and I would never say that, but . . . well, I told you so. Did I not? Don't you remember that little chat we had the night before your wedding? I said, 'Lina, that man has a fair face and a foul heart.' Do you remember?"

"Of course I remember! You cornered me at the rehearsal dinner and told me Graham was after my money."

"Yes, ma'am, I did."

"And I told you that his family had so much money that it made whatever I had earned from modeling look like pocket change."

"Well, that's neither here nor there. The point is, I had a feeling about that one."

"Mama loved him," Karolina said quietly, remembering that night like it was yesterday. Her mother had been shining with a happiness Karolina had rarely seen growing up, her smile so wide it made the crinkles around her eyes look like they were smiling too. And why shouldn't she have been joyful? Her only child—the one for whom she had essentially sacrificed her own life—was marrying a handsome, successful attorney from an established and wealthy family. Her daughter would have everything she hadn't: stability, security, social acceptance, extended family, lots of children, and a doting husband. Her smile that night announced that all those years of work had been worth it, that the debts were all settled, and happily. If Karolina were being honest with herself, so much of her own happiness that weekend had been tied up with her mother's obvious relief and joy: you didn't spend your entire childhood watching your mother work herself to the bone for your benefit without feeling a lifetime's worth of guilt about it.

"Your mother loved you. And she loved that you were settled, and to a man who could provide for you."

"I could provide for myself!"

"She knew that, Lina. She didn't want you to have to."

The two were quiet for a moment, comfortably so. Aunt Agata had practically raised Karolina because Karolina's mother worked as a live-in nanny for a wealthy family six days a week. She would come home Sunday mornings, exhausted beyond description and so excited to see her daughter, and Karolina would spend the time crying that her mother loved the children she nannied for more; that she spent all her time with them; that she was missing Karolina's entire childhood. As if it were a choice. And then, when Karolina was fourteen—after so many weeks and years of this painful separation and brief reunion—a stylish man in a beautiful suit approached her on the street in Kraków and asked if she was interested in modeling. Aunt Agata was certain he was a predator of some kind, but Karolina's mother asked the parents for whom she worked if they could find out more about him, and the word came back: he was legitimate. Not only legitimate but highly respected as having a special talent for finding the most beautiful girls who went on to become the most successful models. He was Italian, from Milan, and he traveled to all the capital cities and small towns and rural villages across Europe to pluck young girls from their ordinary lives and send them on to great money and fame. So when he found Karolina ("Finally!" her mother said, although she'd never before mentioned having such dreams for her child), her mother was nearly delirious with relief.

"But, Mama, I want to become a teacher," Karolina had said when her mother insisted she go to the meeting with the man in Milan.

"Who's saying you cannot? Not me. Not Mr. Italian. What's his name? Fratelli. Just go. See what happens. That's all I ask."

So Karolina had gone. It was thrilling, of course—her first time out of Poland and headed to fashion's capital! Everything was so new, so bright and gorgeous and exciting. And it felt wonderful when the people in Mr. Fratelli's office fawned all over Karolina, examining her from every angle and seeming happy with what they saw. Just one month later, they booked her first job. Three months later came the invitation from Miuccia Prada to headline the fall runway show. Within six months Karolina was on the cover of Italian *Vogue*, and then came the ultimatum: *Leave school if you're serious about this; you'll have the rest of your life to study, but work as a professional model is the shortest of earning seasons, so take advantage when you can.* So at sixteen, right before the start of her junior year in high school, Karolina dropped out. And when she arrived in New York City to live in a cramped walk-up with three other teenaged models and a kind of housemother who cared more about sourcing diet pills than enforcing curfews, Karolina could sense—more than sense, she was certain—that her teacher dreams were over.

"Lina? Are you there?" Her aunt's voice was quiet but insistent.

"Sorry, yes. I'm here." As Karolina always did when she talked on the phone, she was cruising in the far right lane at exactly fifty-five miles an hour. "I can't even imagine what Mama would say now."

"She would be so proud of how strong you're being. That I know for sure. Your mama was smart and capable, and more than anything in the entire world, she wanted her girl to have a better life than she did. I'd say there's no arguing that your mama would be greatly relieved to see where you are now. May she rest in peace."

"May she rest in peace." The words came out as a whisper.

"Okay, that is enough pep for one day. Give Harry a big hug from me, okay? And send me some pictures on the iPad."

"Will do, Aunt Agata. I love you."

"Love you too, sweetheart."

Karolina waited for the call to disconnect and slowly pressed down on the accelerator. Was this how her mother felt on Sunday mornings, when her workweek was finally finished and the bus was making its way to Agata's house, where Karolina perched by the front window, clutching her doll baby and waiting, waiting, waiting? It must have been. Harry's meet didn't start for a while, and he certainly wouldn't be counting the seconds until she arrived—she may not even warrant a hug in front of his friends now that he was twelve—but none of that mattered: she couldn't wait to see her boy.

13

Celebrities Are Fickle and Oftentimes Stupid

Emily

"**Y**ou look so fucking hot in that." Miles's voice was a growl, and it made Emily's stomach flutter.

"What, this?" she asked coquettishly, motioning toward her teensy spandex shorts and strappy sports bra that was cut lower than it needed to be. "I always work out in this."

She accelerated a little, her feet hitting the pavement rhythmically, and she nearly jumped when Miles grabbed her upper arm. Not softly. "I can't wait until we get home."

They had run only twenty minutes or so along the Santa Monica beach, and Emily wasn't ready to go back home yet. But she slowed to a jog, Miles pushed himself against her thigh, and she could feel exactly what he meant.

"Naughty boy! You're like a horny teenager. Stay focused!" She sprinted ahead, but already she had a plan, and she knew he knew she did.

He followed a few paces behind as Emily led the way up from the beach walkway to Ocean Avenue, which had the most amazing views of the coastline stretching from Venice Beach up to Malibu. Wordlessly, she ran toward the entrance of Shutters on the Beach and waved at one of the bellmen when he opened the door for them.

"Welcome back," the man said, clearly assuming they were hotel guests returning from their morning run.

"Thank you," Miles and Emily called out in unison.

They jogged into the middle of the lobby and helped themselves to two cups of citrus-infused water from a console table near the elevators. "Wait here," Emily said, and she ducked into the ladies' room. As she'd known from previous pit stops, it was not only empty but also featured luxurious floor-length doors instead of the usual stalls. She poked her head out of the restroom and motioned for Miles to join her.

He glanced around, looking guilty before ducking behind Emily into the ladies' room. In an instant, he had her pressed up against the full-length mirror and was grinding into her, kissing her sweaty neck and moaning ever so slightly.

"In here," she whispered, dragging him into the toilet room farthest from the door. It was spacious and immaculate but still a bathroom: Emily tried not to think about that part as Miles pulled down her shorts and pushed into her. She held on to the sink for balance, and they moved in their familiar way. Only this time she found herself thinking about Miriam. Did she and Paul really not have sex like this? It was pretty much the only positive thing about marriage, as far as Emily could see: the regularity of sex with someone who knew *exactly* how you liked it. This wasn't even their hottest: when she'd gone to pick him up at LAX after his flight back from Hong Kong, they'd flashed their Platinum Cards and disappeared into one of the computer carrels in the first-class American Airlines lounge. She'd worn a skirt for exactly that reason, and neither needed to say a word when she hiked it up just enough to straddle him in the ergonomic desk chair. No one had noticed them then either. No one ever did. They'd had sex every single day for the ten days he'd been home, and it never would have occurred to either of them that there was any other option.

When they finished, Miles kissed her neck and said breathlessly, "You're amazing."

"You're not so bad yourself." She kissed him back and cleaned herself as well as she could with toilet paper. "Can we finish this run now?"

Miles was laughing when they opened the door, and a woman around their mother's age looked at them in horror. When had she come in? Emily hadn't heard the door open at all, so she hadn't particularly tried to keep quiet . . .

"Excuse me!" the woman said in a pinched voice. "But this is the *ladies'* room."

"I was just leaving," Miles said. He winked at Emily and walked into the lobby.

Emily could feel the woman glaring at her as she washed and dried her hands. She offered the woman a little wave and "Have a nice day" as she left the bathroom.

"Come on," she said, tapping Miles on the butt. "Let's get out of here before we get arrested."

The weather was gorgeous for mid-February, and the sun shone on them as they ran the two miles back to their house on the border of Santa Monica and Brentwood. Emily glanced at Jennifer Garner's house as they passed, to see if any of the kids were playing outside, but since Ben had moved out, there seemed to be a lot less action. When they finally arrived home, both of them were drenched in sweat but grinning.

"That was an excellent send-off," Miles said as he opened their Sub-Zero and pulled out two bottles of vitaminwater.

"I can't believe you're leaving tonight already. It was all too fast."

"Offer still stands, you know. The Peninsula in Hong Kong is not terrible. You could relax a little, go to the spa. Shop. Fuck me. Does that sound so absolutely awful?"

"Of course that doesn't sound awful," Emily said truthfully. "But I have to get back to Greenwich. Karolina needs me."

"Why? Her husband is still cheating on her. She's still banished to *Greenwich*. I'd say she could wait for another week."

Emily took a swig. "All true. But she's getting crucified in the press. Did you see the new *Us Weekly* today? She's on the cover. Looking *hideous*. And the headline says FROM RICHES TO RAGS: THE EXPLOSION OF A FAIRY TALE. The longer these things are drilled home, the harder it is to undo them. And there's custody at stake here. You should hear her talk about Harry. This is a big job for me. Potentially a huge one."

"You have famous clients all the time."

"Yes, but this particular one may be married to the *president* one day. That's a different level. If I can do this right—and trust me, it won't be easy—those little shits Rizzo Benz and Kim Kelly will be begging me. And I will savor every second of telling them to go to hell."

"Sounds about right. I think I saw that Rizzo was interviewed by Breitbart last week? Not good."

Emily laughed. Yet another reason she loved Miles.

"I'm going to go shower," he said. "Join me?"

Emily opened her mouth to tell him that she was going to wait, but he had already left the room. Her phone rang the special shrill version of "Lady Evil" by Black Sabbath as the tune for Miranda Priestly. Staring, Emily knew she had to answer it. Otherwise the junior assistant would keep calling every four to six minutes, around the clock, until she picked up. Emily had invented that little trick herself.

"Emily Charlton," she said crisply, bracing herself.

"I have Miranda Priestly calling. Just a moment, please, while I connect you."

"Emily? Are you there?" Clipped and cold, as usual.

Even after all these years—and despite the fact that Emily was no longer terrified of her—Emily still had a visceral reaction to the sound of Miranda's voice. Her heart beat a bit faster, and her mouth went dry. "Hello, Miranda. Yes, I'm here."

"Lovely." She said the word like she meant its opposite. "Listen, I need you. Gabrielle just announced that she's been put on bed rest!"

"Bed rest?"

"She's expecting her *fourth*. Four children is appalling. Not to mention I've already had to endure *three* maternity leaves."

"Well, you know what they're saying: four is the new three."

"Anything over two is distasteful. I'm sure she won't return."

"Gabrielle's been there for ten years, Miranda. She loves *Runway*. She'll be back."

"I need you to fill in for her, Emily, effective immediately. We are three months out from the Met Ball, and it's not going to oversee itself. Good Lord, how could she have done this?"

Emily suppressed a smile. Even childless, she knew that babies didn't always cooperate with the Met Ball schedule, though she'd bet that Gabrielle had tried her very best.

"Yes, of course she should have. I'd love to help, but—"

"Good. I'll have HR forward you the freelance paperwork. I'll pay you whatever you'd like, but I will plan to own your time for the next three months. You'll start tomorrow?"

"Miranda, I'm in L.A., and I can't—"

"Monday, then. You'll fly first. Or I can get Michael Eisner to give you a lift. That's fine."

"I'm so sorry, I would love to help, but I've accepted a client who's going to require quite a bit of hand-holding. I wouldn't be able to give you what you need for the Met right now. What you *deserve*."

There was an icy pause. "And here I had heard your business wasn't exactly, how shall we put it? *Thriving*."

Emily's stomach dropped. "Is that so?" Word had reached Miranda Priestly—who concerned herself with nothing she deemed beneath her? That little punk Rizzo was probably telling everyone and their mother that he had flown her all the way from Los Angeles in the middle of the night just to tell her she was fired before she was hired. Or maybe it had been Kim Kelly, who had been yapping to everyone that Emily didn't know how to Snapchat. Like it was crucial to know how to turn a selfie into a rainbow-puking piglet. Because *that's* how crises were remedied and celebrity achieved. Perhaps Olivia Belle had something to do with it? Who could ever be sure?

"Allow me to remind you, Emily, although I shouldn't have to: celebrities are fickle and oftentimes stupid. It's a terrible combination and not one that ensures job security. Heading the Met Ball, however? That's the job a million girls would die for."

Everything Miranda said was true, but Emily couldn't return to *Runway*. No matter how many girls would die for the job. Not after all these years. She'd practically saved Kevin Bacon and Kyra Sedgwick from bankruptcy during the whole Madoff drama and had most certainly saved Ryan Phillipe from complete irrelevance. Dealing with Amanda Seyfried's leaked nude photos? Handling the public outcry after Robin Thicke was accused of child abuse? The brilliant way Bruce transitioned publicly to Caitlyn? All Emily. But Emily had enough firsthand Miranda experience to know she should try to smooth things over.

"It's a wonderful opportunity, Miranda. No one knows that more than I. But sadly, I'm not in a place where I can accept it."

"Emily." Miranda's voice was tight but barely controlled. "You'll work with all the top people, but you'll answer only to me. You can hand out business cards on the red carpet for all I care. But I need your organizational genius, that Emily thing you do."

Emily smiled. She knew Miranda must be desperate if she was *complimenting* her. "I'd be happy to recommend a few other people who—"

Click. The phone went dead. Emily was under no illusion that they'd been accidentally disconnected. But the nice thing about being thirty-six years old and accountable to no one was that it no longer left her with that sick feeling in the pit of her stomach.

Finishing off the last of her vitaminwater, Emily grabbed her laptop from the kitchen island and brought it to the couch. She tried to

FaceTime Andy Sachs to tell her how Miranda had just hung up on her midsentence, but it came up as unavailable. Emily texted her instead.

WTF? Just tried FaceTiming you and negged. Don't pretend you have a life. I know better.

The response came back immediately. *Never claiming I have a life, but can't FaceTime. I'm mystery reader at Clementine's school right now.*

Sorry I asked. Just had loveliest convo w/ MP. A peach as always.

Is she still begging you to go back? It's funny, she never begs me.

Emily couldn't help smiling. *Wants me to oversee the Met. G knocked up w/ baby #4. MP called it "vile."*

And you said no??? Liar! Hold on, back to you in a sec

Emily waited, staring at the screen, but Andy never came back. Not even Andy Sachs had time for her anymore! If that wasn't pathetic, Emily wasn't sure what was. Andy, whose new life was the very definition of dreadful, and yet Emily was the one sitting alone on her couch, patiently waiting for Andy to return from gathering eggs or something. If there had ever been any question that Andy was the worst possible fit in the history of *Runway* magazine, her purchase with Alex of a working farm in Quechee, Vermont, had sealed the deal. Milking cows, collecting chicken eggs, and taking the goats out to free-range was disgusting and smelly and all around about as appealing as a natural childbirth. Emily and Andy hadn't seen much of each other—surprise, surprise, Emily sure as hell wasn't going to *Vermont*—but she was shocked that Andy didn't call back about Miranda instantly. Times had changed.

Emily opened Facebook (after reading that only old people in their thirties, like her, ever even used it, she'd been trying to wean herself off) and nearly sprained her thumb madly scrolling past all the photos of babies, babies, babies. Babies sporting those annoying hospital-hat bows and in their coming-home outfits and with cake smashed on their faces as though turning one were some sort of massive accomplishment. Babies in onesies and tutus and swaddle blankets and sucking hilarious fake-mustache pacis and wearing cheeky slogan T-shirts that always referenced MOMMY or DADDY or AUNTIE or MY BFF. Even when they weren't crying next to her on planes or stealing all of her friends' senses of humor, they were still making her life miserable.

Miriam's manic friend Ashley from the baby shower had requested Emily as a friend; before Emily hit "delete," she saw that next to Ashley's psychotically grinning head shot was a photo of the guy from the train a couple weeks earlier. Alistair. Emily quickly clicked on his profile and was irritated to see that he kept it private. Besides his profile picture, which was nothing more than a professional head shot in a less wrinkled Brioni suit, she couldn't access anything—not the About Me, not any photos of his ex-wife or his kids, nothing he might have been unknowingly tagged in years earlier by some nonfriend. Nothing. But it did provide his last name. And when she typed it into Google, she hit the golden trifecta: work bio on his company's page, wedding announcement in the *Times*, and a handful of thumbnail-size party pictures from Patrick McMullan's website. It was amazing how much you could tell about people from those miniature images. A few quick glances and you got everyone's names and faces; the types of parties he'd been invited to and had agreed to attend; and the necessary basics like what he was wearing and how he was described ("socialite," "son of," "heir to," "legendary party boy," or her favorite, "plus one") in the captions. It seemed Mr. Alistair Grosvenor accumulated degrees from Eton and Cambridge and Brown and had an affinity for keeping his hair roguishly long but his suits impeccably tailored. His mother was titled in England—something Emily could never quite figure out—and his father was long dead. And the ex-wife was, unsurprisingly, beautiful. Thin to the point of possible starvation, but Emily wouldn't judge her there: if anything, she admired the commitment. Long-legged and graceful, with straight black hair skimming her angular shoulders, she was nearly always draped in something muted and just stylish enough. *Like a modern-day Carolyn Bessette*. This was not a woman to underestimate. If Emily were single, Alistair's ex-wife would have made for a very worthy adversary.

"Who's that?" Miles boomed from behind her, and Emily nearly jumped out of her seat.

"Why the hell are you sneaking up on me like that?"

He had a towel wrapped around his waist. "I'm not sneaking! I walked in here like a completely normal person to see if you wanted to come take a shower."

"You moved like a puma."

"You're just ogling him so intently you didn't notice me." Miles said this lightly, without the least bit of jealousy.

"I wasn't ogling anyone. He's a friend of a friend."

"Whatever. Are you coming or not?"

"No, go without me," she murmured.

He shrugged and walked back into the bedroom.

She was ready for him to go back to Hong Kong and oddly excited to get back to Greenwich, although gun to her head, she wouldn't admit that to anyone. The sheer amount of money, time, and energy those women could pool among them was astonishing: if they focused their attention to it, Emily had no doubt the town moms could end world hunger or eliminate religious persecution. Just turn those Greenwich mommies loose with their two-hundred-dollar yoga leggings and their Prada checkbooks and their trainer-toned bodies, and there was nothing they couldn't accomplish. The place had a good energy, bizarrely, and she was eager to get started with Karolina. She'd been advising Karolina to lie low, but that was about to end. It was time to fight back.

She group-texted Miriam and Karolina: *Chins up, betches! I'm coming your way tomorrow! And Aunt Emily is going to change your lives forever.*

Part Two

Part Two

14

Viewing of the New German Au Pair

Miriam

"Maybe let's try Zara?" Miriam asked, hoping Emily would agree. Everything else on Main Street in Greenwich was an absolute fortune.

It was one of those bitterly freezing February days that required arctic-wear: snow boots, the heaviest and longest down coat in your closet, and the full collection of hat, gloves, and scarf. The only skin Miriam had exposed to the cold were the three inches between her bottom lip and her eyebrows, and still she thought she might die. Yet somehow super-human Emily appeared not even to feel the whipping winds or icy air. She wore only a cute cropped leather jacket and ripped jeans. Miriam had long underwear beneath her full-length jeans—complete with wool socks and knee-high sheepskin-lined boots—and Emily was wearing flats. Barefoot. And she didn't even seem to notice.

"Stop it," Emily said, taking her by the arm and leading her toward Saks. "I took time off from Operation Karolina for this. You don't buy your birthday dress at Zara. Come with me."

Miriam tried to keep up with Emily, who was booking down the sidewalk. "So, how is Karolina's . . . case?" she asked.

"You make it sound like an STD."

"Well, I don't know how to ask! And to be perfectly honest, it doesn't seem like much is happening."

Emily turned and glared at her. "I can't help Karolina until she wants to help herself. Trip and Graham are playing power games with Harry, and she's not mad enough yet to take action. She's still in denial."

Miriam nodded. She couldn't disagree. "I'll talk to her," she said. And then, because she couldn't stop staring at Emily's exposed skin, "Aren't you cold?" She followed through the store's front doors and directly down the staircase to the contemporary section.

"What are you, eighty? How much can one person talk about the weather? Here, let's start with DVF." Emily plucked two dresses from the racks and examined each one.

"May I help you?" A saleslady in all black approached them.

Miriam murmured that they were just browsing, but Emily barked a "Yes" over her. "We're looking for a great dress that she can wear for a night out in the city with her husband. It has to be something versatile. I'm thinking DVF."

The saleslady ran her eyes up and down Miriam's snowsuit in disapproval. "Would you mind unzipping, honey? I can't tell what size you are."

Embarrassed, Miriam unzipped her parka to reveal a Patagonia wool sweater, which, layered with one of those Uniqlo heat shirts, was the warmest thing she owned.

"Mmmm," the woman murmured, unable to hide her distaste for either the sweater or Miriam's size or both. "I'd guess a ten?"

"I'm an eight," Miriam snapped, lying. She was totally a ten. Formerly a six.

"Ah, yes, of course. I want to show you this great romper I just got in from Alice and Olivia. Oh, and I think you'll love this MILLY skirt I have in mind. We could pair it with a silky tank from Helmut Lang, and it would make a fantastic city outfit."

"Romper?" Miriam said, but neither Emily nor the woman was listening. Each had moved to her own rack and was wildly grabbing hangers like in some frantic episode of designer *Supermarket Sweep*.

A few minutes later, the three women were in the largest dressing room with a mini-stage and a trifold mirror.

"I'm, uh, maybe you guys should wait outside? I'll come out and show you everything once it's on," Miriam stammered.

"Oh, come on!" Emily said. "No need to be shy—we've all seen those Dove ads featuring 'real women.' Strip."

Miriam glared. "Okay, but don't say I didn't warn you . . ." She pulled her sweater and undershirt over her head. Then, without making eye contact with Emily or the saleswoman, she unzipped her jeans, took off her long underwear, and stood, feeling horribly exposed and unattractive, in only her bra and underwear. Thank God she was wearing a pair of cute enough lacy bikinis in anticipation of the night ahead, but the bra was a horror show: nude-colored, full-coverage, and easily something a bosomy eighty-year-old would wear without complaint. Angry red lines from her waistband crisscrossed her pale stomach, and bits of lint stuck in her belly button.

Emily whistled.

Miriam covered her breasts with her hands. "I wasn't expecting to get undressed in front of an audience," she said.

"Nonsense," the saleswoman said, apropos of nothing. "Here, let's try this one first."

It took forty-five minutes of cramming herself into terrible things to stumble on the perfect dress. It was Chloé, which was way more than Miriam would usually spend.

"This one is sixty percent off. In that size," the saleswoman felt compelled to add. Plain black silk with an asymmetrical hemline and a beautiful forgiving drape. It made her boobs look human-size and her waist nearly petite and could easily be worn at the theater or a cool downtown restaurant; plus, she already had great heels to wear with it, and she would definitely wear it again to something else. She felt a pang of panic when she shoved her Amex into the chip reader, and Emily read her mind.

"Stop. It's so on sale, it's practically paying *you*."

They thanked the saleswoman and headed back outside.

"Let's get some lunch?" Emily asked. "I'm starving."

"We have to get the kids off the bus."

Emily sighed. "Right. The kids."

"You're still up for this, right?"

"Yes," Emily said without a hint of conviction.

Was she making a huge mistake leaving her children alone overnight with someone who had never so much as cared for a goldfish? *Probably*, Miriam thought as she drove them both back to her house. But what choice did she have? Neither her parents nor Paul's lived nearby, and they didn't know anyone in town well enough yet to ask them to take their three children for the entire night and get them to school the next morning. Emily was a functioning adult, arguably. She paid her bills and figured out how to feed herself. Besides, if anything went horribly awry, they were just a half hour away and could be home in no time. It would be fine.

"You'll be fine," Miriam said to Emily after they'd collected the kids from the bus and parked them in front of the television.

"I know. I'm not worried. What can be so hard? I've wrangled pop stars barely older than they are. So long as you don't mind if Maisie wears foundation to school tomorrow, then I don't see any problems." Emily laughed when Miriam looked at her in horror. "Go! Be gone. We'll have a great time."

"I left all the numbers for the pediatrician and the police and fire and both our cells and local contacts on the fridge."

"Can't I just call 911? I mean, like, isn't that what it's there for?"

"Emily."

"I'm kidding! It's fine. They're not aliens, just small humans. I've got this, okay? And I promise, I won't even drink myself into a stupor tonight just in case the house mysteriously combusts or a gang of armed men breaks in to murder us all. I'll be on top of my game."

"I can't tell you how much that sets my mind at ease."

Emily grinned. "Go and enjoy."

"You can call anytime, for any reason. We can be home in no time."

"You're not getting out of sex with your husband that easily."

Miriam laughed, perhaps too loudly. The pressure was definitely on. If it didn't happen that night, something was officially wrong with them, and none of the possibilities was good. Either her husband was disgusted with her, in love with someone else, or had been lying to her (and himself) his entire adult life and just realized he actually preferred men. Miriam considered these scenarios during the train ride to the city, and by the time she reached Grand Central, she was more convinced than ever that their entire marriage was riding on this evening. It had taken some effort, but by cross-referencing her calendar, she'd figured out that the last time she and Paul had properly slept together—from start to finish, without falling asleep in the middle—had been two months earlier. Christmas Eve. She'd gone upstairs at her in-laws' house in New Jersey to rest before dinner, and Paul had followed her. The kids had been occupied with their cousins in the basement, and Paul's parents were busy entertaining in the kitchen, and no one had noticed their disappearance for nearly an hour. It had been lovely, but good God—two *months*? The length of time was horrifying, but worse was the fact that Paul had not uttered a single word about it. Not so much as a token "I miss you" or "We need to make time for us." It was as if he didn't notice.

When she joined the short taxi line outside of Grand Central, Miriam tried to forget about all of that. "You need a cab, miss?" called the porter in an official-looking uniform, hailing a cab gracefully. She had forty minutes to get downtown. It was perfect. Plus, he'd called her "miss" and not "ma'am." Things were looking up.

In the forty-five minutes it took to go as many city blocks, Miriam's mind drifted. How long had it been since she'd felt like this? It must have been pre-kids but also pre-pregnancy. Her honeymoon? So she was a few pounds more now than she had been then. Who the hell really cared? She felt gorgeous in her new dress and couldn't wait to show it off.

When the hostess escorted her to the bar area, Paul caught sight of her and actually whistled.

"You look amazing." He breathed into her neck when he pulled her into his arms. "Sexy as hell."

It felt warm and safe to rest her head against his chest. Paul. Her husband. Her best friend. Who'd just called her sexy. They had the whole night, the two of them, and she was suddenly certain that all was fine between them. More than fine—perfect.

"Happy birthday, honey," he said, pulling back a chair at the bar for her. "I ordered you their house drink. Some spicy tequila thing with watermelon. Sounded right up your alley. Damn, I love that dress."

She couldn't keep from grinning. "Emily helped me pick it out. I don't think I would've even tried it on if she hadn't made me. And I texted a picture to Ashley and she freaked out saying how much she loved it."

His face clouded over for an instant but then went back to the solicitous smile and admiring eyes. "Mmm. So does this mean you're all friends now?"

"What was that look?"

"Nothing."

"You got a weird look when I said Ashley's name."

He laughed, and it sounded insincere. "Ashley? What? If you like her, I like her."

There was definitely something he wasn't telling her.

"You seem to like her husband."

"What's that supposed to mean?" Paul took a long drink from his vodka on the rocks.

"Mean? It doesn't *mean* anything. You went over to her house that night I was out with the girls."

"So?"

"Just that it was a little weird to hear from Ashley first."

Another massive swallow. "Why don't you just chip me? Like they do with dogs."

"Maybe I *should* chip you. If you think it's a great idea to ditch your own children on one of the few nights you actually have to be alone with them so you can go drinking and ogling some nineteen-year-old au pair, maybe that's exactly what you need."

"What are you talking about?"

The bartender arrived and slid Miriam's cocktail to her. It was gorgeous: pink, frothy, and sporting lovely green accents of cucumber, lime, and a jalapeño slice. "German? Supposedly gorgeous? And practically a child."

"Miriam." He sounded exhausted.

"Paul."

"Eric texted that he was having a bunch of guys over to play poker and asked if I wanted to join. I don't play poker. I had a new episode of *Game of Thrones* to watch, and I'd just ordered Thai. But you've been on me since we moved to make an effort and meet some new friends, and I figured I probably should."

"This is my fault now?"

"Was their new au pair there? Yes. Was she trotting around the house with no bra? Yes. Am I male and human? Did I look? Shoot me. But this picture that you paint—that we were all over there, staring at her body and making her feel uncomfortable and acting like a bunch of middle-aged perverts, is bullshit."

"What if it were Maisie. How would you feel then?"

Paul's mouth dropped. "Seriously?"

Miriam smiled. She could feel the tension diffuse immediately. "Okay, that was low."

Paul kissed her on the mouth. "Too low."

They finished their drinks and moved from the bar to a table, and Paul did his usual for a special occasion: he ordered one of every appetizer on the menu. She'd thought it was weird when they first met, but she soon saw how awesome it was to taste so many different dishes and not get stuck with a giant meat or fish main dish that you were sick of after three bites. As she dug into the spicy tuna tartare and slices of truffle flatbread and salads with pears and Gorgonzola and the most amazing grilled calamari she'd ever tasted, she was again grateful for her husband. When the waiter brought out an old-fashioned champagne glass filled with chocolate mousse and topped with a single candle, Paul leaned over in her ear and whispered, "Happy birthday, sweetie. May thirty-seven be your best yet."

Together they devoured all the mousse and ordered the check. Miriam left for the ladies' room, and when she returned, she saw Paul furiously typing into his phone. He switched it off as soon as she sat down.

"Who was that?"

"Just work."

Something about the way he said it seemed weird. He never said "work." Miriam knew his entire team, and he always told her who was calling and what it was about.

"What do they need so late? Is everything okay?"

"Everything's fine. Come on, let's get back to the hotel."

"The hotel? We're not going . . . anywhere else?"

Miriam said nothing as they waited for their coats and overnight bags at the coat check.

"Miriam? What were you expecting? You've told me a thousand times that you'd divorce me if I threw you a surprise party."

She followed Paul into the backseat of a waiting Uber. "I thought . . . just from the way you phrased it maybe . . ."

"What?"

"That you made some other plan."

"Other plan?" Again he was checking his phone.

"Like a show or something? I don't know, forget it."

"It's already nine. It's too late for a show. Do you want to go get a drink somewhere? We can go to the bar at the Surrey if you'd like." He reached for her hand and kissed it. "Although, for the record, I'm not opposed to going straight to our room."

Something about the way Paul reached for her sent her mind back to the night he'd proposed to her in Madison Square Park and then taken her to their favorite red-sauce Italian restaurant, where both their families had been waiting for them. Dinner was rowdy and fun, with loads of cheap Chianti and endless toasts to the happy new couple, and by the time they said goodbye and stumbled into a cab, Miriam thought she might die of happiness. She had pretended to be scandalized by Paul reaching for her across the backseat, kissing her neck with a passion she now could almost barely remember, and she'd probably have let him pull her jeans down if it weren't for the cabdriver, who threatened to drop them on the side of Sixth Avenue if they didn't behave themselves. They had stayed up all night long, making love and talking about the future and laughing. Starving again at some point in the very early morning when it was still dark out, they had ventured to the corner diner for omelets and home fries and coffee, and then it was back to bed for another session. Miriam remembered staring at her brand-new engagement ring as the rising sun made it sparkle. When they finally fell asleep, it was fully light outside and they slept through breakfast and lunch, rising only in time for an early ordered-in dinner before heading back to bed.

They could find that again, she was sure of it. That kind of love and passion didn't flame out forever, did it? It took a backseat to small children with super-size needs and careers with endless demands, but somewhere—somewhere—the pilot light still burned. It simply had to, because the alternative was too awful to contemplate.

Now Miriam scooted over to Paul and kissed him so hard she could feel him back away. She bit his lower lip just a little. She stuck her tongue in his mouth.

"Whoa, tiger. What's going on with you tonight?" He pulled away, and Miriam tried not to be offended when he mindlessly wiped his lips dry with his jacket sleeve.

"What's gotten into me?" she asked flirtatiously. "You're right. Screw the hotel bar. Let's go back to our room. I have a surprise for you."

"A surprise for me? It's not *my* birthday."

"Well, tonight it's going to be both our birthdays." Miriam rubbed her hand across the front of his pants, just in case he'd missed her meaning.

They waited patiently for the front-desk clerk to give them the rundown on breakfast and checkout and spa bookings. It felt like an eternity until a bellboy escorted them from the stylish lobby into a too-tight elevator and up to their room on the fourth floor, where they'd been upgraded to a suite with a small but separate living room and a little French balcony with views of the treetops on Seventy-Sixth Street. Someone had dimmed the lights, and low music was playing from the Bose speaker on the nightstand.

Miriam threw her arms around Paul the moment the bellboy pulled the door closed, but he backed away. "I really need to shower first. I've been in meetings all day, on and off the trains and subway. Trust me, you'll be happy I did."

She didn't particularly care if he was clean or not, but that was okay. It gave her time to get everything set up in the living room. "Promise you won't come in here until I tell you?"

"Promise," Paul said. She heard the shower turn on a moment later.

Miriam closed the French doors that separated the bedroom and bathroom from the living area and went to work rearranging the furniture to create an empty space in the middle of the floor. It wasn't quite big enough, but it would have to do. She pulled open the Art Is Love kit she'd purchased for the cost of a round-trip plane ticket to Europe and removed: a massive rolled-up canvas tied with twine; two glass bottles of electric blue paint; a trio of paintbrushes in different sizes and thicknesses; and a coupon to include when it was time to send the canvas in for framing. On the instruction sheet, the only words were these: *Who are we to tell you how to make love? Apply paint to yourself and your lover, and then forget all about it. Lie down on the canvas and do your thing. And enjoy!*

"Well, okay, then," Miriam murmured as she neatly lined up the paintbrushes and glass bottles on the coffee table. She turned on the TV and found a good music channel and then dimmed the lights. She wished she'd remembered to bring a couple of candles, but seriously, she was coiffed and ready, enough was enough.

The shower turned off.

Should she open the gift bottle of champagne the hotel had left chilling on ice or save it for later? Later. A couple glasses of cold bubbly while she and Paul wore their fluffy hotel robes and basked in postcoital bliss would be perfect. She laid out the robes on the couch, surveyed her setup, and stripped down to her lacy black thong.

She opened the French doors quietly, prepared to do a seductive dance for Paul before showing him the kit. He was on the bed. His robe was open and his snores were deep and even. All the lights were on.

"Paul? Honey?"

Who could fall asleep this quickly? It was nine-thirty, for God's sake.

"Paul?" She climbed on the bed, straddled him, and dangled her breasts in his face.

He woke and smiled. "Why, hello there," he said, laughing. He twisted out from under her and rolled to his side of the bed.

"I'm ready for you. In the other room."

"Miriam, I'm not even sure I can pull it together right here. I'm so exhausted."

"Did you really just say that?" Miriam tried to keep her voice light, but his words stung.

"You know what I mean."

"Paul, it's been months. Months. Do you realize that?"

He sat up. "Of course. I think about it all the time."

"And what do you think about it, exactly?"

"I think that although I may not like it, this is what life looks like with three young children and a lot of upheaval. It's normal."

"I don't want this to be our normal," Miriam said.

Paul wrapped her in his arms and spooned her from behind. "I promise I'll make up for it in the morning," he whispered.

She lay there for a minute, long enough for his breathing to even out, before she made a choice. She wasn't going to wonder for the rest of the night what had gone wrong, or regret her birthday night in a gorgeous hotel suite. When she climbed on top of him, he murmured something about being asleep, but Miriam was persistent. She kissed his lips and his neck and pushed against him, and even though it felt like Paul was responding in spite of himself, he responded. The sex was quick, familiar, and functional, and afterward, when he rolled over and immediately fell asleep, she didn't wake him.

15

Exactly Like Rehab, Only Different

Karolina

"**O**h. My. God. I can't walk. I'm crippled. Permanently maimed. Who the hell does this for fun?" Emily asked, collapsing onto a wooden bench in the Pilates studio's lobby as the other women streamed past them.

Karolina smiled. "I do it in Bethesda all the time." She paused. "Did it all the time. The megaformer of death."

"I mean, you look phenomenal, don't get me wrong, but is it worth it? I'd so much rather just starve than have to put myself through that five days a week."

"I starve too," Karolina said with a smile. "Come on, let's go get a coffee or something. If we stay here, people might talk to us."

Emily jumped with the energy of a child. "That's really all you had to say. Walk. I'm right behind you."

Karolina clicked open her SUV. "Where to?"

"Take me anywhere we can have a private conversation and decent coffee. We have a game plan to discuss."

"I don't know this town much better than you do, but when I want to hide somewhere, I go to the library."

"The library?"

"The only people I ever see there in the middle of the day are retirees and nannies who take babies to story hour. But that's upstairs, so you don't really see them either. And there's a café with espresso."

"Sold! This thing you call a library sounds perfect."

Once there, they each ordered a large coffee and a KIND bar, which Emily noticed Karolina only nibbled before pushing away.

"You're thinking about today's *Star* headline, aren't you?" Emily asked.

Karolina sighed. "I know it's trash, but it bothers me when they say I have an eating disorder. I don't. I'm just careful."

"I know, but I'll say it again: the truth is irrelevant. Step one of our plan is to tweak your appearance. You've gotten too thin—even for me. I think you should gain some weight," Emily said. "Nothing crazy, just a few pounds. Make you look slightly less heroin-chic. Just so you'll be, you know—more relatable."

"That's your brilliant plan to reinvent me, save my reputation from ruin, and get my son back? I should fatten up?"

Emily rolled her eyes. "You're not listening. I'm not suggesting you morph into some heifer, just that you put on a few pounds to look a little more . . . maternal."

"Maternal?"

"Look, I recognize that Greenwich, Connecticut, is hardly the home of maternal-looking women. But still—even here you look like an alien with those gazelle-like legs and crazy perky tits and sexy, wavy hair down to your ass. And if the Greenwich moms are threatened by you—and trust me, they are—imagine how you're playing in Topeka.

I've never been to Nebraska, but I've heard that the Walmarts there look like carnival freak shows."

"Isn't Topeka in Kansas?"

Emily exhaled a loud, annoyed sigh.

"Sorry. So you were saying. Weight gain. Anything else?"

"A haircut."

"Stop it!"

"I'm serious, Karolina. It doesn't have to be all-out butch, but shorter and less sexy is mandatory. And I know you don't want to hear it, but we need to talk rehab."

Karolina started to protest, but Emily cut her off. "I know, I know, you don't have a drinking problem. You're practically a nun. I did look and could not find a single piece of dirt on you regarding drinking or drugs before this particular . . . incident. You're, like, the only clean supermodel in history. Not even diet pills! As a nod to your impeccable record, I think a week will be sufficient."

"I am not going to rehab!" Three nannies with three toddlers at the next table turned to look at her.

"Keep it down, Amy Winehouse."

"Emily." Karolina knew she sounded exasperated. "How will I ever get custody of Harry if I admit I have a problem? I'm *innocent*, and I will *not* admit to something I haven't done!"

"It's simple, Karolina. We need to turn public opinion in your favor. Only once you're redeemed in the public eye can we go to court for custody, and from a much better position. As it is—as Trip told you— you've got nothing. Zero. So rather than be the quiet, good wife un-complaining about this baseless witch hunt, let's be proactive. Think of Harry."

Karolina peered at Emily, who she knew was right. "How would your fake rehab work?"

"We put out an announcement. You're going 'out west' to 'contem-plate your actions.' If we're coy, everyone will assume rehab. You're not actually confirming or denying, so they'll be certain that's where you're headed."

"And where will I be going?"

Emily took a sip of her coffee and frowned. "You'll hide out for a week at Amangiri. I know the GM, and he will guarantee you complete privacy."

"Where?"

"Are you serious? You haven't been to Amangiri?"

"I told you, Emily. I don't drink. How am I supposed to know about rehabs?"

Emily held up a hand. "Oh my God. Okay. It's a super-luxurious hotel in the middle of fucking nowhere. Like, private-plane nowhere or drive-five-hours-from-the-nearest-city nowhere. In the canyons of Utah. There are maybe twenty rooms built into the side of a mountain with private pools and fireplaces. Spa is insane. Food is ridiculous. There are all sorts of outdoorsy things you can do if you're into that, which of course I'm not. But trust me: you want to go."

Karolina sipped her coffee and considered. Already she felt like she'd been banished to a foreign land without friends or family nearby. For the first time since before she'd married Graham, she felt like she was floating. Rootless. As though no one in the whole world cared where she was or how she was doing—except Miriam and possibly Emily. Aside from her mother dying, Karolina couldn't think of a single time in her life when she'd felt more helpless or alone. And while some celebrity retreat in the middle of the desert in Utah wouldn't be her first choice, it wouldn't be her last one either. No paparazzi. No Bethesda-people run-ins. No tabloid mudslinging. No supervised visits with Elaine. Hopefully no Internet, so she wouldn't be able to keep hitting "refresh" on Google News to see if any new pictures of Graham and Regan together popped up. All of that and it would count as a step toward repairing her reputation?

"Okay," she said slowly, nodding. "I'm in."

"Excellent!" Emily said, slapping the table, which rattled enough to spill Karolina's coffee. "Sorry, but I knew you were smart enough to listen to me. We leave Friday."

Karolina's head snapped up. "We?"

Emily smiled. "Oh, yeah. We need to move on this. We leave from JFK at nine, nonstop to Vegas. Then there's some hideously long drive through the desert. I could be convinced to book a car and driver, so just say the word. There are charter and private-plane options, but I have to say, I'm not feeling those lately. Too risky from a leak perspective. So we'll drive. Or we'll make Miriam drive. Look at some Mormons. Listen to some bad music. And then we'll arrive in heaven."

"Miriam?" Karolina asked. She had so many questions. "Mormons?"

"It's Utah!" Emily cackled. "You watched *Big Love*, right? Oh, and yes, Miriam's coming too, I already asked her. She was predictably irritating about arranging babysitters, but even she couldn't turn down an all-expenses-paid trip to Amangiri."

Karolina swallowed. Why was this sounding way more like a girls' spa trip than a necessary step toward putting her life back together? "How much is this costing me?"

Emily outright guffawed. "Trust me, you do *not* want to know. It's obscene, like, even in my world. But look on the bright side: it's cheaper than thirty days inpatient somewhere! And the linens will be soooooo much nicer."

"Fine. If it's not rehab, I'm in. I'll think of Harry."

"Between now and then, we need to work on a few things. Most important, I'll work up some language and email it to a few key people. Implying rehab but not saying it. Then we'll need to practice your nondenial denial. I'll lead you through every step." She paused. "And then we will get busy legally. Miriam told me she's reviewing your divorce papers?"

"Yes."

"She says the prenup is pretty clear-cut?"

"Yes."

"We could fight it."

Karolina shook her head. "I don't want his trust fund from Daddy."

"We'll find a way to remind the public about that," Emily said. "Next we've got to get you more active on social media. It's time to get your social accounts back up and running. But we need to lose the throwback modeling photos. And no more of you dressed like a senator's wife. We're going for accessible, warm, engaging."

"You mean chunky?"

"Try wearing something a little more down-home."

"Because you're such an expert at that?"

"Jiggly thighs and pleather shoes. That is your golden ticket right now."

"Has anyone ever told you you're crazy?" Karolina asked.

"Yeah, just, like, every minute of every day. Listen, we need to talk Graham for a minute."

Karolina's mind flashed to the picture she'd seen from a party the night before benefiting a pediatric cancer unit at Children's National Medical Hospital. Regan Whitney was on the board, naturally, and Graham had gone as her date. It was their first public appearance together. She held his arm as they walked into the restaurant.

The color must have gone from her face because Emily said, "Yes, I saw it too. Low-key, under the radar, but still touching each other. Testing the waters. They'll probably show up at a few more local events together before issuing any kind of formal announcement. At least that's what I'd advise them to do."

"He's going to marry her, isn't he?"

"Sure is. The second your divorce goes through. She's his ticket to the White House."

Karolina touched her fingers to her forehead. "This is a nightmare."

Emily grabbed Karolina's arm. "Forget about that for a minute. Right now we need to discuss Graham's past. I want the dirt."

"He's irritatingly clean."

"That's bullshit!" Emily said. Once again, women turned to stare. "There is no way a man can be that much of an asshole and not have secrets. Illegitimate children? Juvenile crimes that got expunged? A drug problem? Run-ins with escort services? Hell, it's not sexy, but I'll take white-collar crime at this point. Insider trading? Anything."

Karolina thought of one night in particular, a couple years into their marriage. Graham had always been meticulous, from the way he kept his closet to the manner in which he conducted his relationships. It had taken him over a year of dating Karolina before he'd trusted her enough to confide even the smallest colorful detail about his parents' marriage. She remembered thinking he could have been one of those dorks in high school who'd never gone to a party where people were drinking. And then he had completely rocked her world. He told her a story she could barely believe. A story she would never, ever tell another living soul.

Most definitely not Emily.

Emily saw something in Karolina's eyes, because her own narrowed. "What are you thinking right now?"

"Nothing!" Karolina's voice got an octave higher.

"Come on! You were married to him for *ten years*! No man is a saint. This man set you up. Ruined your reputation. He keeps you from your son. So spill."

Despite her fury at Graham, Karolina held back. It might ruin Graham, but it would also ruin Harry. "There's really nothing. I'll tell you if I think of something," she lied.

"Damn right you will. Think long and hard about whatever secret of his you're keeping right now. Is it in your best interest?" She glanced at her phone. "I'm out. I have a highlights appointment in the city in an hour."

Karolina looked up in surprise. "Wait. Are we really doing this Utah thing?"

"We sure are. I'll text you all the info." Emily gathered her things and tossed off a wave, saying, "Remember. Don't answer your phone if you don't know who's calling. Don't put anything in an email or a text that you wouldn't want plastered on the front page of the *Post*. And go get a cheeseburger! Call you later!"

Before Karolina could say another word, Emily was gone.

A Greenwich mom with a slight twist on the classic uniform (Athleta jacket paired with Lululemon leggings and headband instead of the full double L's from head to toe) approached Karolina's table.

"Hi, sorry to interrupt, I just wanted to say—"

"I have to leave," Karolina blurted out. Avoiding eye contact, she too grabbed her coat and headed toward the door, but not before the woman murmured to her friend, "I was just going to compliment her bag."

Christ, you're losing your mind, Karolina thought. Maybe a trip to the desert was exactly what she needed.

16

Just a Friend and a Blue Glitter Condom

Emily

Emily marched down the wood stairs as well as she could in four-inch heels to the freezer across the kitchen, pulled out the Tupperware of Carvel cake, and dumped it in the garbage.

"What the hell are you doing?" Miriam yelled. Immediately she heard a child's footsteps above her. "Matthew! Back in bed! Everything's fine. Mommy didn't mean to scream!" she yelled again, and miraculously the footsteps stopped.

"Just try and tell me you weren't going to eat that the second I left." Emily shook her head. In the week since Emily had been back from L.A., she'd walked in on Miriam shoving food into her face at night at least three times. Once had been leftover kid mac and cheese, and Emily had almost vomited.

"Please." Miriam sounded exhausted. "Not everyone is meant to look like you. Why don't you try having three kids in three years."

Emily snorted. "Fat chance." Emily did a little twirl. "How do I look?" Her LBD was tight and short, but neither excessively so, and it had the most subtle cutouts right at the waist, making her midsection look even tinier than usual. The chances of her getting in a bathing suit were small, but just in case she ended up drunk enough and the party was more fun than she expected, she had packed a tiny, elegant Eres bikini in a Ziploc bag in her clutch.

Across the kitchen, Miriam also pirouetted. She wore actual elastic-at-the-bottom-and-not-in-a-cool-way sweatpants from what looked like the 1990s, a massively oversize men's undershirt, and those fluffy grandma socks. "How do I look?"

Emily forced a smile and remembered the old Miriam, the Miriam of Manhattan: slim, put together, professional, totally on top of her game. Where had that woman gone? Did it mean she was depressed? Emily made a mental note to inquire sensitively—or as sensitively as she could manage.

"Well, I'm off. You sure you don't want to come to this thing?"

"What, and miss the newest *This Is Us*?" Miriam laughed. "When are you back?"

Emily grabbed her clutch and her rabbit-lined leather coat and walked into the mudroom. "They're here, I'm leaving! Have a great night with your Netflix and your binge!" and she stepped out into what felt like a wall of cold air before climbing gingerly into the backseat of the waiting Audi sedan.

"Hiiiiii!" Ashley squealed from the front. "Oh my God, you look A. MAZE. ING!"

"Thanks, you too," Emily said, trying to sound like she meant it.

"Emily, this is my husband, Eric," Ashley said, grabbing him by his sport-coated arm.

Eric backed the car out of the driveway and revved the engine more than was necessary. "Nice to meet you. Ashley has told me all about you."

"Is that so?" Emily wondered what could possibly be included in Ashley's summary. After that horror of a sip 'n' see Miriam had dragged her to, Ashley had glommed on to Emily like a desperate freshman. She had friended Emily on Facebook, followed her on Twitter and Instagram, and had invited her to join Snapchat. If all that wasn't irritating enough, she'd taken to emailing and texting Emily daily with all sorts of asinine updates on things going on around town. Emily had deleted most without reading them, but the invitation for that night had caught her eye: POOL PARTY! it blared. Zachanda was throwing the fete at his or her house and promised a very special surprise. Back in Greenwich for nearly a week, heading to a practically dry state in two days, Emily hadn't hesitated to accept. Yes, it was likely the party would be boring and WASPy, with the women on one side of the room, wearing Lilly Pulitzer and talking workouts and children, and the men on the other, humble-bragging about the new car or boat or plane they'd purchased. In Los Angeles everyone would be jockeying to talk to such-and-such studio head or the agent who'd just signed the hot new star. Douchey people were douchey everywhere. But she couldn't deny that there might be someone interesting to meet from a business perspective. Besides, she hadn't left Miriam's house in days. If worse came to worst, she'd Uber home and call it a night, but at least it would get her out of that house for an hour.

"So, who is Zachanda?" Emily asked, more to make conversation than because she actually cared. "Male or female?"

"Oh, Zachanda?" Ashley said with a laugh. "It's not one person, it's two. Zach and Amanda."

"Wait—on purpose? Like they think they're Brangelina?"

Ashley giggled. Her blond bob bobbed just so. "They're not movie stars, but they sure are A-list billionaires. Trillionaires, maybe."

Eric, who had been silent while stealing occasional and not subtle glances at Emily in the rearview, scoffed. "Hardly. He's done well with his fund. Very well. But he is nowhere close to being a billionaire."

"Okay, fine, then. Multi-multimillionaires. Like, hundreds of millions of dollars," Ashley said.

Emily rolled her eyes. What was it with people around here counting everyone else's money? There was no shortage of wealth in L.A. or
New York, but it just didn't seem so all-defining. She would sooner take
a job at *Runway* than live in a town where bored housewives sat around
all day calculating each other's net worth.

After what felt like an eternity in the car, driving around dark streets
flanked on all sides by gated mansions, they pulled up to the largest one.
A security guard who wore a dark suit and a Secret Service–agent ear-
piece checked their IDs at the gate while a second guard supervised.
There were two more at the main house near the valet stand, and a fifth
who checked licenses one final time at the door.

"Ohmigod, did you see that? The last one has a gun!" Ashley whispered. Emily immediately smelled the alcohol on her breath. Nice.
Nothing wrong with a little pregaming. She regretted she hadn't done
the same.

A uniformed maid escorted them through the triple-high foyer and
through the kitchen, past a staff the size of a busy midtown restaurant,
and out to the backyard. A massive tent was lit by assorted string lights
and jewel-toned glass lamps, and heat lamps made it feel like they were
in Marrakech during the summer and not New England in winter. Huge
woven floor cushions and poufs in every imaginable color took up much
of the floor space, and they were draped with what appeared to be silk
and cashmere throw blankets. Elaborate glass hookahs with ornate gold-
painted designs and sweet-smelling charcoal burbled all over as guests
inhaled on their pom-pommed tubes and silver-plated mouthpieces and
exhaled the smoke in long, languid streams.

The centerpiece of the tent was a kidney-shaped pool whose water
was lit a sexy red color and looked to be kept at such a high temperature
on this cold early-March night that actual steam rose from its surface. No
one was swimming or even dressed for it, but Emily had a feeling people
would end up in the pool sooner than later. She swiveled once more to
take it in, determined to tune out Ashley's insipid prattling, and she had
to admit: this place was a blow-away. It was as though they'd stepped

through a time-space warp and into an authentic underground Moroccan hammam. There was no Lilly Pulitzer. No pearls. No business suits. Just a few dozen beautiful people sipping hand-mixed mint mojitos and smoking hash mixed with apple-flavored tobacco and laughing and relaxing and flirting.

"You picked the perfect party," Ashley said as she surveyed the room.

"My God. This was . . . not what I was expecting."

"Yeah, Zachanda always throws the best parties. Last year they brought in professional porn stars to do a cabaret show and give private lessons."

Emily's mouth dropped. "You're lying."

"I'm not! It sounds sketchy, but it was actually super-fun. I'm just saying you picked the right party to come to without your husband. It's generally understood at a Zachanda event that you say goodbye to your significant other at the beginning of the night."

Eric had already taken off without a word. "Wait—this is a *swinger* party? You brought me to a fucking *swinger* party?"

"Of course not!" Ashley sounded offended. "We're not swingers. Nobody *cheats*. You just flirt a little."

"Porn stars giving private lessons?"

"To couples, silly! To spice up their sex life. Like, a tutorial. But we're not swingers." Emily leaned in a bit closer. "Although I'd be lying if I said there weren't rumors."

"Rumors? Don't be an idiot!" Emily said. She lowered her voice when she saw Ashley's hurt expression. "This town has a reputation," she said, though she wasn't entirely sure that was true.

Ashley waved her hand. "Every suburb has those rumors. And no one ever knows anyone who actually swings."

Emily couldn't stop staring at a waiter's tight jeans. Was there any chance it was actually body paint and not denim? Was it humanly possible for someone to be that gorgeous and straight?

"Ma'am?" the waiter said. His Southern accent was as thick as honey.

This snapped her out of her daydream. *Ma'am?* "Excuse me?"

"I was wondering if I could get you a cocktail, is all?" He brushed a flop of blond hair off his forehead and grinned to reveal dimples. Of course.

"You called me '*ma'am*.'"

"Pardon?"

Ashley placed her hand squarely on the waiter's chest and leaned in so close Emily was certain she was going to kiss him. "Sweetheart, we would looooove cocktails," she sang in a god-awful imitation of a Southern drawl.

"Yes, ma'am."

"Stop saying 'ma'am'!" Emily shouted.

"Don't mind her," Ashley said, literally batting her eyelashes. "Bring us whatever you think is best. But make them both doubles, please."

He feigned tipping a nonexistent hat, flashed his dimples again, and headed toward the bar, which was tucked discreetly in the back of the tent and featured three bartenders, two female, one male, all total knockouts.

"Mmmm," Ashley said, scanning the scene. "I love it here."

"I can't believe this is a Monday night."

"We know how to have a good time in Greenwich," Ashley said, giving her a playful poke in the side that made Emily want to smack her. "Come on, I'll introduce you around."

Emily allowed Ashley to take her hand and lead her around the tent, rattling off everyone's biographical facts. Mom of five, ran eleven marathons, was screwing around with her tennis instructor. Bald but amazingly funny dad who used to have his own show on Comedy Central; rumored cocaine problem; big family money. The stories seemed to get longer and less interesting until Emily had sucked down the last of her third mint mojito, at which point things took a noticeable turn for the better. Emily looked around and realized the party was in full force. When had that happened? A pair of models wearing only mermaid tails glided through the water, perfect breasts bobbing in unison while everyone watched but pretended not to. Someone had built and lit a gorgeous bonfire right outside the tent doors. Couples were draped across cushions and poufs, legs entwined, making out. European lounge music and hundreds of candles and burning incense added to the sexy boudoir vibe. Some people were dancing, and others were easing their way into the pool. Ashley had gotten caught up in some inane conversation about volunteer opportunities, and Emily had sneaked away, heading toward the bar for her next mint mojito, when she heard a familiar voice behind her.

"Why, look who we have here."

She knew who it was before turning around, but she couldn't ignore the little leap she felt in her chest. He looked familiarly rumpled, only this time in a pink shirt with rolled sleeves and a pair of well-worn jeans. His tan was spectacular and, come to think of it, problematic for March. It would be such a turnoff if he tanned. He couldn't possibly, could he?

"Please tell me you were sunning in Saint Barts and not at Beach Bum," Emily said, eyes wide, hopeful she'd pulled off appearing not too thrilled to see him.

"What, this?" Alistair said, motioning to his forearms. "What about this isn't natural?"

"Oh, I don't know, just that it's March and there's slush on the ground and this must be the grayest, most depressing place on earth right now. Not that you'd know it from looking around here."

"Don't judge me because I have a lovely woman named Allegra who comes to my house once a week and spray tans me in my basement."

Emily stared in horror. "Just when I was beginning to find you somewhat attractive . . ."

"*Somewhat* attractive?" Alistair leaned over and whispered, "I know you love me. And my golden-bronze spray tan."

She reeled backward, unsteady on her feet. When had she gotten so drunk? "You better be joking," she said. Or rather, slurred.

He laughed and said something about being on vacation in the Caribbean without elaborating and then the hot blond waiter walked by holding a tray of drinks that may have contained only dirty glasses, but Emily grabbed one and downed the contents.

"Ah, the Caribbean. It's like everyone on earth who's ever gone to Harvard saying they went to school in Boston. When you press, they say Cambridge. It takes, like, five more tries until you can get them to say Harvard."

"Yes. And then you can't get them to stop."

Emily barked out an unselfconscious laugh that quickly turned into the kind of hysterical, uncontrollable laugh that made her sides ache. Alistair looked delighted with himself.

"I was in the British Virgin Islands, if you must know."

"Ah, sailing in the BVIs. How original."

He cocked his head. "How did you know I was sailing?"

Emily looked him up and down. "You're British, exceedingly preppy, and living in Greenwich. What else would you possibly be doing there? Taking cooking lessons?"

"Glad to know I'm a walking cliché."

"We all are. Some of us are just better at hiding it." Emily looked around for another drink, but it seemed like the waiters had stopped serving and had started dancing. With the guests. Like, *dancing* dancing.

"Unlike the rest of us, you don't strike me as a stereotype."

"What do you know about me?" Emily said.

"I know you're confident enough to come to this party without a date but too hot to not have some sort of boyfriend or significant other waiting at home. Though for some reason you haven't so much as mentioned his existence. How am I doing so far?"

No, she hadn't mentioned Miles, but it was just too irresistible and delicious. This feeling of being wanted. Untethered. Sexy to someone other than your own husband. Besides, there was no harm in a little flirting. It wasn't like she was going to sleep with him.

"Go on," she said.

"The real question is what are *you* doing here tonight?" he said. "What are you doing in Greenwich at all?"

"I'm helping out a client who lives here, so . . ."

"So you have no choice?"

"Right."

"And you're not going to tell me who that client is or how you're helping him or her?"

"Correct."

"Okay, then."

"Can we sit for a minute?"

He nodded and she followed him over to a patch of empty floor cushions. A hookah was lit and wafting the most delicious-smelling smoke. "Tobacco, you think?"

Another good-looking guy with his shirt unbuttoned slightly too much leaned over from his own cushion perch, where he was fondling the upper thigh of a very young-looking girl. "It's hash. Just so you know."

"Oh, really? Thanks," Emily said, and put the hose down. She'd never gotten into drugs, despite making a concerted effort to like them when she was younger. After all, cocaine kept you skinny! But she hated the tweaked-out feeling after she came down from it and how impossible it was to sleep. She'd never smoked hash and was surprised when Alistair took the hose and inhaled so deeply that the coal ember lit up a fiery orange.

"Hmmm, maybe you're not a total cliché. I never took you for a hash smoker," she said.

"Gap year in Egypt. I spent a fair number of weekends in Sinai, and smoking hookah was the local pastime. They shouldn't call this hash, though," he said, exhaling the smoke languidly. "It's more like Jamaican beach weed. Super-chill, very relaxed. Like having a martini, nothing more than that."

Hmm. A martini sounded perfect right about then. Their hands touched as he gave her the hookah, and she felt a jolt. The hash washed over and she felt instantly relaxed, almost liquid, and there was none of that totally stoned or incapacitated feeling she hated so much.

His phone rang. "Sorry, I have to take this. I'll be right back." He stood up and walked to the edge of the tent, near the bar.

Irritated that he'd answered his phone while they were sharing a moment, Emily shakily stood up and realized that she was now both drunk and high. And yes, she was starting to feel a little paranoid too. A bathroom break. That was what she needed. And not the wedding-level Porta-Potties with marble sinks and attendants they did here. She needed to be alone.

Doing her absolute best to appear collected and sober, Emily made her way to the house. Just before she walked into the brightly lit kitchen, still buzzing with staff, Ashley intercepted her. "You okay?" she asked.

"I'm fine!" Emily said, peeved to have been caught.

"There are bathrooms outside, you know, and they're gorgeous."

"Can you leave me alone? For, like, five seconds? Just not keep track of me?"

Ashley wheeled back. "I was only making sure you were okay."

Emily turned and headed for the stairs, again trying to appear like she knew where she was going. At the first bedroom she came to—a young boy's room, judging by the outer-space theme—she crept over the plush rug and into the bathroom, which featured glow-in-the-dark stars and a toilet that lit up blue when it sensed her walking near it. Exhausted from the effort of trying to appear sober, she practically fell onto the toilet lid and focused on controlling her breathing. There was no denying it now: the spins had taken over.

A knock on the door made her sit straight up. How long had it been? A minute? An hour? She called out, "Just a minute," as she hoisted herself up and considered splashing some water on her face, but a familiar voice came through the door. "Emily? You okay in there?"

"I'm fine!" she sang out, wondering how he had found her.

The door cracked open. He popped his face in, grinning. "Can I come in?"

"Um, hello, stalker." She stood and braced herself on the sink. "No, you can't come in."

She was relieved he didn't listen to her, and when he shut the door behind him, they were in near-darkness save for the glowing stars and the comet night-light.

"I came back and you were gone."

"I needed a moment."

"Apparently. It took me forever to find you. I thought you'd left."

"You know, that sounds like a good idea. It is about time I left."

"What, and miss all the action downstairs? You should see the scene down there. It's like a strange cross between the staff dance cottage at Kellerman's and the Box in the East Village. With a little Middle Eastern opium-den vibe thrown in for good measure."

They both froze as they heard a noise come from the other side of the door. A rustling of some sort, which stopped almost as soon as it started.

"Probably someone checking to make sure no guests are hiding in any of the bathrooms," Alistair whispered, stepping closer to her. He pushed his body firmly into hers. She could smell him, a combination of sweet-apple tobacco smoke and hashish mixed with expensive cologne. And although she didn't want to, she could feel her body react.

She knew a hundred percent that he was going to kiss her. There was no question anymore, not with them standing in a strange dark bathroom, the lower halves of their bodies pressed together so tightly that she could feel everything. By whispering into her ear and rubbing his cheek against her own, he was merely teasing her by delaying the inevitable. She knew this. Could sense it. How long had it been since she'd been this close to a man other than Miles? She did the math: six years. No one was awarding her any ribbons for best wife—or him for best husband—but she had kept her vows of fidelity and never cheated on him. When, after what felt like an eternity, Alistair reached down to take her chin between his thumb and forefinger and tip her face up toward his, she was physically desperate to kiss him. But the moment his lips touched hers, the sensation of it—not at all unpleasant, just so *different* from what she was used to—pulled her from her languid, sexy buzz and sobered her right up.

Suddenly she was clearheaded. The spins were more like sways, and that syrupy-body feeling she'd gotten from the hash had dissipated. All she knew was there was a strange guy—a hot one, yes, but still not her husband—pressing in to her, and it didn't feel right. She pushed him away with flat palms on his chest.

"I can't," she whispered.

"You can. You want to."

"I don't. Let's go back downstairs."

There was a crash from the other side of the door, and they froze again in the darkness.

"What do we do?" Emily asked.

"I guess we just have to wait for them to leave," he whispered before pinning her back against the sink and kissing her neck.

Had she groaned audibly? Her entire body was screaming for him, but there were a million thoughts she couldn't ignore. Her husband, for one. And the fact that they were about to be caught in a super-compromising position despite the fact that nothing exceptionally awful had actually happened. She needed some time to think.

Her phone beeped with a text message from Ashley. *Where r u? Entire cast of hamilton here incl lin-manuel. Performing soon. Don't miss it!!!*

"What? I feel like I'm losing my mind. Am I losing my mind? *Hamilton* is here?"

Alistair nodded. "Last year they flew in Serena and Venus to play a private exhibition match on their tennis court. The year before that, they had all the industry's top porn stars come do 'demonstrations.' Or 'lessons.' Or whatever they called it. This year is on a Monday because Broadway is dark and they got the entire original cast to come and perform three numbers. We really should go down there."

"I really didn't expect this in a . . . a *suburb*."

"Shhh." He pressed his finger to her lips. "We'll stagger ourselves at the stairs so no one sees us walk down together, okay?" He opened the bathroom door and Emily followed him out to the bedroom, where she promptly tripped and nearly fell on what felt like a dead body on the darkened floor.

"You okay?" Alistair whispered at the exact same time a woman's voice—not Emily's—asked, "Who is there?"

"Wait, hold on a second," said another male voice.

By this time Emily had pulled herself off the body and lit the flashlight on her phone. It took a second for her eyes to adjust to the darkness, but she could make out that there were two bodies on the floor, not one, and neither was dead. In fact, one looked very, very familiar.

"Emily?" The man's voice was pleading, desperate.

"Yes?"

"This is not what it looks like."

Alistair must have found the overhead light switch, because abruptly they were bathed in light from the hanging planets, and it was easy to see that it was exactly what it looked like. In the middle of some grade school boy's shag carpet lay a young woman with her denim skirt hiked around her waist. Ashley's husband's very naked and very white ass covered the girl somewhat but didn't conceal quite enough real estate: not only was she naked, but Eric was wearing a condom. With blue glitter. And some sort of spiky latex bits sprouting in seemingly random directions.

Emily burst out laughing. Perhaps not the best reaction when you literally fall over your friend's friend's husband having (protected!) sex with someone other than your friend's friend, but come on—this was too good.

"Emily. Please. Ashley would——" He rolled off the girl, and everyone averted their eyes for a second until he managed to pull his pants back up. The girl didn't make a single move to cover herself. If anything, she may have been stretching for effect.

"Eric, I don't know anything about you or her or your marriage, and guess what? I don't want to. Nothing. Nada. I've got ninety-nine problems, but your drama isn't one of them, okay?"

Eric looked skeptical.

Alistair reached over and pulled her arm. "Why don't we give them some privacy?"

Emily followed him out of the room but not before she saw the look of realization dawn on Eric's face. Which was shortly followed by delight. *That cheating asshole*, Emily thought. If he thought he had something on Emily, he was going to bitterly regret it.

Emily was sobering up, but the party was off the hook. All pretenses of control and good behavior were gone: everywhere people were grinding, making out, dancing, and gyrating. Someone had killed most of the lights, and the hookah smoke had turned the tent into a virtual hotbox.

"What are you doing?" Alistair asked as Emily furiously typed into her phone.

"Getting an Uber. I'm done."

"Done? But the *Hamilton* cast is just about to start."

Emily looked at him and raised her eyebrows. "This place is crazy. You people are all insane."

"Hey, don't group me in with them."

"You *live* here. You *are* them."

Her Uber was five minutes away. She couldn't decide what was more appealing at that moment: calling Miles to hear his voice and confirm for herself that she'd done the right thing, or making a huge ruckus in Miriam's kitchen in hopes of waking her so she could tell her every single unbelievable detail about the entire night. Well, perhaps not *every*. But most.

"I'm going to wait out front," Emily said.

Alistair gave her a strange look and shrugged. "Never a dull moment with you, is there?" he asked.

"What's that supposed to mean?"

"Not a thing. Have a good night, Emily Charlton. See you around sometime." Then, without another word, he gave her a dry kiss on the cheek and walked away.

What the fuck?

"Emily? Emily! WHERE ARE YOU GOING?"

Emily turned around just in time to see Ashley literally racing toward her as fast as her slutty dress would allow.

"Oh, hey. Listen, I'm headed out. I called an Uber, so don't worry about me."

"You can't leave!"

"Oh, I definitely can."

"But you're going to miss—"

"*Hamilton*, I know. I desperately hope Lin-Manuel will forgive me."

Ashley nodded as though this were likely although not guaranteed. "Listen, have you seen Eric? I don't want him to miss the show either." While she asked, Ashley squinted and swiveled her gaze around the tent, trying to make out faces through the darkness.

"Eric? Nope. Not me," Emily said, not missing a beat. Ashley, Eric, and Eric's potentially underage blue-glitter-condom-loving girlfriend would have to fend for themselves.

"Hmm, okay. I'll keep looking."

"Sounds good. Ash? Thanks for tonight."

A look of sheer joy spread across Ashley's face, and she flung her arms around Emily's neck. "You had fun? Really? Oh, I'm so glad! I mean, I'm sure it's not like any of the super-cool parties you go to in L.A. or New York or wherever, but hopefully you weren't too bored."

"You know what? I was a lot of things tonight, but bored wasn't one of them."

Ashley appeared to ponder this and then obviously decided it was a compliment. "Kisses!" she trilled, giving Emily double-cheek kisses.

Emily flashed her a massively fake smile as a Toyota Camry with an Uber sign pulled into the circular driveway.

"Same location you entered, miss?" the driver asked. He gave her a lovely, totally noncreepy smile, and Emily wanted to hug him for not calling her "ma'am."

As if on cue, her phone rang. It was Miles.

Answer it, she urged herself, her thumb hovering over the green button. *Answer it!* She wanted to—or rather, she wanted to want to—but it all seemed so exhausting. Instead, she silenced the ringer, dropped her phone in her bag, and leaned back against the cool leather seat.

"Sir? Can you just drive around for a bit? Thanks." And she closed her eyes and tried not to think at all. But the thoughts kept coming like cold, unwelcome riptides. Olivia Belle had basically stolen Los Angeles out from under her. She was crashing at a friend's place in a batshit-crazy suburb. New York was right around the corner, but it felt so very far away. Her career was in the toilet. Her husband was across the planet. Was it time to call Miranda? Tuck her tail between her legs and return to *Runway?* At this, her eyes flew open, and she gasped so audibly the driver checked his rearview.

"You okay, miss?" he asked, looking concerned.

It took every ounce of her energy to respond in a measured way, like a sane person and not like a crazed, panicked animal. "Yes," Emily said, her voice shaking. "I'm doing great."

17

Pinterest's Mom
of the Year

Miriam

Miriam was a big believer in the pick-your-battles school of parenting, and what kindergarteners wore to a kid's sixth birthday was not going to be one of them. However, as soon as she pulled into the parking lot and joined a long line of luxury SUVs waiting to park, she could see that she had vastly misjudged. Again.

The invitation's "to the nines" clearly translated to miniature humans in all manner of ball gowns and bow ties eagerly rushing toward a bright red carpet flanked by velvet ropes while their mommy chauffeurs yelled at them to watch out for other cars. Matthew was the first one to undo his seat belt, although Maisie actually beat him out the door.

"Do not go inside without me!" Miriam yelled, helpless to do anything but wait for the other cars to move. "Hold hands—it's a parking lot!" But like everyone else in her life, they ignored her and rushed toward the action. Thankfully a valet materialized to take her High-lander (was that a sneer she detected when she handed him the keys?), and she speed-walked to her children. A man holding a clipboard and wearing a purple crushed-velvet blazer with coordinating velvet slippers beamed at them.

"Well, who do we have here?" he asked.

"Kids, tell the nice man your names," Miriam prompted, but they were busy watching the other children strolling down the red carpet, turning and posing for a gaggle of what looked like actual paparazzi holding massive flashing cameras and calling out the children's names.

Miriam was suddenly self-conscious about her own outfit, a pair of admittedly not great mom jeans and a lumpy down coat. "Sorry," she murmured to the doorman. "This is Matthew and Maisie Kagan," she said.

"Terrific!" the bouncer boomed as he checked their names off his list. "Schuyler will be so happy her classmates are here. I'm Ron, one of Schuyler's dads."

"Thanks for having us," Miriam squeaked, trying to hide her surprise that this extremely young and very attractive man was the father of a six-year-old girl.

"And you are?"

"Sorry." Miriam blushed. "I'm Miriam Kagan. Their, uh, mom."

"Step right up, kids. Parents' entrance is around the other side. Only kindergarteners get to walk the red carpet." He motioned toward the start of the walkway, marked with a massive gold-plated frame standing on a three-foot-high easel that read VIP ENTRANCE.

Maisie, who was just starting to read, asked, "Mommy, what does 'vip' mean?"

"Oh, it's another word for 'kid,'" she lied.

The father-bouncer gave her a funny look but didn't say anything as he pinned a corsage on Matthew's track jacket and slipped a wrist version onto Maisie's hand. Both children beamed. "Go pose for the cameras now, gorgeous ones!" he told them.

That was all the encouragement they needed. Someone must have fed the "photographers" their names, because they all began shouting, "Matthew, over here! Maisie, show us your outfit!" in such convincing ways that Miriam couldn't help but stare. She wondered if she should pull them out of there—after all, this wasn't the message she was dying to convey to her five-year-olds—but she couldn't for the life of her think of a decent exit strategy. Maybe she'd get lucky and one of them would throw up. Her heart nearly stopped when Maisie, her baby girl, broke into a dance for the cheering paparazzi and the other watching parents. "Show us your moves, Maisie!" one of the women called. On cue, Maisie shook her butt in the same way she did during family dance parties, when Paul would blast "Call Me Maybe" and they would all dance like crazy in their pajamas. *No. No. No.* Miriam wanted to throw her coat over her daughter's head and whisk her away from this insanity.

She didn't wait around for the parents to stare at her daughter. She pushed her way through the parents' entrance and found her children in the "entertainment" area with two attractive twentysomethings.

"Maisie? What a cute name!" one of them was saying. "Would you like me to do your hair and makeup?"

"Yes!" Maisie squealed, although Miriam was nearly certain she had no idea what she was agreeing to.

"She's only five," Miriam said to the makeup artist, who was plugging in a flat iron.

"Oh, I know. Don't worry, we won't do lashes or anything. Just some lipstick, blush, eye shadow, maybe a touch of tinted moisturizer. Then I think we'll flatten her hair and maybe weave in some tinsel. What color would you like, sweetie?"

"Pink and purple, please." Maisie looked like she would faint from excitement.

"Tinted moisturizer?" Miriam asked.

The girl looked up at her, frowning. "It's just for fun. Dress-up. But if you don't want me to—"

"Mommy! I want to! Don't say no!"

"Of course not, love. It's just . . . I think you're beautiful exactly the way you are."

"I want pink and purple in my hair!"

Miriam sighed. "I know. Go ahead."

The makeup artist gave her an unmistakable look: *Go away, overbearing mother*.

She pulled out an old-school Caboodle filled with more Chanel and Armani cosmetics than they stocked at Bergdorf.

"I'll be right back, sweetie." Miriam was going to kiss Maisie on the cheek, but the stylist swooped in front of her with a hot iron.

Most of the tables had been removed to make room for an enormous professional-looking stage complete with a sound system and light show. Red velvet curtains hung in swooping drapes from the ceiling and the walls, and another red carpet—this one with gold stars, each with a child's name—wove its way through the main room and up to the stage.

"Miriam!" A woman with wild curls whom Miriam recognized from the sex-toy party stepped in front of her. "It's so good to see you."

"You too!" Miriam said loudly to compensate for the fact that she couldn't remember the woman's name.

"How *amazing* is this? I mean, what I wouldn't have given to go to something like this when I was a kid. All we ever did for birthday parties were pony rides or Chuck E. Cheese's."

"This is definitely not Chuck E. Cheese," Miriam murmured, catching sight of a male dance teacher who was giving the boys dance lessons in the back room. He couldn't have been a day older than twenty-one, and his abs were so defined that Miriam stopped in her tracks and stared.

"Not bad, huh?" whispered another mom beside her.

"Oh my God." They all stared at the shirtless, spandex-bottomed human Gumby gyrating in front of the boys.

"Yeah, I know. I used to think a birthday party was good if they served adult beverages. Now I'll never be happy again unless there are half-naked man-boys who can move like that."

"Are these really Justin Timberlake's backup dancers?" Miriam asked, certain she should already know the answer.

"One of Schuyler's dads—not the one by the door, that one over there—is some big executive at Justin's record label."

"There is no way Matthew is going to agree to dance," Miriam said with a mother's authority. "He hates dancing. He thinks it's a girl thing. Nothing we say can convince him otherwise."

As though on cue, Matthew started moving his hips. Slowly at first, and then madly, in every direction. As the teacher added arm movements, so did Matthew. Within a minute, twenty boys were thrusting all over the stage.

A flash of blond hair in the back of the room caught Miriam's eye. Looking like she was trying to disappear, was Ashley.

"Excuse me, I just have to say hi to a friend," Miriam said. As she got closer, it became obvious Ashley was crying. "Hey, are you okay?" Miriam asked.

Ashley's eyes were bloodshot and mascara streamed down her colorless cheeks. She was so pale that Miriam was certain she'd just received some sort of horrific medical prognosis.

"Oh, honey, come here." Miriam took her hand and led her friend to a table that was shielded from the dancing boys and the watching parents. She pulled a chair out and Ashley collapsed into it. "What's going on?"

"Oh, Miriam. It's . . . too . . . awful." Ashley hiccupped. "My kids are never going to recover from this."

Miriam took Ashley's hands in her own and was shocked by how cold they felt. "Tell me, sweetie." Miriam squeezed her hands.

"I think Eric is cheating on me. No, scratch that—I know he is."

Miriam was surprised only by how completely unsurprised she was. She cleared her throat. "Why do you think that?"

"There have been a lot of signs lately. Nothing definitive, but things have just been . . . different."

"Every marriage has ups and downs."

"I know, and that's what I kept telling myself. But Eric is totally checked out in the bedroom. It's like he's doing it out of obligation." Ashley offered a small, bitter laugh. "We're the ones who do it out of obligation, not them!"

"Oh, honey. He could be tired. You said yourself he's been working like crazy."

"And then there's the trainer. Eric's always been an athlete, so it wasn't that strange. He's always loved team sports. Or running. Not going to the gym. But, like, now he's there every day."

Miriam's mind flashed to Paul and his newfound interest in working out. Ashley kept talking, though Miriam was quiet. "Do you remember when that whole Ashley Madison hack happened?"

Miriam nodded. She'd known a mom from their preschool in New York who had discovered her husband's account during the hack and had promptly divorced him, taking him for everything he was worth.

"Okay, boys! Let's take it from the top!" the dancer yelled into a headset microphone. "One, two, three, four!" A too-loud rendition of "Can't Stop the Feeling!" blasted from the speaker.

Ashley went on, "I remember reading about it. But it never even occurred to me to check Eric's email address. What was that, like, three years ago? The baby wasn't even born yet! I remember reading all the horror stories of women finding their husbands on it. I felt bad for them, but I was certain Eric would never do something like that."

"And?" Miriam croaked. She was trying to focus on Ashley, she really was, but it was hard when all she wanted to do was get to a computer.

"I was reading some super-old copy of *Women's Health* at the dentist's office yesterday, and there was an article about what you should do if you find your husband on Ashley Madison. Like, everything from what therapist you could see to which STDs you should get tested for."

"Okay . . ."

"And I don't know what came over me. I can't explain to you why I did it." With this, Ashley started bawling again. "But I Googled that database where you could check someone's email address, and sure enough. He was there—both his work and personal email! Does that mean he has two accounts? Like one account for cheating on your wife isn't enough?"

Miriam was thankful for the loud music, because Ashley's sobs had turned into wails, and she seemed entirely unconcerned about who heard her.

"I remember when that whole thing happened, and—"

Ashley cut her off. "And Fairfield County, Connecticut, had, like, the most registered users per square mile of anywhere in the U.S., I think."

"Some men were just curious what all the fuss was about. They'd go on to check it out but never actually contact anyone on it."

Ashley turned her tearstained face to Miriam's. "Well, not my husband. I left the dentist's office without even getting my checkup and went straight home. I dug out the old credit card bills, which I never, ever look at because it makes me sick to see how much money we spend every month, and there it was, plain as day. The random numbers-and-letters combination that the article tells you to look for on your billing statement. It's totally innocuous if you don't know what it is, but if you type it into Google, you can see that it's a cover for Ashley Madison billing. I counted thirty-eight months of billing. You think it was just fleeting curiosity?"

Miriam looked down at her hands.

"Miriam, what do I *do*?"

"Well, first I think you need to figure out what *you* want. What is the best possible outcome for *you* in this situation."

"A *divorce*?" This word Ashley whispered, like "cancer." "You think I should get a divorce?"

"No! Unless you want to. I didn't say either way. Just that it might be good to do a little thinking about what you want before you talk to Eric about it."

"Ohmigod, what if *he* wants a divorce?"

Miriam didn't want to point out that the entire purpose of Ashley Madison was for married adults to have affairs with other married adults, working under the assumption that neither wanted to implode his or her marriage.

"You can't know until you talk to him, sweetheart. I'm sure there's going to be—"

"Mommy! I have to go potty!" Ashley's son called out from the stage.

Ashley wiped the tears and makeup from under her eyes. "Am I a mess? Can I even be seen in public?"

"You're okay. You might want to hit the ladies' room just to touch up," Miriam said.

Ashley offered a hand to her son and helped him down off the stage. Miriam watched and tried to swallow a near-overwhelming wave of nausea. Was it possible? Until the move to Greenwich, she had never once in all their years of marriage seriously considered the possibility that Paul might cheat. But how could she deny that Paul sounded just like Eric? The preoccupation with working out, the lack of sex, the newfound interest in hanging out with douchey guys, like Ashley's husband . . .

Of course. Paul was cheating on her. Maybe it wasn't Ashley Madison—she desperately hoped he wasn't *that* stupid—but it was someone. It had to be.

"Mommy? Mommy!" Matthew called from the stage.

Miriam's head snapped up, but she still couldn't focus.

"MOMMY!"

She jumped. "What, love? I'm right here."

"Watch me!"

Like a happy zombie, Miriam grinned through a choreographed and highly inappropriate dance show featuring her five-year-old son's pelvis thrusts and watched her sweet, innocent daughter, who had been transformed into something straight out of *Toddlers & Tiaras*, practice her "fashion walk" down the red carpet. At the end of the party, Miriam

even said thank you and managed to seem genuine, instead of horrified, when the children got their party favors: for Maisie, a thoroughly
bedazzled, personalized tote bag stocked full of lotions that smelled of
cake batter and vanilla and makeup laced with glitter; and for Matthew,
a biker-style pleather jacket signed across the back by Justin Timberlake
in silver fabric marker. At her twins' last birthday party, Miriam had
handed out cellophane bags full of M&M's and had felt like Pinterest
Mom of the Year because she'd tied them with personalized ribbons that
read: THANK YOU FOR CELEBRATING WITH US! LOVE, M&M.

"Mommy, that was so much fun!" Maisie said as Miriam buckled her
into the car seat. "I am going to wear my new makeup every day."

"No, sweetie, it's for dress-up. We don't wear makeup outside of
the house."

Maisie burst into tears. "It's not fair! It's mine! I decide!"

"Mommy's the boss, not you," Matthew said from his seat.

Miriam tipped the valet and eased the car onto the road.

"Mommy! Maisie said a bad word! She called me buttface!"

"Maisie."

"I did not, Mama! He is lying!" Maisie screeched.

With this, Matthew started to cry. "I am not!" he wept. "You never
believe me!"

"So did you both have fun at the party?" Miriam asked. The twins
recounted their favorite activities, and Miriam's mind wandered. *Did
that really happen? Who are these people?*

As Miriam drove home, she felt a mounting chill of fear. Had they
made a mistake by moving to Greenwich and exposing their kids to
this lifestyle? Should she have left her job? Were she and Paul drifting?
Could he possibly be having an affair? When was the last time she'd
made him a coffee the way he liked it, with the milk steamed instead
of just dumped in cold? Or taken the time to make her specialty turkey
chili that he loved even though the kids wouldn't touch it because it was
too spicy? When had she put on lingerie instead of an oversize cotton
T-shirt? It was no wonder he was cheating. He'd be crazy if he weren't.

These thoughts occupied her the entire ride home, but it took turning onto her road to confirm, beyond any shadow of a doubt, that she was right. Standing in the driveway, side by side, not seeming to notice the cold drizzle, were her husband and son. Ben was jumping up and down, waving his hands like a maniac. And there it was—a red Maserati convertible, all sleek lines and shiny new paint. The dealer's temporary plates still on. And it was all Miriam could do not to crash her big, ugly SUV straight into her husband and his brand-new car.

18

Road Trip

Karolina

"It's only a hundred extra per day to upgrade. It's a no-brainer," Emily said, her back pressed against the red car.

The three of them stood in the executive line at the National Car Rental in McCarran airport. They'd just stepped off a Virgin America flight—where Emily, unsurprisingly, had booked all three of them in first class—and had been debating whether to drive a Ford Explorer (Miriam's vote), an Audi sedan with a nice sunroof (Karolina's), or the BMW convertible that Emily had been hawking as if her life depended on it.

"We're going to be driving five hours through the desert. Anything could happen. A convertible isn't safe," Miriam announced, sounding very momlike.

"Isn't safe how, exactly?" Emily asked.

"Isn't it obvious? If the car flips over, there's no top to protect us. We'd be crushed."

Emily rolled her eyes. "When was the last time you flipped your car?"

Miriam rolled hers right back. "I'm just saying. Nobody rents a convertible for a five-hour drive through the desert."

Karolina held up her hand. "It's like neither of you remembers that I'm headed to 'rehab'! The A4 is a good compromise, and I'm paying, so no more arguing. Come on, guys, let's get going." They gathered their rolling suitcases and carry-on totes, but a minute before they made it to the car, a young couple tossed their lone bag into the trunk, swooped into the front seat, and roared out of the garage without a word.

"They knew we wanted that one!" Miriam cried, reaching after them.

"Sign from God that we were meant to have the convertible," Emily said, popping the BMW's trunk. "Not a ton of room, I admit, but we'll make it work."

"And get melanoma," Miriam murmured.

"Have you heard of this amazing thing called sunscreen? It's so cool! You rub a little on your face and you don't get sunburned. And guess what? I have some right here in my bag!"

Miriam glared at Emily but climbed into the backseat. "When we're picking bugs out of our teeth and our hair is wrapped in knots and our scalps are burnt and we've lost our voices from screaming to be heard over the wind, I'm going to say I told you so."

Emily gave Miriam the finger, and despite herself Karolina smiled, realizing she had never taken a road trip with friends in her life. Karolina had been modeling by age fourteen. She and Graham had traveled extensively—it was one of the things they both loved—but Graham had always balked at renting cars in foreign countries. Flying all over the world was a different kind of adventure, but still, how was it possible that in thirty-seven years she'd never taken a proper road trip?

Karolina slid behind the wheel and, once they hit I-15, set the cruise control for eighty-five. They flew down the open road in the midmorning

March sun. When they passed the Vegas Strip, Emily cracked them all up with a highly detailed description of her newest business idea, which involved selling tours for men to travel to Vegas with their friends, where they'd get a group discount on vasectomies, after which they'd recover in a luxe hotel room while strippers iced their balls.

"Oh my God. It's brilliant," Miriam screeched from the backseat. "Not only is it an easy sell for the husbands, but you don't have to take care of them afterward. You are definitely onto something."

"You haven't even heard the best part. We offer a two-for-one rate and call it the Vegasectomy. I think it's going to be a massive hit."

Karolina wanted to laugh with them, but she couldn't ignore the queasy anxiety and uncertainty that seemed to plague her all day, every day. Not that it stopped her from eating like a whale for the first time in her life. Hours later, when they were all so starving that the only possible thing to eat besides gas-station snacks were giant, oozing McDonald's sundaes that they ordered from the drive-through, Karolina inhaled hers. "I can't believe I just ate dairy," she moaned, clutching her stomach.

"You didn't!" Emily said. "It's all chemicals. No milk whatsoever."

Just after dark they arrived at Amangiri and were met by the general manager, Emily's "old friend." He promised them complete discretion.

"I chose our most private accommodations," he said after leading them outside and swinging open glass doors to reveal a suite that looked like it had been carved from a single slab of gray cement. A huge sitting area in the middle featured all-white divans and chairs facing the desert. A small bonfire roared on their porch. The private lap pool glittered like an oasis from the sand, flanked on all sides by mountain ridges. White lounge chairs and white umbrellas with perfectly folded white towels. The master bedroom had a king-size platform bed and a bathroom with a double-rain indoor-outdoor shower and an oversize tub looking out floor-to-ceiling windows.

"You can have this suite," Emily announced. "Miriam and I will take the double next door. You'll need all that extra space and solitude to focus on your sobriety."

Miriam and Emily went to their room to get ready for dinner, but Karolina changed into a swimsuit and lowered herself into the lap pool, which felt more like a hot tub. Almost immediately, her phone rang with a 212 area code. She took a deep breath. She was ready. Emily had told her exactly what to say.

"Hello? This is Karolina Hartwell."

"Karolina?" The voice on the other end was young and female and sounded surprised. The woman probably never expected to have her call answered.

"Yes."

"This is Susanna Willensky from the *New York Post*. Is it true you've left Greenwich and are giving up visitation rights to your son?"

Karolina inhaled. She'd been prepared for the rehab question, but the accusation of abandoning Harry? That wasn't supposed to be part of the equation.

"Ma'am?" The woman was insistent.

"I haven't and won't give up visitation. Nothing could be further from the truth."

"And the rehab? For a problem with alcohol? After your arrest? Is it fair to say you're seeking treatment?"

Karolina paused to make sure she remembered Emily's exact wording. It was important to be precise—not lying but not telling the whole truth either. "I have taken some time to travel out west to clear my head. I think the fresh air and the change of scenery are what I need right now."

"Out west? Can you elaborate?"

"No, I'm afraid that's not possible." Emily had been insistent on those two words: "not possible." It implied that Karolina would happily share her location if only there weren't strict confidentiality rules regarding her stay (in rehab). There was no way any remotely intelligent reporter could hear that and not bet her entire life savings that Karolina was checked in to the ultra-luxe treatment center in Montana that was part high-end dude ranch and part luxury hotel.

"I see. Anything else you'd like to add about—"

"Thank you, that's all the time I have now." Karolina pressed "end" and was relieved it was over. Emily would be pleased.

"Would you ladies like to join us in the desert lounge?" asked Tim, the waiter. "A local astronomer will be giving a stargazing demonstration."

Karolina looked around the table.

"There will be a s'mores workshop as well. Dark chocolate, milk, Reese's, peppermint—"

"I think we can stop by for a few minutes." Emily smiled sweetly. As he walked away, she gazed after him. "If this joint weren't charging five grand a night for a room, I might think they were running a male whorehouse."

Miriam laughed. "He's a child, Emily! Like, twenty, maybe."

Emily held up her hand. "I'm just saying . . . one is more gorgeous than the next. And Timmy here is my personal favorite."

"Yes, well, if you hadn't noticed, there are an awful lot of single women around here," Miriam offered. "Maybe they switch up the staff according to their guest profile each week."

All of them turned to the nearby table and stared as the group of a dozen women—girls, really—broke into laughter. It was clear they were a bachelorette party, since the bride wore something emblazoned with BRIDE every chance she got, but beyond that, they were a loud, attractive mystery.

"Just so long as they're focused on themselves and not us. The last thing we need is for one of them to recognize Karolina and leak it to the press that we're hiding out at a luxury hotel and not a twelve-step program."

"I don't understand who has a dozen friends that can afford to come here," Karolina said. "And they're young. Like, twenties."

"I'm sure one of their fathers or fiancés is paying for it," Emily said.

Karolina turned to her and raised her eyebrows. "Well, that's sexist! We're all here together, and it's not my father or husband who's paying for it."

"Emily's right, though," Miriam said, downing the last sip of her wine and motioning for yet another glass. They were on glass number five, and no one could catch the slightest buzz. Finally, Tim had clued them in to the statewide drinking laws that allowed only four ounces of wine to be served at a time. They called it the "Utah pour."

"I am?" Emily asked.

"Her father is paying for the weekend. Although her fiancé certainly could. But he's currently treating his friends to a weekend in Ibiza."

"How did you figure that out?" Emily asked.

"It wasn't hard," Miriam said. "They've been taking selfies like crazy. I searched hashtag 'Amangiri' and found a few pics they'd posted. I followed the one we know is the bride back to her page. From there, it was easy to see who her fiancé is, since there are make-out and proposal pictures all over the account, so I Googled him because his Insta was private and saw he's a managing director at the largest hedge fund in the U.S. Incidentally, they got in some legal trouble a few months ago over accepting money from some Bahraini sheik on the terrorist watch list, but that's neither here nor there."

"Wow," Karolina murmured.

"I haven't even told you the most interesting part. I saw on her account that an older man, presumably her father, had tagged her on a photo he posted on Facebook. Or actually, whoever runs the social-media accounts for the Swedish royal family. Long way of saying that she's a Swedish princess who grew up in a palace in Stockholm and came here for boarding school and her MRS degree."

Emily whistled. "I'm officially impressed."

Karolina's eyes widened. "You found out all of that without know-ing any of their *names*."

"Digging up dirt was a fairly big feature in my previous life, before I only wore spandex and went to sex-toy parties."

Emily said, "Your skills are needed now. By *us*. Can you find out anything about Graham that we can use against him? No one—espe-cially douchebags like him—is totally clean."

Karolina recoiled at Emily's casual viciousness and then got angry with herself. She shouldn't feel badly about *anything* in light of what Graham had done to her.

Miriam leaned across the table. "Tax evasion? At the very least, you probably had a nanny or a cleaning lady at some point who wasn't legal."

"Are you kidding?" Karolina asked. "He's had political aspirations forever. You think he was going to risk hiring an illegal alien?"

"Okay, then what about drugs?" Emily asked. "He seems like a co-caine kind of guy."

"Not really. Maybe a couple times when we first met? But who cares? Obama admitted to trying coke."

"Karolina. I know there's something. You need to tell us." Emily's manner had switched from lighthearted to angry.

Karolina's mother had always told her it was a good quality to be a bad liar. "I don't know what you're talking about."

"You have something on him, I know you do. It's written all over your face."

Karolina met Emily's gaze. "I've told you everything I know," she said.

Two or three years into their marriage Graham lay in her arms after they'd made love, and he'd wept. She'd never seen him cry before that night or after—not when his father died, or on the anniversary of his first wife's death, when he took Harry to the Hamptons beach where he'd scattered her ashes. After nearly an hour of soothing and promis-ing, he told Karolina, and when he did, she couldn't breathe. It was the twenty-fifth birthday of a girl named Molly. Or would have been, had she lived to see it. More than twenty years earlier, when Graham was seventeen, he hit and killed four-year-old Molly Wells near his parents' summer home in Amagansett.

Emily slapped her hands on the table hard enough for their wineglasses to rattle. "We're all the way out here in the middle of fucking nowhere, talking about some Swedish princess, while your husband—the man you are refusing to sell out even now—has basically kidnapped your child, ruined your reputation, and thrown you out like yesterday's garbage."

"Emily," Miriam warned.

"It's bullshit," Emily hissed. "She has something on him. I can tell! *We're* trying to get *her* life back, and she's not willing to help."

"I'm tired," Karolina said, trying to suppress the tears. It had been an amazing day filled with rock climbing and hot-stone massages and floating in the pool, and she didn't want to ruin it. "I'm going to sleep. Have a s'more for me. I'll see you guys at breakfast."

"Lina, sweetie, Emily and I are worried about you. You seem awfully tired and lethargic. I know things are hard right now, but are you holding up okay emotionally?" Miriam asked, placing a hand over Karolina's.

"What she's trying to ask is if you're planning to jump off a bridge," Emily added.

Karolina looked between her two friends. "I really am just tired," she said, standing up. "Thank you for your concern, but I promise I'm not planning on swallowing a bottle of pills anytime soon."

As soon as she stood, Tim reappeared like magic, helping Karolina move her chair out of the way. "You're not going to miss s'mores, are you?" he asked.

"Maybe next time," she said, and he made an adorable pouty face but moved on to the next table.

Emily nodded. Miriam gave her the thumbs-up. As if on cue, Tim turned around and grinned at her.

"I'm going back to my room. I love you both, but I've had enough,"

Karolina said. She heard Miriam call after her, but she pretended not to and walked out of the restaurant. A handful of glass lanterns lit the path to her suite. The bed had been turned down and the lights lowered, and the outdoor fire pit on her private patio had been lit. Karolina pulled a bottle of Perrier out of the minibar and settled onto the cushioned sun bed next to the fire. The desert stretched out before her, completely silent, but she couldn't see much beyond the tall cactus a few feet away. *Harry would love this*, she thought. She had tried him before dinner her time, which was right about when he went to bed, but he'd rejected her FaceTime and replied with a text: *sorry mom cant talk sleeping at jasons 2nite call you tmrw.* She wondered why on earth Graham was letting him sleep at a friend's house the night before a game. But of course she knew. Regan.

Karolina heard knocking off in the distance. A woodpecker? It came again, more insistent this time. She walked back into her room and realized someone was at her suite's door. "I'm already in bed!" she called to Emily and Miriam, despite the fact that she was fully dressed.

"Sorry to disturb you," a male voice replied.

She turned the deadbolt and opened the door. There, with a shy smile, stood Tim. The waiter. Who was now freshly showered and looking better than ever in an untucked button-down with rolled sleeves and a pair of jeans.

"So sorry, Mrs. Hartwell. I hope I'm not disturbing you. Your friends said you needed help with something in your room?"

"Something in my—" She stopped. She wanted to murder Emily. This had her name all over it.

Tim's smile widened, and he gave her what could only be described as a mischievous look. "I think they said it was a bug? Perhaps a scorpion? I'm here to, um, help you remove it."

"A bug? Yes, that's right. A bug." She stepped back to let him pass, and she knew exactly what was transpiring. "It's a very big bug."

"Yes, that's what they said. I'm so sorry about that. Let me see what I can do." He kicked the door closed behind him and started to kiss her. It happened so fast, and there was so much to process—the sensation of kissing someone with a beard, someone who wasn't Graham, and how instantaneously turned on she was, literally, like a light switch—that she couldn't do anything except kiss him back. In a minute he'd scooped her up, movie-style, and laid her on the bed, and when he lowered himself on top of her, she thought she might lose her mind.

"What?" he asked gruffly, running his hands through her hair.

"Wait one second," she whispered.

He stopped instantly. "You okay?"

Karolina smiled. He was even cuter up close, if possible. "Just one thing."

"Anything."

"Please don't call me Mrs. Hartwell. Like, ever again."

Tim laughed and buried his face in her neck. He slowly undressed her. When, finally, they were both completely naked, he stopped, sat up, and looked her up and down with obvious appreciation. "Wow," he murmured, and it was obvious he meant it. "You are one beautiful woman, Karolina."

Karolina reached up and pulled his face down to hers. "Shhh."

They made love twice. After the second time, they fell asleep, and when Karolina woke up, the gas fire pit outside was still burning. It was five a.m., the sky just starting to lighten. She slipped out of the bed and walked, naked, to the glass door that offered a spectacular desert view. She was thirty-seven years old. And this was her very first one-night stand. Of course, they would be there for two more nights, there would be ample opportunity to . . . Karolina stopped herself. No. It had been perfect, exactly what she needed. One amazing night of sex without emotion.

An hour later Tim had sneaked out of her suite with the finely honed skills of someone who did so all too frequently. The night had been too delicious to share, to dissect, to listen to Emily's probing questions, or to watch Miriam sit in quiet judgment. *No, thank you*, Karolina thought. This would be hers and hers alone.

19

America Wants to Forgive You

Emily

Emily took a drag off her cigarette and slowly exhaled. It was an unusually warm day, one of those teasers that had you believing spring had arrived, and Emily and Karolina were sitting on Karolina's back patio, overlooking the winterized pool. The trip out west had been highly successful. An *Entertainment Weekly* poll had Americans willing to forgive Karolina at fifty-two percent. "Rehab" had gone great, and it was time to move forward on the rest of the plan. Not to mention that Kyle had fielded three calls for Emily from new clients and flowers from Miranda Priestly.

Karolina held up the latest copy of *People*. "Well, it's finally official," she said, her voice cracking.

Emily snatched it. The cover featured Graham and Regan, smiling broadly. They were cheek to cheek, with more perfect white teeth between them than looked normal or necessary. HOW I FOUND HAPPINESS AGAIN was emblazoned across the bottom and, under that, a small byline: Graham Hartwell. She'd seen this coming from a mile away, but still, she had to give him credit: his rollout was perfect; he was doing everything beautifully. And incidentally, the tip-in story featured Kim Kelly's disastrous fashion choice on the red carpet. Emily couldn't help but feel a surge of delight.

"They'll be engaged by late fall and married by next spring, mark my words," Emily said.

"We're not even officially divorced yet!"

"You will be."

"Emily! Take it down a notch," Miriam said, walking in from Karolina's kitchen with a plate of homemade Rice Krispies treats she'd brought.

"Well, it's true, isn't it?" Emily turned to Karolina. "Hiring Miriam to represent you is the smartest thing you've done since hiring me."

"She didn't *hire* me," Miriam said. "I'm helping out on the legal side of things, is all. Unofficially. But officially."

Karolina and Miriam exchanged grateful smiles. She waved her hand. "You can tell Emily what you told me. About the prenup," Karolina said.

Miriam took a bite of a Rice Krispies treat. "I'm sure you know that it's iron-clad. And pretty self-explanatory. They each get what they came to the marriage with, and they split whatever was earned in the last ten years. She keeps Greenwich, he keeps Bethesda, the apartment in New York gets sold, and they each take half."

Karolina shook her head. "It's all clear. Except for Harry."

Emily studied her friend and hoped—no, prayed—she didn't cry.

Karolina started to weep quietly.

Miriam enveloped Karolina in one of her mom-hugs, and Emily reached across the table and awkwardly patted her hand. "It's okay."

"It's not okay! I'm the only mother Harry has known for ten years. The poor, woe-is-me single-dad card plays too well. Dead wife. Widower. Motherless child. All part of his master plan!"

Emily plucked a cigarette from the pack, lit it, and handed it to Karolina, who wordlessly accepted it.

"Listen," Emily said. "It's going to work out. I promise. I have some ideas."

"You have some ideas for helping me not be a social pariah. And they're all lies anyway. What about getting my kid back? When technically he's not even my kid?" Karolina wailed. "And what about the truth? Shouldn't my name be cleared? Wouldn't that help with custody?"

Emily and Miriam exchanged glances.

"I agree with Karolina. It would help. It's time to clear her name," Miriam said.

"Have a little faith, okay?" Emily said.

"Faith?"

"Did you not tell me that in ten years he has never taken Harry to a doctor's appointment? Or gone to more than one baseball game a season? Has never taken him away alone anywhere? Doesn't know the names of any of his friends? Doesn't attend parent/teacher conferences?"

Karolina nodded, wiping away tears from her eyes.

"I get that I'm not exactly the authority on all things parental, but those sound pretty basic to me. Things that, like, ninety percent of remotely decent parents manage to handle."

"Yes, but—"

"Stop defending him! I'm wondering why he really wants to take this all on now. What, he's suddenly going to morph into Dad of the Year because you're out of the picture? Not likely."

"Yeah, well, he has *her* now," Karolina said, waving the copy of *People*.

"Oh, and twelve-year-old boys are *so* accepting of brand-new stepmoms." Emily took another drag and followed it with a sip of wine. "She's going to want her own kids. Not yours."

Karolina's eyes widened.

"Am I wrong?"

"No, of course not. She's young." Karolina refilled her glass.

"Unless it's him?" Emily suggested. As soon as the words were out of her mouth, she regretted saying them, if only because she desperately didn't want to get into a long conversation about Karolina's infertility. She knew that Karolina had tried everything, from acupuncture to Clomid to crystals to multiple rounds of IVF, and nothing had worked.

"If only," Karolina said with barely disguised bitterness. "He was tested twice. It's me."

"What's wrong with you?"

Karolina gave her a look.

"What? Sorry, I didn't mean it like that. I'm not . . . well versed in these types of conversations."

Karolina sighed. "Unexplained infertility, they call it. They ran a thousand tests and my eggs were fine and my progesterone was a little low but nothing unworkable, and I don't have endometriosis or polycystic ovarian syndrome or—"

Emily held up a hand. She was trying not to look disgusted but wasn't sure she was succeeding. "So what is it?"

"I literally just could never even get pregnant. No miscarriages. Nothing. No positive pregnancy tests ever. Even with IVF, we never made a viable embryo, so we couldn't even get a surrogate."

"I'm sorry," Emily said. It was difficult to imagine trying so hard to get pregnant when she'd expended so much effort to stay unpregnant.

"It doesn't matter now because I have Harry. *Had*."

"And you'll have him again!" Emily lightly touched Karolina's arm. "Trust me on this, Lina. This is all about Graham's appearance. It's only been a couple months. We need to let it play out."

Emily reached for a copy of the *Post* and flipped to "Page Six," holding it out to Karolina. "Look!"

"I can't believe it," Karolina said. "They did exactly what you said they would."

"It's the press. They're not so mysterious. You got a DUI. You're a high-profile person in your own right, married to a U.S. senator. Naturally, everyone wants to see you repent. Step one, implied rehab, check! Step two is a total makeover, and step three is a high-profile appearance where you announce to the American people how sorry you are and beg for their forgiveness."

"How high-profile?" Karolina looked alarmed.

"Like *Ellen*. *The View*. *GMA*. High."

"Oh God."

"You've walked in the Victoria's Secret fashion show six times!"

"Seven."

"Practically naked! And every legitimate pervert and teenaged boy and bored husband in the Western world has watched you. You can't possibly be nervous about going on *Good Morning America*!"

"No, it's going on national TV and lying to the world about my nonexistent alcoholism."

Emily shrugged. "America wants to forgive you! We forgave Hugh Grant his prostitutes. Ben Affleck screwing the nanny. Even Brad cheating on Jen. We can certainly give you a second chance too."

Karolina's face darkened to an alarming shade of red. "My God, I hate him so much."

"Emily can handle the public," Miriam said, "but there's no way I'm allowing a fake crime to stay on your record."

Emily nodded. "See? And after you do your makeover and look-how-healthy-and-sympathetic-I-am interview, we'll get you affiliated with a cause. The obvious choice is Mothers Against Drunk Driving, although a case could be made for Driving While Distracted or something similar. We'll get you on the board of something prestigious and based in New York, and of course you'll host an event at the Greenwich Yacht Club. It would be a really nice touch if you could publicly offer your support and congratulations when Graham and Regan get engaged—that'll play really well. After that? It's smooth sailing. In the meantime, we're hiring a decent social-media consultant, and we're going to show the public who you really are."

"And who is that?"

"Remember what I said about putting on some weight, changing your image? I think you should get a bob."

Karolina shuddered. "Stop."

"I'm serious! Do you want your hair to say 'drunk seductress' or 'dependable mom'? Because right now it's screaming the former." Emily felt badly for even suggesting Karolina cut her long, gorgeous hair, but, well, drastic times . . .

"This is insane."

Emily nodded and placed her hand on Karolina's ever-shrinking wrist. The stress was taking a toll. "Listen. I can change your image, and it will work. But if you're serious about wanting a stronger case for custody, or"—she waved her hand dismissively—"clearing your name, I need that dirt you're holding back from me. Judging from your sulky lower lip, it's something salacious."

"It's nothing."

"He wasn't fazed in the least by ruining your life!"

"It's . . . It's not that simple, Emily. I have Harry to think about."

"I understand," Miriam said.

Emily said, "Graham sure as hell isn't thinking about Harry's well-being in any of this, so I'm not sure why you are."

"Well, you wouldn't be sure, would you," Karolina whispered, her voice quivering. "You're not a mother, Emily. I know you think it's, like, some bourgeois thing or something, but can't you understand why I wouldn't want to get back at Graham if it means hurting my son too?"

Emily considered this for a moment. "So there is something."

"Emily, leave her alone," Miriam said.

Karolina stood up. "I'm done. Have your pick of the guest rooms, they're all clean."

"We're not done!" Emily called, but Karolina had already walked out. Emily exhaled a loud sigh.

"You're too rough on her," Miriam said, gathering her coat and bag. "Try to imagine what she's going through."

Emily massaged her temples.

"I'm heading out. I'll call you tomorrow," Miriam said.

When Emily heard the front door close, she lit another cigarette. Kids did nothing but complicate things. The night she met Miles, they'd fallen drunk into bed together following some charity event and he had bolted awake at six in the morning, terrified that he'd knocked her up.

"You have a what?" he'd asked, head resting on his bent arm.

"An IUD."

"Is that like the pill?"

"No, it's not like the pill. Seriously? You've never even heard of it? Men have it so easy."

"Well, is it as reliable as the pill?" He was really looking worried. "Because I definitely don't want a kid. I mean, no offense. Of course I want them later. But definitely not now.

"A college buddy had a one-night stand with a United flight attendant on a layover in Chicago. He was twenty-two. He didn't even know her name. She tracked him down from the flight manifest eight weeks later and called him out of the blue. She didn't expect anything but couldn't live with herself if she didn't tell him that he would have a son."

Emily raised her eyebrows. "You're comparing me to a flight attendant?"

"He's got a fourteen-year-old now! It's crazy."

"Not to worry. I won't be getting pregnant now. Or ever."

"You don't want kids?"

"Of course not. You do?"

Miles squinted and, incidentally, looked very cute doing so. "Yeah, I do."

"Mmm, maybe," Emily had said, but only so he didn't think she was a heartless bitch devoid of all maternal instincts when they'd just met. And she wasn't! A heartless bitch? Perhaps sometimes. She thought babies were cute—who didn't? She liked holding other people's sometimes, if they smelled good. And the clothes? They were to die for. That amazing Chloé fur vest she'd just seen at Bergdorf and pair it with the Ralph Lauren jodhpur leggings. What wasn't absolutely adorable mini-size? But throw away her life and career on a crying, pissing, spitting thing that would inevitably grow up to hate her as much as she hated her own mother? Hell no. Why was that so hard for everyone to understand?

She stubbed out the remaining cigarette and texted Miles. *You up?*

He responded right away. *It's 11 in the am here. Yes, I'm up!*

I can never remember

12 hrs ahead. Not hard.

I know, I know. I'm working on it.

U at Miriam's?

Staying at Karolina's now. One of the kids got sick so I bailed. It's ok tho—conditions better here. No dog, no kids, more booze. How is all there?

Speaking of kids . . .

There was a pause followed by the three dots that indicated Miles was typing. *Here we go*, Emily thought.

Just got an email from Betsy. She's due in oct—twins!!!!!!

Wow. Good for them.

Could be us you know, just say the word

Emily snapped a selfie holding up her pack of Parliaments and sent it to him.

She watched her screen for a few minutes: no response. She tossed her phone next to her on the couch. Then, reconsidering, she grabbed it, pulled up her T-shirt, and took a picture of her bare breasts. She cropped her face out just in case he was in a meeting or something and sent it.

Three dots. Thumbs-up emoji.

Thumbs-up? A fucking *emoji*? That was what their marriage had come to when she tried to apologize with a quick sexting session?

Emily went into the photo album on the phone and again selected the picture. This time she used an editing app to remove the bit of flab in front of her armpit and enhance her cleavage just so. She cropped in a bit closer on her left breast, the fuller one, and switched the entire photo to black-and-white to hide any stray hairs or freckles. Then she scrolled her contacts until she found the number Alistair had given her the night of the Moroccan sex party, or whatever the hell they were calling it, and hit "send." *At least he'll know what to do with a photo of a beautiful naked woman*, she thought as she sat back on the couch and waited for his response.

20

Make It
Stop

Miriam

There was a Le Pain Quotidien in Greenwich, of course—
two, actually—but something about sipping a full-fat latte on an uncomfortable stool packed in like sardines in the West Village felt better.
Miriam glanced at all the people jammed into the sitting area and smiled.
Some had strollers, yes, but plenty of others had laptops and messen-
ger bags and bike helmets. There were men. And people speaking foreign languages. All different shades of hair and skin. The entire place
hummed while its patrons met, worked, brainstormed, discussed. The
energy was palpable in a way that did not exist on the main drag at
home, where most of the spacious seating went unoccupied and the only
customers who did stop by were clad in activewear and biding their time
until school pickup.

She'd taken the train in for her annual eye exam and had dragged a tote bag full of Karolina's bills and statements, figuring she may as well work in a Manhattan coffee shop as long as she was there. Okay, and maybe shop a little, which had brought her down to the West Village, where she was hoping to convince Paul to grab a quick burger at Corner Bistro before heading back to Connecticut.

"Miriam? Is that you?" She heard a familiar voice behind her.

"Stephanie! Hi! Oh my God, it's been so long!" Miriam jumped from her stool, nearly knocking it over, and hugged her former co-worker. They'd both started as associates right after law school, until Stephanie had taken an in-house job at MTV a couple of years later.

"You look . . . great," Stephanie said.

"Liar." Miriam laughed. "I'm, like, twenty pounds heavier. Come here, sit."

Stephanie looked pretty and professional in a perfectly tailored cream Theory suit that highlighted her smooth tanned skin, a silk blouse, sky-high heels, and a blowout so bouncy and shiny it would have made Kate Middleton jealous. She slid between Miriam and a glaring hipster wearing headphones the size of cereal bowls. She turned to Miriam. "I only have a minute before I have to get back to the office for a conference call, but I'm so happy to see you!"

"You too!" Miriam said. "Are you still at MTV?"

"Yep, still plugging along. I escaped to get my hair blown out because I have an event tonight at Gagosian and won't have time after work. You know how it is." Stephanie scrunched up her nose. "Wait, why are you all the way down here?" She was polite enough not to comment on Miriam's outfit: ripped jeans that she suddenly felt too old to wear, paired with a cardigan and last year's booties. Flat, of course, for city walking.

"Me? Oh, I'm just getting some paperwork done while I wait for Paul. He had a meeting in the city today, so he's giving me a ride back to Connecticut. We have parent/teacher conferences this afternoon." Why was she blathering on like that? Couldn't she have stopped after "paperwork"?

"Connecticut? What?"

Miriam laughed uncomfortably. "Oh, you didn't know? We left the city last fall. Greenwich. So the kids could have a backyard, you know, the usual."

"I had no idea! Wow. That's amazing. I've wanted to move out of the city since we had Dashiell, but I'm too scared of the commute. I barely see him now, and that's with me living on the Upper West Side. How are you managing?"

Miriam could feel the flush start in her chest. "I, um . . . I'm not working right now."

Stephanie clapped her hand to her mouth. "I'm so sorry! I had heard some rumors about Skadden, but I never figured it would affect you. As a partner and all."

"I wasn't pushed out."

Stephanie's eyes widened. "You quit?"

"Yes," Miriam said with more conviction than she felt. "Paul sold his company, and I thought it might be good for the family if—"

"Right," Stephanie said. "It makes total sense. I'm sure you'll go back when you're ready."

"Yes, I'm sure," Miriam said, and although there wasn't the slightest hint of condescension or envy in Stephanie's tone, Miriam sensed herself being hyper-vigilant to it. She had quit her job to stay home and be more present with her children. She had zero plans to go back to work, even if there were days when she missed it like an amputated limb.

"Well, you remember what it's like when you duck out and all hell breaks loose?" Stephanie held up her phone to show her twenty new emails.

They waved goodbye, and it was all Miriam could do not to put her head down on the table. The entire interaction had just been . . . exhausting. She turned back to her pile of papers. When she'd volunteered to help Karolina sort through all of the legal and financial documents surrounding the divorce, she'd been appalled to find that they had a slew of unpaid bills between them. Karolina had given her the password to their online bill-paying account, and Miriam could barely believe what she saw: cable bills, electricity, insurance, credit card bills, home repair, doctors' bills—all either unpaid, overdue, or paid twice. One Verizon bill had been paid three times.

When Miriam asked Karolina about it, she'd just shrugged. "Sometimes I pay. Sometimes he pays. Sometimes we both pay. Sometimes neither of us does. It always works itself out."

"Why don't you have your accountant do this?"

"Why? He does the taxes. But we can pay our own bills."

"Clearly not. Some of these have gone to collections. Do you have any idea what that does to your credit?"

"What do I need credit for?"

So there it was. They were just too wealthy to care. Too rich to need a mortgage or be concerned if they'd paid three times for the same thing. She would sort through and organize her finances, pay the outstanding bills, and, most importantly, get a handle on what Karolina and Graham had as a couple and as individuals. Make sure Graham hadn't stashed anything in an offshore account in the Caymans or Geneva. Or hell, didn't own a property somewhere that he'd failed to mention. God only knew what else this man was capable of.

So far Miriam had made her way through nearly all the household bills for the Bethesda home in the previous year, and there was only one small manila envelope left to sort through. It was labeled HART-WELL FAMILY BILLS in Sharpie script and showed a return address of a concierge medical practice in Bethesda. Karolina had explained that Dr. Goldwyn was a dear family friend who acted as the overseer of medical care for both her and Graham, and the last time she'd stopped in to say hello, his receptionist had handed her a pile of unpaid bills. Miriam began to sort and pay. The medical dermatologist for Karolina's full-body scan; the cosmetic dermatologist for her Botox and Fraxel treatments; the concierge pediatrician they used for Harry; a whopping figure to the Mayo Clinic for something called an "executive physical" for Graham during which, it looked like, they tested pretty much every cell, organ, and membrane in his body; an orthopedist for Harry's broken arm; a private rehab facility where Graham worked on an old knee injury twice a week; charges for Karolina's annual Pap smear. It was a mess but all pretty self-explanatory. It wasn't until Miriam ran across a bill from a surgeon's office in Manhattan that she needed to pick up the phone for clarification. In addition to spelling Graham's name wrong, the bill didn't describe the treatment, and Miriam couldn't understand why, if he had no existing medical condition that she could see, Graham would meet with a surgeon in Manhattan. Her heart skipped a little beat: was this going to be where she stumbled across Graham's secret face-lift plans? That would make the day *so* much more interesting.

She called the office and asked for accounting. If she had to tell a small white lie and mention something about power of attorney in order to get the information, she would—after all, Karolina had given her permission to investigate—but the young woman who answered sounded bored, overworked, and interested only in getting off the phone as quickly as possible.

"Hello, I'm a lawyer representing the Hartwell family. Karolina Hartwell has asked me to settle any unpaid pills, and I have something here that reads 'Unspecified' with code number 394. Could you please tell me what that was for?"

"Yeah, one sec." The account girl put her on hold. She was back about two minutes later. "Is that invoice number 635380101?"

Miriam scanned the bill. "Yes."

The sound of typing came through the phone. "That's super-old. Like, five years ago old. And I show here that it was paid. In full at the time of treatment. In cash, actually. So I'm not sure why you even have a bill."

Interesting. Miriam said, "This is from Blue Cross. And now that you mention it, it isn't a bill, it's a statement. And I didn't realize how old it was. Sorry about that."

"No problem," the girl said, although she wasn't convincing.

"Just one thing: what was the procedure that took place? I need to make sure I've accounted for the correct one," Miriam said, stringing together a bunch of nonsense words in what she hoped sounded like an authoritative voice.

"The code listed here is for a laparoscopic inguinal hernia repair."

"Oh, okay," Miriam said, unable to keep the disappointment out of her voice. "Thanks for your help."

She was just about to hang up when the girl said, "Wait. Oh, never mind, it's nothing."

"What's nothing?"

"It says here they also did a vasectomy. But they didn't code it separately, so it didn't show up on the statement. Whatever. They tack the vasectomies on to a lot of the hernia surgeries these days, it's not a big deal."

Miriam nearly dropped the phone but took a deep breath and forced herself to stay calm as the girl continued. She thanked her lucky stars that this person appeared never to have heard of HIPAA. "Are you sure?"

"Yep. Says so right here. October nineteenth, 2013. Performed by Dr. Hershberg at Mount Sinai at eight-thirty in the morning."

"Got it. Okay. Thank you so much. You've been very helpful." Miriam quickly hung up before she could say anything suspicious.

It was unfathomable. Had he been sitting across from her, she may have murdered him.

Violating every ethical/professional bone in her body, she reflexively dialed Emily, not Karolina.

"Why are you *calling* me? What couldn't be discussed over text?"

"Graham had a vasectomy."

"What!"

"A vasectomy! He got snipped! Like, permanently."

"How do you know?"

"I just got off the phone with the doctor's office. He did it *five years ago*. Right when Karolina was trying to get pregnant! Getting IVF shots!"

"Christ. He's such a scumbag!"

Miriam smacked the table so hard her coffee splashed over the side. People around her stared, but she didn't care. "Karolina still doesn't know! You're my first call."

"No way, Miriam. Not me. You're out of your fucking mind if you think I'm going to be the one to tell her this."

"You wanted the dirt!"

"You're her lawyer. And a friend since childhood. I'm her freaking image consultant! You think I should be talking to her about her husband's surprise snipping?"

"Emily. I'm just saying that we are *both* helping her recover from this, so we should tell her together."

Emily laughed. Not nicely. "No, thank you. Did I tell you I tripped over Ashley's husband climbing all over some teenager? My policy is no drama. No way."

"Wait—what?"

"Ashley? Your friend?"

"Yes—I know. I meant . . . you saw her husband flirting with a teenager?"

"No."

"I'm confused."

"Not flirting. Fucking. Pardon the crassness, but there's really no other way to describe it."

Miriam rested her head in her palm. Her skull was suddenly throbbing sharply on one side. "You're sure? Where? Why didn't you tell me?"

"At that weird *Eyes Wide Shut* party she dragged me to. And I didn't tell you because I don't want any involvement whatsoever. But it was him."

"Oh God. What do I do?" Miriam moaned.

"Nothing! You do nothing! This has nothing to do with you. She'll hate you if they get divorced because she'll be convinced it was somehow your fault, however irrational that is. And she'll hate you if they stay together because she knows you know this humiliating thing about her. Trust me. The only way to play this one is to pretend you don't know a goddamn thing."

"She's already worried he's cheating. She found his email address on the Ashley Madison leak site."

"Shocking."

"Emily!"

"Do nothing. Karolina, though, you *have* to tell. I've always felt she doesn't hate Graham as much as she should in light of what he's done to her. This will help that. Plus, you're her lawyer."

Miriam's stomach dropped. Her call waiting rang. "Em?" she said. "It's Paul. I've got to run."

"Okay. Let me know how it goes."

Miriam clicked over. "Paul? Hey, where are you?"

"Outside. And I'm double-parked in a no-standing, so can you come out?"

"I need a second to pack up and everything."

"If I'm not here, I'm circling the block and I'll be right back." And he hung up.

Okay, then. He was a half hour early and she still had a list of things to do, but she packed up her laptop and papers and threw out her coffee. He wasn't outside when she got to the sidewalk, but he pulled up within a minute. In the red Maserati. With the top down despite the chilly day, music blaring. At least a dozen people on both sides of Bleecker turned to look.

"Can you turn that down?" she asked, trying not to sound as peeved as she felt.

"It would be criminal to turn down a sound system like this," Paul said, not noticing her irritation.

"Everyone's *staring*." She knew this was New York and no one remotely cared what car she and her husband were driving, but she hated feeling so conspicuous.

"Who cares? Come on, get in before I get a ticket."

Miriam tossed her laptop bag in the back—which was about all that could fit—and got into the passenger seat. The leather felt cold but plush, and the music beat in her chest.

Paul leaned over and gave her a kiss on the cheek. "Hi."

"Hi. Are you still up for Corner Bistro? I'm dying for a decent burger."

"Can't," he said. "I have to jump on a call before we go to the conference." He started weaving around cars and taxis in an aggressive way, in and out of his lane with no turn signals and no regard for right of way.

"Paul—"

"What? I'm driving like a New Yorker."

They didn't say another word until they were on the West Side Highway, first passing Chelsea Piers and then the giant lot where the city stored all the towed cars and finally stopping at a red light next to the *Intrepid*.

"Can we put the top up? I'm freezing," Miriam said.

Paul looked displeased. "Sure." He punched a button and the convertible instantaneously did its thing.

"Can I ask you something?"

He glanced over. Looking nervous? Dubious? Or was she imagining it?

"What do you know about Eric?"

He squinted almost imperceptibly but kept his eyes fixed on the road ahead. "In terms of?"

"Paul."

"What? That's a really vague question. I don't know him that well at all. He's made a decent effort to be friendly. He's called me to come over for poker nights and that kind of thing. You know that."

"Yes, but has he told you anything about . . . him and Ashley?"

Paul smiled. "I've told you before, honey. Guys don't talk like that. We don't sit around talking about feelings. Or our marriages."

"So you don't know . . . anything?"

Paul gazed ahead, but Miriam could've sworn she saw the briefest flicker. "Anything about what? Whether or not he's happy with her? No."

"Or if he's cheating on her?"

Paul shook his head. "He's just a local guy, I'd barely call him a friend. I'm not saying he is or he isn't cheating, just that he's not telling me about it either way. Why?"

"No reason."

"Whatever is going on, don't get involved. These things never end well."

"That's exactly what Emily said."

"Well, then she's smarter than I give her credit for."

Miriam considered Emily's noninvolvement policy. If Paul were cheating, she would want to know . . . wouldn't she? Although she could think of a few scenarios in which she actually might not want to know. How could she decide whether Ashley would or wouldn't want to know? She sighed, which Paul didn't seem to notice, and they drove the rest of the way in silence.

Later that night, as Miriam was tucking Benjamin into bed, he asked her to get under the covers and snuggle with him. How long had it been since he'd allowed this? she wondered. Six months? Longer? She nuzzled her face into his neck and breathed in his smell. Some days, as a stay-at-home mom, she wanted to slam her head against a wall from the monotony, but she couldn't deny the comfort from moments like this—moments she rarely had when working eighty-hour weeks.

When she closed his door behind her, Paul was waiting in the hallway.

"Twins down?" she asked.

He nodded. "I'm going to hit my computer for a couple hours. I have some work to catch up on."

Miriam was quiet for a second. "What about dinner? I brought home enough rolls from Yama to feed ten people."

"I'm not really hungry."

Time to trawl your Ashley Madison account? she thought. Forcing herself to act normally, she stood on tiptoe and wrapped her arms around his neck, hoping for a quick make-out, but he wriggled away and murmured something about a call.

"Even our son lets me kiss him," she murmured, but he pretended not to hear and walked downstairs. She was standing there, unsure what to do next, when her phone rang.

"Miriam?" Emily's voice was breathless, panicked. "You need to come quickly. I'm at Karolina's house. Now!" The call disconnected. Miriam immediately tried calling both Emily and Karolina and was met with voicemail.

Christ. Had Karolina swallowed a bottle of pills or something? Should she call the police? No, Emily was capable of dialing 911, this was obviously the kind of emergency that required a friend. She dashed off a text to Paul, grabbed the Yama bag from the fridge, and jumped in her car.

She barely remembered the drive to Karolina's. She tore through the front door and saw Karolina in the foyer, looking stricken.

"Oh, honey. I'm so, so sorry," Miriam said, hugging her. Karolina stood eerily rigid.

"What are you doing here?" Karolina asked.

"Oh, Emily called and said you two needed . . . would like . . . some company." She held the bag aloft. "I brought city sushi."

Karolina scrunched her perfect nose. "Um, okay. The fill-in cleaning lady took pity on me and made some salmon tonight. Did you know the caretaker couple who used to live here moved to Arizona with their daughter full-time? I didn't want the company, but now that they're gone, I want them back."

Miriam looked at her friend. There were the faintest dark circles under her eyes, but otherwise she looked as gorgeous and chic as usual in a pair of tight joggers, a cropped sweatshirt that exposed her navel and slid off her shoulder, and an adorably messy bun. "Well, you look okay . . . ," Miriam mumbled.

"Thanks, I guess?" Karolina said.

Emily appeared in the doorway behind Karolina and put a finger to her lips.

Karolina swiveled her head from one friend to the other. "What's going on?"

Emily said nothing. Karolina turned to Miriam. "Why are you here? What's so awful that you two are acting like this?"

Miriam's stomach dropped. She could *kill* Emily. "You bitch!" she said, pointing to Emily.

Emily shrugged. "This is something she should hear from one of her oldest friends, not some chick she just met."

"Oh my God, you two are scaring me! Is Harry okay?"

"No, no, it's *not* about Harry. But why don't we pour some wine and get this sushi laid out and we can all talk like reasonable people?" Miriam said in her most soothing talking-to-toddlers voice.

But Karolina wouldn't budge. "Nobody's moving until I know what's so horrible that you both had to come here to tell me."

"Graham had a vasectomy five years ago," Miriam blurted. It seemed to fly out of her mouth against her will.

A long moment of silence followed.

"No he didn't," Karolina said, sounding less angry than confused.

"Yes he did," Emily said.

Miriam could see Karolina's eyes fill as she looked her straight in the eye. "It's true," she said softly. "I'm so sorry. I spoke with the doctor's office, trying to reconcile an old bill. They told me the exact date, time, and surgeon who performed it."

"That's impossible," Karolina said. "He was tested two or three times. And they always said his sperm were fine and that the problem must be . . ."

There was a brief pause while she appeared to process this, and then, without any warning, Karolina vomited on the floor. Emily must have seen it coming because she jumped backward like a gymnast, but Miriam hadn't and her sneakers were covered. She slipped them off and peeled off her socks for good measure before taking Karolina's hand and leading her to the living room. "Here, sit. I'm going to clean that up and get you some water."

"I'll help," Emily said, and then promptly headed for the pantry to grab some bottled water, leaving Miriam to mop up the puke.

When they returned, Karolina was perched on the edge of the couch, looking slightly green. She accepted the water but made no move to open it.

"I tried Clomid and herbs and took my basal temperature and acupuncture and tested my discharge consistency, for God's sake! Seven IUIs, two egg retrievals, and three rounds of IVF. Four years of my life were spent in doctors' offices, getting poked and prodded and injected, and so many people stuck their hands inside me that I barely even noticed anymore. All of those people must have known Graham's sperm was useless, and they lied for him! I saw a fortune-teller for two hundred dollars an hour. A shrink. And the whole time, Graham *knew* none of it would work?"

No one moved.

Miriam patted Karolina's arm. "Let's talk it through."

"Talk?" Karolina said, looking directly into Miriam's eyes. "No. I don't want to talk anymore. I need to go upstairs and start preparing for jail, because I'm going to find a knife and cut the balls off that motherfucker."

21

Munching Xanax
Like Gumballs

Karolina

Karolina bolted upright in bed. The clock read 2:22 a.m. *Make a wish!* The thought popped into her head automatically. *I wish he dies.* Suddenly it didn't seem hard to understand how regular, law-abiding people became cold-blooded killers. She and Graham had fought before, and Karolina had felt every degree of anger toward him, but this was different. This was *hate*.

Shouldn't two Xanaxes last longer than two hours? She should have been mercifully blacked out until at least five. But it was as if the pills had amped her up instead of knocking her out: her heart was pounding arrhythmically, and her entire body was covered by a thin layer of sweat. How on earth was she expected to *sleep* when that monster had literally ruined her life?

What happened next wasn't so much the result of a conscious or even rational decision; Karolina barely remembered showering or pulling on jeans and a sweater, and she wasn't entirely sure she was even awake as she rooted around in the kitchen, looking for car snacks and bottles of water and stuffing them in a backpack. Which was probably why she almost had a heart attack when the lights blazed on around her.

"What the hell are you doing?" Emily asked, squinting. She was wearing a half-tee and a Hanky Panky thong and had a satin sleep mask pushed up on her forehead.

Karolina whipped around. "Leave me alone."

"Gladly," Emily said.

"It's none of your business." Karolina took a Diet Coke from the fridge.

"If I knowingly let you murder him, it's going to ruin my life too. I'm not sure how, but I'll definitely get arrested for being an accessory or something. So please, can we back off the psycho routine and cycle it down to regular crazy?"

Karolina stopped and stared at Emily. "Do you really sleep in a *thong*?"

Emily glanced down. "What else would I sleep in?"

"I bet Regan sleeps in a thong too. No, no, that's not right. She probably sleeps in one of those *Little House on the Prairie* nightgowns that make you look like a teenaged virgin. A totally innocent schoolgirl except for the fact that she's sleeping with my sociopath husband." Merely saying the word "husband" made her heart beat faster.

"Seriously, why are you packing a bag at three in the morning?"

"It's none of your business." Karolina tried to slide past Emily and through the doorway, but Emily put her arm against the frame.

"You've already said that. You can't go kill Graham. That's bad optics. The new Quinnipiac poll has your popularity above Bella Hadid's! Remember—feelings over facts! People care how you make them *feel*. Killing Graham is not a feel-good ending to this story, at least not to the general public."

Karolina's laugh sounded borderline maniacal. "I'm not going to kill him. I just need to . . . talk to him."

"Uh-huh. Talk. I'm sure. And have you thought about how Harry is going to react when you break into their house in the middle of the night and go ballistic on his father?"

Karolina stopped. She hadn't considered Harry. Emily led her by the arm to the kitchen table and poured her a glass of cold white wine.

"Shouldn't you be making me chamomile tea or something?"

"Oh, yes. Tea really helps everything." Emily sat next to her with her own glass of wine. "The only reason I'm not giving you vodka right now is because I saw you munching Xanax like gumballs a couple hours ago. And I don't need your overdose any more than I need Graham's murder."

Karolina somehow managed to laugh. Emily could make anyone laugh.

Emily said, taking a slug of wine, "You were fully going to get in your car and drive to Bethesda and show up in your old house like a total stalker and what? Shoot him? Cut his throat?"

Karolina sighed. "I hope you know me well enough to realize that if I were going to murder Graham, I'd at least hire someone."

"Well, that's a relief." Emily smiled.

They each took another sip. Karolina could feel her pulse slow.

"It's time to tell me that dirt you weren't willing to divulge before," Emily said.

"It's too awful to be delicious. It's really, really sad."

"Noted. Now tell me anyway. I can work with awful."

"You have to swear not to—"

"Stop it!" Emily said. "Next time you have one single impulse to protect him, I'd like you to remember in vivid detail shooting yourself full of hormones and going under general anesthesia to harvest your eggs so they could be fertilized with sugar water."

Karolina dug her nails into her palms.

"Exactly," Emily said. "Now dish."

"Graham was involved in a fatal car crash in high school," she said quietly. "I only know what he told me, since there's nothing written about it anywhere, but he was seventeen and had just gotten his license. He was driving home from football practice and a four-year-old girl bolted from behind a bush. He didn't even have time to step on the brake. It was instantaneous."

"No!"

"The parents were family friends and they were all out on the Hartwells' porch having cocktails when the little girl ran in front of the car."

"Oh my God."

Karolina nodded. "All I know is the girl's parents decided not to press charges. The whole thing was a terrible accident."

"They didn't press charges? *In the death of their daughter?* I'm no lawyer, but I don't think that's even their choice. Shadesville. This reeks. There was definitely a deal cut."

Karolina took a sip of water. "I really don't know. He didn't give me a lot of detail. Apparently his parents pulled a classic stiff-upper-lip WASP move and told him to buck up and move on. That he was innocent. That it was a tragedy but it wasn't his fault."

"That'll fuck you up," Emily murmured.

Karolina nodded. "He needed counseling. And what did he get? A ride to football practice the next day and a lecture from his father on 'staying focused.'"

"They sound like lovely people," Emily said. "Now I'm *certain* they paid hush money."

"Graham did say his mother visits the little girl's grave on the anniversary of the accident every year. Has never missed one. A few times she's run into the girl's mother there, and they don't really talk, they just cry together. It's so, so awful."

Emily was silent, but Karolina could see exactly what she was thinking. "You're not using this in your takedown plan," Karolina said. "It's nothing more than a terrible tragedy."

"The Hartwell family—American royalty, if we ever had it—are likely complicit in a cover-up of epic proportions. Who was bribed? What were the circumstances of the accident? Why on earth has nothing ever been reported about the accident? You think the public wouldn't be *interested*?" Emily took another sip of wine, appeared to consider something, and then drained her glass. "What's our goal, Karolina? It's Harry. It's custody. To clear your name. But we won't get there without leverage. Graham and his people are too connected. And . . . there's something else I have to tell you."

"Oh God. What now?"

Emily refilled both their glasses. "You said Graham refuses to work out at the Senate gym, right?"

Karolina squinted. She hadn't remembered mentioning that. "Yes. He said it's too cliquey. Everyone talks shop. It's not relaxing."

"So instead he goes to the Equinox near Dupont, yes?"

Karolina nodded.

"I'm happy to report that Graham has made a new friend at his gym."

"Meaning?"

"Meaning Graham has recently become enraptured with a very pretty, *very* fit brunette named Ana. Last week he began coordinating his gym visits around hers. Yesterday he asked if she wanted to get a juice together when they'd finished their workouts."

"How do you know all this?" Karolina asked.

"Because Ana works for me."

Karolina's eyes widened. "She works for you how?"

"I hired her to seduce your husband."

Karolina's laugh sounded more like a bark. "I hope you didn't pay her too much, because that's just about the easiest job in the world."

"You're paying her, actually, and she does charge quite a bit. But it's fair, I think, considering she's going to get pictures, sexts, whatever it takes."

"You hired a *prostitute* to seduce Graham?"

Emily appeared horrified. "First of all, *I* didn't hire anyone. *You* did.

But I didn't hire a *prostitute*. She's a former police officer who now does private work. Lots of corporate things and political stuff. And she's got an excellent reputation."

Karolina rested her head in both hands. "This isn't happening. This is like a bad episode of *Housewives*."

"They're all bad. But I disagree—this is brilliant! You of all people know Graham can't keep it in his pants, not even for a president's daughter and his ticket to the Democratic nomination. He's going to self-sabotage one way or another—we're merely helping it along."

"Is this even legal?"

"Karolina, get a grip! He certainly has the free will *not* to try to have sex with her. But what do you think are the chances he's not going to try?"

"Zero." Karolina sighed. How had they gotten to this point? It was gross on so many levels, but a small part of her was relieved that he would get what he deserved. A sex scandal à la Anthony Weiner. Public humiliation. Exposure for what he truly was. But what about Harry?

"They're going on their juice date today. I give it a week. The only questions are when and where."

"They'll go to her place," Karolina said. She sounded tired. "He's not a total idiot."

"I agree," Emily said. "Which is why a friend of mine has already been there and set up more spy cams than first-time parents have focused on the baby nurse. How do you think Jude Law got taken down? Or Ben Affleck? Do you really think those so-called nannies were civilians? Hell, no. They had backers like us."

Suddenly, it felt every minute of three a.m.

Karolina reached over to take Emily's glass and put it in the sink, but Emily snatched it back and finished the bottle.

"Try to sleep," Emily said. "The wine, the Xanax, the plan. You should be good for at least a few hours."

Karolina watched Emily take another long slug. During all the time they'd spent together, Emily had never opened up about herself. Her business was clearly flagging. Her husband was in Hong Kong. She seemed worn out and maybe depressed.

Karolina was about to ask her but thought better of it.

"What were you going to say?" Emily asked.

"It was nothing."

"Please, don't hold back."

"No, it's not like that. It's just . . . Are you happy?"

"What, you don't think I'm enjoying drinking refrigerated white wine at three in the morning in Greenwich, Connecticut? Olivia Belle is taking over my industry, and I'm not even making friends in the *suburbs*." Emily glanced at Karolina. "No offense."

"Listen, Emily. I remember you from the *Runway* days. You were amazing. A bitch on wheels."

Emily's face softened. Karolina saw the curl of a smile.

"You kept everyone in line. The models would talk about you, you know. You scared us."

"I did," Emily agreed. "And I ran that woman's life. New York, Paris, Milan. We were everywhere."

"Well, nothing's changed! You're still that same person. Still every bit as bitchy, unstoppable, and intimidating as the senior assistant I remember from *Runway*."

A look crossed Emily's face. "Miranda even wants to hire me back."

"For real?" Karolina asked. "What would you do?"

"Head up special events. Which basically means run the Met Ball."

Karolina whistled and suppressed a memory of her first Met Ball with Graham. She'd worn Versace. He'd looked so handsome in Tom Ford. The night had been magical, hadn't it? Or were all her good memories now suspect? "Wow."

"Yeah. If she'd offered this five years ago, I would've jumped. Now I can't really imagine it. The hours. The twenty-four/seven drama that is *Runway*. Yes, it would mean New York, but maybe L.A. has made me soft. I'm not sure moving back is worth it if it means working there again."

Karolina went to the cabinet and pulled out a packet of chamomile tea. "Have you thought about the fact that maybe it's just called growing up? Priorities changing? Which is actually a good thing." She filled the mug with boiling water from the instant hot and placed it in front of Emily.

"You sound creepily positive," Emily said, "for a person on the brink of homicide."

Karolina laughed. "I should start a new feel-good Instagram page. Post things like 'Choose happiness' and 'Be the reason someone smiles today.' Hashtag 'blessed.' Hashtag 'humbled.' I could be the next Glennon Doyle Melton. A woman of the people! Everyone will love me again. How's that for a master plan?"

Emily was nodding. "I like it. I do. I'll get right on it first thing in the morning."

"Before or after you touch base with the professional you hired to entrap my husband?"

"After. Plus, you hired her, not me. And stop calling him your husband!"

Karolina laughed, and it felt like something released inside her. "I'm really going back to bed now."

"And I'm really going to dump this tea you so kindly made for me in favor of a Valium. But thank you for the thought."

Back in her bedroom, Karolina climbed into bed. The sheets were cool and soft on her skin. She opened her Kindle and read a few pages before she felt her eyelids get heavy. Just as she was drifting off to sleep, a thought came so suddenly that she gasped. What she'd missed in all the drama of the previous day was that there wasn't a damn thing wrong with her body. Maybe, just maybe, she could have a baby after all.

22

Not the Only One
Who Can Google

Emily

The instructor in front of her was gorgeous: ripped, with longish hair he kept brushing off his square-shaped jaw, a sheen of sweat covering every inch of exposed skin. Every thirty seconds or so he would lift his head and look directly at Emily and give her that smile, the one that confirmed she was the only one in the room. Which of course she was, because she was riding on Karolina's Peloton, and the hot instructor was on the screen, and his direct eye contact with Emily was actually shared with 1,294 other home riders. No matter. She could sweat with him and his alt-country playlist all night long. She had no idea what had inspired her to get off her ass in this beautiful, empty house and get on the bike at ten o'clock in the evening, but she was going with it. This beat SoulCycle any day of the week: no people, no socializing, and she could spin in her sports bra and a pair of ripped spandex shorts. Plus, no one would have a word to say about the fact that she planned to enjoy a vodka soda during the cooldown and stretch.

Her phone rang. She wouldn't have answered it for anyone except the cop, which was who caller ID showed was calling.

"Belinda?" she said, jabbing "speaker" on her phone while simultaneously lowering the volume on the bike's screen. "What's up? Do you have an update for me?"

"Ah, Emily Charlton. The one and only. I'm delighted you picked up." The voice that came through the line was male. Older and refined. Supremely confident.

"Who's this?" Emily asked, trying to hide her surprise. Her legs began to slow.

"I'm surprised you don't know. Perhaps you should check one of your Dropcams."

"Drop—" Emily nearly dropped the phone. She stopped pedaling and unclipped from the bike.

"I'll save you the suspense, since I'm sure you're wondering. Your friend Belinda, if that's really her name, has nothing to offer you."

"Is this Graham Hartwell?"

"Senator Hartwell. Show some respect."

His voice was so authoritative, Emily actually almost apologized. Then she remembered whom she was talking to and she laughed. "Whatever, *Graham*. I'll show some respect when you do something to earn it."

There was a beat before he said, "I don't know who you think you are with this little plot of yours, but it took all of three seconds to figure out. Next time you want to send a former New York City police officer after me, I will press charges. Do we understand each other?"

The line disconnected. Emily was grateful no one was there to see how badly her hands were shaking.

Dammit. That did not go well. And if Emily were being honest, she should have predicted that very outcome. Graham was no teenaged-starlet idiot. She'd vastly underestimated him.

She walked to the kitchen and helped herself to a can of cherry-flavored seltzer she found in Karolina's fridge. After a few sips, she poured it into a glass, tossed in some ice cubes, and added enough vodka to fill it to the top. Difficult times called for extreme measures. She took a long, deep sip and, realizing it tasted like cough medicine, poured the rest in the sink. The clock on the microwave read 10:28. Where could she get a decent drink at this hour in this damn town? Were there even any actual bars? She texted Karolina, who was in Bethesda for the night visiting Harry, and the answer came back immediately:

No clue. Why? I have enough booze in that house to intoxicate a football team.

Emily wrote back: *Please never put that in writing again.*

Sorry, forgot I'm supposed to be a recovering alcoholic . . . !!!!

Emily texted Miriam next. Her reply was also instantaneous: *I can't meet you at eleven on a Tuesday night for a drink. Who do you think I am?*

Not inviting you per se—just asking where I can go.

Ah, thanks. In that case, try the Italian place by the train station. Haven't ever been later than dinner but I've heard they stay open until midnight.

Thnx. LMK if you change ur mind.

Nope.

Decades of habit forced Emily into the shower and a decent pair of jeans with a cute silk T-shirt, an open cardigan, and a swipe of lip gloss. Her only concession was her hair: if she sprayed it with enough dry shampoo to degrease an ocean oil slick and wrapped it on top of her head, hopefully no one would notice how badly it needed a wash. She waited outside for her Uber driver, a much too chatty older woman whom Emily had to ask to stop talking, and within fifteen minutes she was contentedly settled on a high stool with an admittedly excellent dirty martini in hand.

"Can I get you anything else?" the bartender asked. He was in his thirties and cute enough. "Maybe an appetizer before the kitchen closes?"

Emily offered him a real smile. "Thanks, I'm good with this. I'll be asking you for another soon."

"I look forward to it," he said and walked to the other end to help another customer. Was he flirting with her? Was she even still flirt-worthy? Alistair had seemed to think so, but then he'd dropped off the face of the earth. *Don't think about it!* she willed herself, to little effect. *Ugh*, she cringed just thinking about the Photoshopped boob pic, texted to him right after her own husband hadn't even bothered reacting to it. And nothing. Nothing! It was mortifying. She'd checked a hundred times to make sure she'd sent it to the right person, but their text history didn't lie. And if that weren't enough, he had his freaking *read receipts* turned on. It hadn't vanished into the ether; it had gone exactly where it was intended and been opened and evaluated and then . . . nothing. Not so much as a fucking thumbs-up emoji.

"I'll be right back," Emily told the bartender with a wink, placing a napkin over her martini, although there was barely a sip left. She was heading toward the back of the restaurant, looking for the ladies' room, when she noticed a couple tucked into a booth with high wooden walls. In front of each of them was a plate of heavenly-looking pasta and a bowl-size glass of red wine. There was a personal lamp mounted on the wall right above the table, and the glow lit up the man's face at the exact same second that he glanced up and looked directly at Emily. It was Alistair. Jesus Christ. What were the freaking chances?

"Emily," he murmured with a smile that she couldn't quite read. "What a surprise seeing you here."

"I could say the same," she said, sneaking a peek at the woman he was with. Brunette and attractive. She was dressed in a nicely tailored suit, probably Theory, and her hair was in need of a highlights refresh, but her skin was perfection. Why did she look familiar?

"Haven't I told you that I come here three nights a week for din-ner?" Alistair said, his dimples showing. "Tonight's a bit later than usual, but we both had late meetings."

For a moment Emily figured they worked together, but then something clicked: this woman wasn't his coworker, she was his ex-wife. Granted, Emily had only Googled her briefly, just long enough to know she wasn't still a threat, and yet here she was, tucked into a cozy booth with her supposed ex-husband, sharing a romantic late-night meal.

"I'm Emily Charlton," she said with a broad fake smile. "You must be Alistair's ex. Don't worry, he only has nice things to say!"

The woman made a face like she'd spotted a dead rat. "Excuse me?"

"Oh, it's not like we sit around talking about you, but he showed me pictures of the kids and said what a great mom you are."

"Emily." Alistair's voice was grave, as if he were announcing a death. "This is Louisa. She is not my ex. And we are on a *date*."

Emily's hand flew to her mouth. "But they look . . . so . . . My God, when they say men have types, it's really accurate."

"And you are?" Louisa asked. She had regained her composure and looked like she sensed a fight and wasn't planning to back down.

"I'm Emily Charlton," she said.

Alistair helpfully explained, "Yes, Emily is married to a friend of mine. Miles is a good bloke. Haven't seen him in a while. Tell him not to be such a stranger, okay?"

Emily felt her mouth fall open. That *asshole*. Who did he think he was? And more to the point, how did he know?

Alistair turned back to Louisa and clinked his wineglass to hers. As Emily continued walking to the bathroom, she could hear him say, "She's a little mental, that one. But she means well." Louisa's laugh tinkled like a wind chime.

She'd barely finished washing her hands when her phone lit up with a text.

You're not the only one who can Google

Followed by a thumbs-up emoji. Emily tried not to scream.

She had no choice but to walk past the happy couple on her way back to the bar and was irritated to overhear them discussing Trump's Russian involvement. Louisa was engaged with current events too? How lucky for him.

"Can I get you another now?" the cute bartender asked.

240 · LAUREN WEISBERGER

Emily drained her drink and pushed the glass toward him. "Yes, please. And an IV if you have one."

"Is this seat taken?" The voice behind her was a whisper; the only reason she could hear it at all was because it was so close to her ear. She whipped around and nearly fell off her bar stool.

"Miles? What are you doing here?" She jumped off the stool and threw her arms around her husband's neck.

"I couldn't let my baby drink alone," he said, helping her back on her stool and then taking the one next to her. He tucked his overstuffed garment bag at their feet and placed his laptop bag on the bar.

"Oh my God. This is crazy! When did you get here? How long are you staying? And how did you know where to find me?"

He grinned and Emily thought: *He is really freaking good-looking. Why am I always forgetting how much I want him the second he's out of sight?*

"I landed at JFK an hour ago. I wanted to surprise you. I'm here for two nights. And I showed up at Miriam's house with a giant bouquet of baggage-claim flowers, but she said you're staying at Karolina's now, and that I could probably find you here. I left the flowers for her after one of the kids came downstairs crying. I think I woke them."

"Why are you only here for two days? How can they do that to you? It's not even long enough to get over the jet lag." Emily took his hand in hers.

"Because I'm not here for work. I missed my girl. I have a meeting on the twelfth that I can't miss, so it'll have to be a quick visit." He leaned over and kissed her, and Emily immediately felt her body respond. "Is Karolina going to mind if I stay with you tonight, or should we get a hotel room for some privacy?" Miles murmured.

"Karolina is in Bethesda for the night. The place is all ours."

This time when he kissed her, he slipped his tongue in her mouth and lightly bit her bottom lip the way he knew she loved. "That is very good news." And then to the bartender: "Check, please."

Emily took his hand and followed him to the door. She couldn't help but give one final look around the restaurant.

"Did you forget something?" Miles asked, holding her hand with one of his and slinging his bags with his other.

"What? No, of course not. Come on, let's get back home and I'll show you this new lace thingy I got. Only there's not much lace. And the crotch seems to be missing . . ."

23

Home to the Custom-Fit Vagina

Miriam

What do they put in these Goldfish to make them so addictive? Miriam wondered for the thousandth time as she shoved a handful in her mouth. It wasn't like they were Reese's peanut butter cups. Hell, they couldn't even compete with a good old-fashioned Dorito. They were a toddler's snack cracker! But she found them so damn delicious.

So much for the calories burned on that three-mile walk-run, she thought, chewing loudly and enjoying her quiet, empty kitchen. Click, click, click. Miriam typed and clicked, typed and clicked, allowing only a few seconds to study each result before moving on to the next. She was a master Googler, researcher extraordinaire, and her investigation into Graham's little doctor visits had yielded excellent results. Next up: the arrest. She needed all the intel available before suggesting a meeting with Trip, Graham's lawyer, and decided she'd start with an exhaustive history of DUIs in Maryland—specifically anyone who had managed to clear his or her name after refusing a sobriety test. After that, she'd start trying to find out the names of all the cops on duty the night Karolina was arrested—not just the ones who'd brought her in—and see if anyone remembered anything suspicious. It wasn't going to be easy, but she was sure she could uncover *something*.

Paul walked down the stairs in jeans and a fitted T-shirt, looking freshly showered.

Miriam clicked off the sordid Graham headlines.

"Whatcha looking up?"

"I just finished an article on how progressive certain towns in Montana are. Maybe we should move there?" she said, unsure why she didn't want to talk about Graham and Karolina with him. It wasn't a lie—she had just read that article—but what did she think she was hiding?

Paul peeled the top off a yogurt, licked it, and tossed it in the garbage. "Didn't you just complain bitterly about how hard it was to get a drink in Utah?"

Miriam nodded. "Our kids would have a huge geographic advantage when applying to college. They could name their Ivy."

"Benjamin is only eight!"

"Yes, but it's never too early to think about these things. While all these Greenwich crazies spend the next ten years and tens of thousands of dollars on tutors and coaches and camps, we can move to Montana. And our kids will be just as likely to get in, if not more so."

Paul scooped the last of his yogurt. How could he finish an entire cup in three spoonfuls? "You sound like an insane person. You might have gone to Harvard and I went to Arizona State?"

"So?" she asked.

"So . . . we're both doing fine."

"Uh-huh."

"Come here," he said, wrapping his arms around her. "What are we fighting about?"

Miriam didn't say anything.

"We have a great home in a great town. The kids are thriving. You've made friends. What's so awful about where we're living?"

"Nothing's awful. That's not my point."

"Well, then what is your point?"

"I don't know . . . I just feel like we need a change."

Paul nudged her chin up so she was looking at him. "Maybe what we need is to relax and enjoy it. Three kids in the span of three years. My company took off. You left your job. We moved out of the city. I'm not sure more change is the answer."

"You're right," Miriam said.

"Good." He kissed her on the cheek. Always the cheek.

"Where are you off to?" she asked when he pulled his fleece off the hook in the mudroom.

"Oh, a few of the guys are meeting up at the gym. For a squash game before work."

"At ten in the morning?"

"Yeah, one of the younger guys thought it would be good team building."

"So . . . where's your gym bag?" Miriam asked as innocently as she could manage.

Paul looked momentarily confused. "Gym bag? Oh, it's in the car already. I'll be home in time for dinner, okay? Love you, honey."

"You too . . ."

Miriam listened as the garage door opened, Paul's car started, and the garage door closed. She watched through the mudroom door as the Maserati pulled away before she typed in the website that revealed all the hacked Ashley Madison user information, and then she searched every email address she knew for Paul. Once again, nothing turned up. Why did she keep doing it? She liked to think that if he were going to cheat on her, he'd at least be smart enough to use a fake email address. She'd never know if he didn't want her to know, it was time to accept that. But did she really think Paul was capable of it? Then again, had you told her a couple years earlier that he'd be all but retired, living in the suburbs, playing squash and poker, and driving around a Maserati, she would've laughed herself to death. There was something contagious about suburban living that she didn't remember from the city. When everyone you spoke to all day, every day, wore glitter headbands and yoga pants, it became normal.

Miriam glanced at the clock. It was time to get dressed or she was going to be late to the breakfast. When Ashley had asked Miriam if she'd like to join a weekly breakfast chat with a group of local moms, Miriam had initially begged off. Breakfast chat? What the hell was that? But then she tried to figure out what else she was doing at ten-thirty in the morning on a Friday. Or any day, really. Ashley had assured her a hundred times that it was fun and relaxed and super-casual—that everyone came in workout clothes—but Miriam knew better by now. Even though it took nearly an hour, she showered, shaved her legs, blew out and straightened her hair, applied full makeup, and dressed in a pair of newly ripped jeans and a rag & bone cold-shoulder sweater. Was she trying too hard to look twenty-five instead of thirty-five? she wondered as she grabbed her purse and jumped into her Highlander. Probably. But so was everyone else.

The moment she walked into the hostess's dining room, Miriam could see that once again she had seriously miscalculated. Eight women clad exclusively in dry-wicking stretch fabrics sat around the table, nibbling on blueberries and throwing back Bellinis. All had their hair pulled into ponies or buns or glitter stretch bands; all wore cropped Lululemon leggings and tanks with built-in bras; the only thing that varied was the shade of neon on their Nike sneakers. No makeup. Sweaty-looking. Just as Ashley had promised.

"Oh, didn't Ashley tell you?" Evie, their hostess, asked Miriam as she handed her a Bellini. "We schedule our breakfast meetings for ten-thirty so everyone can come right from their nine a.m. Soul classes or CrossFit or SLT or Bar Method or Orangetheory or beach boot camp or whatever."

"Yes, and it gives us plenty of time to get drunk then sober up before pickup at three!" another woman called, raising her champagne flute in the air.

"Can't pull a Karolina Hartwell," Claire said, rolling her eyes. "My God. A DUI with kids in the car? Life-ending."

"You'd have to move," Evie said, sipping her cocktail. "Just list your house and get the hell out of town, because it's over."

Ashley said, "Karolina is actually a friend of Miriam's."

The room got so silent Miriam could hear someone swallow. This was almost an entirely different group of women than the ones who were at the sex-toy party she'd attended. Ashley had told her these women were a sort of rival clique with little overlap.

"She's a really good person, and this whole situation is just . . . a giant misunderstanding." Miriam took the only empty seat, at the head, and helped herself to a bowl of yogurt and a blueberry mini-muffin.

The women exchanged glances and moved on.

"Di, did you get Andrew to agree to Jamaica for Christmas next year?" said a tall, thin woman in all-black spandex. "I have to pay the deposit this week."

Di, a pretty blonde who looked to be in her early thirties, shook her head as though something grave had happened. "I keep trying! I can't reach him at all during the day when he's at work, and when he comes home at night, he doesn't want to talk about any planning. It's so frustrating!"

Nods all around.

"I'm sure he'd rather rent the villa with you guys than go to my parents' in Scottsdale again. Go ahead and count us in."

This got everyone talking about their Christmas plans, despite the fact that it wasn't yet Memorial Day: Montego Bay, Turks and Caicos, the new Aman in the Dominican. Which quickly segued into plans for Presidents' Week (Galápagos, Alaska, fjords in Finland, shopping in Paris) and ended in a heated debate about the best place for spring skiing out west: Deer Valley, Jackson Hole, or Aspen.

Evie walked around the table, refilling champagne glasses. "Would anyone prefer a Bloody Mary? I can ask Mina to make up a batch."

A handful of women, including Miriam, raised their hands. Why not? Champagne gave her a headache, and what else was she going to drink at eleven in the morning? Coffee? Juice? She lived in Greenwich now. *Please.*

The woman sitting to Miriam's left turned and introduced herself as Josie. "How old are your kids?" Josie asked.

"Oh, I have an eight-year-old boy and five-year-old boy-girl twins," Miriam said, barely noticing the assumption that she had children, something she never would have assumed of anyone in New York City. "What about you?"

The woman smiled and Miriam couldn't tell if it was one of bitterness or exhaustion or joy. "Five, actually."

"Wait—five children? Or five years old?"

Another indiscernible smile. "Oldest boy is four. Then a three-year-old girl and a two-year-old girl. Of course we thought we'd roll the dice for one more boy—my husband's idea—and we got twins. Identical boys, eighteen months. I think we're probably done."

"What—probably?" Miriam hated to sound so horrified, but never in her life had she met someone with five children under four. How was this woman even alive right now?

"Well, you never really know, do you? I'm only thirty-three."

"Yes, of course. You have lots more time. Lots," Miriam hurried to say, but Josie had already excused herself to refresh her drink.

"Don't let her get to you," Ashley whispered, leaning in.

"My God," Miriam said, shaking her head. "How does she raise all those kids?"

"She doesn't."

"Doesn't work?"

"Doesn't raise the kids," Ashley said. "She's one of those who thinks of kids as a status symbol. Like, the more you have, the more money you have. She has two au pairs, a full-time live-out driving nanny, and weekend help all day Saturday and Sunday. She's not exactly overextended."

"Still. Five kids under four? And she looks like that? It's so epically unfair."

"You set up a meeting with Dr. Lawson and you could look like that too," Ashley murmured under her breath. "He has offices in the city and in Greenwich. Does beautiful work and is very discreet. Even his waiting rooms are totally private. Just say the word."

"There is no way plastic surgery gave her that body." Miriam looked at Josie's long legs and the nearly nonexistent hips and the long, flowing beach waves.

"No, not all of it. Good genes gave her the legs. Near-starvation and three hours a day of cardio make her skinny. But the tight abs? The pert nose? The cheerleader breasts?" Ashley cupped her own breasts here and pushed them up toward her neck. "Those are all Dr. Lawson's. Not to mention the well-Botoxed forehead and the plumped-up lips. Tammy, a nurse in his office, did those."

"Wow," Miriam breathed. "No wonder everyone looks so much better than me." She'd always figured it was stunningly obvious when someone had plastic surgery: the Jennifer Grey nose, the Renée Zellweger lips, the Joan Rivers pulled-too-tight face, the Heidi Pratt boobs. But every last inch of Josie looked natural and in proportion.

Ashley glanced around the table. "By my count, every single woman at this table has had *something* done except one."

"Who? Evie? She doesn't seem like the type."

"You."

"Oh, come on. You can't be serious," Miriam said.

"I'm completely serious. Every single one."

"What did you have?" Miriam couldn't envision that a single thing about perky blond Ashley wasn't God-given. Except maybe the highlights. But even those looked sun-kissed and natural.

"Me?" Ashley sipped her mimosa. "Please. What *haven't* I had done? I was scheduled to get my eyes done in eight weeks, but I think I'm going to do my vagina instead."

"Your . . . vagina?"

Ashley nodded. "I've been thinking about it forever, ever since Claire did it. You remember meeting her for the first time there, right? At the sex-toy party?"

Miriam squinted. She vaguely recalled the hostess saying she'd just gotten her vagina "done," but no one had elaborated.

Ashley continued, "Things with Eric are still up in the air. He knows I know about Ashley Madison, and he's saying all the right things. It's going to take some time to figure out how we move forward, together or separately. So I figure do the vag now and it'll pay dividends no matter what: either for Eric, who may think twice about affairs with married women if his own wife is like a teenager down there. Or for the next man. If I have to be back out there dating again"—with this, she shuddered—"then you better believe I'm going to give myself every advantage."

"I . . ." Miriam coughed. What did it mean to have one's vagina done? Which part, exactly? And what did they do? "I'm not totally sure what you mean."

"About what?"

"About having surgery on your . . . you know. Is it because you pee when you sneeze? My OB said that happens to everyone after kids."

Ashley smiled and patted Miriam's hand as if she were seriously impaired. "There's no right fit for everyone. Some fix the outer area strictly for aesthetics. Others have their pelvic floor rebuilt. And others have everything tightened to make sex better. It's all perfectly normal. Commonplace, actually."

Miriam laughed. She couldn't help it.

"What, you think I'm kidding?" Ashley turned to face the rest of the table. "Ladies? Sorry to interrupt, everyone, but my friend Miriam here needs a bit of clarification. Do you mind participating in a little informal survey?"

Seven heads swiveled toward them and Miriam felt herself blush. "Forget it, I believe you," she whispered to Ashley.

"Now, we are totally off the record here. But we're all friends, right?" A few of the women looked nervous. "How many of you have had plastic surgery?"

There was a brief hesitation before three women raised their hands.

"Ladies, come on, now," Ashley said with an encouraging smile.

The remaining four raised their hands.

"And how many of you would do it again?"

All seven hands remained raised and Ashley added hers.

"Now, how many have done your lady parts? I only ask because I'm scheduled for surgery with Dr. Lawson in just a few weeks, as soon as camp starts. And I'm a little nervous," Ashley said, letting the last part hang in the air.

"Oh, don't be nervous," said a pale redhead in some sort of strappy workout sweatshirt. "You'll love how you look in a bathing suit. And *Eric* will love how it feels."

"Agreed," said the petite blonde with blindingly white teeth next to her. "It's almost annoying how much Roger wants it now that I've had it custom-fit."

There was so much to unpack there—so much that sounded utterly and completely mysterious—that Miriam didn't know where to start.

"I have to say, though, that I would actually recommend Dr. Fine-Steinberg instead of Dr. Lawson. I don't know about your husbands, but mine was much more comfortable having a woman handle him down there than a man," said a strikingly beautiful woman with a deep tan and a heart-shaped face.

"Agreed a hundred percent," said the woman next to her.

Everyone looked to Ashley, who turned to Miriam. "See? It's pretty standard fare."

"Wait. I still don't understand. What does she mean, you'll like how you look in a bathing suit? Don't you, like, wear a bikini bottom to cover that part up?"

"She means a little snip and sew and you don't have to be super-self-conscious anymore that your labia is hanging down like the meats at a deli counter," Evie said, and the table broke into appreciative—and understanding—laughter.

"I don't think my . . . I don't think it, um, hangs any lower than it should." Miriam couldn't bring herself to say "labia" in front of all these people.

The pretty redhead spoke up. "Look, I'm obviously not familiar with your labia, but if you're in your mid-thirties and you've had a couple or three kids, then it's likely things aren't where they should be."

"Yeah, and I challenge you to find something less attractive than camel toe," Josie added.

"Camel toe?" was all Miriam could say.

"It's when you're wearing something really fitted and—"

"No, I know what it means," Miriam said. "I just didn't really realize it was something to consider."

"Well, it is," Ashley said. "Men hate it."

"I didn't know that." Miriam drained the rest of her Bellini. "So they . . . fix it in this type of surgery?" she asked, clearing her throat.

"That and more," Ashley said with an authoritative nod.

"You said that men feel more comfortable with a female doctor? What do they have to do with this?"

There was a beat of silence, and then the pretty, petite blonde asked in a sugar-sweet voice with a hint of a Southern accent, "Where are you from, Miriam?"

"From? Oh, everywhere, really. My parents were diplomats, so we moved all over. But I, um, we actually moved out here last fall from New York."

"And none of your New York City friends had their lady parts custom-fit?" the blonde asked.

"A bunch had episiotomies and various stitches after childbirth, but I'm not totally sure what you mean by custom-fit . . ."

The women exchanged glances as though silently debating who

was going to field this one. Finally, Evie said, "So long as they're putting you under and getting everything on the outside in tip-top shape, it makes sense to have them tighten up everything on the inside too."

"Of course." Miriam nodded like she was cool and got it.

"So your husband gets himself aroused, and the doctor measures his length and girth, and then he can customize your vag to fit your husband perfectly. Not too loose, not too tight. Just right."

"Wait—is that even legal?"

The women laughed. Ashley asked, "A show of hands, please?"

Four women raised their hands. And Ashley was planning to do it, which would make a clean fifty percent of the room.

Ashley faced Miriam. "See? There's no way that only women in Greenwich do it. Everyone does. We're just the only ones who are honest about it."

The pale redhead laughed. "I'll have to disagree with you there," she said to Ashley. "I don't think we're exactly honest about it, at least not outside this room. There are more women in this town with 'diastases' "—she air-quoted the word—"than can be medically warranted."

"Diastases?" Miriam whispered to Ashley.

"When the stomach muscles become separated from pregnancy. It can be a real thing, like a serious problem for some people, but everyone I know says they have it so they can justify their tummy tucks."

"And hernias," Evie called out. "Have you noticed how many women between the ages of thirty-five and forty-five desperately need hernia repair? If that's not a euphemism for a tummy tuck, nothing is."

Everyone laughed. "I told people that," the petite blonde said.

"Me too," Josie added.

"My personal favorite is when you say you're having a lift just because you got a little saggy after babies. Um, I'm sorry, if the doctor is putting silicone into your breasts, it no longer qualifies as a lift."

More laughter. Suddenly, the conversation shifted to summer camp, and Miriam couldn't wait to tell someone about this new development.

Paul? Emily? Karolina? It was something they all needed to hear: it was totally insane.

"What are you, like, Orthodox or something?" Emily said when she called her on the drive home. "Yes, it's super-trendy now. Big deal. News flash: girls kiss other girls, and it doesn't mean they're lesbians. Buckle your seat belt for this one: people meet each other on Tinder and have random sex. Like, totally random. No one even calls the next day! Can you imagine?"

"Emily, I'm not that bad!"

"Hey, if the penis fits . . ."

"Really?"

"Sorry. But seriously, Miriam, nothing you're telling me is remotely surprising."

"Having it custom-fit to their husbands?"

"Bespoke vaginas are the new Birkin bags."

"Lovely, Emily. Do you sit around and worry about your camel toe in a bathing suit?"

"Of course not. My vag is pristine. Pure as the morning snow."

Miriam swerved a bit to avoid clipping an oncoming car on the narrow two-lane street. "I can name twenty guys off the top of my head who I know for a fact sullied your snow," she said.

"At least I haven't pushed three eight-plus-pound babies out of there!"

"I worry about every single freaking thing on my body—except for the way my vagina looks in a bikini bottom."

There was a moment of quiet on the line, and Miriam wondered if they'd been disconnected. But then she heard Emily say, super-slowly and with obvious delight, "Well, maybe you should."

"Ha ha. Listen, can we please talk about Karolina for a minute? She told me about the ex-cop setup. Emily, you'll get yourself sued—or arrested. Please stop it. We need leverage, but it's not helping anyone to toe the law."

"Spoken like a lawyer."

"Spoken like someone with half a brain! Seriously, Em. We're close. I'm sure I'm going to find something soon, and we can get Harry back."

"Good. You keep working like an eager lawyer beaver, Miriam, and I'll keep doing what I do. Because I'll tell you this right now, I'm not stopping until Graham is *finished*."

24

The Tides Are Turning and the Tears Are Terrific

Karolina

"I love you, Mom. I'll see you at visiting day?" Harry asked, his brow furrowing in that way it always did when he was uncertain.

"Of course, honey. Have the best time, and I'll see you in a few weeks." Karolina moved her lips close to the phone's camera and kissed it. She could see Harry blush, but he smiled too.

"Mom? You'll definitely be there, right? Even though Dad will be too?"

"Yes, love. I wouldn't miss it for the world. You remembered to pack extra Claritin, right? In a package labeled for the nurse? The dissolvable tabs?"

"Uh-huh. I got them. I checked off everything on the packing list you sent. I have it all."

"I'm so proud of you. Packing yourself up for the whole summer isn't easy," she said, her voice cracking a bit. "Next summer I promise I'll be there to help."

They said goodbye, and when the FaceTime disconnected, Karolina exhaled. She missed Harry desperately, but somehow it was easier knowing he'd be out of Graham's clutches too. Plus, getting him safely tucked away at camp was perfect timing for the rollout Emily had planned.

The makeup artist, a surprisingly unattractive, overweight woman with both bad skin and bad makeup, sighed loudly. "Please hold still. Just a bit longer."

Karolina watched as the woman applied dots of concealer the size of marbles under her eyes and spread them around with a spackle-like tool. She tried not to stress about her too-short hair. "Isn't that, ah, a bit heavy? I mean, I know I must look tired these days, but that seems . . . I don't know . . . excessive."

The woman said nothing.

Emily swept into the room, bringing with her the smell of cigarette smoke. "Looking good, ladies," she said without looking.

"Really? Because I have *never* had makeup done like this," Karolina hissed.

"That's *exactly* the point," Emily said, hanging a half-dozen outfits on a wheeled garment rack. She held up the skirt suits one by one. Each one was a solid jewel color with a knee-length skirt and zero shape.

"They all look like something my Polish grandmother would wear to Christmas services," Karolina persisted.

"Yes. Not a single woman in this room will be threatened by you today. And that's what matters."

"Threatened? I may scare them!" Karolina said, now eyeing the bright rouge the woman was circling into her cheeks.

"That's fine too."

"Seriously, Emily, this is going too far. I chopped off all my hair, like you said. I'm in full old-lady makeup. Can't I at least wear something decent? A simple dress, even?"

Emily sighed. "I can agree to Lilly Pulitzer. Nothing else, I'm afraid."

"I cannot wear Lilly Pulitzer!" Karolina said, thinking of a recent photo of Regan and Graham at the golf club where Regan was in head-to-toe Lilly.

"Your call." Emily shrugged.

"Hold still," the makeup lady said with obvious irritation.

Karolina raised her eyebrows at Emily, who just laughed. "Seriously, Emily. Are you sure about all this? It seems extreme. And it makes me nervous that Graham figured out that whole thing with the ex–police officer. I just don't know if—"

"Listen!" Emily held up her hand. "Feeling over fact! No one cares what actually happened. No one cares if you're guilty or innocent. No one cares about legality and details. The only thing that matters is how they *feel* about you. How they viscerally react to you when they see you, hear you, meet you. The rest of it, for better or worse, is noise. And the sooner you accept that, the better off we'll be."

Karolina nodded. Emily said everything with such confidence. She reminded herself that Emily was her best—and possibly only—shot.

"Okay, let's review," Emily said. "Donna will introduce you right before lunch is served—"

"I smile in an accessible but not sexy way. I talk about how my most important job is to be a great mom, and that's exactly what I'm going to focus on, and how I want to empower other, less privileged moms toward the same goal. How's that?"

Emily was typing something into her phone. "What? Oh, good. That's good." She looked up. "Remember: these women can sympathize with too much drinking. This is Fairfield County, Connecticut, which must have more functioning alcoholics per square foot than anywhere in the world except maybe Moscow. Don't be ashamed to admit it. But whatever you do, don't mention Graham's name! Not only are we look-ing to disassociate you from him, but it's too risky with this audience. Plenty of women who pretend they're liberal secretly vote Republican, but you can't depend on it—a fair number really are bleeding hearts, even when it goes against their own financial interests. But their husbands would murder them if they knew. Basically, everyone lies. It's impossible to tell. So don't even go there, okay?"

"Okay."

"Otherwise, I think you're ready. I called the local media; the event raises a boatload of money and they have nothing else to do. I have commitments from a few city and two national outlets who would never waste their time with this but are here because I leaked it would be your first public appearance since the arrest. So this is an opportunity to practice. Got it?"

"Yes," Karolina said, although her stomach churned with nerves. Why was it that she could walk a catwalk in front of celebrities or half-naked, but she felt intense anxiety standing before a couple hundred housewives?

"Good. And remember: Miriam is working on getting the Breathalyzer lie debunked. But until she's there, you have to make nice with the audience. Don't admit it, but don't be confrontational and accusatory until we have proof. Okay, finish up here and put the clothes on. I'm going to check on a few things, and I'll be back in a minute."

Karolina changed into the electric blue skirt suit, the least hideous on offer, and followed Emily down the hall to the banquet room of the Greenwich Golf and Yacht. She wondered if she was doing the right thing.

"Darling!" the blond woman in charge of the luncheon called out when she saw Karolina. "Don't you look . . . different! My, I have to say, I love what you've done with your hair."

"You do?" Karolina asked, touching it self-consciously.

"Love."

Karolina shot a glance to Emily, who smiled back at her knowingly. *Of course she loves it*, Emily's smile said.

"Thank you so much for having me today," Karolina said with as much grace as she could muster. "I helped raise money for underprivileged children in Bethesda, and it means a lot that you invited me to help out here today."

"Oh, please. We should be thanking you," the blond woman said, waving at the crowd, all of whom seemed to be watching from the round luncheon tables. "Your appearance filled the room."

Karolina suffered through a few more passive-aggressive comments before the woman finally led her to a staging area with a podium.

"Ladies, may I have your attention, please?" the woman said, tapping on the microphone. "Can you hear me?"

There were murmurs and nods.

"Wonderful. Thank you for taking time out of your busy schedules to join us for this very important lunch today. Without your continued support, we would not be able to fund our children's program so generously. Thanks to you, deserving children from less privileged families in our community and the surrounding neighborhoods have access to quality after-school care, summer camps, and nutritious meals on weekends and in the summer, when they aren't able to access their free lunches at school."

The room clapped politely.

"Now I'm delighted to introduce you to our guest of honor. Ms. Karolina Hartwell was an accomplished fashion model, as you all know, and now she works tirelessly on behalf of underprivileged children. She is a stepmother herself, to a twelve-year-old boy, and the wife"—here she paused and looked to Karolina with a questioning expression, which Karolina pretended she didn't understand—"of the esteemed junior senator from the state of New York, Graham Hartwell. Please join me in welcoming her."

Karolina inhaled at the sound of Graham's name—Emily would not be happy. The applause was not exactly overwhelming, but Karolina was too nervous to care.

She cleared her throat and leaned toward the microphone. Her accent became more pronounced and her voice shook when she spoke in front of crowds. The women peering up at her were all probably thinking of Karolina, in a drunken stupor, driving their own children home.

"Good morning, everyone," she said shakily, and immediately realized it was afternoon. "I'm honored to be invited here today. This is such a wonderful organization, and it does so much to help children. As so many of you surely know, I, um . . ." Karolina's voice cracked and she felt herself flush with embarrassment. "I have struggled myself recently. But I can promise that I'm doing everything within my power to make it right again."

Karolina saw the women's expressions turn from suspicious to sympathetic instantaneously. She hated the idea of copping to a lie, but she trusted Emily's strategy, and she desperately hoped Miriam would find something to clear her name. She didn't know what it was, exactly— the relief she felt when she realized they didn't all hate her after all, or the embarrassment she felt at having to admit to something humiliating in front of all these people, or maybe the nerves—but the swiftness of her tears surprised her so much that she could barely speak. Her body was wracked with sobs, fat tears falling from her face directly onto the microphone. When she tried to wipe them away, her hands came away streaked in black mascara.

"I'm so sorry," she managed to choke out just before the blond lady came rushing onstage like a flowery linebacker.

"Mrs. Hartwell, thank you so much for your honesty," the woman said into the microphone. Then she turned to Karolina and whispered into her ear, "Why don't you head to the ladies' room for a few minutes and I'll take over here? I'll come check on you just as soon as I can."

Karolina nodded and tried to hold her head high as she walked off the podium, but at the very last moment her heel caught the bottom step and she pitched forward. She regained her balance before she fell, but not before the entire room could see her matronly skirt tear from the slit in the back.

"I'm sorry," she said again, louder this time since she didn't have a mic, and fled toward the back doors. She could feel the stares of two hundred women strike into her like a laser. Thankfully the bathroom was directly outside the banquet hall and was empty when she ran in. She felt like she might throw up. Had she ever made a bigger fool of herself? For a day that was supposed to be her practice for the real thing, she had screwed it up beyond description.

Karolina forced herself to look at her reflection in the mirror as she splashed cold water on her face. To say it was a horror show was an epic understatement. Her eyes were bloodshot. Black mascara streaked down both cheeks. Her new haircut was stuck to her face from the tears and her nervous perspiration. The ridiculous round circles of blush had run into sad-clown streams.

When Emily rushed in, Karolina braced herself.

"I just, I—" And before Karolina could say another word, she dissolved into tears again.

"You bitch," Emily said with a slow smile.

Karolina looked up. "What?"

"That was fucking brilliant, Lina! Brilliant."

Emily was doing an actual jig in front of the sinks. "That was so well played, I don't even know what to say!" she crowed. "I mean, a tear or two—fine. But actual hysterical sobbing? That was masterful. I bow down to you." And she did just that.

"I didn't do it on purpose," Karolina tried to say, but it came out more like a whisper. "I just . . . lost control."

"Yeah, I'd say so! In the best way possible at the best possible time. You're a goddess." Emily seemed to notice Karolina trying to clean herself up and rushed over. "No, no. Don't fix it all. You look like something the cat dragged in, and that's exactly how we're going to keep it."

"You can't possibly think I'm going back out there," Karolina said, backing away from Emily as though she were a rabid raccoon.

"Of course you are. Come on, I'll go with you," Emily said, and clamped her hand firmly around Karolina's forearm, walking her toward the door.

"No way. I made a complete idiot of myself! And didn't you say

New York and national media are here too?" Karolina covered her face with her free hand as they exited into the hallway. "I want to die."

"Oh, please, stop with the dramatics. I literally couldn't have scripted it better. I'm the one who should be ashamed that I didn't think of tears first. Now you have to march back in there, take your seat, nibble your lunch, and answer all their questions as they approach you to offer their sympathy. I wasn't going to go here yet, but I think in light of the day's developments, now would be an excellent time to let slip that Graham isn't letting you see Harry. And how it's breaking your heart."

Karolina had to run in her heels to keep up with Emily's pace. "But that's not really true," she said. "He's not forbidding me from seeing him. I've gone to swim meets and had solo dinners with him. He's going to stay with me for the weekend after he gets home from camp."

"Details," Emily said, waving her hand. "I have one word, Karolina. Vasectomy. Let me do my work."

As Emily predicted, she was practically swarmed when she returned to her table. Women crowded around her, vying for space.

"You poor thing. My mother drank too much too. Now my husband does. I can completely relate."

"Oh my, I'm going through a divorce right now also. It's so hideous, isn't it?"

"I got a DUI when I was in college. Thank God I didn't have children yet, but I would die if my mom friends knew about it."

Karolina nodded and tried to enjoy the sympathy. After all, she deserved it.

One gaunt woman with a traumatized expression grabbed Karolina's arm and whispered, "Whatever you do, don't give him an inch with the custody agreement. They all know that's the only thing you care about anyway."

Emily stepped in before she could answer. "That's very good advice," she said, apropos of nothing. "I hope you don't mind if I steal her away? Her ex-husband is trying to keep her from seeing their son, and we need to make sure she keeps her energy up for that important battle."

"He is not! What is he, some kind of monster?"

"Senator Hartwell should be ashamed of himself, using the child as a pawn like that."

"Go on, now, and make sure that man knows who's in charge."

Again the tears streamed from Karolina's eyes. These women did understand, did care. They couldn't stomach the thought of a father coming between a mother and child. They were on her side, and for the first time in forever, Karolina felt grateful.

"Thank you all for your support," she managed to eke out, meaning every word.

"Brilliant again," Emily hissed into Karolina's ear as she led her from the room and toward the parking lot.

"I meant it." Karolina didn't try to mask her annoyance. "They were all so kind."

"Of course you did," Emily murmured, marching toward Karolina's Mercedes SUV. "If there was a single group of people worth winning over, it was this one. You're part of the community now. And trust me, they will mobilize faster and more efficiently than a Navy SEAL team to defend one of their own. They're wealthy and well connected, and they'll get the word out to all their other wealthy and well-connected friends: you're the victim here and Graham's the . . . What did that one woman call him? *Monster.* I have to say, that was a smashing success."

Karolina climbed into her car, wanting to believe Emily. Wanting to hold Harry, watch a movie with him, make him breakfast and listen as he told her details of his day . . .

"Be ready for the calls to start rolling in. You're going to get questions from everyone. Just do exactly what you did here: be sympathetic and human and admit to your flaws. No need to attack Graham if you keep playing your cards right—let everyone read between the lines and do it themselves. The tides are turning, Lina, and not a minute too soon. It's time people saw him for exactly what he is."

Karolina started the car. Her phone rang with an unknown 917 number.

"Answer it," Emily urged. "Answer all of them." Her face was alight with excitement.

Karolina switched over to Bluetooth and pressed "accept." As she reversed, she started to talk. Reporters from what felt like every city in the U.S. called and asked the same questions. Was it true that she'd gone to rehab? Was she remorseful and repentant? Was she working with Mothers Against Drunk Driving? Is Senator Hartwell keeping her from seeing her son? Did she believe in second chances? What did the future hold? Had she heard from the mothers of the other boys who were in her Suburban that evening? Karolina talked her whole drive home and then straight through the next four hours of sitting on her couch, sipping cup after cup of Earl Grey, trying to be as honest as she could—or at least as honest as possible when she was lying about everything. Whenever Karolina faltered, she thought of the vasectomy. Still, she was surprised—no, downright shocked—to see how the reporters' tone had changed from hostile and accusatory to understanding. Her very real tears of terror and sadness in front of all those beautiful, privileged women were a public absolution. Karolina the Drunk Model had become Karolina the Suffering Human Being.

So long as things with Harry were uncertain, and she didn't know what Graham might blindside her with, she could not completely relax—but she no longer felt like the entire world hated her.

She was doing the best she could. It wasn't perfect, it wasn't everything, but for right now it was enough.

25

The Cocaine of the Kindergarten Set

Emily

How long had it been since Miles had done something so spontaneous as fly back unannounced from Hong Kong and surprise her? Emily wondered as she tried not to touch the mud mask she had assiduously applied to her face, neck, and décolletage. She didn't know if it was the complete surprise, or the familiarity, or what, but the last forty-eight hours had been amazing. And not just the sex this time but all of it: they stayed up late into the night and talked about Miles's frustration with the travel his job demanded, Emily's feelings of failure, the fact that they both felt distanced and estranged for reasons beyond geography. Sure, he'd still slept like an asshole for fifteen hours straight, but she supposed she could forgive him when he'd flown more collective hours to see her than they would actually spend together.

"Do you realize you haven't stopped smiling for days?" Karolina said, walking into the living room and dropping her bag on the sofa. Karolina had taken Emily's advice and switched from her eight-thousand-dollar Hermès Kelly to a much more accessible Michael Kors tote. The supermodel had successfully downgraded herself to something resembling normal—still beautiful but warmer and more relaxed.

"I think that's an exaggeration. But it was a good visit."

"Good for you guys, I'm glad. You needed it."

"What is that supposed to mean?"

"People were starting to talk."

Emily's eyes widened. "Are you fucking kidding me? There are people in this loser town talking about *me* and *my* personal life?"

Karolina laughed. "Of course there are. I was just with a group of them. My new best friends, and they are so pleased to see you reunited with your husband."

"You go to one Moms' Night Out and now you're the Doyenne of Greenwich?"

"Isn't that what you wanted?" Karolina batted those L'Oréal lashes.

Emily sniffed. "Yes. I suppose." There was a pause. "Are you going to make me beg?"

"Yes."

"You can keep your stupid small-town gossip to yourself, then."

"Oh, come on, Em. You and Alistair?"

"Alistair?" Emily could feel the now-dried mask cracking around her forehead. "What the hell do they know about Alistair?"

"Everyone thinks he's gorgeous, and he's been after you. I have to say, I'm a little hurt you didn't say anything."

Emily laughed bitterly. "I sent him a half-naked selfie and he didn't even bother to respond."

Karolina stared with those shocking blue eyes.

"What?" Emily said.

"So they were right."

"How so?"

"They said something was going on between you two. Someone

saw you together at a party." Karolina was obviously trying to keep the judgment out of her voice, but she was failing miserably.

"Those women are bit players in our bigger plan to get you back to your former life, with your son, where you belong. Forget the other stuff. It's just noise."

Karolina appeared to think about this. "I'm going to change into sweats. Want to watch something? *Handmaid's Tale?*"

Emily shrugged. She was trapped for at least the next thirty minutes, until her mask was ready to come off. "Sure."

Karolina disappeared up the stairs, and Emily considered changing into something with an elastic waist. Never for a day in her life had she felt a pound overweight. She did it old-school—cigarettes and Diet Coke and vodka sodas with limes—and so long as she kept her mouth shut, she didn't even really need to work out that much. But now? This was Greenwich. The suburbs were threatening to tack five pounds to her hips like she was some sort of common housewife. It was unacceptable.

A ringtone that wasn't her own bleated from deep in the couch, and Emily dug it out. Karolina's phone showed a handsome, smiling photo of Graham across the screen. Of course Emily knew she should ignore it, but that didn't seem like any fun.

"Hello? Graham?" Emily asked as sweetly as she could manage. She had no idea what she was going to say to him.

"Karolina, you listen and listen closely," Graham said, his voice deep and serious. "I will not have you disparaging me in the press. I will not have it! Your implication at that charity thing that I am keeping you from seeing Harry? How dare you! Do you need attention and sympathy that desperately? Well, then let's make it official. I didn't want to have to do this—not for you, me, or Harry—but you've left me with no choice. You may not come to visiting day next month. And if you breathe one word about it to the press, I'll make the arrangement permanent."

"Graham, this is—" Emily tried, but he had already hung up. She sat there, dumbfounded, until the anger came rushing back. She dropped

Karolina's phone and picked up her own. She texted Graham twice. The first one simply read: *Vasectomy.* She gave that a full minute to sink in and followed it up with: *Karolina will expect to visit Harry as planned. That's all.*

Emily heard Karolina's footsteps and dropped both phones back on the couch. Even with her hair shorn, Karolina looked predictably spectacular in a pair of flowy pajama pants and a coordinating camisole.

"Is that, like, from Victoria's new Here Are My Nipples collection?" Emily asked, rolling her eyes.

Karolina squinted. "What's your problem?"

"Nothing, never mind. Here, watch whatever you want. I changed my mind. I'm actually really tired. I'm going to bed."

"Okay," Karolina said, looking a little hurt.

"I'm headed into the city for an early work breakfast." Emily could tell that Karolina was waiting for her to say who with, but she wanted to escape as quickly as possible.

"'Night," she heard Karolina call as she made her way to the stairs.

The guest room Emily had decamped to was a soothing oasis of plum, gray, and navy. Matouk sheets, Frette towels, the softest silk and wool rug her feet had ever touched. Every detail was comfortable and perfect, right down to the television hidden in the bathroom mirror. Emily had never been the lounge-in-the-bath type, but she was feeling restless and bloated and bored and stressed all at once. What could possibly be better than feeling weightless while watching a *This Is Us* from the comfort of heaps and heaps of Molton Brown bubbles? But even with Milo Ventimiglia on the television to distract her, Emily couldn't focus. If everything went as planned the following day, she'd be making a deal with the devil. She dialed Miriam's number.

"Em? Hi. Wait, one sec— Benjamin Kagan! Undo that belt from your sister's neck right now. Do you hear me? RIGHT THIS SEC-OND! Get upstairs and back to bed NOW!" Emily heard a scuffle and then some crying.

"Much as I love the sound of screaming mothers and bratty children, maybe you can call me back?" Emily said. On the muted television in the bathroom mirror, the young Mandy Moore was singing in her band. Through the phone, she heard a door slam.

"Hi, sorry, I'm here now," Miriam said breathlessly. "Please tell me why I thought leaving my job was a good idea?"

"Because your babies are growing up so fast and you feel every second slipping through your fingers like the sand in an hourglass? Or some other bad metaphor like that? I think that's what you told me when I asked you this exact question two weeks ago."

Miriam sighed. "It's hell some days. You're not calling to cancel your date with Maisie tomorrow, are you? Because she would be devastated. She wanted to sleep in her dress tonight."

"Of course I'm not canceling! We'll meet at the train station at eight, right?" Emily needed to bring Maisie with her; nothing would unsettle Miranda more than dragging a child into the office. She was hoping it would make Miranda more susceptible to manipulation.

"Have you decided what you're doing yet?"

"We're going to hit all the favorites: Alice's Tea Cup, Serendipity, Dylan's. Shop. Roam. Maybe get a mani. You know, girl stuff."

"Okay," Miriam said. "Please no American Girl store, okay?"

"Why not? Too commercial? Anti-feminist? Made with phthalates? What could possibly be your complaint against dolls?"

"She's only five, and I don't want to get her hooked too early."

"Yes, the Cocaine of the Kindergarten Set. I've heard that. No drugs, no sex, no American Girl. Gotcha. Listen, can we change the subject, please?"

"I only have a second. Paul is going to—"

"Okay, good." Emily lowered her voice to a near-whisper in case Karolina was listening. "I just happened to answer Karolina's phone and it was Graham. Only he thought I was Karolina, and he—"

"You just *happened* to answer Karolina's phone? Seriously?"

"That's not the important part! He thought I was Karolina, and he freaked the fuck out about her badmouthing him at the charity event. He told her she couldn't go to Harry's camp visiting day next month, and if she doesn't get in line, he's going to completely cut her off from Harry."

"Oh my God, he's mentally ill. There can't be any other explanation."

"How about he's a straight-up asshole?" Emily suggested.

"Not only that, but Trip is avoiding making a mediation appointment. Says Graham's too busy. Luckily he put it in writing so I can present that to the judge when we finally drag him into court. And now he's threatening to keep her from her own son? He's a monster."

"That does seem to be the word of the day. And I might have texted him from my own phone," Emily added.

"What do you mean?"

"I texted Graham 'vasectomy,' and I'm guessing he got my point."

"Do you really think threatening a sitting United States senator is a good idea? What do you think he's going to do? Quit? Retire? Beg you to keep it quiet? I mean, come on, Emily—no offense, but this isn't a fashion magazine. There might be legal consequences to your actions. Did you think about that?"

Emily considered this and felt a brief wave of panic. "Of course I did."

"Does Karolina know he called?"

"No."

"And the cop you hired to ensnare him or entrap him or whatever you want to call it? Did you have her sign an NDA? What if she turns around and blabs about how you hired her?"

Emily dug her nails into her palms. It wasn't the first time Miriam had been condescending, even if she didn't necessarily mean to be. But accusing *Emily* of not taking Karolina's plight seriously? When she'd practically moved from Los Angeles to the *suburbs* to help? It was just too much. "I'm hanging up. If there's anything else I need to consider from a legal perspective, please chime in." Surprising herself, Emily ended the call.

She waited, seething, her hands slightly shaking. She would fix this. It's what she did; it's who she was.

It took two minutes, but then a text popped up on her screen: *Sorry. Rough night. We'll fix this. I got you. Love you.*

And then, immediately following: *Please say you'll still take Maisie tomorrow????*

Emily smiled. She wrote back: *I would never punish the daughter for the mother's crimes. See you tom am, even if the mother is a complete bitch. xo*

"You'll remember to buckle her seat belt if you take any cabs, right? Because she really should still be in a booster, but I know you won't want to drag one around all day."

"Absolutely correct," Emily said, wrapping both hands around her venti skinny latte despite the early-summer heat. She'd woken up dreading the day but then remembered how much Maisie adored her and how excited the girl was. "Negative on the booster. And I'm not such an asshole that I can't remember to use a seat belt for a five-year-old."

At this, Maisie's head swung around and she stared at Emily.

"What?" Emily asked her.

"Even the five-year-old knows that's a curse word," Miriam said, giving Emily one of her Miriam looks.

There was a whistling noise in the distance.

"You girls have fun! Mommy will be home all day calling the Bethesda Police Department," Miriam called with a wave.

"Come on, honey," Emily said, grabbing Maisie's hand. "Tell your mommy you love her and that we'll both do our very best to survive the next six hours without her constant and incessant meddling."

"I love you, Mommy! We'll both try our best to—"

Emily clamped her hand over Maisie's mouth. "I'll bring her back in one piece, I promise. And with no more than one American Girl doll, okay?"

"American Girl?" Maisie asked, sounding almost frenzied. "We're going to the American Girl store? And I'm going to get a doll? My very own American Girl doll? Oh, Aunt Emily, I can't wait!"

Emily was almost scared to face Miriam after that, but a quick glance confirmed that her friend had essentially given up: Miriam stood there, shaking her head, looking defeated. Then she blew them both a kiss and headed back to the car.

Maisie chatted all the way into the city, telling Emily about the girls in her camp group: who had the most friendship bracelets, which one was a bully, who could do the silliest impression of their counselors. She discussed why she loved *Wild Kratts* and which teacher she was hoping to get for first grade and what she planned to ask the Tooth Fairy for when she lost her next tooth (and by the way, four were wiggly—four!). Who knew the child could talk like this? When she was home, Emily barely heard her do anything except fight with her brothers and ask for snacks. Did Miriam know what a gem she had on her hands? What an adorable little girl? When Maisie reached up and took Emily's hand on the escalator in Grand Central, Emily felt a little rush of emotion. She squeezed the girl's hand and kissed the top of her head.

"Where are we going first, Aunt Emily?" Maisie asked excitedly.

"Where else? American Girl!"

"But Mommy said I'm not allowed until I'm seven. She said their clothes cost more than hers and I have to wait for a special occasion."

"Well, we're having our very own girls' day in the city—that's special, isn't it? And of course the doll's clothes cost more than your mommy's—have you seen what she wears?" They speed-walked toward Fifth Avenue. "Life is short, honey. Let's have fun now."

Ninety minutes later, the two of them had had more than their fair share of fun. Five hundred and twenty-two dollars' worth of it, to be precise. Not only had they bought a Gabriela doll, but Emily had coached Maisie through selecting a wardrobe: a smart wrap dress for work, an all-black romper for cocktails, a frothy pink ball gown for awards ceremonies, two different tennis outfits for visits to the club, and a pair of skinny ankle-length jeans and a blousy top for weekend brunches. Maisie kept suggesting workout clothes of some sort—leggings, running shorts, sweatpants—but with patience and persistence, Emily talked her out of them. It wasn't Maisie's fault. When all you saw modeled at home were hideous garments with elastic waistbands, how could you possibly know the alternatives? They finished their visit by debating whether to choose a horse and stable for Gabriela to practice her equestrian moves or a pool with a swim-up bar where she could entertain her friends in the summer; unable to decide, they purchased both.

"It's all coming to my house? Pinky swear? All of it?" Maisie asked anxiously as she followed Emily outside, clutching only the doll.

"I promise, sweetheart. I paid extra for overnight shipping, and they said it would go out today. Here," she said, handing Maisie a plastic bottle and a cup of ice from the corner bodega that they had popped into after leaving the store.

"My mommy doesn't let me drink soda," Maisie said, staring at the bottle.

"Don't worry, sweetie. It's diet. This kind is actually good for you."

They sipped their drinks in contented silence for a couple minutes as Emily watched Maisie watching everyone else. Emily was filled with such protective love for the little girl, it surprised her. It was embarrassing to admit, but she couldn't remember the last time she'd had this much fun on a girls' day in the city. She told Maisie as much and the little girl's face lit up. "Me too," Maisie said, hugging her new doll and squeezing Emily's hand.

"Oh shit," Emily said, looking at the time.

Maisie's mouth opened into a perfect circle.

"Don't worry. We're just going to be late. And you know who doesn't really do late? Miranda Priestly."

"Who's Miranda Priestly?" Maisie asked.

"She is the woman to whom I'm going to sell my soul," Emily explained.

"What does 'sell my soul' mean?"

Emily scooped up Maisie and the doll. "Come, honey, we have to hurry."

When they finally arrived at Elias Clarke, Emily breezed through the glass doors without bothering to talk to the shocked secretary in the lobby and headed straight for Miranda's suite, where she was met with a death look from Miranda's junior assistant.

"Can I help you?" asked a pretty gazelle in a pencil skirt, white silk shell, and sky-high open-toed sandals; she clearly meant to offer anything but help, even though Emily had a tired Maisie on her hip and an American Girl doll hanging from one hand.

"I have a meeting with Miranda," she said in her most irritated voice, which she was pleased to see got a reaction from the girl. "Emily Charlton."

"Oh, Emily! Of course!" the girl said, nearly toppling over in her effort to stand up. "I've heard so much about you. You're, like, a legend around here."

"Are you saying I'm old?"

The girl looked panicked. "What? No, of course not. Not anything like that. I just meant—"

Emily forced a smile. Oh, how she remembered those days. "Listen, where can I stash this one for a few minutes?"

"That one . . . what, um, is that?"

"This? It's a child. Surely you've seen one before?"

The assistant blushed. "Yes, of course. I didn't know you had a daughter. She's precious."

Two phones began ringing at once. The junior assistant grabbed one instinctively and said, "Miranda Priestly's office. No, I'm afraid she's not available right now. Yes, I will take his number, and she will try him back if and when she's able to." The girl nodded as though actually writing something down. "Mmm-hmmm. Thank you. Goodbye."

She turned to Emily. "Never gonna happen," she said as she grabbed the second call and repeated the same script.

"Juliana!" Emily felt the hair on her arms stand up. "Is Emily out there? I'm ready for her now."

Emily was trying to arrange Maisie in Juliana's chair when Miranda swung open the doors. Her dusty rose dress was Alexander McQueen and the sling-back stilettos were, as always, Manolo. A featherweight cashmere cardigan, likely Prada, hung off her shoulders as a defense against the corporate air-conditioning, and her hair was flawless, as always.

"Did anyone hear me? Anyone?" She peered at Emily first, acknowledging her with a nearly imperceptible nod, and then turned on Juliana. "I said I'm ready for her *now*."

"Yes, Miranda," the assistant said, an unnatural redness mottling her neck and face.

Miranda swiveled around expertly and strode into her office.

"Thanks, Juliana. Just give Maisie your phone if she starts to get upset," Emily whispered.

"My name is Elle," the girl whispered back. "Juliana is the senior assistant."

It was bizarrely reassuring to see that nothing ever changed.

"Emily! Bring the child in with you. Juliana has plenty to keep her busy right now. We don't need to add babysitting to her responsibilities."

"Certainly," Emily said, reaching for Maisie's hand. But the little girl bolted into Miranda's office, where she immediately grabbed a crystal paperweight off Miranda's desk.

Emily felt a prickle of sweat. What the hell was she thinking, bringing a five-year-old into Miranda Priestly's office?

Miranda gazed at them impassively. "The girl has excellent taste," she murmured. "What's your name?"

Maisie peered up at her, one of the few people on the planet seemingly unafraid to meet Miranda's eye. "Maisie Kagan."

"Well, Maisie Kagan, would you like to play on my computer while Emily and I have a chat?"

Maisie's eyes widened and she nodded.

"Come here."

As Emily tried to hide her shock, Miranda got up from her metal desk chair and helped Maisie climb onto it. She quickly typed a few keystrokes and waved her hand at the screen. "Have a ball." Miranda turned to Emily and motioned for them both to take a seat on the couch by the windows.

Emily tried to arrange herself on Miranda's couch, but she couldn't deny that nothing was sitting right. Now that she was back at *Runway*, she felt like a cow. Her Helmut Lang dress had hiked up too far on her legs, which looked a little meaty, and thanks to lunch, her belt was feeling like a straitjacket. Emily sat as straight as possible and pledged that she would commence a juice cleanse immediately upon arriving back in that fat-inducing suburb.

Miranda looked Emily in the eye and said, "I'm firing these idiot girls left and right, and I don't have time for it anymore. It's time for you to return to *Runway*, Emily. The Met Ball last month was a horror show."

"Everyone raved about it! The Strong Female theme in honor of #metoo was a home run. Even the haters all admitted it was brilliant. E! called it the 'the starriest night in May,' if I remember."

Miranda appeared to consider this. "Brilliant, yes. But it was stressful. Disorganized. And you know how much I love that. It should have been *you* in charge. It's June already. By this time we always have the theme chosen for next year's ball, and we are well on our way to planning *Runway*'s big parties during New York and Paris Fashion Week. And what do I have now? Zilch."

"I'm flattered, Miranda, but I—"

"Enough," Miranda said with barely contained exasperation. "I want to hire you, pay you handsomely, and obviously work you to the bone."

"And I'm tempted." Emily nodded. "But I've made a commitment right now to another client."

"Karolina Zuraw?"

Emily nodded. She realized she was speaking to one of the few people who thought of Karolina as her own person, not Mrs. Graham Hartwell.

"And how is that working out for you?" Miranda's smile was almost imperceptible as her hand went to the Hermès scarf around her neck.

Emily cleared her throat. Here it was: her one chance. "You know Karolina—too sweet for her own good. And the tabloids haven't helped. But I do think we've turned a corner—"

Miranda took off her Prada reading glasses and pinched the bridge of her nose. "Emily. Save the shit. We've known each other too long."

Emily nearly fell off her chair in surprise—Miranda never cursed. Never. She thought it crass and unladylike, something reserved for stupid people.

"Okay, you're right," Emily said slowly. "He's made her a victim, and humiliated her in front of the whole world, and taken away her life as she's known it. I want to give it back to her. I want to destroy him. He's a monster."

"I will help you. And then you will help me," Miranda cut her short.

Bingo. Emily's eyes narrowed. "She needs custody of her son, and for America to forget about the DUI."

"What do you have?" Miranda asked.

Emily sat up straighter. "A couple of things. But Karolina isn't willing to go public."

Miranda made a tsk-tsk sound. "So unimaginative." She closed the newspaper and turned her full attention to Emily. "Send me an email. Bullet points, please."

"Miranda?"

"I will handle this."

"I appreciate that, but it's really not so simple. You see, I—"

Miranda's hand went up. "That's all."

"Miranda, you asked me here to discuss how I could help you—"

"It's settled," she said, rising. "Run along, darling. Go with Emily."

"Maisie, say goodbye and thank you to Ms. Priestly," Emily stage-whispered, but Miranda ignored them, picking up the phone.

Emily shut the double doors behind her and Maisie.

"Thank you for being such a good girl," she said to Maisie once they were safely inside the elevator. "You were very well behaved in there. Sweetheart, can you please do me a favor and not tell your mother that we came here today? How about it be our little secret?"

Maisie placed her pointer finger to her bottom lip exactly the way Miriam did.

"Thanks, sweetie. That means a lot to me."

"Emily?" Maisie's voice was childlike, but her pose—now with one hand on her hip and the other extended in front of her, palm out—was anything but.

"Yes, sweetheart?"

Maisie looked her straight in the eye. *"That's all."*

26

The Thousand-Dollar
Throw

Miriam

When Miriam opened her eyes, she noticed two things immediately: first, her husband was on top of her, naked. And second, the room was still pitch-black, so it must have been the very middle of the night. Was she dreaming? Was he? No, he seemed very much awake as he kissed her neck and tried to shimmy her nightshirt over her head.

"What are you doing?" she asked dumbly. It was obvious, of course, but so damn foreign! Hot, spontaneous middle-of-the-night sex?

"What does it look like I'm doing?" Paul murmured, working his way down her stomach.

"Um, I'm not sure you want to do that," she said, yanking on Paul's head with both hands.

He brushed her aside. "I know what I want."

So she let him. Gladly. She let him do everything else he wanted to also, the darkness of the room and the drama of the late hour making her feel freer. Afterward, when they lay in a sweaty embrace, both breathing heavily, she couldn't help but smile.

"That was really nice," she said.

Paul laughed. " 'Nice'? I was hoping for something more like 'mind-blowing' or 'life-changing.' "

Miriam rolled over and kissed him. "By 'nice,' I actually meant 'That rocked my whole world.' "

"Better."

"Paul?" She could tell he was starting to drift off, but this was the closest she'd felt to him in months.

"Mmm?"

"What brought that on?"

"What brought what on?"

"That. Lovemaking. What we just did."

"What do you mean?" His eyes were closed and his breathing was slowing.

"I mean why now? After it's . . . been so long. I'm not trying to ruin anything. It's just that . . . I don't know. It feels like that kind of came out of left field, things have been . . . different between us lately. Not different, I shouldn't have said that, but maybe distant. Like we haven't been entirely on the same page. Take work, for instance—" She was interrupted by a snore so loud she thought he must be faking it in a jokey way of shutting her up, but as she listened for another minute, he continued snoring steadily.

An hour later Miriam was still awake. None of the usual things worked—reading the free version of *Moby-Dick* on her Kindle, surfing only sports websites, not even listening to NPR on her phone—so she climbed out of bed and headed to the kitchen for a snack. She didn't know how she ended up in Paul's office, exactly, but it was as if a magnetic force pulled her from her perch in the pantry, where she had inhaled two fistfuls of potato chips, and directly into Paul's sleek rolling Aeron chair.

Miriam expected he had changed the password to his computer, so she was surprised that their shared password logged her right in. She nosed around a little, scanning his inbox, outbox, and trash for anything unusual, but nothing stood out. She hit up his iPhoto. Nothing. There was a folder ominously named PRIVATE in his Dropbox, but inside were only copies of the family's passports, Social Security cards, credit cards, and driver's licenses. Twenty minutes into her little search, and Miriam was feeling guiltier by the minute for invading his privacy like this, but the palpable relief she felt was worth it. She jumped a little when the computer dinged and a new email came in. It was from American Express, and it included his June credit card statement, along with a confirmation that he'd chosen to go paperless.

Paperless? she wondered, clicking on it. If anything, she and Paul were both extraordinarily anal. They went over their statements with color-coordinated highlighters each month to catch any fraudulent charges before paying them in full and scanning them into both cloud-based and hard-drive filing systems. She couldn't imagine why he would go paperless if he would end up printing out the statements to review every month anyway. Another click revealed the statement from Paul's individual card. Each of them maintained a personal credit card and a checking account, since they agreed on the importance of financial freedom and privacy—plus, how would they ever buy each other a gift or a surprise if everything was shared?—but most everything was charged to their shared card and paid for out of joint checking. Aware that she was violating everything they'd agreed on, Miriam clicked open Paul's statement.

The first dozen charges were typical. Two restaurants they'd visited together. A charge for strawberry picking that weekend they'd taken the kids to a nearby farm. Sunoco, Foot Locker, Jamba Juice, the fish place in town. A charge for having his racket restrung. Thirty dollars at Barnes & Noble when she'd sent him to pick up a last-minute kid-birthday present. The recurring monthly charge for his fancy new gym. The largest single charge, nearly three thousand dollars, was for Delta, and she remembered that it was the plane tickets to Florida they'd bought for the coming Christmas. It was number thirteen that caught her attention, a charge from Lofted, a small, insanely expensive design store on Main Street that Miriam was too intimidated to enter. She'd ogled the gorgeous area rugs and the dramatic lighting fixtures from the street, but each time the imperious owner met her gaze and didn't offer a smile, Miriam scuttled along. The charge was for eleven hundred dollars, and the only description of the purchase was THROW BLANKET. What the hell was Paul doing buying eleven-hundred-dollar throw blankets at Lofted? As far as she knew, he wasn't aware the store existed. Was it an impulse purchase, something he'd bought because he could, like the Maserati? She wouldn't have thought so before, but apparently that was a yes. A super-fancy gym? Again a yes. But still, it seemed impossible that he'd spend over a thousand dollars on a *blanket*, when Paul was neither remotely interested in home design nor particularly cold. Which meant it was probably a gift.

For whom?

Her birthday wasn't anytime soon. Paul didn't usually buy ahead like that, and it wasn't as though she'd asked for a criminally expensive blanket as her present. Or anything, for that matter. He hadn't bought his mother a birthday gift since his wedding day, when all gift-buying and thank-you-note-sending responsibilities had instantly become Miriam's. Gun to her head, she couldn't think of one person on earth Paul would buy it for. Except the obvious. She'd have to be an absolute moron not to see it. Not to accept it.

She went back to the statement. There were a handful of more ordinary charges, a couple of questionable ones (a hefty charge from Benjamin Moore for primer and paint; an even bigger one for an online framing company), but the very last item took her breath away. Right there, the final charge of the month, on June 30 to Coastal Realty, and again only two menacing words for the description: JULY RENT. $3,300. The address listed was for a management company located in town.

A collage of images flashed through her mind: a love nest, painstakingly painted in Benjamin Moore's Burnt Ember and Smoked Truffle, adorned with various pillows and blankets and floor cushions to ensure every possible surface was soft enough for the constant, unrelenting sex it hosted. And although she wasn't a puker—never had been, not through two pregnancies and plenty of questionable street food abroad—without a moment's warning, Miriam leaned over and vomited directly into Paul's pristine walnut trash can. She must have passed out right in the chair, because when she next opened her eyes, Paul was staring down at her with a worried expression, his eyes darting between the computer, the barf-filled trash can, and Miriam.

"Miriam, what's going on? Why are you sleeping in here? Are you sick?"

The taste in her mouth was so repugnant and her tongue so dry that she could only glare at him.

Paul helped her over to his leather man-couch as though she were an elderly patient. The feeling of his warm, capable hand wrapped around her upper arm made her stomach roil again.

"Here, rest," he said. "I'm going to give the kids some cereal and get them on the bus. I'll be back in a few minutes, okay?"

Miriam slung her arm over her eyes to block out the light, as though she were suffering from an ordinary hangover instead of realizing that life as she knew it was over. Even this felt strange, the level of drama. Miriam didn't do drama. She did capable and dependable. She gave the kids well-balanced meals of fruit and yogurt and protein-rich eggs each morning, even when she herself ate donuts. She put on brave fronts when she was tired or upset, firmly convinced that her children didn't need or deserve to shoulder any of her own adult burdens, and she stuck to a well-worn routine that gave her and her family the kind of predictability and stability they all required in today's crazy, frenetic world. But collapsed in a heap on her husband's couch after having great sex with him only to discover that he'd been cheating on her, as she'd suspected? And not just cheating but preparing to *leave her* by renting and decorating his own apartment? No. This was not her scene. And the longer she lay there, listening to the familiar sounds of her house as Paul scrambled to get all three children dressed, packed, fed, and off to school, the angrier she became. *He* had done this to her.

Thirty minutes later, when he finally returned from the bus stop, she spat, "How *dare* you?" The nausea faded. The weak, jittery feeling that had kept her from standing or talking had disappeared. And in its place was cold, hard anger. "How dare you do this to all of us? Because you know what, Paul? That's the true tragedy here. It's not just me who has to deal with the fallout of your cheating. Because let me assure you, I *will* get over it. I will *not* be a victim. But our children? That's a different story entirely."

Paul stared at her, astonished. What? Was he surprised to see the fire in her? Had he started to think of her as a suburban mom who lunches, like all the rest of them? Did he not recall that she had outearned and outperformed him with her superior education and better job right up until he happened to get lucky and win the jackpot?

"Stop looking at me like that and say something," she said, her tone venomous. "Actually, on second thought, don't. You know what we're *not* going to do right now? We're *not* going to sit here for the next two hours with me begging you for every last detail—who is she, how did you meet, how does she like it in bed, is she prettier than me?—and you pleading for my forgiveness. We're better than that, Paul. Or at least I am. Let's save ourselves even more heartache and not go there. Go pack a bag and get the hell out of this house, and after we've both had some time to think things over, we can have a conversation like rational people."

"Are you finished?" he asked, his voice quavering.

"Yes." Although she desperately wanted him to leave so he wouldn't see her cry, she also secretly hoped he'd do what she had ordered him not to: namely, throw himself at her feet and beg for forgiveness. Announce that he was willing to do anything to save their marriage and piece back together their family. She was giving an Oscar-level performance, but underneath the brave exterior, she was terrified.

"I can't believe what I'm hearing right now," he said, raking his hair.

"Oh, *you* can't believe—"

Paul said firmly, "It took me a minute to figure out what the hell is going on here—or really, what *you* think is going on here—but I've got it now." He pointed to the computer screen, where his Amex statement was still up. "You see charges you don't recognize. A rented property you can't explain. And it's curious, I get it."

"Curious? I'm not sure that would be my first choice in words."

He glared at her with such distaste that it almost took Miriam's breath away. "Get in the car. Right now." Paul strode over to the couch and grabbed her wrist. He pulled her up to stand so roughly she yelped. "I mean it, you crazy person. The car. Now."

Miriam looked down at her vomit-spattered nightshirt. "I'm not even wearing underwear," she said, motioning to herself.

"You have two minutes. Go throw something on, it doesn't matter what. I'll meet you in the garage."

Her mind was surprisingly blank as she grabbed a pair of ripped jean shorts from the floor and a clean T-shirt. The kitchen looked like a hurricane had blown through it, but Paul was standing in the connecting mudroom, holding open the door to the garage, challenging her to even think of mentioning the mess.

Although she would've thought it impossible in light of what had gone down, they rode in absolute silence for ten minutes before Paul pulled into a parking lot. Surrounding it was a two-story building, horseshoe-shaped, with a gray-washed exterior and white wood-framed doors and a shingled roof. It looked like it belonged more in Nantucket than in a suburb of New York. Miriam had driven by it a hundred times but hadn't really noticed how charming it was.

"Why are we here?" she asked, looking around. On the first floor were a yoga studio, a landscape design firm, and an organic market that advertised a juice bar in the back.

Paul held open a door that read COWORKING SPACE, and she followed him up a staircase to a cheerfully lit waiting area. On the three doors here, she saw signs announcing their occupants as two child psychologists and one speech therapist. Past that area and down the hall were more doors, each adorned with a person's name, and at the very end of the hallway, a door with no name. Paul typed a four-digit code—their shared ATM pin, she noticed—into the keypad and swung it open. Inside was a small but surprisingly spectacular open-plan office with washed-oak floors and modern but warm furniture: desk, leather swivel chair, bookcases filled with framed family photos and Miriam's favorite hardcovers and tchotchkes she'd collected from her travels over the years. Best of all, it was filled with the most incredible light, from the two enormous overhead skylights and the back wall of windows that looked out over a small tributary of the Byram River. There was a Juliet balcony that overlooked the idyllic grassy river spot and, down below, a picnic table where a woman in her twenties sat reading, a cup of coffee in hand.

"What is this?" Miriam asked, although now that she could see the contents of the bookshelves, it was rather obvious.

Paul just stared at her.

"What for? I'm not working enough to justify having an office. Especially not one this pretty," Miriam said, admiring how the space felt both modern and uncluttered yet cozy and inviting at the same time. She couldn't have pulled that off if she'd tried.

"You're an incredible mom—don't get me wrong—and the kids are so lucky to have you at home with them, but we both know it's not making you happy."

"That's not true, it's just that—"

Paul reached up and touched her lips with his finger. "I wanted you to know that I've been hearing you. A lot has changed since we've left the city. Things are weird out here. Good, I know, but weird. You don't want to go back to working eighty hours a week and commuting to and from a demanding firm in the city, but I can also tell that going to gym classes and PTA meetings all day long isn't doing it for you. You're always happiest when you're busy, so I thought if you had a proper dedicated space to escape from the rest of us, you could take on more legal work in town. Only if you wanted to, of course. There's no pressure. You always said no when I suggested you get your own office, and I completely took over the home office. So I'm sorry I've been secretive and had to do all this behind your back—and I'm doubly sorry if you don't like it, but Ashley picked the decorator—but I really wanted you to have this. Because I love you. And I'm here for you."

"So you're not cheating on me?" Miriam didn't know when the tears had started, only that they were streaming down her cheeks.

"I'm not cheating on you." Paul opened his arms, which she gladly collapsed into.

"You didn't find someone with a better vagina?"

Paul gently pushed back her shoulders and peered at her. "What did you say?"

"I figured that's why you weren't so interested in sex anymore. One of the reasons, at least. I mean, you should hear the way these women talk about it."

"My God, Miriam. Is that what you've been thinking? That we have less sex now because there's something *wrong* with you?"

She could only manage a nod.

"Come here, baby. I'm so sorry. I don't know what's been going on exactly, but I think it's kind of normal for people who have been married this long. These things wax and wane, you know? Not that I like it, but it's something we can work on. This whole adjustment to the suburbs hasn't been easy for either of us."

Miriam reached up to kiss Paul on the lips. And as she took Paul's hand and walked around her gorgeous new office, painted in soothing shades of Burnt Ember and Smoked Truffle, she spotted something else. There, draped over a fabulous little love seat upholstered in a rich eggplant velvet, was a throw blanket. It was gray with an off-white ikat pattern, and the cashmere was so rich and plush, she felt like she could wrap her entire body in it and sleep comfortably on the hardwood floor. The tag read: CASHMERE AND SILK, HAND-LOOMED BY ARTISANS IN NEPAL, BROUGHT TO YOU EXCLUSIVELY BY LOFTED, although Miriam could have guessed as much before she even read it.

"I'm sorry" was all she could manage to choke out before the sobs started to accompany her tears.

"I love you, Miriam. I love our family. I love our life together," Paul said, enveloping her in a full-body hug that made her feel everything in the whole world was exactly how it should be.

"I love you too."

27

The Dalai Lama of Blackmail

Karolina

Karolina took a sip of her nigori sake and checked her phone. It wasn't like Trip to be late, especially when he was the one who had pleaded to meet in the first place. She knew Miriam had been trying to set up a meeting and he'd refused to see her. For better or worse, Karolina's curiosity about what her former "friend" had to say meant she'd agreed to meet him. Without her lawyer. Miriam might kill her. Emily certainly would. The waiter came by to refill her shallow sake bowl, and Karolina promptly downed that too. When Trip finally did arrive, he wore an inscrutable expression.

"Thank you for meeting me. I'm sorry I'm late," he said as he sat down next to her. The four-top was set for two people to sit across from each other, but Trip merely dragged the place mat in front of him. He leaned over to kiss her cheek, but she ducked.

"I ordered a drink without you. Are you offended? Or totally expecting it?" Karolina said.

"Oh, please. I know you don't have a drinking problem."

"Weren't you the one who told me I had a DUI in the first place? I had to pretend I went to rehab, for God's sake. My 'friends' in Bethesda haven't spoken to me since the night it supposedly happened. Since the night your BFF used his political and civic connections to frame me for a crime I didn't commit so he could look like the victim instead of the cheating scumbag he actually is."

Trip grimaced, and it made Karolina want to punch him.

"So is this the meeting when you tell me that it was all a big misunderstanding? That Graham is sorry and we can be *civilized* now? Because if it is, you can turn around and head right back outside. I'm not interested."

The waiter returned and Trip sounded desperate as he asked for a vodka on the rocks with extra olives. "Something's come up. And we need to discuss it."

"Continue," Karolina said.

Trip cleared his throat. He was actually nervous. *How dare he*, Karolina thought. And then the words Emily had drilled into her for months: *No mercy*.

The waiter arrived and they ordered. Then there was an awkward moment of silence. Clearly they had plenty to say, but they hesitated to jump into the heavy stuff.

Trip placed his hand over Karolina's. And for some reason, she didn't remove it. "First, I owe you an apology."

"For what? I want to know."

"I stood by him while he did these awful things to you. And I don't know why. Out of some misguided sense of loyalty, maybe? He was always there for me from the day we met as undergrads. When my parents died six months apart. When the twins were born prematurely and we spent weeks in the NICU. When Ellen left me. He's always been there, and I guess I thought I owed him for that."

The waiter appeared with two small bowls of soup and two salads with ginger dressing, and they had to rearrange the table to accommodate it all.

"I have to ask you something," Karolina said, feeling a familiar lump in her throat. "And I need you to be honest."

"I swear." He peered at her.

"Did you know about the vasectomy?"

Trip crinkled his nose. "The what? Whose vasectomy?"

Karolina studied his face: he was telling the truth.

"Graham had a vasectomy five years ago and never told me."

"Jesus Christ, Lina. That has to be bullshit."

"I didn't believe it either. But it's true."

Trip placed his fingertips to his forehead. "Oh my God. I don't even know what to say. I swear to you, I had no idea."

"No wonder it was so hard to get pregnant, huh?" Her laugh was mirthless.

Trip hadn't lived through the day-to-day while Karolina desperately tried to have a baby, but he knew the broad strokes. He'd helped Karolina arrange a consultation with a fertility specialist who was visiting from Switzerland and had the highest success rate in the world.

Trip was quiet. "He told you about the, um, the incident in high school?"

Karolina nodded, sipping some miso soup from the outsize wooden spoon. "Yes. He told me when we first married. I didn't know he told you too."

Trip exhaled. "I don't think he meant to tell me. We were seniors at Harvard and he got trashed one night. More than usual. I guess it was the anniversary of the girl's death, and he got so shitfaced that he came home from the bar and broke down. Sobbing. It was one of the saddest things I've ever seen in my life. But the next morning he either didn't remember or he pretended he didn't remember, and we never spoke of it again. I think he shut down. Maybe forever."

"Wow. Did he tell you what happened?" She lowered her voice to a whisper. "Was it his fault? Was he speeding? Drinking? I didn't ask and he didn't say."

"I don't know. He just said she ran out in front of his car, and he hit her before he ever saw her. I never told another soul."

"I didn't either." Karolina paused, remembering she'd recently told Emily. "Well, only one person. But I swore her to secrecy."

"Nothing would ruin his political career faster. He might have had a chance to overcome it if he'd admitted it from the beginning, explained it, repented for it—basically done exactly what he feels—but it's too late now. He's made it this horrible secret, and it would ruin him."

"I agree. And as tempting as it is to go public with it, I never would. I don't want Harry to have to make sense of something like that. And to drag the girl's parents through it all over again? It's too cruel." She paused. "The vasectomy, however, is tempting."

They finished their soup in silence. It wasn't until Karolina took her first bite of salad that Trip looked at her. "Lina?"

Something in his tone made her set her chopsticks down.

"Graham asked me to tell you that he's considered it all carefully, and he thinks the best thing for Harry is to go to boarding school. Like he did, and his brothers."

Karolina pushed back her chair to stand, furious. "That animal! How can he even think of sending our son to—?"

"Lina, just *wait*." His voice was steely. "He has made arrangements for Harry to start at Choate in the fall."

Karolina could feel her eyes widen. Choate? That was right here in Connecticut. What sort of fresh hell was he planning to torture her with now? "Okay . . ."

"And he thinks it would be best if you stayed at the Greenwich house indefinitely so Harry can visit you on weekends and holidays, and perhaps you can go up there during the week sometimes to see him. Take him and his friends out for dinner, that kind of thing."

"Why would he voluntarily choose to send Harry to school near me?"

"I'm not so sure it was voluntary," Trip said quietly.

Karolina leaned in. "What do you know?"

"Nothing beyond what I just told you. So my suggestion would be to enjoy this victory. Because that's definitely what it is."

It wasn't the first time Karolina had cried in front of Trip, but for some reason she felt more self-conscious now about the tears than she had in the past. "You really think he means it?" She tried to wipe the mascara from under her eyes but figured she was probably streaking it.

Trip nodded. "He already completed the paperwork to arrange for the transfer. Sidwell is making him pay for the entire year because it's too late to withdraw. And he's still doing it."

"I, I . . . I can't even speak," Karolina said, pushing her salad away.

"He asked me to tell you myself. Said you hung up on him when he called."

Karolina could barely describe the rush of elation pulsing through her. She still had rage—five years lost to his lies, if not more. But knowing that she would continue to be Harry's mom, to be part of his life, to see him on a regular basis . . . The other worries faded into the background.

This time Karolina took Trip's hand. "I have to get home. Can we finish another time?"

Trip would have to wait. Everything would have to wait. Right now the only thing that mattered was getting home to talk to Emily. Never in her entire life could she remember feeling as grateful as she did at that moment; as she raced to her car, she could practically feel her son in her arms. She drove as quickly as she could.

Her call to Miriam went straight to voicemail, but by then she was already pulling onto Honeysuckle Lane.

"Emily! Emily! Em! I! Lee!" Karolina shouted as she ran through the kitchen as fast as her wedge espadrilles would allow. "Emily!"

Karolina looked around. There was a half-drunk bottle of Whispering Angel on the coffee table, accompanied by a pack of Marlboro Lights. That inane Bravo reality show about yachts was blaring from the television. All the lights were on. And the pair of nude Chloé sandals that Emily had been wearing since Memorial Day were on the carpet. Clearly she was here. So why wasn't she answering?

"Emily! Are you up here? You need to hear this," Karolina called, racing up the carpeted stairs. She checked the two guest rooms that Emily had been switching between, depending on her mood and a number of other factors Karolina couldn't quite understand. "Where the hell are you?"

"I'm in the bathroom!" Emily yelled back, her voice muffled.

"I have the most incredible thing to tell you!" Karolina called back. She was high, absolutely flying, with joy. She wanted to scream her news to anyone and everyone; to go salsa dancing with strangers; to stay up all night for three nights in a row.

"Can you give me a minute?" Emily sounded as irritated as Karolina was excited.

"Sure. You okay?" Karolina waited directly outside the bathroom door.

"Seriously?" Emily called. "Can you give me, like, five seconds of privacy?"

Karolina grinned. At no one. For no real reason. "Sure. Clock starts now."

In under a minute, Karolina heard the sink turn on and then off. The door swung open and Emily, looking like she'd been dragged through a tornado by an open-air cruise ship, emerged.

"What the hell is so important that you are literally staking out the bathroom?" Emily asked, walking straight past Karolina, who hurried to keep up with her.

"Emily, I have no idea what you said or did, but whatever it was, thank you! Graham is sending Harry to boarding school—in Connecticut!"

Emily stopped and turned around, her expression neutral. "And?"

"And what? I'll stay in Greenwich and Harry will come *here* on weekends. Plus, I can go there to see him. I'm basically going to be his primary parent!"

Emily sighed loudly.

"What?" Karolina asked.

"This is why I like to handle things by myself. But when she offers her assistance, you really can't control her."

Karolina resumed following Emily, who plopped herself back down on the living room couch and reached for the remote. "Wait—turn that down. Who are you talking about?"

"She got you Harry back. She stepped up when I needed her. It's not perfect, but at least it's done."

"Who?" It was all Karolina could do not to wrap her hands around Emily's neck. "Emily. Tell me what happened. Right now."

Emily pressed her palm against her forehead as though her head was pounding. "Miranda is harping on me to come back and oversee events. It's flattering, don't get me wrong, but she just doesn't seem to—"

"Emily? Can you please tell me about my *son?*"

Emily waved her hand. "I told her I couldn't work for her right now because I was too busy with you. She asked what was up with that—basically why I hadn't fixed this already. I told her it wasn't so easy going head to head with a sitting U.S. senator. Then she pretty much laughed in my face like I knew she would. She told me she would handle it, and it would take her approximately sixty seconds. I told her to go for it."

"Go for it? What does that mean, exactly?"

"She asked what it was you wanted. I said Harry. She wanted to know if I had any dirt she could use on Graham. So I emailed her a list. Then she handled the rest."

"Handled the rest?"

"You keep repeating everything I say."

"You really told her about the girl in high school when I swore you to secrecy?" Karolina's warm feeling of complete happiness was quickly giving way to outrage.

"Yes."

"And about the vasectomy?"

"Oh, I had already confronted Graham on that. So maybe it was the one-two punch that got him to do this."

"Emily! That was *private*. Between us."

"Because of Harry. I know. I'm not an idiot. Miranda didn't take it to the press. She took it to Graham. Called him straight up out of the blue, I'm sure, and reminded him how she served for a few months as President Whitney's social secretary. That's Regan's father, President Whitney. Remember him? And how tight Miranda and the president are socially? And I'm guessing she told him point-blank that President Whitney would be *very* unhappy to hear about some of the things his daughter's soon-to-be fiancé had been part of. I imagine she gave him a lot to think about."

"Oh my God." It was all Karolina could say.

"No media, no public pronouncements or unsavory scrutiny. Just a good old-fashioned shakedown from a woman who operates at the master level. She's like the Dalai Lama of Blackmail. The Grande Dame of Extortion. The Priestess of—"

"I got it." Karolina reached for the bottle of rosé, filled Emily's glass to the brim, and then drank the entire thing down herself.

"Help yourself. I feel like shit anyway," Emily said. "Still, I don't think weekends are good enough, do you?"

Karolina stared at Emily. "I've seen him exactly five times since New Year's."

"Karolina." Emily said this as though merely uttering her name was exhausting. "When are you going to stop looking at the world as a place where you owe it something and start acting like it owes *you*? Have you done anything wrong here? Hurt anyone? Are you looking to screw anyone over? No. You just want to live a normal life and see your son. It doesn't sound particularly exciting to me, but hey, to each her own."

"What are you saying?"

"Just because Miranda Priestly would be happy with weekends and Graham agreed to that doesn't mean *you* have to! Pick up the goddamn phone and tell him the deal's off unless Harry goes to Choate as a day student and lives with you. Or some other school. This is fucking Greenwich, for Christ's sake, there have to be a dozen schools around here willing to take fifty grand a year off your hands to educate a seventh grader. Make it happen!"

It was as though someone lifted a weighted blanket from her chest. Karolina could only stare at Emily, in awe of this woman who instinctively knew how to get what she wanted. Emily was right: if Graham was so desperate to preserve his relationship with Regan that he'd let Harry go to boarding school in Connecticut, she should be able to push a little bit harder and get Harry full-time. She whipped out her phone and started typing but quickly erased all of it after deciding that short and strongly worded was better. She added Trip and Miriam to the chain.

There's been a misunderstanding. I want Harry living with me full-time in Greenwich. You can pick the school. You can tell everyone he boards if that saves face. But he doesn't—he sleeps at home with me, every night, every year, until he graduates. He can come see you in Bethesda whenever you two decide, but otherwise he lives with me. And I want it done legally and in writing.

She had to physically restrain herself from qualifying all of her statements with further justifications. She hit "send" and couldn't breathe.

The three dots appeared within thirty seconds and stayed blinking for nearly two minutes. Then they vanished. They reappeared and vanished again, and Karolina thought she might have a heart attack. Was he going to renege on the whole deal? Decide that he'd rather keep Harry in Bethesda than marry Regan? Call the bluff and tell her to go to hell? Karolina literally paced, clutching her phone, her palms so sweaty that she dropped it two times.

When his reply came in, Karolina didn't even realize she'd been holding her breath. She had exhaled, preparing for the inevitable crush of disappointment to wash over her, when her eyes focused through the tears and fixed on the only two letters he had written. *OK*. Both in caps. No qualifications, no threats, no negotiation, no argument. Just acquiescence. Her son was hers again.

28

One Little
Ambien

Emily

Emily watched as Karolina bounded out of the living room and up to her room, presumably to call Miriam or her aunt or whoever else would want to know the good news about Harry. Emily was happy for her, of course, but she also felt like a failure. *Probably because I am one*, she thought, mindlessly flipping through the channels. Emily had put the whole plan in place. She had brilliantly orchestrated Karolina's mommy makeover and new messaging; she'd gotten her rehabbed in Utah—not to mention laid—and she'd relaunched her to the ladies who lunch in Greenwich, who could surely take things from there. But what she hadn't done—couldn't do, apparently—was get Karolina what she wanted most. When push came to shove, it was Miranda who'd stepped up and gotten it done. It might give Emily's business a boost in the end—if she didn't hear from Kim Kelly's people in the next week, she'd be shocked—but it wasn't her win. And one thing in all of this was absolutely certain: Miranda hadn't done anything out of the goodness of her heart, her affection for Emily, or her concern over the well-being of a child she'd never met. How long would it take Miranda to collect payment for what she was owed? She had literally made a deal with the devil.

Not having the energy to reach across the table and reclaim her wineglass, Emily hoisted the new bottle Karolina had opened to her lips and took a long drink. It didn't help get rid of the queasiness she'd been feeling all night, nor give her anything approximating a decent buzz. Irritated and tired and already half-hungover, she hoisted herself off the couch and headed for bed. She squirted toothpaste on her toothbrush and began to brush in an overly aggressive way that was certainly receding her gums when something caught her eye. That stick. Just resting there by the sink, waiting for someone to notice it. Emily spat and gave it a perfunctory glance. There, clear as day, were two bright red lines. Exasperated, she tossed it in the trash and proceeded to floss and pee and wash her face without a second thought. What good were these fucking pregnancy tests when they were always wrong?

She'd fallen asleep watching *Narcos* on Netflix—the iPad had hit her face and she hadn't woken up—when she felt someone shaking her awake.

"Emily. Emily! Get up." Karolina sounded frantic.

"Mmm. What?" It somehow felt like she'd been unconscious for three seconds and also for three days.

"Get up! Right now. Open your eyes!"

Emily obeyed, and Karolina's pure panic caused her to bolt awake. "What? Is it Miranda? Are you sick? What's happening?" she asked, ripping the headphones from her ears as her iPad clattered to the floor.

"How could you not tell me you're *pregnant*?" Karolina asked, her face so close that Emily could smell her minty breath.

With this, Emily could only laugh. "Because I'm not! Did you really have to wake me?"

"Emily. I SAW THE POSITIVE PREGNANCY TESTS IN THE BATHROOM!" Karolina was hysterical now, really out of control. Why was she screaming like that? It was enough to make someone crazy.

"Calm the fuck down, will you, please?" Emily said, pulling the comforter up under her arms. "I'm not *pregnant*."

"You're not? Then whose tests are in the bathroom?"

Emily looked at Karolina. "You have your own bathroom. Hell, you have your own seven bathrooms."

Karolina's eyes looked like they could pop out of her head. "I was out of toilet paper! I went to the nearest bathroom to get a roll. And lo and behold, it looks like a Duane Reade pregnancy-test aisle exploded in there! And they're all freaking positive! You were clearly not trying to hide anything, so don't give me this privacy crap right now. Oh my God, Emily, I'm so happy for you." The last words came out in a squeak, and Emily could tell Karolina was seconds away from tears.

"Before you start with the waterworks, please hear me out. I am not pregnant. I have an IUD! Well, I had one. Up until recently. And my periods never went back to normal because of all the hormones. I couldn't remember when I had one last so I peed on a stick. God knows you stock them like tissues. It wasn't a serious thing—because there's no way I'm pregnant—and sure enough, it was a false positive."

"A false positive?"

Emily nodded.

Karolina sprang off the bed, her arms flapping wildly. It was maybe the only time Emily had ever seen this gorgeous woman look completely ridiculous. "Emily! THERE IS NO SUCH THING AS A FALSE POSITIVE!"

The way Karolina said this, with such certainty, gave Emily pause. Could she be right? No, no, that wasn't possible. "Of course there is."

"Oh my God, I can't even!" Karolina was breathless. "Emily. There is a hormone detectable in your urine when you're pregnant. That's what activates the second line on the tests. It's totally possible to get false *negatives* because the test misses detecting the hormone, but you cannot get a false *positive*—the test is not going to detect something that's absolutely not there."

Emily felt like someone had punched her. "You're sure?"

"I spent the better part of the last five years trying to get pregnant. You don't think I know exactly how a drugstore pregnancy test works?"

Emily grudgingly lifted her gaze to meet Karolina's.

"You're pregnant. There is no room to argue here."

"But—"

"I'll go with you tomorrow so you can have it officially confirmed at a doctor's office, but I've never been more certain of anything in my entire life."

Again that gut-punch feeling. Emily sucked in her breath. "That can't be."

"Why not? There's not really some huge mystery here."

"Yes, but I had an IUD!"

Karolina looked incredulous. "You *had* an IUD? As in, you *used* to have an IUD but currently you do *not* have an IUD?"

"For ten years!" Emily snapped. "Two of them, actually. And I planned to put another one in when she took the last one out, but the one I wanted was back-ordered, and when the office called to tell me it was back in stock, I meant to schedule an appointment . . ."

"But you didn't."

"I was busy! Helping you, for one thing. Besides, Miles always pulls out. Almost always. And I probably have three eggs left, if that."

Karolina pressed her hand to her forehead and appeared momentarily contrite. She sat down next to Emily on the bed. "I know—I am sensing—this is not what you wanted. But it . . . it doesn't have to be a bad thing."

"Please. Just stop. I'd like to go back to bed now." Emily studied her hands as though they were fascinating parchments.

"And I'll make an appointment for first thing tomorrow."

"A waste of everyone's time."

"I insist."

Karolina paused before leaving. But when Emily sneaked a peek a moment later, Karolina was gone and had shut the door behind her.

Emily exhaled. If she were being totally honest, she'd had an inkling for a while now. The question was how long? When had the near-constant queasiness become all-out nausea? When had the once-delicious smell of cigarette smoke started to make her stomach roil? When had her boobs begun to ache in a completely foreign way? When, exactly, had her pants gotten so tight that she'd taken to wearing Lululemons like some suburban-mommy robot? When had a simple spicy tuna roll become revolting? She'd been denying it to herself for weeks already. Possibly longer? Christ, it was hard to say. But tonight, when she'd rooted around under the bathroom sink looking for more hand soap and had hit the motherlode of all pregnancy tests, she figured she'd try one. Just to confirm that this was bad PMS or a virus or something. Food poisoning. At worst, mono. But one had come up positive and the next one had too. Six more after that. Maybe if all the tests were from the same batch, then that particular batch was screwed up in some way?

She reached for the bottle of sleeping pills she kept in her nightstand for emergencies like these and shook a bunch into her palm. She had 5-milligram Ambiens, 5-milligram Belsomras, 2.5-milligram Lunestas. There were over a dozen Ativans, courtesy of her shrink friend in L.A., and half as many Xanaxes she'd scored from a kindly old lady she'd sat next to on her last flight. Even a few stragglers of Valium, which she still considered the gold standard of excellence despite their being hopelessly out of fashion. When life got particularly stressful and it was more than a cocktail could handle, this bottle of magic pills was her only salvation. Eagerly, she sorted and counted and debated the pros and cons of each: fun high but hangover the next morning versus straight-to-bed boredom but no dry mouth. She decided on Ambien, her trusty old friend, and was uncapping a bottle of water when a gruesome image popped into her head: a cute little baby face and torso with no arms or legs, wailing like crazy, wearing a look that said, *You did this to me.* Emily tried to shake it off, to tell herself it was ridiculous, that heroin addicts gave birth to babies with arms and legs every single day and one little Ambien wouldn't make a lick of difference, but try as she might, the image stuck.

"Fuck," she said, carefully pouring the handful of pills back into the bottle, securing the childproof lid, and then promptly throwing it against the wall. She turned the lights off and pulled the pillow over her face. This was going to be a very long night.

Dr. Werner pressed, not gently, from inside Emily with one hand and looked skyward, as though deep in concentration, like an intrepid explorer working her way through a pitch-black cave.

"I can venture a guess. I'd say close to sixteen weeks, give or take. But we'll do an ultrasound next, and that will give me a much better idea." The doctor removed her hand from Emily, snapped off her glove, and jotted some notes on a chart.

Miriam squealed. "Sixteen weeks? Oh my God, that's, like, real. Like, four months along! Like, almost halfway there!"

"Can you stop that, please?" Emily snapped at her. Her heart had just done some sort of flip-flop thing, and she was trying to figure out if it was nerves or excitement or morning sickness.

"Sorry. I'm sorry. I'm just *so excited for you*."

Emily glared at her. "You're here right now because Karolina couldn't keep her shit together in an OB's office. What I could really use right now is some *quiet* support."

"Understood."

"Make that *silent* support."

Miriam nodded.

Dr. Werner was pretending that she didn't hear them, but Emily could see she was trying to suppress a smile.

"Okay, Emily, this will only take a minute," the doctor said, encasing a white wand in a condom and squirting clear goo over the top. She dimmed the lights, pulled a screen on a rolling pedestal closer to Emily's exam table, and inserted the wand.

Emily held her breath. It didn't hurt. She could barely feel anything, actually. But this was what would make everything real. Up until now, it could all be explained. The dozen home-pregnancy tests. The positive urine dip at the office this morning. The pelvic exam. All vulnerable to error or at least interpretation. But seeing a little embryo on a screen where one wasn't before—hearing that embryo's heartbeat—well, that was a bit harder to deny.

"Emily, I'd like you to look right here." Dr. Werner pointed at a black blob on the screen. It lolled about like a jellyfish afloat in rough water.

The sound of a horse stampeding filled the room.

"What's that?" Emily asked, alarmed.

"Sorry, that was turned up really high." Dr. Werner turned a switch, and the horse stampede sounded a whole lot more like a very fast heartbeat. "You are looking at a healthy pregnancy, Emily." She moved the wand around more and used the keyboard to mark and measure the image on the screen. "I was close. You're measuring at fifteen weeks and two days. Would you like to know the gender?"

"No!" Miriam shouted before clamping a hand over her mouth. "Sorry. I just think it's so great to be surprised. There aren't many true surprises left in life, and I loved not knowing with any of—"

"Dr. Werner?" Emily asked sweetly in a voice loud enough to drown out Miriam. "Being that it's my body and my baby and my decision, I would like to know the gender."

The doctor moved the wand to the far left, enough to give Emily a small jolt, and pointed again. "You see? Right there. A girl. You're going to have a girl."

"Oh my God. A girl? For real?" The words had tumbled out before Emily could stop herself. Already she'd been feeling woozy from uttering the phrase "my baby," but this was almost too much to handle. There was an actual girl baby inside of her? That had a beating heart and a growing body and would turn into a real, live human if she allowed it?

"I can't say with a hundred percent certainty until the blood test is back, but yes, I'd say that's clearly a girl."

"Oh my God. Oh my God. Oh my God." Emily just kept repeating it over and over, unwilling or unable to say anything else. When she finally remembered that Miriam was there too, and she twisted her head around to find her friend over her shoulder, Emily shouldn't have been surprised to see Miriam crying.

"Sorry," Miriam wailed, wiping at her face. "I'm so sorry. This is your moment. I'm supposed to be the calm one, I know. But I'm just so happy for you. A baby girl! What's better than that?"

The doctor closed Emily's file and opened the door. "Congratulations. Why don't you get dressed and then we can meet in my office to discuss everything, okay?"

"Okay," Emily said, but it sounded like a squeak.

As soon as the door closed, Miriam nearly threw herself on the table. She whipped out her phone and began typing furiously.

"What the hell are you doing? You're not telling anyone, are you?" Emily asked. She hadn't even told Miles yet.

"Of course not. Wait, hold on a sec. There. I have it. The due-date calculator. If it's August twenty-eighth today and you really are fifteen weeks and two days pregnant, that means your baby is due . . . February twentieth!"

"February? As in the dead of winter? The darkest month of the year? It's even depressing in L.A. then! I don't want her birthday to be February!"

With this, Miriam belly-laughed. "You're crazy beyond comprehension. But I'm still happy for you."

Emily jumped up, feeling newly energized, and pulled on her underwear and jeans.

Miriam watched her. "Get ready to throw out all your thongs. And your sexy bras. All your lingerie, pretty much. Think cotton and stretch.

Elastic waistbands. Eating as much ice cream as you can shove down your gullet without feeling even a twinge of guilt. My God, I'm so jealous right now."

Emily made a gagging sound. "There is precisely zero percent chance of any of that happening." Only fifteen weeks in, and already she'd had to force herself into jeans this morning when all she'd really wanted was to pull on her most indulgent stretch Lulu leggings.

"I have to call Miles. Oh my God, I am literally going to make his life with this news right now."

"Will he be even happier than you?"

"I'm not happy!" Emily said automatically. She tried desperately to look bitchy—usually something that came so naturally to her—but she couldn't keep the smile off her face.

"See? I knew it! I knew you'd be thrilled when you got the official confirmation. Karolina said you were a delusional wreck and that you were going to throw yourself off a building if it were true, but I *knew* that wasn't the case."

Emily glanced at her watch. "What are you doing for the next hour?" she asked Miriam.

"Me? Nothing. Well, actually, I was going to go to my new office—"

"Mmm-hmm. Interesting. But today's about me. After the doctor gives us my list of dos and don'ts, will you come with me somewhere?"

"Of course. Anywhere. Carvel? Dairy Queen? McDonald's? Let's get the party started!"

Emily looked at Miriam with disgust. She held up her hand. "Stop."

"What else can you do for fun when you're pregnant besides eat? No drinking, no smoking, no drugs. No vigorous exercise, not that I ever minded that restriction. No crazy sex. Again not really a problem for me. But it doesn't leave a whole lot," Miriam said.

"I can still shop," Emily said, tossing her Goyard over her shoulder. "We're going to Bergdorf. To buy a very miniature, very expensive, extremely impractical fur Chloé vest. In an infant size. Are you in?"

Miriam beamed. "I'm in."

29

Willing to Do
Whatever It Takes

Miriam

Miriam gazed out over the river from her desk in her new office and smiled to herself. It was mid-November, and even though the leaves had finally fallen and there were nighttime frosts, this day was gloriously sunny and warm. She was just about to meet Ashley for lunch at the salad place downstairs when her office phone rang.

"Miriam Kagan," she said, pleased by her professional tone. It had been only a few months since she'd settled into her new office and taken on new legal work, and she was surprised by how much she was enjoying it.

"Um. Hello. May I please speak with . . ." There was a pause as the male voice sounded like he might be reading something. "Miriam Kagan?" He pronounced Kagan like "Ka-GAHN."

"This is she. Who, may I ask, is calling?"

"Hi. This is Officer Lewis from the BPD. The Bethesda Police Department, that is."

"Officer Lewis, how kind of you to return my call," Miriam said, although she wasn't hopeful that the call would be any different from the dozen or so she'd already made and received. Through the Freedom of Information Act and a few well-placed lawyer friends—and fine, she'd admit it, her highly tuned Facebook-stalking skills—Miriam had pieced together a near-complete list of the officers who had been on duty the night Karolina was arrested. She'd left dozens of messages over two months' time. She'd spoken to nearly all of them by phone, when they chose to call her back, and not a single one had anything illuminating to say. Yes, they remembered Karolina spending the night in the holding cell. Why wouldn't they? It wasn't every night you got a former Victoria's Secret Angel—or, depending on your area of interest, a current senator's wife—in jail. Yes, they knew at the time that she was being held for driving under the influence. A few of them remembered seeing Harry and his friends and then Elaine, when she'd come to pick them up, but others did not. No matter. Not a single officer had anything to say that was different from what had been shared in the papers: namely that Karolina was brought in drunk, semi-hysterical, and refused at first a Breathalyzer and then a blood test. They all assumed one was administered after a court order was obtained, as would have been standard procedure, but none of them would swear to it.

"You're welcome. And I know I said I was calling from the BPD, but I retired last month. Really to join my father's business, since he's been ill. But legally speaking or whatever, you should probably know that I'm no longer a member of the force."

"Okay," Miriam said. "That's fine."

Officer Lewis cleared his throat. "Yes, thank you. Anyway, I feel terrible that I didn't tell someone this earlier, but it would have been . . . complicated. With my superiors and all."

Miriam inhaled sharply and hoped the ex-cop couldn't hear her excitement. "Okay," she said, stretching out the word as soothingly as she could.

"Are we off the record?"

"Of course."

"Well, I read all over the news that Mrs. Hartwell refused various sobriety tests. And that is not my recollection from that night. It was the very opposite, in fact."

"Are you sure?"

"Yes, ma'am. She asked repeatedly to be administered a Breathalyzer. Begged, in fact."

"She did?" Miriam asked, although this was exactly what Karolina had been claiming all along.

"Yes, ma'am. Multiple times."

"And you're sure of this?"

"Very, ma'am. I was the officer on duty who completed her booking. The field officers left at shift change, and I was responsible for finishing her paperwork."

"I see," Miriam murmured. "And you clearly remembered her *begging* for a Breathalyzer?"

"Yes, ma'am."

"And may I ask why you didn't administer one? Isn't that protocol for all suspected DUIs?"

"Yes, usually. But in this case, Chief Cunningham said that we were forgoing the sobriety tests because Mrs. Hartwell was a VIP."

"Meaning?"

"That Senator Hartwell wouldn't be too pleased if his wife was arrested for drunk driving. I wasn't entirely comfortable breaking with protocol, but I did understand it was a sensitive situation."

"Yes, I can understand that," Miriam said, trying to sound sympathetic.

"I should have called earlier . . ."

Miriam nodded, even though he couldn't see her. "Of course, Mr.

Lewis. I think anyone could understand your hesitation. But will you do the stand-up thing and set the record straight? You're off the force, there will be no personal fallout for you. And Mrs. Hartwell—who just so happens to be a lovely person who has suffered a great deal—will be forever indebted."

There was a moment of silence. "You would use my name?"

"Yes," Miriam said definitively. "That's the only way."

Another moment of silence, during which Miriam held her breath, and then she heard: "Okay. I'll do it."

They arranged a time and a place to meet that coming Friday, and Miriam pumped her fist when they hung up. She grabbed her purse and coat and flew down the stairs, not even bothering to lock her office. She and the others who shared the space were like a dysfunctional family. They complained about the weather over coffee each morning and drinks occasionally after work. They signed for each other's packages and greeted each other's clients and shared news updates and weight-loss tips. The psychotherapist named Dara, whom Miriam adored, had started dragging her to some insane Pilates-meets-kickboxing class three times a week, and Miriam had already dropped two sizes.

When she raced into the salad place, breathless, Ashley looked up from her phone with a strange expression.

"Sorry I'm late. I—"

"Miriam?" Ashley interrupted, leaning across the table far enough to stop Miriam midsentence. "I have something to tell you."

"You and Eric are getting back together?" Miriam asked, nearly certain that would be the outcome, when being the only question.

Ashley twisted her mouth into a look of pure disgust. "Eric? Oh, hell, no!" she said loudly enough for the people behind the counter to turn and look. "He can go screw each and every one of his Ashley Madison girls for all I care."

"Okay." Miriam laughed. "Noted."

"I've met someone. More than met, I guess I should say. I'm in love.

"He's a local dad, actually." Ashley lowered her voice, although they were the only two customers in the entire place. "I can't believe I never knew him, but I suppose Greenwich is bigger than we think. And our kids aren't the same age."

"That sounds great," Miriam said genuinely. A divorced dad who lived locally sounded like one of the best possible outcomes from this whole horrible ordeal.

"And I haven't even told you the best part." Ashley leaned in and whispered, "He's British."

"Nice!"

"He's gorgeous. And so, so sexy."

"Good for you," Miriam said. "I'm really happy for you."

Ashley nodded. "Thanks. I know it's a little awkward with you and Emily being friends and all, but I think we can all be grown-up about this, right?"

"Emily? My Emily?"

Ashley peered at Miriam. "She didn't tell you?"

"Tell me what?"

"Normally I'm not one to gossip—and Alistair has assured me there's nothing going on between them—but I did see a naked selfie she sent him on her phone."

"Wait—Emily Charlton? Some guy named Alistair? That's ridiculous. She would never do that," Miriam said with more confidence than she felt.

Ashley pulled her own phone from her bag, scrolled, and held up the screen for Miriam to see.

Miriam narrowed her eyes. "Those are just naked breasts. They could be anyone's!"

"Please, Miriam. I have her number in my phone. Just so long as she doesn't think I stole her man or something. Whatever they had isn't any of my business—and you know how much I admire her—but, well, I don't want her thinking there's still anything between them. Because there's not."

Something about the way Ashley was looking at her made Miriam want to laugh. Suppressing the impulse, she said, "Is that maybe something you'd like me to convey to Emily?"

Ashley appeared to think about this. "If *you* want to. So long as you don't think she'll be offended."

Miriam smiled. "You can never tell with Emily, but I'll do my best." Her phone buzzed and she glanced at it. It was a text from Paul.

Have you had lunch yet?

Here now w/ Ashley. She has a new man.

That's good b/c Eric has three new women.

Paul!

Sorry. Anyway made a rez for date night tonight.

Where we going?

Miriam was so caught up in her text exchange, she didn't even notice Ashley stand up. "Sorry, I have to run," Ashley said. "The hair place just called that they can fit me in. I want to get a blowout before my date. Thanks for listening, Miriam. You're the best."

"Anytime. And I'm happy for you, Ash. You deserve it." Miriam watched as Ashley walked to her slate gray Range Rover with a bounce in her step. *Good for her*, she thought.

This time her phone rang. "Hey, baby," she answered. "I was just about to text you back."

"Time for a quickie?" Paul asked, his voice gruff and sexy.

"No!" Miriam laughed, although she was delighted he'd asked. They were both trying to make more of an effort at spontaneity. "Ashley just left and I'm headed back upstairs."

She was updating him on the new development in the Karolina case when Miriam felt a strong hand clamp down on her shoulder and she jumped. Paul stood just behind her, grinning.

"What are you doing here?" she asked, standing up to kiss him.

He didn't say anything. He threw out her empty coffee cup, collected her purse from the back of the chair, and took her by the hand.

"Where are we going?" Miriam asked, practically giggling like a little girl. "I haven't even ordered yet."

"Shhh. Can't you keep quiet for a minute, woman? We're going to check out that insanely expensive throw blanket in your office. Let's see if it delivers the quality it promised."

30

The Girl
Has Balls

Karolina

Outside were low, slightly decrepit stone walls, a beautiful flagstone terrace with a fire pit, and climbing ivy on the brick facade. Inside it had a massive farmhouse sink, three wood-burning fireplaces—including one in the master bedroom—and the most exquisite exposed beams in all the common rooms. There was a small but lovely saltwater pool and, best of all, a lavishly finished basement rec room complete with an indoor sports court and a theater room where Harry loved to entertain his new school friends.

Karolina stretched out on her brand-new club chair, an oversize and overstuffed monstrosity from Restoration Hardware that gave her an almost inordinate amount of happiness. Everything from its plush velvet fabric to its ability to recline made her smile. It was three times the size of what she needed, but no matter: it was perfect. She felt that way about the whole new house, actually. It was still mostly unfurnished; when she'd listed the old house, she'd been eager to sell everything that Graham had chosen. But even empty, this house had a warmer and more inviting feel than she could have hoped. With an accepted offer for the old house, Karolina had pounced on a brand-new listing after spying it online. It was in the so-called Back Country part of Greenwich, which felt more rural and private, and it maintained a lovely French-country feel.

Karolina could hear the thump-thump of the basketball as Harry and two other kids shot hoops downstairs, and she smiled. It would be hard to improve on this Saturday, she thought, spreading open the *New York Times* for what might have been the tenth time that morning. The final chapter of Operation Karolina had come to a boldly beautiful end that day with the publication of ten simple words on the front page, right below the fold: NEW INFORMATION EMERGES IN THE CASE OF SENATOR HARTWELL'S WIFE. The story detailed how Officer Lewis, no longer with the Bethesda Police Department, had confirmed Karolina Hartwell's claims that she not only "requested but actually begged" for police to administer a Breathalyzer test. Questions remained about why such a test was not administered, per protocol, and both the Department of Internal Affairs and the Bethesda DA's office were investigating. Officer Lewis went on to say that Karolina "appeared distraught, as one might expect after being arrested in front of one's child, but in no way appeared intoxicated or otherwise impaired. It occurred to me then—and probably to others, although we did not discuss it—that it was highly unusual for her to be kept overnight with no corroborating evidence."

Karolina picked up her phone to text Miriam yet another thank-you, but it rang before she could dial and displayed an unfamiliar 202 area code. Figuring it was someone from the media, and today was a day she would *gladly* make a statement, she answered it.

"Karolina Zuraw," she said confidently, pleased to have officially switched back to her maiden name.

"Karolina? This is Regan. Regan Whitney." The voice on the other end was higher-pitched than Karolina would have expected. And anxious-sounding.

"Hello, Regan," Karolina said magnanimously, proud of how she'd managed to disguise her shock.

"Graham asked if I could call you to discuss Christmas. He thinks it would be a good idea for us to get to know each other—to establish a working relationship—so we can make decisions that are best for Harry."

"My lawyer, Miriam Kagan, already reached out with a schedule of visits, and Trip agreed—I'm surprised Graham didn't tell you," Karolina said, trying to suppress a smile. She kept waiting to feel the predictable pangs of jealousy or at least awkwardness, but they never came. In their place was a confident calm and a newfound sureness that she could handle whatever Graham and Regan might throw at her.

"Yes, well, we were very much hoping that Harry could join us at Elaine's for her traditional Christmas Eve dinner. And of course, if you don't mind, to stay for Christmas morning to open his gifts. We could have the driver take him back to you in Greenwich so you could have him for the evening meal?"

"I believe that works with the schedule, Regan. Perhaps you can ask Graham for a copy?" Karolina said.

There was a moment of silence. "I guess our wires crossed," Regan said. "But thank you." Her relief was palpable even through the phone.

"You're welcome."

"Well, I won't keep you any longer," Regan said.

"There's something else you should know," Karolina said. The words were right there at the tip of her tongue. She knew she shouldn't get involved—no one would think she was being anything but vindictive—but Karolina couldn't help herself. She had *been* Regan. And if someone out there—anyone—could have saved her all those years of heartbreak, she would have wanted to know. "Regan?"

"Yes?"

"I know this is going to be very hard to hear. Graham had a vasectomy over five years ago. He never told me. He let me believe that I couldn't get pregnant because we had fertility problems. He let me undergo *surgery* knowing it would never work. It's certainly none of my business, but if you do want kids of your own one day, you might want to consider what I'm telling you."

The silence was shockingly complete. Not a rustle nor a ping or a breath. "Regan? Did you hear me?" Karolina asked.

"I heard you," Regan said quietly. "Please excuse me, because I am going to hang up now."

And then a click.

"Mom! Hey, Mom!" Harry called as he raced into the living room, practically hyperventilating from excitement.

"Hi, sweetie," Karolina said, her heart still doing a little tumble each time she caught a glimpse of him. She folded the newspaper and tucked it under a couch pillow.

"Mom, will you take me and Andy and Ethan to the movie theater on Prospect? A bunch of guys from school texted and said they're meeting to see *The Rocky Horror Picture Show*."

"Isn't that a scary movie? And what about lunch?"

"Mom!" Harry said, exasperated. "I'm *thirteen*. Please." Andy and Ethan appeared behind him, furiously nodding.

"Are your mothers okay with this?" Karolina asked, trying not to smile at the fact that Harry had turned thirteen two days earlier.

Again they nodded.

She sighed. So much for a quiet day at home. But it would be a good excuse to run some house errands while the boys were at the movie. "When do we leave?" she asked.

By the time Karolina got back to the house that afternoon, it was nearly dark outside. She'd dropped Harry at Ethan's for dinner and had stayed for a cup of coffee with Ethan's mother, a surprisingly normal woman who bustled around her kitchen, stirring pots of pasta and trying to convince Karolina to join them for dinner. But it was a relief to get home and unwind, to slowly unpack her shopping bags of faux-fur throw pillows and bed linens and two brand-new sets of guest towels. She'd bought the most beautiful porcelain Buddha to place on the mantel in her bedroom, and a lovely textured rattan bowl to fill with fruit on the kitchen island. *This is what nesting must feel like*, she thought. Maybe someday she'd like some help, Emily continued to suggest. But for now it felt right to do it all herself. Karolina was so caught up in removing price tags and examining her purchases and placing her items that she didn't even notice the half-dozen missed calls on her silenced phone. When the doorbell rang, she assumed it was Harry, getting dropped back at home.

"Hey," she said, swinging open the front door. But it was Emily who stood on the porch, looking semi-hysterical and, well, large. Working for Miranda in the autumn off-season had allowed her a bit more "leisure" time, but the baby was due soon.

"Em! Are you okay? Is the baby okay? Here, come in."

"I'm not so fucking huge that I can't walk by myself," Emily hissed, pushing her way past Karolina and refusing her hand for help. Emily glanced around. "Is the kid here?"

"No, he's at a—"

"Why haven't you been answering your phone? My God, it's like the Dark Ages around here! How am I supposed to reach you? By carrier pigeon? No, instead I have to drag my gigantic fat ass into the car and drive here *in person* from New York City."

"What's going on? Is Harry okay?" Karolina asked, the panic starting to creep in.

"I don't know one damn thing about Harry. What I do know is that the entire world is talking about your ex-husband."

Karolina looked hard at Emily. She'd heard pregnant women sometimes lost their minds. Got forgetful, absentminded. She would be gentle. "Yes, they are. That article in the *Times* this morning was great, wasn't it?" she said, to show that she knew and she'd read it a hundred times.

"That's old news, you moron. Here, turn this on," Emily said, thrusting the remote to Karolina and collapsing into the overstuffed club chair. "Christ, this thing is huge."

"What channel?" Karolina asked, but she didn't have to wait for an answer. It was on every channel.

"If you're just tuning in, we have some breaking news. Multiple sources confirm that Senator Graham Hartwell, junior senator from the state of New York, was responsible for the death of a four-year-old child nearly three decades ago. Cause of death is said to be vehicular manslaughter, although sources do say that Senator Hartwell—a high school student at the time of the accident—was not under the influence. Why this story has never been revealed is part of CNN's exclusive investigation. Now we are going to Poppy Harlow, who is in Bethesda with the latest. Poppy?"

"Oh my God. This isn't happening," Karolina said, walking closer to the television. "Oh my God. That's my house. Emily! You swore you wouldn't say anything!"

"Whoa, hold on there for a minute. First of all, I didn't swear to anything. I have always supported this sordid little story coming out, and I haven't made any apologies for it. But you made it quite clear that you didn't want it out there for Harry's sake, so against my better judgment, I respected yours."

"So what are you saying? That this wasn't you?"

"Correct. As much as it pains me to say it, this wasn't me."

"I can't even . . ." Karolina's voice trailed off as it hit her. Of course. If the little girl's family hadn't uttered a word in thirty years, and neither had Elaine or Trip or Karolina, then there was only one other person it could be.

"Can't even what?" Emily said, looking newly interested.

"Maybe we should be friends with her?" Karolina said, a smile starting to spread.

"Who? I have no idea what you're talking about."

"I told her this morning about Graham's vasectomy—don't ask, I didn't mean to, it just sort of came out—and then this. It can't be a co-incidence."

"Regan!" Emily laughed. "No, I wouldn't think so. Wow. I'm impressed. The girl has balls."

"Right? Look at this," Karolina said, waving toward the throngs of reporters. "There must be a hundred of them. More than even the day I got arrested. I am so glad Harry isn't there right now."

"I think it's safe to say that Graham and Regan's fairy-tale wedding is likely on hold. Forever. Not to mention his presidential aspirations." Emily pressed all five fingers together and kissed the tips. "Buh-bye."

As if on cue, the front door of Karolina's former Bethesda house opened, and a hush fell over the crowd on TV. Out walked Trip and Graham in nearly identical navy suits and blue-and-white-striped ties. Had they coordinated that? Karolina couldn't take her eyes off the screen. What could Trip possibly say to defend Graham now? Would he pretend he never knew? Claim it was all a big misunderstanding?

Trip and Graham approached a podium, and Graham pulled a note card from his pocket. He began to read: "Ladies and gentlemen. I ask that you please give my family and me privacy at this sensitive time. We will try to answer all your questions in due course. Thank you for your understanding."

Literal shouting commenced immediately. "Senator, is it true that you are responsible for the *murder* of a girl named Molly Wells?"

"Can you confirm that your family paid the Wells family in exchange for their cooperation?"

"Did Harvard University know of your crime when you were accepted? Did anyone else in the Senate?"

"Has your future father-in-law, President Whitney, offered his support?"

"Do you expect the Senate to commence impeachment proceedings in light of this new information?"

"What would you like to say to your constituents now? To the American people?"

On and on it went, while Graham looked increasingly uncomfortable. Trip stepped in and said, "No further comments," and shooed Graham away.

Karolina's doorbell rang. She and Emily exchanged a look, convinced it was the press looking for a comment, but both their phones vibrated with a text message at the same time. *Open up, it's me*, wrote Miriam.

Karolina pulled open the front door and was relieved to see only Miriam and no cameras. "Come in," she said, ushering her friend in. "Why are you so dressed up?"

"Who's dressed up?" Emily called from the living room. "Can you people please come in here for this conversation? I'm a beached whale. Don't make me get up!"

Karolina gave Miriam a look and they both smiled. "By 'beached whale' she means she's put on thirty pounds," Miriam said, following Karolina.

"I heard that!" Emily shrieked. "And I haven't gained anywhere *near* thirty pounds, so fuck off!"

Miriam gave Emily a cheerful wave. "I can't stay," she said, pointing toward the television. "But I had to be here for all this. I think it's fair to say this entire nightmare is over."

Miriam was right—it was over. Finally and completely over. There would be too many questions from too many reporters and too many cameras pointed in her direction, but this time they wouldn't concern her. Harry was safely under her roof again. The *New York Times* had announced she wasn't guilty of drunk driving. And now, even though Karolina wouldn't necessarily have done it herself, Graham was discredited. His career, over. There was satisfaction there, and happiness, but most of all she felt a deep and calming sense of relief.

"I couldn't have done it without you," Karolina said, looking first at Emily and then at Miriam, wondering what she'd done to deserve two such real and loyal friends. "Seriously, you guys are the best."

"I'm just so happy that it's all worked out," Miriam said, embracing Karolina in a full-body hug. "I love you, honey."

"Blah, blah," Emily said, waving her hands. "Enough of the feel-good crap. You love us. We're the best. We know. Now, Miriam, can you tell us something more interesting? Like, who on earth picked out that outfit? Because—and I hesitate to say this, trust me—but you look almost cool. High-waisted jeans that you didn't buy at J. Crew? A heel over an inch and three quarters? Even *foundation*? I applaud you."

Miriam gave Emily the finger and they all laughed.

Karolina ran to the kitchen and came back with a bottle of red wine. "This was the bottle Elaine bought Graham and me on our wedding day. She said we were supposed to drink it on our tenth anniversary, which of course we didn't. Graham said he had to work that night, but he was probably seeing Regan. Anyway, who cares about that now? What I do know is that I Googled it, and this bottle is worth three grand. Anyone want some?"

Karolina poured the wine into plastic cups, since the glasses weren't yet unpacked. She felt guilty handing a pregnant woman a cup of wine, but Emily snatched it from her and said, "Third trimester is fully cooked. Move along," and together they held their plastic cups toward the ceiling, cackled like witches, and toasted one another.

Later that night, after her friends had left and she'd checked that Harry had turned his lights off at a reasonable hour, Karolina climbed into bed. It didn't feel real—this gorgeous, good-feeling home, her son once again hers, an impromptu night spent drinking wine and laughing with close girlfriends—and she wondered if this was the first time in her entire life she'd felt truly happy. There had been moments. She'd never forget those Sundays she spent with her mother, walking through the park or helping her cook or sharing a bath, but they'd always been tinged with the imminent sadness of her mother leaving again. Getting her first magazine cover, being selected to walk in the Victoria's Secret show the first time, being named the face of L'Oréal—all of those career accomplishments had filled her with pride but left her feeling somehow empty. Even the early days with Graham, when they'd made love frequently and traveled often, were tinged with her own questions and doubts: Had Karolina honestly loved him? Had he loved her? Had either of them even known then what love was? Or had she been so young and naive and desperate to please her mother and her husband that she'd convinced herself it was love when it was really something else?

When Karolina's phone rang beside her, she jumped. The lamp beside her bed was on and the clock on her nightstand said it was 11:48. And a quick glance at the caller ID announced it was Graham.

"Hello?" she said. "Graham?"

"There you are," he said breathily. "I'm sorry if I woke you. I wanted to wait until morning, but I couldn't. I can't sleep, I can't eat, I can't do anything but think about you."

Karolina inhaled and held her breath. Why, when she hated him so much, did it still feel good to hear him say that? "Graham . . ."

"Please, just listen. I screwed up, Lina. I know I did. The whole thing with Regan was an awful mistake. I never loved her, not like the way I love you. What you and I have is different, Lina. I know you feel it too. We built a family together, a home. A *life*. And I'm the first to admit that I put it all at risk because of my ambitions. You know it wasn't because I loved her, right? I let my career aspirations be the priority, and in doing so, I jeopardized us. I realize that now, and I can't apologize enough. But I'm going to get help. I've been in touch with a world-renowned psychologist who specializes in high-powered men and infidelity, and I'm certain she's going to fix this. I'll take a leave of absence from the Senate. I want to be a better man. A better father to Harry. And hopefully, a better husband to you."

"You want to be a better husband to me?" It came out like a squeak. So many thoughts raced through her mind—the planned DUI, the night in jail, and most of all, the completely wasted days and months and years spent trying to get pregnant—but those were the only words Karolina could utter.

"Yes. You deserve that, and so does Harry. I'm going to work very hard to prove that to both of you, because you two are all that matter to me in the entire world."

Her throat tightened. How many times had she imagined this moment? Fantasized about the time he would come groveling back to her, saying all the right things so they could finally put their life back in order? To recognize his shortcomings, to admit his guilt, to announce his willingness to change? And to beg for her forgiveness? Here it was, happening almost exactly the way she'd envisioned it dozens of times—hundreds?—over the past months, and she wanted only to cry. She would shed tears for babies she had so desperately wanted and for the fear she'd felt about losing Harry and for the old Karolina, the naive and innocent one, who hadn't been able to predict or even imagine that Graham was capable of doing such hideous things. But here it was, and there was no satisfaction, no feeling of victory, nothing but a strong certainty that this chapter of her life was closed forever.

"Graham, I want you to listen closely," Karolina said, not even trying to disguise her crying. "You and I no longer exist to each other as anything more than co-parents, and we never will. Harry and his well-being are all we'll discuss, ever again. Outside of being the father to our son, you are dead to me. Now and forever."

She clicked the "end call" button and collapsed against the pillows. The tears felt cathartic, almost cleansing, and Karolina allowed herself to let it all out, as her mother had always encouraged.

"Mom? Are you okay?" Harry's voice, which alternated these days between a little-boy squeak and a manlier baritone, surprised her. He was standing in her doorway.

"Oh, honey, come here. I'm fine," she said, motioning for him to join her. Karolina felt a surge of love as her beautiful, lanky boy—now nearly taller than she was—climbed on the bed. He wore plaid pajama pants and an old camp T-shirt, and his left cheek was bright red and warm with sleep, as it always was when he was a little boy.

"What's wrong? Why are you crying?"

Karolina reached for him, and when he folded his warm body into hers, and she wrapped her arms around him, she believed she could know no greater happiness. "I'm crying because I'm happy, love." She buried her face in his hair and inhaled his familiar, delicious smell. "Right now everything is exactly as it should be."

31

Goodbye Wheatgrass, Hello Sarcasm

Emily

"I still can't believe this is happening," Miriam said as she helped line up baby bottles filled with pink jelly beans. "How did she agree to this?"

Karolina laughed. She had just finished tying pink ribbons on the guest favor bags and was about to start filling the champagne glasses with sparkling rosé. "It's not our fault. Everything we suggested was cool and understated and anti-baby, and *this* is what she chose."

"I can hear you, you know," Emily called from her perch on the couch, where she was directing her baby-shower setup like a bellicose air traffic controller while a girl from Drybar blew out her hair. "I'm starving. Can someone please bring me something to eat?"

Miriam materialized in front of her. Her floral dress was cinched at the waist, and her over-the-knee boots made her legs look long and glamorous. "You look thin in that," Emily said accusingly.

"Nice, right?" Miriam twirled around and finished with a little bow. "I'm back to my pre-kid weight. Who knows? I may be in a bikini by next summer."

"Please no," Emily said, looking disgusted. "You've had three children. No one needs to see your bare stomach again, ever. Or mine." She motioned to her own enormous midsection, which was nothing like the cute basketball-under-the-shirt she'd imagined. Instead, she looked like she'd swallowed a whole goat. Maybe even a buffalo. Her ass had spread into the shape of a half-deflated beach ball, her breasts were bulging out of the double-F nursing monstrosity she'd wrapped them in, and her cankles were textbook, only puffier. Even her face had swollen to nearly twice its size, and her necks—plural—unfurled themselves every time she dared move her chin in a downward motion. She hadn't seen her feet in six weeks. Karlie Kloss had asked her last week if she was having *twins*. There was no point of obvious delineation between her breasts and her belly or her right boob from her left. She was straight up, no denying it, *huge*. And the worst part of the whole wretched thing? She was okay with it.

"What can I get you, honey?" Miriam asked. "The caterers brought a gorgeous-looking arugula and farro salad. Let's see, I also saw them setting up an enormous fruit platter. There's grilled salmon over spinach, a quinoa dish with cranberries and feta, and a—"

"I want a burger!" Emily barked, irritated beyond description that she couldn't just get up and help herself. She had special permission from her doctor to get out of bed solely for the baby shower, but she had to sit the entire time. The woman was such an alarmist! Something about her cervix being too far opened and the baby almost falling out. Emily wasn't entirely sure of the details, although Miles had taken notes and asked questions and policed her every move as if she were about to give birth to the next queen of England.

"We decided against the sliders on the menu, remember, honey?"

Miriam said soothingly. "Too many vegetarians. Oh, we have mini–
tomato bruschetta drizzled with—"

"I. Want. A. Burger!" Emily growled. "*Not* a slider. *Not* a piece of
salmon. A real, juicy burger. With cheese. And fries. And I want it *now*."

"Got it," Miriam said, and Emily could see she was barely suppressing a smile. "I'll order one for delivery. Should be here in no time."

"That's my girl," Miles said, emerging from their new bedroom
wearing jeans and a cashmere hoodie. He stood over her and rubbed her
belly. "And that's my other girl."

"Your girls are starving," Emily said, offering her face for a kiss.
"All this prissy girly baby-shower food isn't going to cut it."

"I have to run out now to pick up the balloons, so tell Miriam that
I'll grab your burger on the way home, okay?" He kissed her again,
grabbed his coat, and walked out the apartment door. There was nothing Miles wouldn't fetch or find or assemble now that there was a baby
in the picture. He was so ecstatic and so damn attentive, Emily worried
she might have to get pregnant with a second baby just to keep his attention. She relaxed back into the couch and watched everyone set up
around her. They moved so quickly! Like gazelles. She could barely remember a time when it wasn't an effort to get from the bedroom to the
bathroom.

Emily had been skeptical that they could move into the new apartment by December 1 and have it set up enough for her New Year's Day
shower, but even she had to admit the place looked pretty good. When
Miles had heard from his company that his transfer from Los Angeles to
New York had been accepted, Emily had almost screamed with happiness. Peace out, L.A.! Goodbye, wheatgrass and early-morning mountain hikes and hideous highway traffic and surfing culture and most of
all people who either didn't understand or didn't like sarcasm. Hello,
dirt and bagels and taxis and self-deprecation and *edge*. It was good to
be home.

She wanted to move back to the West Village, on a ground-floor
brownstone apartment with a backyard area like they used to have, but

334 · LAUREN WEISBERGER

Miriam and Karolina had gotten hysterical when Emily said so. They moaned about staircases and strollers, about safety and security, and how moving into an apartment without a doorman to sign for diaper deliveries and hail cabs was basically akin to child abuse. So against her better judgment, she and Miles had signed a lease on a three-bedroom condo in a brand-new high-rise in West Chelsea, where the High Line jutted through the third floor of the building and out the other side. The lobby looked like a Mandarin Oriental, the gym could be mistaken for an art installation, and the roof-deck pool switched between indoor and outdoor with the press of a button. There was even a communal play-room designed by child-development specialists and staffed round-the-clock by Columbia students. It wasn't what she would have chosen, but Emily had to admit that so far it was pretty sweet living.

"I still think you should have moved to Connecticut," Karolina said, walking into the room. "Now that you're going to be a mom and all."

Emily stared at her. "I'm not even going to dignify that with a response." She turned and smiled at the woman who'd finished her hair and was gathering her dryer and brushes.

"I have to say, I really like it there now," Karolina said. "It gets a bad rap—and there are some crazies, of course—but overall . . ."

Emily held up her hand. "Stop. Please. If I hear you or Miriam say another word about how beautiful and lovely and civilized the suburbs are, I'm going to vomit. Mark my words: I will never live in the suburbs."

Karolina smiled as she placed a final pink rose in the crystal vase on the pink-draped buffet table. "Yeah, no one's ever said that before."

Emily's phone rang and caller ID announced that it was Helene, Rizzo Benz's manager. "Hello, Helene?" Emily said, dripping kindness. "Long time, no talk. What's it been? A year since Rizzo's Nazi prank?"

"Hi, Emily. So sorry to call you again on New Year's Day. I promise this isn't going to be a thing, but well, I'm calling with some good news. Rizzo would like to hire you, effective immediately. Not for any particular problem this time, but to be added to your roster just in case."

"Sounds like someone else isn't happy with Olivia Belle's little . . . situation."

"You could say that. Rizzo fired her immediately upon hearing the news, and yours was the first name that came up."

"Well, isn't that flattering," Emily said sweetly. "I'd be more than happy to work with Rizzo. I just need him to call me himself—tomorrow, please, not today—and tell me that he's sorry he was such an asshole and from now on he'll do whatever I tell him, no questions asked. Can you pass that along for me?"

"Um, I can tell him that, but I'm not sure—"

"Well, those are my terms. Happy New Year, Helene. And thanks for the call." Emily hung up and smiled. She'd be hearing from him first thing the next morning. In the forty-eight hours since news of Olivia Belle's accounts getting hacked—resulting in endless client images, emails, texts, home addresses, even some medical information (aka plastic surgery plans) being splashed across the Internet—Emily had fielded calls from each and every one of her clients who had deserted her for Olivia. And she'd taken each and every one of them right back into the fold, after extracting both protracted apologies and promises of loyalty going forward. Not that Emily would forgive and forget. She wouldn't. But it was damn nice to have a full roster again, and it would make leaving Miranda and *Runway* permanently after her maternity leave that much easier. Helping Miranda sort out the Met Ball and Fashion Week the last couple months hadn't been as hellish as Emily had originally thought—as promised, the perks were plentiful and the pay was impressive—but it was definitely not a long-term career option. Miranda had basically accused Emily of getting pregnant to get out of *Runway*, and Emily hadn't disagreed. It was the least confrontational way to end her temporary stint there while maintaining a good relationship with Miranda. It must have worked, because Miranda had accepted Emily's insincere invitation to the baby shower, and now all Emily could think was that she needed Miranda today like she needed another ten pounds.

The phone rang before she could consider this further. It was the doorman, announcing that the first guests had arrived. "They're here," Emily bellowed from the couch. "Can someone get the door?" She texted Miles: *where r u? need my burger!*

One by one, women streamed into the modern Italian-design-style living room. Each so chic and pulled together. So stylish. So *thin*. And each and every one lied through her teeth, telling Emily how gorgeous she looked, how much her skin glowed, how she barely looked like she'd gained a pound. Emily glanced down at her black maternity leggings with the waistband that stretched over her belly and straight to her bra strap and the poly-blend shapeless black tunic she wore over them, and she forced herself to smile. If only any of them realized that she didn't give a flying fuck how she looked. There was a real, live human being growing inside her—a daughter, no less! So what if she was fat now? That was why God invented personal trainers and private nutritionists, wasn't it? Some proper starvation and a ton of exercise and she'd have her body back in no time. And whatever didn't go back exactly where it belonged would be easily remedied by Dr. Feinberg, right in the privacy of his lovely office on Park Avenue. Why did women get so *stressed* about all this?

When nearly all of the invited guests had arrived, Miriam distributed sheets with color photos of two dozen babies. The goal was to see who could write the names of the celebrity parents underneath each photo in the least amount of time. A player could earn extra credit if she also knew the name of the baby.

"You seriously want to play Celebrity Baby with me?" Emily asked, and everyone laughed. She put her pen to the paper the moment Miriam called "Go!" and had completed the entire worksheet in one minute and thirty seconds.

"Done!" Emily called, holding her paper above her head. She looked around the room: no one else had filled in even half.

"Fine, I'll go back and do my extra credit," she mumbled as she scrawled "Luna" and "Boomer" and "Rumi" as though signing her own name. Thirty seconds later, she said, "Done! What do I win?"

Out of the corner of her eye, Emily saw the apartment door open and Miles walk inside clutching a Shake Shack bag. Oh, how he loved her! To stand on that line all the way across town in January? She couldn't remember ever feeling so lucky. But her gratitude was cut short when she noticed who had followed him inside and was looking around the apartment with such obvious disgust that Emily felt a wave of humiliation wash over her. What was so repugnant to Miranda right then? Emily wondered. It could be the couch—she knew she should've gone for gray linen and not that tacky velvet the decorator had insisted on. Or was it the rug in the foyer, with its abstract pattern and contrasting colors, that Miranda hated? Or perhaps it was all the women, teetering on heels and balancing mimosas and laughing a little too loudly over an insipid baby-shower game? *No*, Emily thought. That level of Miranda revulsion could be saved for one and only one thing: Emily's pregnancy. It was one thing to procreate; Miranda seemed to understand that was unpalatable but necessary. But to let oneself nearly double in size while undertaking the aforementioned procreation? That was just obscene. Emily placed both hands on the couch and heaved herself to the standing position. It was important to greet Miranda properly. And besides, she *needed* that burger.

"Miranda, I'm so pleased you could make it," Emily said, hoping the lie didn't sound as transparent as she thought it did. Still, while it wasn't enjoyable having Miranda attend a get-together in one's own home, it did say something about Emily, didn't it? Something good.

"Emily." Miranda nodded. "Due any moment, I see."

"I actually still have six weeks to—"

Miranda waved her right hand at nothing. "Do me a favor and fetch your friend Karolina for me, dear."

"Karolina Zuraw?" What could Miranda possibly want with Karolina? She wasn't going to bring up the whole messy Graham thing, was she? Try to take credit for it? Because Emily was over that entire situation and really didn't want anything to distract from her day.

"Do you know another one?"

"I'll get her. Can I bring you back something to drink? Some Perrier? A mimosa?" Emily felt the familiar wave of perma-embarrassment
that she always felt in Miranda's presence.

"I'm on my way out," Miranda said, even though she had yet to
remove her long fox coat.

"Of course, I'll be right back."

Emily hurried from the foyer to the living room as fast as she could.
It felt like a ten-pound kettlebell was pressing against her pelvis, but
Karolina wasn't there. She wasn't in the powder room or the kitchen
either. It wasn't until Emily peeked into the nursery they had decorated in soothing shades of cream and beige that she found Karolina,
absentmindedly stroking a cashmere crib blanket while staring at the
midcentury-modern rocker so intently that Emily just knew Karolina
was envisioning how it would feel to feed a baby in that chair.

"If you're picturing me nursing, you can stop right now," Emily
said, although she knew that Karolina was imagining herself nursing
and didn't care one whit how Emily planned to feed her daughter.

"The nursery is beautiful," Karolina whispered.

"You're going to have one just like it one day soon," Emily said,
grabbing Karolina's arm. "I know it."

Karolina shook her head. "I hope you're right. I've never stopped
wanting it, not for a single second."

"I'm always right. Now come with me. Miranda Priestly is asking
for you."

"Miranda's asking for me?"

"I have no idea why, if that's what you're wondering. But hurry,
Miranda doesn't wait."

Probably only ninety seconds had elapsed since Emily had left Miranda standing in the foyer—only three total minutes since Miranda had
followed Miles through the door—but Miranda shot Emily one of her
classic how-dare-you-make-me-wait glares.

"Karolina," Miranda acknowledged, not bothering to hide her obvious once-over of Karolina's figure and outfit. Then, as though relieved

that yet another person wasn't pregnant, she said, "You can take over for Emily during her maternity leave."

"What?" Emily asked at the same time that Karolina said, "Pardon?"

"It's not really a difficult concept, girls," Miranda said. "Emily, I can no longer have you in the office looking like . . . that. Karolina can fill in for you in your absence. The Met Ball is once again five months away, do you think it's going to plan itself?"

"Of course," Emily said, because it was the only thing she could think to say. If she'd had to guess, she would have said Karolina would be horrified at the suggestion. After all, she certainly didn't need to work. And why would she want to work for Miranda, of all people? But there was no denying her expression of pure joy.

"I would love to," Karolina said, clasping her elegant hands together.

"Excellent," Miranda said crisply. "Then you will be an ideal replacement."

"Excuse me? Miranda, that's not at all what—"

This time Miranda's left hand went up. "Please stop. You aren't planning to come back. Don't insult me by denying it."

Emily closed her mouth and nodded.

Miranda cinched the fox coat tighter and turned to the door. "I'll have Juliana send you whatever you like for your baby gift, so be specific with her. Karolina, be in my office Monday morning by nine and ready to work, yes?"

"Yes." Karolina beamed, her cheeks flushed with excitement, looking at least ten years younger.

And with that, less than five minutes after she'd arrived, Miranda was gone.

"Where is she?" Miriam asked as she joined Emily and Karolina in the foyer. "I'm dying to meet her."

"I got a job!" Karolina practically squealed. "Working at *Runway*. On the editorial side."

"Let's not get carried away here," Emily said. "It's not like you're going to be writing cover stories. The Met Ball is important, don't get me wrong, but I can't have you thinking—"

"Oh, shut up, Emily." Miriam and Karolina said it right at the same time and dissolved into laughter.

Miles peeked his head in. "Can I get some help out here, please? There's an entire roomful of women in high heels stomping around every inch of our apartment, and they all look very hungry."

"We'll be right there, sweetie," Emily said. "Miriam will dazzle everyone with her size-four waist and the fact that she's having sex with her husband again, and Karolina here can tell us all how to live our best life in the suburbs. If anyone needs me, I'll be in my usual spot on the couch, trying not to break it."

Miriam laughed out loud and Karolina turned to Emily. "Can I get you something to eat before we head back in? Another burger, maybe?"

Emily considered this before reaching out to take both Miriam's and Karolina's hands, leading them down the hallway and back toward the party. "Yes, please," she said, squeezing them both. "I thought you'd never ask."

Acknowledgments

I feel lucky to have spent the last decade looked after by the finest in the business: Sloan Harris. Words cannot express my gratitude to you for always being my champion, my adviser, my friend. At times, my shrink. I couldn't do it without you. Thank you also to Jenny Harris, my behind-the-scenes reader and cheerleader. I adore you both. To everyone at ICM, who works tirelessly to support authors and artists each and every day, but especially: Alexa Brahme, Diana Glazer, Josie Freedman, Patrick Herold, Jenn Joel, Heather Karpas, Kristyn Keene, and Maarten Kooij.

I'm so grateful to have an amazing publishing team behind me. At Simon & Schuster in the U.S.: Kelley Buck, Elizabeth Breeden, Cary Goldstein, Jon Karp, Zack Knoll, Carolyn Reidy, Sarah Reidy, Katie Rizzo, Richard Rohrer, Jackie Seow, and Beth Thomas, thanks to each of you for working your magic to help bring this book to fruition. But most of all, Marysue Rucci, editor extraordinaire, who can skillfully offer a line edit, a major plot overhaul, and everything in between—often on the same page. At HarperCollins in the UK, the book may have a different name, but it also has a crack team to skillfully and lovingly shepherd it to the shelves. First and foremost, an enormous thank-you to editor Lynne Drew, who makes each and every word of my manuscript better. My tour visits to London are always the highlights of my publications, due entirely to seeing and reconnecting with all of you: Charlotte Brabbin, Isabel Coburn, Elizabeth Dawson, Anna Derkacz, Kate Elton, Jaime Frost, Damon Greeney, Hannah O'Brien, Emma Pickard, Charlie Redmayne, and Claire Ward. At Curtis Brown, I send both hugs and thank-yous to Sophie Baker and Felicity Blunt for everything you do.

Oddette Staple, Ludmilla Suvarova, Kyle White, thank you for helping me keep it all together—and making me smile along the way.

To the kick-ass strong and whip-smart women who, whether near or far, IRL or on FB, offer constant support ("This is going to be your best one yet!"), unwavering patience (even when I vanish into a manuscript for weeks or months on end), and the perfect mix of cocktails, sarcasm, and laughs (always perfect so long as there's all three): Heather Bauer, Jamie Bernard, Alisyn Camerota, Helen Coster, Lisa Cummings, Anne Epstein, Jenn Falik, Vicky Feltman, Jane Green, Anne Greenberg, Julie Hootkin, Audrey Kent, Micky Lawler, Mandy Lewitton, Leigh Marchant, Pilar Queen, Arian Rothman, Jena Wider, and Lauren Taylor Wolfe.

Most of all, thank you to my family, without whom none of this would be possible. To my mom, Cheryl, and my dad, Steve, you have been my biggest cheerleaders from day one, and you have taught by example what it's like to love reading and writing; and to Bernie and Judy, my supportive stepparents. To Jackie and Mel, my parents-in-law who are more like a second set of parents, you inspire me every single day with your commitment to family and your love of adventure. Dana, you render most everyone else irrelevant with your sense of humor, loyalty, and our shared sister thing of being able to complete each other's sentences. Seth, Dave, Allison: there are not three other people on earth with whom I'd rather raise our families and share our lives.

To my sweet and dazzling R and S, you are my everything. Watching you grow each day, in every way, is the greatest joy in my life.

And finally, to Mike. You of all people know I'm not the type to write a love letter for the world to see, but this one time I can't resist. Thank you. For your constant love, patient support, and killer editing skills (are you sure I can't slide a "just" in there just one more time?); for being the kind of dad every child should be lucky enough to have as his or her own; for being the husband who's even more loving than the perfect guy I'd always imagined. There is nowhere I'd rather be than by your side.

About the Author

LAUREN WEISBERGER is the *New York Times* bestselling author of *The Devil Wears Prada*, which was published in forty languages and made into a major motion picture starring Meryl Streep and Anne Hathaway. She is also the author of the *New York Times* bestselling novels *Everyone Worth Knowing*, *Last Night at Chateau Marmont*, *Chasing Harry Winston*, *Revenge Wears Prada*, and *The Singles Game*. Her books have sold more than thirteen million copies worldwide. She lives in Connecticut with her husband and two children. Visit laurenweisberger.com to learn more.